The

Voice

In

The

Dark

Printed in the United States of America

First Printing, 2016

ISBN-10: 069263729X

ISBN-13: 978-0692637296

Published by: Charmed Hearts Books

Table of Contents

Dedicated

To

Hopeless Romantics

Lost Soul Mates

Dreamers

Chapter One

The large grandfather clock in the hall ticked away as the keys jingled loudly in the lock of the front door. Everyone had been fast asleep in their beds, until the disruption from downstairs roused them from their slumber. As the front door slammed open, it banged into a pedestal, knocking the vase of flowers that sat upon it to the floor with a crash. Loud laughter and noisy stumbling footsteps echoed across the foyer floor, announcing that Addison and his fiancé had made it home from their night out. They didn't seem to be concerned about the noise they were making in the nighttime hours.

Elizabeth woke with a start, and looking at the clock, realized what had woken her. The man in the bed next to her reached into the bedside table, and pulled out his pistol.

"Put that away, Arthur. It's our grandson, not a burglar. Go back to sleep. I'll take care of this myself." She patted her husband's arm. Still half asleep, he put the firearm away, and rolled back over. She threw her covers to the side, slid on her slippers and robe, and went to address the disturbance personally.

"What in the world do you think you're doing? Do the two of you have any idea what time it is?" She snarled, as she descended the stairs. She was joined at the bottom of the grand staircase by her steward, Roger, still dressed in his pajamas.

"Sorry, Grandmother...I didn't realize." He tried to say it as clearly as possible, but the slurring of his words made him hard to understand. "Lena and I just got home. What are you still doing up? You didn't have to wait up for me. I am not a child."

"You could have fooled me...And, no, I didn't wait up for you. You could've woken the dead, with as loud as you were being." She spoke sternly to her grandson. "Now, I suggest that you get to bed, right now. Roger, would you please escort Ms.Thorton to one of the guest rooms?" She motioned to the gentleman next to her.

"She can just stay with me in my room tonight..." Addison tried to step in front of Lena, but tripped and fell, setting their laughter off once again.

"Not in my house, she won't...now, get yourself to bed, Addison Xavier Thatcher!" The older woman pointed at the young man on the floor, who was still chuckling. "We will address this in the morning." She turned on the spot, grabbing Lena's arm. "I will take care of Lena, myself." She turned to the aging man to her right, and her tone softened. "Roger, please get my drunken grandson to his room." As she ascended the marble staircase, she dragged the stumbling blonde up with her.

When the two women came to one of the guest rooms, Elizabeth swung open the door, and shoved the younger, scantily-dressed girl into the room. Lena stumbled forward and fell to the floor, her hair flying forward to cover her face.

"That wasn't necessary!" Lena screeched, flipping over, and glaring up at the silver-haired lady in front of her.

"Yes, it was. You will sleep in here tonight, but in the morning, you *will* go home. Ever since you came into my grandson's life, there has been nothing but chaos and destruction, disobedience and disrespect. I will not stand for it any longer." She grasped the door handle. "And, when I said that you will go home in the morning, I meant it. When the sun rises, you will be dressed and out the door. And, don't even think about sneaking into Addison's room." She slammed the door behind her, Lena still on the floor.

*****

Roger had flung Addison's arm over his shoulder for support as they approached the large Oak door. With very little effort, he swung the solid door open and walked across the room, and laid the drunken young man on the bed.

"Thanks, Roger. It's been a long time since someone has tucked me into bed."

"I'm not tucking you in, Sir. I am simply doing what I was told…to assist you to your bedroom." He took the young man's waistcoat, and hung it in its place in the wardrobe nearby. He did the same with his shirt, and his slacks. He removed Addison's shoes, and put them on the shelf with his other footwear and closed the doors to the wardrobe. Clothed only in his undershorts, Addison maneuvered himself into his bed, and covered up. No sooner did he hear the door shut, and his head hit the pillow, that he was out like a light. All was quiet in the large house once more.

*****

It felt like he had only just fallen asleep, when he was startled awake by a blinding light in his eyes. His head felt like it was being beaten with a mallet, and his mouth was filled with cotton balls. He tried to cover his eyes, but something or someone ripped his covers from him, and his pillow was ripped from his grip.

"What is the meaning of this? I was sleeping!" Addison screamed, which only made the pounding in his head worse.

"Your grandparents require your presence in the office…immediately. Get dressed, sir." Roger barked, as he threw the curtains open wider, letting in the early morning sunshine.

"Can I, at least, take a shower or something? I feel positively disgusting."

"You smell like it too. I will have Becky come change your sheets, and clean up your mess." He had a revolted look on his face, as he spotted the mess that had been made, obviously from Addison getting sick at some point. "The least you could have done is aim for the waste basket I left for you. This is why you shouldn't drink." Roger walked over to the wardrobe, took out a set of clothes and took them to the bathroom. He set out fresh towels and then returned to the side of the bed. He yanked the blankets off of Addison, once again, and heaved the young man upward. "Get washed up, dressed, and meet with Ms. Elizabeth and Mr. Arthur. There is aspirin on your nightstand if you need it." He stomped out of the room.

Addison quickly popped two caplets in his mouth, washed it down with the glass of water, and stumbled his way to the bathroom to get cleaned up. While he was standing under the running water, he couldn't hear the front door slam. He must have been in the shower for a good fifteen minutes before his head became clear. He quickly dried off, clumsily put his clothes on, and descended the stairs.

Approaching his grandparents' office slowly, he raised his hand to knock. The door opened before his knuckles could make contact with the wood. His grandfather stepped aside, allowing him to enter, before he closed the door behind him. Elizabeth motioned for him to have a seat on the couch, opposite of the chair she was sitting in. Arthur stood against the bookcase, puffing on his pipe.

"Roger told me that you wanted to speak with me. Are you going to lecture me about last night? Because, if you are, Grandmother…I have heard it a million times before." He stood in his spot, refusing to sit down on his grandmother's command.

"I have no intention of lecturing you, Addison. I told Roger that we wanted to speak to you, because I wanted to inform you that we have contacted our lawyer about changing our wills." She spoke calmly, though she felt like screaming.

"Did you finally decide to add Lena? After all, she will be my wife in a few months' time." He sat down on the couch, and stretched his arms, lazily, across the back of it.

"Quite the contrary, Addison. In fact, we have decided to remove you from our wills, entirely." Arthur removed the pipe from between his teeth. Elizabeth nodded, and folded her hands in her lap.

"I'm sorry…I don't think I heard you correctly. I could have sworn that I just heard you say that you were going to *remove* me from your wills." He gave a chuckle, believing that his grandfather must have worded his statement wrong.

"You heard me right, Addison. In light of recent events, we've made the decision to remove you as a beneficiary from both of our wills." This statement took Addison from slightly amused to confused and angry.

"You can't do that!"

"We most certainly can, and we will, as soon as our lawyer, Mr. Robertson, arrives later this afternoon."

"Why are you doing this? Because I came in late last night, and woke everyone up?" He got up, and folded his arms over his chest. "I apologize for that. I am truly sorry. However, is that a valid reason for disinheriting me, your only grandson?"

"I assure you that this has very little to do with last night. Last night was just the tipping point for both of us." Elizabeth shifted in her chair, and motioned for him to return to his seat, as she was not close to being done. "Your behavior, both here and outside of the walls of this home, have become quite a problem. You have been in the local papers…more than once…exhibiting behavior unbecoming of the Thatcher family name. For generations, we have been one of the most revered families in society, looked upon with the utmost respect, and in a matter of a year, you have tarnished a reputation that has taken decades to build." She pulled out the drawer of the table next to her, and removed a stack of newspapers from it, laying them on her lap. "This headline reads: *Drunken Addison Thatcher Causes Disturbance at City Council*." She flipped that paper up, revealing the next paper. "*Thatcher Heir: Is he Above the Law?*" She gave her grandson a look, glanced to her husband, and then proceeded in reading off five more headlines, all highlighting his behavior in a less than savory manner. When she had read the last headline, she gathered them back into a neat pile, placed them back into the drawer, and slammed the drawer shut.

"What do you want me to say, Grandmother? I am young, and everyone watches me like I am the King of England. There are other guys, just like me, who do the same things I do, and sometimes worse. It isn't my fault." He sat back down on the couch, and glared at the woman in front of him.

"You know that's not true…at least not completely. Lena is just as much, if not more, to blame for all this. You have brought shame to this family, to our reputation, and we will stand for it no longer. That is why we are removing you from our wills, boy." Arthur took two steps forward, and pointed the mouth piece of the pipe at his grandson.

"If this is because of Lena, as well, why isn't she here, being reprimanded?" He crossed his arms over his chest again.

"She is not our grandchild. She is not a Thatcher! If she wants to flaunt herself all over town in those tight outfits, and street walker shoes, she will only bring shame to her family, not ours."

"She will be a Thatcher, though. We will be married in a few months." His fists clenched. He looked to his grandmother, to his grandfather, and then back again.

"That will not happen…not as long as I am alive. She has turned you into a delinquent, a nuisance, a menace to society. You were brought up to be a model citizen, a fine young man…destined to carry on the Thatcher family Legacy. You had everything, but then she came into your life, and destroyed any chance for you to be what you were meant to be." Arthur stepped forward, and towered over him, his chest puffed out.

"Say it, Grandfather…Say you are forbidding me to marry the woman I love. I dare you!" He was back on his feet.

"You have no idea what love is, Addison! And, as far as Lena Thorton is concerned, you are just a meal ticket. The only reason that she has latched onto you is because she thinks that she can earn a higher social standing. The Thortons are conniving, vindictive people. They will do anything and everything they can to climb the social ladder. All she had to do was bat those eyelashes at you and you were hers to mold and manipulate. That is why we are doing what we must…even if that means disinheriting our own flesh and blood. I refuse to let her get her hands on our family's money. I refuse to stand by and allow her to tarnish our family name." Now, Elizabeth was up on her feet. "However, if you choose to not marry Lena, but a woman worthy of a young man of your standing…we would very happily be willing to reconsider our decision."

Though she was in her early seventies, she neither looked nor acted like it. The only thing that gave anyone the indication that she was up there in years was her silvery hair, which she kept in a very stylish up-do. Confidence and elegance seemed to radiate from her, as she always dressed as a proper lady should, with limited exposure of skin. No one ever saw her without her face made up and her hair done, even those she lived with.

Arthur, on the other hand, looked his age. He was very grey, and the wrinkles on his face were like a road map, which was rather symbolic for the life that he had lived. He worked hard to maintain the family's traditions and beliefs, and it had aged him. His skin was like leather, tanned and stiff from countless hours outdoors. However, his appearance and age, didn't have any effect on his body. He was as spry and mobile as a twenty year old, and his physique was lean and muscular. He stood like a tower, in comparison to his grandson.

Addison began to pace in his effort to work through, mentally, what his grandparents had just explained to him. His mind was reeling, feeling as though both of them were giving him an ultimatum; Marry Lena and lose everything, or dump Lena and keep his inheritance and social standing. He turned on his heels and looked at the elderly couple in front of him, a defiant look in his eyes.

"So, in other words, I must choose between you and my fiancé. If I marry Lena, I lose my inheritance, and my place in this family. If I choose to betray her, I can keep everything as it is."

"Not in so many words, but yes." Elizabeth walked over to Addison, and laid her hand on his shoulder, but he shook her off. "It is for your own good, Addison."

"Lena does love me, despite what you may think. She doesn't care about our family's fortune, or social standing. You are wrong about her, and I will prove it. I am going to get her right now, and she will tell you herself. Is she still in bed?" He turned to head for the door.

"She's gone. I told her that she needed to leave, and so she went home early this morning." Elizabeth sighed.

"You did what?! How could you do that? You had no right!"

"I most certainly had the right! This is my…our house. I could have sent her home last night, but chose to let her sleep here, out of the kindness of my heart. I didn't even have to tell her to leave this morning. She left on her own, and obviously didn't feel the need to say goodbye to you." Elizabeth walked over and stood between her grandchild and the door. "You have a choice to make, Addison. You can give up your whole life for a woman that thinks only of herself, and what she can get from you. Or, you can choose to think for yourself, and your future."

"That is precisely what I am going to do, Grandmother." He pushed past her, and right before he closed the door behind him, he looked to her and then to his grandfather, giving them a saddened but determined stare. "Goodbye."

Addison immediately ran up to his room, and began shoving things into a suitcase. He refused to be told what to do.

"I am not a child anymore. I am twenty-nine years old, and I can marry whom I like, regardless of what they have to say." He grumbled, shoving his undergarments, half-hazardly, into one of the pockets of the large case.

There was a knock at the door, but Addison chose to ignore it. A few moments later, the knocking continued. When Addison didn't answer it the second time, the door swung open, and Roger sauntered in.

"What do you want? I never said for you to come in." Addison grumbled, still packing his things.

"Well, sir, I couldn't help but notice that your grandmother was upset. And, usually, when she is upset...it has something to do with you."

"She...and grandfather pretty much told me that I had to choose between them and Lena. I am choosing Lena, end of discussion. So, if they sent you up here to convince me otherwise, save it!"

"No...Let me help you pack. After all, you are a full grown adult." Roger pushed him aside and began to repack his things neatly.

"Thank you, Roger. At least someone else understands how I feel." He stepped back, and let Roger do all the work.

"I do, sir. You are more than capable to take care of yourself, and more so, someone else."

Addison stopped dead in his tracks and looked at Roger. Suddenly, he felt like he had a bunch of rocks in the pit of his stomach.

Chapter Two

Addison banged on the front door of the Thorton home, a shabby house on the edge of the town. The paint on the door chipped off in chunks as his fist hit the wood with force. He heard what sounded like the thud of footsteps coming toward the other side of the door, and he stepped back, and straightened his hair and clothes. The wood barrier was yanked open, and an older, balding, heavy-set man answered the door.

"Oy! What do you want?!" The man barked, and then looked up. Clearing his throat, he spoke with a softer tone. "Mr. Thatcher! It is quite a pleasure to have you visit our home. Oh, where are my manners? I am Harvey Thorton, Lena's father. Would you care to come in?" He moved aside, and allowed Addison to enter the house. It was in shambles, and quite dirty compared to his home. He avoided touching anything. "May I offer you something to drink?"

"No thank you, sir. I have come to see Lena. Is she home?"

"Of course…LENA!!!" The man screamed down the hall, and then turned back to Addison, smiling, his teeth brown and decaying.

Like sunshine on a dreary day, Lena came out from around the corner. She looked like something completely out of place. Her whitish blonde hair shined in the light of the flickering bulbs, her ivory skin glowing. She was a vision of beauty to Addison, and he reached out to Lena, offering her his hand.

"What are you doing here, Addison?" She looked at him, nervously, almost embarrassed to have him in her home in its current state.

"Pack your things, Lena. We are leaving."

"Wait a minute, Addison…What are you talking about, leaving? Where are we going?" She laughed, and looked at her father and then back at Addison.

"I don't care where we go…let's just run away…elope." The sound of desperation in his voice was like a red light in her head, and she pulled her hand away.

"What about our big wedding? It was going to be the social event of the season. The newspapers were going to be there…" She began to act like a spoiled child, having something they wanted taken away.

"You love me, and I love you. We don't care about that stuff, because we have each other."

"What has gotten into you, Addison? I do want all that stuff…and you do, too." She took a step back, and crossed her arms over her chest. "Have you been drinking this morning?"

"No, I haven't been drinking. My mind is the clearest it has been for a long time. I love you, Lena May Thorton, and I want to marry you and run away to some exotic island together, where we can live on coconuts, and rum, and bask in the sun…without anyone there to tell us we can't….Please, Lena…"

"No, Addison! I have worked too hard to get where I am at, to run away and leave all of it behind." She let out a giggle, her expression softened, and she straightened the collar of his coat. "You are being silly. We will have our big wedding, which will be the talk of the century, and then we will live in a huge mansion, and we will be invited to all of the most exclusive parties and events…"

"I don't care about all of that…I just want you. Now, go pack your things…" The last part came out of Addison's mouth as more of an order, than a suggestion.

"Maybe he wants a private wedding, my sweet. The point is that he wants to marry you *now*, rather than later. Do as he says, kitten, and go pack your things." Harvey coaxed his daughter, giving an apologetic look to Addison for his daughter's stubbornness. "You will get married on some remote island, and then come home and sell the exclusive photos to the highest bidder, am I right?" He nudged Addison with his elbow and gave him a grin and wink.

"No photos, no cameras…just Lena, and myself, and a pastor…" He stated, ignoring the shocked look on the man's face. "And we won't be returning back here…Wherever we wind up, that is where we will make our life…out of the public eye, and in perfect happiness."

"No! I want to be in the public eye! I want to be on the front page of the Gazette…I want them to make a moving picture show about me… '*From Rags to Riches: The Lena Thorton-Thatcher Story.*' I want the fanciest clothes, and my own chauffeur, and invitations to parties and events that only the crème de la crème get invited to. I want it all!"

"So…you want what being married to me will bring…" Addison's heart seemed to stop, and he felt as though he was falling. His grandparents were right, after all. "Do you even love me? Or is it my family's money and reputation that you love?" It felt like a knife had just gone through his chest, and his face hardened. She saw the look in his eyes and stepped toward him, wrapping her slender arms around his shoulders. She kissed his nose, and looked into his eyes.

"My darling, Addison…You are my knight in shining armor. You are taking me from this dump to live in your castle. I get the hunkiest guy in all of Woodcrest. I love you more than I have ever loved anyone, but I just happen to love everything that comes with you, too."

"Prove it…" He pushed her from him.

"Prove what, Addie-bear?"

"Prove that you love me more than anything else…but more so…prove it to my grandparents. If you can convince my grandmother and grandfather that you are marrying me because you love me and for no other reason, then we will have your big wedding and all of it…I promise." He stepped toward the door. "Meet me at my house in an hour, and we will go see them together."

"Addison, they hate me!" She whined.

"Well, I guarantee that, if you convince them that you truly love me and only me, then they will embrace you with love…One Hour, Lena!" He leaned forward, kissed her cheek, and raced out the door.

Lena looked at her father, wiped the spot where Addison had just kissed her, and sighed.

"Daddy, I have got an hour to prepare for the greatest performance of my life. The poor guy…If he wasn't so gosh darn rich and good looking, I would just say forget it…"

"Lena, my sweet little temptress…" He grabbed her arm, and squeezed. "You wouldn't have to prepare if you had just gone with him when he asked you to. Are you as incredibly daft as you look? You had him right where we wanted him, and you made such a scene…"

"Daddy…you're hurting my arm!"

"Good…now, hear me, girl. Arthur Thatcher won't really be a problem, but that woman is not as naïve as her grandson, so you better give it everything you've got, or you have ruined it for both of us. Marrying into the Thatcher family is the key to our rise in society."

"Yes, daddy, I promise…I will have that old bat like putty in my hands by the time I am done." She gave her father a devious look, and he released her arm. She walked to her room, and began to prepare to meet with the one person standing between her life now, and the life she wanted, the life that her father insisted that she have.

*****

The phone in the foyer rang, and rang. Roger, who was nearest to it, picked up the receiver, and spoke to the man on the other end. With a look of horror, he hung up the phone and went to Elizabeth's office, and began to knock. When she didn't answer the door, he opened the door, and stuck his head in.

"Mrs. Thatcher, it is quite urgent…" He whimpered, when she gave him a stern look for coming in without invitation. She had been in a very unhappy state since Addison had left.

"Very well, what is so urgent?"

"You and sir just received a phone call…from the hospital. It's Mr. Addison…" At his words, she jumped up and sped across the room.

"What's happened to my Addison? What's happened to my grandson?" She pleaded with him to tell her, her eyes filled with tears.

"He's been in an accident, ma'am."

"Dear Jesus above…he's not…"

"No, Ma'am…He's alive…but he's unconscious. They called you because there are reporters swarming the hospital already. They said that you are to use the hospital staff entrance."

"Get my coat, and then get the car. My grandson needs me." She went to her phone and phoned her lawyer, canceling the meeting for later that day. Retrieving her husband from the dining room, where he was reading the day's paper, they rushed to the front door where Corrine, one of the maids, was waiting with their coats. They sped out the door, promising to give everyone an update as soon as they knew something.

*****

As Elizabeth and Arthur raced up the corridor toward Addison's room, thoughts of their earlier discussion ran through her head. She felt partially responsible, believing that he had driven carelessly because of the ultimatum they had given him. The nurse pointed them to the room, where there were officers from the sheriff's department waiting. Seeing them there made them believe that he had not only driven recklessly, but also intoxicated. Elizabeth walked into the room first, and the doctors were there, adjusting the machines hooked to his I.V.'s. She cleared her throat and they turned to her.

"Mrs. Thatcher, I am Dr. Kramer." One of the men held his hand out to her, and she shook it. The doctor proceeded to tell her what they think happened, where they found him, and what tests that had been run.

"Was he driving under the influence of alcohol? Is that why the police are outside his room?" She reached down, and took her grandson's hand in hers.

"Actually, Mrs. Thatcher, all of his screens came back negative. He had alcohol in his system, but he was below the levels of intoxication. The police are outside his door for his protection and privacy. The news reporters outside are ready to pounce, and we know how delicate the situation is."

"Was anyone else hurt? Did he hit anyone else?"

"Ma'am, he wasn't driving. The police said that when they found him, he was just parked. The keys were in the passenger seat. Someone hit him head on, probably coming around the corner. The driver of the other vehicle has yet to be found. They fled the scene."

"My poor Grandson…"

"Aside from some broken ribs, and a mild concussion, he seems to be fine. It is quite shocking that he wasn't injured worse, considering the circumstances. What we can't figure out is why he hasn't woken up. We did a CAT scan, and there is minute swelling, but nothing to explain it. He seems to have slipped into some sort of a self-induced coma."

"What should we do, Doctor?"

"As I said, aside from those few minor injuries, which we have treated, there is not much else we can do here. Our hospital isn't equipped to keep him protected from the vultures outside, though. We can't keep them out forever."

"Can we take him home? What I mean to say is, it would be much easier if he woke up in his own room, and not here. He *will* wake up, won't he?"

"Honestly, that is up to him now. He could wake up tomorrow, or a week from tomorrow. It is completely on him. We can arrange to have him transferred home, and receive in-home care, if that is what you wish. He would be safer from prying eyes and ears in your home. Is that what you want to do?"

"Yes, doctor, that is what I want to do."

"That's fine. Come with me and we will make the arrangements and you can sign his discharge papers." She followed him out of the room. Arthur was sitting in a chair in the hall, and Elizabeth had the doctor explain the situation to him. She proceeded to follow the doctor, and Arthur went into the room to see his grandson.

"You are a Thatcher. You are our legacy. Don't give up on us now, boy. Come back to us. When we lost your father, we only managed to pull through the grief because we still had you. Don't you dare leave us…not like this." He took his grandson's hand in his, and sat down on the chair next to his bed.

Memories of his son, Landon, floated through his mind as he sat next to the young man in the bed. It felt like an old wound had been reopened. It was hard enough to cope with the loss of his son, daughter-in-law and granddaughters to a car accident, but to possibly have lost his grandson the same way was more than he could bare.

Landon, his wife Maddie, their twin daughters, Cassandra and Alicia, and Addison had been on their way to visit when the weather got really bad. The storm was so horrible, that there was barely any visibility on the road; Landon hadn't seen that he had drifted into an oncoming lane of traffic, and they crashed into another car. Landon and Maddie were killed on impact, but the girls and Addison were rescued by another driver. The girls' injuries were severe and they both passed away at the hospital, but Addison made it through, seeing as he was in the center seat. His sisters took the impact when the car rolled, therefore saving his life.

Not a day passed that they weren't thought of, and a beautiful picture of the family still hung in the foyer of the Thatcher estate to this day. Arthur was often found talking to the portrait.

As he sat there in the hospital room, Arthur thought of nothing but what he would say to Addison, and how he wished that he could take back the morning's discussion.

Chapter Three

The afternoon came, and the hospital had transferred Addison by ambulance to the estate. All the equipment had been delivered and set up before he arrived.

Just as the Ambulance was leaving, Lena arrived at the door, as she had promised Addison she would, though she was several hours late. Part of her hoped that something had happened to Mr. or Mrs. Thatcher. However, when she walked in the front doors, she saw them standing at the top of the grand staircase, in front of Addison's door.

"What happened? I just saw an ambulance pull away. Are you alright?" Lena acted like she was concerned for their well-being.

"Now is not a good time, Lena." Arthur chimed in, as he descended the steps.

"Addison asked me to come by here this afternoon. He said that he wanted the two of you and the two of us to have a sit-down and get things out in the open. Where is he?" She looked around for any sign of him.

"The meeting has been cancelled. Addison was in an accident." Arthur puffed at his pipe, and gave her a look.

"An accident?! Is he alright? Oh, my poor Addison!!! Where is he?" She was genuinely shocked, and that surprised Arthur, immensely.

"He's unconscious. They don't know why, and there is nothing that they can think of to do for him. We had him transferred here, so that we could oversee his care."

"Well, is there anything that I could do?" She asked, thinking that just asking would earn her brownie points with them. If Addison wanted her to prove her "love" to his grandparents, she was going to make them believe that she cared with very little effort possible.

"Now that you mention it, Lena. Would you like to oversee his care? After all, you are his fiancé...Who better to make sure that he is taken care of than the woman that loves him." Arthur gave her another look.

"Arthur, she is neither trained in how to care for him, nor is she mentally equipped to do what is required of her. I want him to come back to us...." Elizabeth came stomping down the stairs, appalled at her husband's idea of Lena caring for her grandson.

"As he said, I am his fiancé...it is my duty to make sure he is cared for properly. You will have nurses coming to care for his medical needs, so I don't need to be trained." Her indignant tone infuriated Elizabeth. "You have made it clear that you don't believe I love him. What better way can I prove you wrong than to make sure that he regains consciousness as soon as possible." She stepped around them and headed for the steps, but Mrs. Thatcher grabbed her by the arm. "You think that I am just a stupid, airheaded, gold digger. Let me prove to you that I am more than that!" She yanked her arm free, and began to ascend the stairs.

"Lena, if you can prove me wrong…I will never doubt your intentions again. None of us will. You know what is at stake if you don't do what you should to ensure that he is cared for." Elizabeth could not believe that those words came out of her mouth, but at this time, she was desperate.

A full month had passed since his accident, and there had been no sign of Addison regaining consciousness. Lena sat with Addison, read to him, talked to him when she had witnesses. However, as soon as they were left alone, she would snoop in his things, and steal small, yet valuable trinkets, stashing them in her handbag.

She didn't touch him except for when there were others around, to which she would sit at his side and hold his hand. The hair on his face began to grow in, and the hair on his head began to look greasy and unkempt. Elizabeth figured, after just a week of no change or improvement in his condition, that Lena was just putting on a show, hoping to earn respect from her, but her mild efforts only infuriated her further.

Not having any other options, she put an ad in the papers, requesting someone to care for Addison while he was laid up. She made the ad very discreet, not revealing for whom it was for, avoiding any crazy applicants. It was at least a week before she got any responses from the ad, and she began to set up secret interviews. Most of the people that she spoke to were either under-qualified, over-qualified, or just plain out of their minds. She had almost lost hope of finding someone who fit the description, until she got a message from Roger that someone she knew had called about the perfect person to fill the position, and had dropped off a letter in the post office box for the ad. As she looked through the letter, she felt a glint of happiness, and picked up the receiver to her phone, and began to call her friend.

"Hello, my dear. I got your letter, and she sounds marvelous, and perfect for the position. May I speak with Miss Alison, please?"

Chapter Four

The firemen rushed back and forth from the smoldering building as Alison stood outside the caution tape, watching the last few years of her work literally go up in smoke. As she observed the fireman work to pull people from the burning building, she couldn't help but worry about the residents. The brave firefighters were working exceptionally hard and fast to make certain that no one was left inside, but it was only when she heard the men say that the building was clear, that she let out a sigh of relief.

She rushed over to the crowd of elderly people who had been pulled from the building. They were covered in soot, and ash, and looked purely terrified. She looked around and made sure that all of the residents in the west wing were accounted for, and when she had counted all of them, she smiled, knowing that no lives had been lost there. She was sure that everyone one else was accounted for as well, as she saw many of her coworkers mixed in with the rest of the people.

"All my things were in there…the pictures that my grandchildren made me…my photographs. They are all gone!" One white-haired lady cried, hugging the blanket around her.

"It'll be alright, Lorraine. The children can make you brand new pictures, and I am sure that your kids have copies of all your photographs." A kind gentleman with a toupee patted her on the shoulder. "We are alive…"

"Yes, you are, and I am so grateful for that!" Alison came up behind the elderly couple, and wrapped her arms around them both.

"Miss Alison! Oh, look what has happened to our home…it's gone…all gone!" The woman sobbed.

"I am so sorry…but everyone seems to be safe and accounted for, and that is all that matters to me. Do they know what caused the fire?" She offered the woman a tissue.

"No, not yet, Miss Alison…but I have a feeling it has to do with Herb and his stinky old cigars…" The man mumbled.

"Oh, now, Victor…Herb knows not to smoke his cigars except for in the garden. Besides, he would never do anything to put anyone in danger…you know that!" She gave the man a stern look, and then looked around at the other people pulled from the building. Through the smoke, she spotted a couple more of the workers, some of which were in the building at the time of the fire. "I'll be back. I am going to go talk to Miss Maddie. Stay warm." She pulled the blankets around the people, and then went to find her boss.

Madison was wiping soot and ash from one of the older men when Alison walked up. She hugged more of the people, reassuring them, and then pulled her aside.

"What happened? We just had the Fire Marshall out here last week, didn't we? How could this have happened, and what is going to happen to all these people?" Alison began to rattle out questions, not allowing Madison to answer before asking another.

"Alison, you need to slow down. I know you are panicked, but everyone is just fine. No one was hurt, with the exception of some minor smoke inhalation. We don't know what started the fire, but it started and spread so quick that we barely had time to get everyone out. Were it not for those firemen, and our newest over-night orderly, we would have lost about twenty people. That orderly got half of the residents out all on his own, bless his heart." The mention of the new worker barely phased Alison, as her heart was still thumping from the catastrophe before her. "This is absolutely devastating. However, both Happy Meadows and Pleasant Palms have room for all of them, so at least they have someplace to go." Maddie sighed, and looked at Alison. "As far as the workers, some of you will be out of a job."

"Some of *us*? What do you mean?"

"Both of the facilities are almost fully staffed, and are only offering jobs to those according to seniority...those who have been here the longest get first dibs on the open positions.

Unfortunately, we have more staff here than open positions. I'm so sorry, sweetie."

"These people are my life…I have invested five and a half years of my life to them, and now what?"

"Alison, I wish that there was something I could do, but I have no control over it. I will give you a shining letter of recommendation for any job that you apply for, though."

"The problem is that there are no jobs out there, Madison. And if I don't have a job, I don't get paid. And if I don't get paid, I can't pay my half of the rent. I am going to have to move back to Philly with my folks…I am not looking forward to that."

"Oh, I am sure it isn't as bad as you think. From what you've told me, your parents would love for you to come live with them."

"Ha! My dad is a strict, overbearing, overprotective retired soldier…and he's Mexican. My mom is an Italian woman who believes that, if you aren't three hundred pounds or more, you are too skinny." She laughed at the thought of living back at home. "Enough of my pity party, I am gonna check on our people, and then go home and start packing."

After an hour of checking on the elderly people that she had formed bonds with over the last few years, and saying her goodbyes, she got in her beat-up, mint green car and drove the four miles to her apartment. She felt horribly, telling her roommate, Jeanie, that she couldn't pay the rent, and suggested that she put an ad in the paper. After they had their girlie cry-fest, Alison went in her room, and began to pack.

A week later, Jeanie helped take boxes of Alison's belongings to her car.

"You could stay here until I get a new roommate, you know." Jeanie stated, as they slammed the trunk shut.

"That wouldn't be very fair. I can't live here, and not contribute. I just wish that I didn't have to go so far away."

"Philadelphia is not that far away." Jeanie giggled, hugging Alison.

"Yeah, I suppose you are right. We'll keep in touch." She got into her car, and rolled down the window. "I really wish that I could stay. I have looked into other jobs…sent out my résumé to so many places, but no one is hiring. So, off to mommy and daddy I go…wish me luck." She laughed and started the car. After waving goodbye to her friend, she headed down the road.

After an hour of driving, she heard a dinging, and looked down at her console, realizing that her fuel level was teetering above empty. She looked down the road, and began to panic, as she saw nothing but open road and no signs for gas stations.

"Just great…I'm gonna be stranded out in the middle of nowhere…my luck just keeps getting better and better." She pulled her phone out of her purse, but it died just as she got ready to call her parents. "Really...REALLY!?" She got angry, and began to pound on the steering wheel. After a moment, she composed herself, and started praying that she could get to a gas station before she broke down.

All of a sudden, her car began to rattle and shimmy. The radio began to make funny noises and bounced between radio stations. She reached over to shut it off, but got a static shock from the knob, and suddenly got very light headed. Her eyes became fuzzy and she blinked a few times. When everything came back into focus, she spotted a sign fifty feet ahead, directing her to a gravel road off to the right.

"Now Entering Woodcrest, Penn. Population: 877"

"Woodcrest, Pennsylvania? Did I take a wrong turn somewhere?" she spoke aloud. "I have never even heard of Woodcrest?"

She looked around, and she noticed that the main road she was on was closed ahead. Maybe there was an alternate route through this mysterious town. She pulled off to the side of the road, and tried her phone again, but there was no juice left. Deciding that she really had no choice, she turned onto the dusty road and drove straight, heading for a line of enormous trees. Confusion set in as the road seemed to lead into them, yet there was no opening. She slowed slightly as she got closer, and then something weird happened. For a moment, she thought her eyes were going funny again, as the wooded towers in front of her seemed to part, revealing more dirt road.

The next thing she saw made her think that she was completely out of her mind. Just as she thought she was driving into the middle of nowhere, a town materialized before her very eyes. Needing to get her head straight, she brought her car to a stop on a cobblestone street.

"What in the world just happened?" She shut off the engine, and closed her eyes, and laid against the wheel. "I just drove into a town hidden behind a forest of trees. It just appeared…out of nowhere…maybe I need to eat something." She took a couple deep breaths, and then sighed. As if the hidden town was not enough for her, she started to notice that there was something very bizarre about this hidden place.

People in odd clothing walked past the front of her car, stopping and staring at her. The buildings in front of her were not like buildings she had seen before, they looked as though they belonged in some place out of old movies. There was a post office, a city council building, and a town center with a decorated Gazebo. The grass was the greenest she had seen in a while, and she felt as though she had been sucked into a time tunnel. She rubbed her eyes, and looked again, and yet nothing had changed.

"This cannot be real. I was just driving down the interstate and there was nothing for miles, except those trees. Now, I am smack dab in the middle of some strange place." She whispered to herself. "Maybe it is a set for a movie…" She rolled down the window, and tried to get someone's attention. A gentleman, dressed in a grey suit and what looked like a fedora approached the car.

"Did you need some assistance, miss?" The man asked, looking at her as if she were an alien.

"Yes, please…I seem to be lost. Could you please tell me…where am I?" She asked as politely as she could.

"My dear girl, you are in Woodcrest, Pennsylvania. Where were you trying to go?"

"I was going to Philadelphia. How far out of the way have I gone?" She tried to ignore the stares and whispering.

"I can tell you, with certainty, that you are a long way from Philadelphia, sweetheart."

"I figured as much. Is there a detour coming through here? The main interstate seems to be closed back there." She turned around, to point in the direction she had just come from, but the trees were positioned just right, that she couldn't tell where she had come through them to land up here. "Well, that's strange..."

"What's strange?" The gentleman looked in the direction that she was staring.

"There was a road there, going right through those trees, but I can't see it now. You must think I am absolutely mad."

"You are as sane as I, my dear. Although, you do look weary and from the sound of the growling, you also are in need of some nourishment. What's your name?" The man asked, putting his hand on hers.

"Alison Moreno."

"Well, Miss Moreno…My name is Thomas Gentry. I am the Mayor here." He cleared his throat, stood up, and waved some gawking folks along, then bent back down. "I am sure that we can take care of what ails you, before you find your way to where you are heading. Miss Grant has an inn down on Main Street."

"Maybe I do need to get some sleep, and something to eat…" She put her hands to her head, and felt as though she was hallucinating.

"Of course…poor thing. I do, however, suggest that you let me, or my wife, accompany you. Your outfit will only draw unwanted attention."

"What is wrong with my outfit?" Slightly offended, she became defensive. She surveyed her clothing, and aside from the strap from her lavender bra sticking out from under her blue cotton tank top, she seemed to look alright.

"I am sure that it is acceptable attire from where you are from, wherever that may be, but outfits such as yours, here, are only worn by..." he leaned in and whispered the rest of his sentence. "…well, let's just say that it is quite odd. You are showing entirely too much skin."

"I'm sorry…too much skin, sir? Where I come from, I am quite covered compared to some."

"Well, that is a relief, I suppose, but still, I would ask that you wear something befitting our town and customs, at least while you are here. A nice, sweet girl such as yourself doesn't deserve a bad reputation." He stood up again, and opened her car door. She unbuckled her seatbelt and grabbed her purse, before stepping out of her car. Mayor Gentry waved over at the kind looking woman standing twenty feet away. She walked over to the car, and smiled at her husband, then looked at the young woman with him. She gave a slight smile at Alison, quickly surveying her apparel. "This is my wife, Odette. Odette, this is Miss Alison Moreno. She is a long way from home, and is need of rest and a meal. However, she is also in need of new clothes. Would you be an angel and take her to Ms. Morton's?"

"Of course, darling…Come with me, honey. We will get you taken care of." She reached for Alison's hand.

"What about my car, Mayor Gentry? I can't just leave it here, can I?"

"I will have someone bring it to the Inn for you. The walk will do you good." He caught the stares of more of the townsfolk, and took off his jacket, and handed it to Alison. "Put this on…until you get to the dress shop." Alison took the coat, put it on and followed his wife as she crossed the street.

Chapter Five

The town was unlike anything she had ever seen with her own two eyes. It was busy, with people in very old fashioned clothing. They passed by some old cars, some of which are only seen in a museum. Everyone was very friendly, greeting each other as they passed by.

"So, my husband seems to have taken a liking to you, Ms. Moreno. You intrigue him. Where did you say you were from?" Odette spoke as they walked.

"I'm from…" She started, but was interrupted.

"Here's the shop…come along." She scooted Alison in ahead of her.

"If you don't mind my asking, Mrs. Gentry…"

"Please, dear, call me Odette." She smiled at the young woman, as they took a seat and waited for Miss Morton to come over to assist them.

"Alright, Odette. If you don't mind my asking, what year is it…here?" Alison felt foolish asking such a preposterous question, but she feared the answer.

"I'm sorry? Did you just ask me what year it is?" Odette gave a small chuckle.

"I know it sounds silly, and I probably sound crazy, but I look at everything around me, and it just seems like I…"

"Well, I assure you, my sweet…it is nineteen thirty-eight…the twentieth century here, just as it is for the rest of the world. There could be nothing sweeter than living in the thirties, especially now that things have gotten back to normal after the Great Depression." Odette patted Alison's hand, in reassurance. Odette's words made Alison very dizzy and she sat, eyes wide, and stared at the woman in front of her.

Miss Morton, a sweet older lady with freckles and a sweet smile, approached them, and Odette leaned in close. "This young lady is in need of proper clothing for her age."

After having a brief conversation with the elderly woman, they got straight to work. The young women working there were instantly put to work, picking through the racks for appropriate clothing. Odette went through the pile of clothing that were brought, and picked out four or five dresses for Alison to try on.

Sure that she must have heard Odette wrong, or that they were trying to play a joke on her, she tried on the dresses without argument.

"As lovely as these dresses are, Ms. Odette, I am unemployed and am unable to pay for them." Alison muttered, after she had tried on the last one.

"You needn't worry about that, my dear. Think of these as a gift."

"Oh, Odette, I couldn't possibly…" Alison stepped out of the dressing room with a very flattering pale yellow dress on.

"I will not take no for an answer, young lady. Now, let me tie that ribbon, and then we can head to the house." She turned her around, and gently pulled the ribbon around her waist and tied it into a bow just above Alison's derriere. She retrieved the other dresses off the hook in the dressing cubicle, and handed them to Alison, and proceeded to the register to pay for them. She also grabbed other clothes in Alison's size such as pajamas, loungewear, and so on. With a smile, she reached into her pocketbook and pulled out the money and laid it on the counter, grabbing the boxes of shoes that she also purchased, before heading out the door. Alison followed quietly, and gave the ladies in the shop a nod, before exiting.

Alison and Odette walked down the street, back in the direction that they had come, but Alison could sense a slight difference between the looks she was getting before, and the looks she was getting now. Young men were now stopping and staring, waving, and smiling at her, and she could feel her cheeks getting flushed. When she had first gotten to Woodcrest, people had been staring at her, but not in a good way. Some people even approached Odette, inquiring about Alison's presence, as they hadn't seen her in town before. Odette would politely tell them that she was a visitor, and then continue on her way.

Soon, they came upon the mayor, and he smiled a wide, welcoming hello, obviously pleased at the change in Alison's apparel. Odette kissed her husband, handed him the shoe boxes, gesturing for Alison to hand him the garment bag as well. He took them, and placed them into the car awaiting them, and then held the back door and front passenger doors, for the two ladies to get in.

There was not much talking done in the car, as they drove to the home of the Mayor and Mrs. Gentry, but after the afternoon that she had just had, she wasn't really in the mood to converse. As they drove down the streets, she took in all the people and sights.

It was a very quiet and quaint town, and for a moment, Alison could picture herself living here. The buildings were all brick and mortar, and very closely built together. At the last turn, which took them past a park, there was a large statue of four very regal men.

"Is that a memorial statue, Mayor?" Alison found herself asking the kind man in the driver's seat.

"Those, my dear, are Woodcrest's Founding Fathers; Patrick Flannery, George Ballimore, Nathanial Thatcher, and Andrew Cunningham. Woodcrest owes them everything. They were good men, who wanted a better life for their families, and the families of those around them." The pride in Thomas' voice made Alison smile.

"And if you take the time to meet some of the people of Woodcrest, I am sure that you will find that they live on through their children, and their children's' children. A few of the families, such as the Flannery's and Thatcher's still reside here." Odette added to her husband's informative speech.

This town had a history, and the more time that she spent here, the more she wanted to know.

There was a feeling deep in her gut that told her that there were forces beyond her knowing that had led her here. Her finding this place was not an accident. Something had happened to her, out on the road, something that she couldn't even begin to explain or understand. Something or someone had pulled her through time, and she was going to find out why.

The preconceived notion that Odette was trying to be funny, or play a joke on her, had long since been dissolved. Her heart raced as she thought about her day. She had woken up in Pittsburg that morning, in the year Twenty-fifteen, and was now in a small community called Woodcrest, in the golden age of nineteen thirty-eight; She had traveled back in time seventy-seven years without realizing it. *How did this happen? When did this happen? I didn't go through smoke, or see anything to indicate that I was passing through a wormhole in time.*

Alison realized that Woodcrest was a lot bigger than she first thought. Her pulse sped up slightly as she witnessed history as it passed the window of the small automobile. No one her age would ever get this opportunity in their lives; to see the world in a different time, when life was far less complicated.

Sure, a lot of things had changed through the years that made the world better, in her opinion, such as integration, and marriage equality. However, a lot of things in this time period molded the world that she had been misplaced from.

Alison's deep, contemplative thought was suddenly interrupted, as the car came to a stop.

"We are here." Odette chirped.

Chapter Six

The house was tall and gorgeous, and befitting the mayor and his wife. It was very well maintained and the landscaping was beautiful. It reminded Alison of houses that she saw in pictures from her history books. There were beautiful apple and cherry blossom trees in the front yard, surrounded by flowers of many colors.

They had pulled up to the curb, and Thomas quickly exited and opened the doors for the ladies.

"Why are we here? I thought I was going to the inn."

"You will be, but we have decided to invite you for dinner with us, in our home. We would love to know more about you." Thomas smiled, as he offered her his hand.

"Are you sure that that is what this is really about? I am sure I am not the first newcomer to Woodcrest. Do you always invite strangers to your home?"

"Not usually, no…but there is something special about you, Miss Moreno." Thomas sighed, and watched her body language and mannerisms rather closely.

They settled in the sitting room, while dinner was being prepared in the kitchen, and there was a deafening silence that seemed to surround them. Alison sat as lady-like as she could, considering that she was not used to wearing a dress as daytime attire. She looked around the sitting room, and everything was so clean, and elegant. She could tell that there were no children, as there was absolutely no evidence of anyone young. Then again, sitting rooms were not the place for children back then. With a deep sigh, she looked to her host and hostess, and caught them trying to urge the other to speak first. Finally, after a few agonizing moments, Alison opened her mouth to speak. Thomas beat her to it.

"So, Alison, what do you think of our fine town? Is it anything like…" He thought back on where she said that she was going when she first arrived. "…Philadelphia? Are things different there?"

"Yes…and no." She tried to be vague, not wanting to tell them of her thoughts.

"Obviously, the fashion is different. I apologize if I may have come off a little demeaning or judgmental at first. I would hate for you to think that I meant to cause you insult." The apologetic look in his eyes was sincere.

"I understand what you meant, Mayor Gentry, and I am not insulted." She answered, partly fibbing to the nice man. It became silent for a few minutes more, and then Odette spoke up, fully knowing that her husband was not going to ask her what was weighing heavy on both of them.

"I have a few questions, based on things that you said earlier." She paused as Thomas cleared his throat, and tried to detour her from inquiring of it so soon. She rolled her eyes, and continued. "When we got to the dress shop, you asked me what year it was, which I found strange at first, but your reaction to my response was what really set off a red flag in my mind." She put her hand to her lips, and leaned forward, her eyes squinting slightly. "Why would you need to know what year it was? What year do *you* think it is, sweetheart?"

"It is 1938, like you said, Odette. We are in 1938." She tried to say it without looking absolutely foolish.

"Alright. It is, in fact, 1938, but that is not what I asked you. You don't have to be afraid to tell us. I am sure that there is some logical explanation."

"I don't think that it's as simple as just saying it…I don't quite understand it myself." An odd sort of fear seemed to overwhelm her.

"There is nothing to fear, Alison. Whatever you say here, to us, will stay between us." Thomas tried to reassure her that whatever she was about to tell them would be alright.

"Alright, but don't say I didn't warn you." She took a deep breath, and then kind of blurted it out, and then flinched, curling herself into a ball on the corner of the couch. "When I left my apartment and roommate this morning from Pittsburg, it was April 10th, 2015! And now, I have found myself here, in Woodcrest, seventy-seven years in the past!"

The mayor and his wife took a moment to absorb what the girl in front of them had just said. At the moment that the words finally sunk in, their eyes became wide and they looked slowly back to Alison, who was still flinching, teeth clenched, eyes squeezed shut.

"My dear girl, you must relax. We are not going to attack you." Thomas approached her, and laid his hand on her shoulder. She opened her eyes, and looked at them. They stared at her, not because of what she said, but the way she reacted after she said it, as if an explosion was going to happen at the mere words of time travel.

"I don't understand. I just told you that I came back in time, and yet you haven't phoned the men in the white coats to come haul me away." The confusion over their reactions hurt her head. "Why aren't you calling the men in the white coats to come and haul me away?"

"Do they have them where you come from? We have doctors that specialize in altered reality disorders, but they don't necessarily make house calls."

"I am not delusional, I swear!" Alison panicked. "True, my reality is slightly altered, but it has nothing to do with my mental state."

"Darling girl, we didn't say that you were delusional." Odette jumped in, trying to calm her. "In fact, I have a confession of my own to make. While you were in the fitting room, trying on dresses, I felt compelled to go through your bag." She blushed, and bowed her head in shame. "After I saw your reaction, I couldn't help myself." She looked to her husband, who was shaking his head at her.

"Regardless of your reasoning, my dear wife, you had no right to snoop through her things. She is no danger to us, nor is she a danger to anyone here in Woodcrest. Tsk Tsk."

"I know it was wrong, but I was left with more questions than answers after I looked inside of her purse. There are letters, receipts, and papers…all collaborating that she is not from…here. But she also had other things in there that I have never seen except in the moving picture shows or in scientific magazines."

Alison was taken aback at the conversation's direction. As Odette explained what she had found in her investigation, Alison pulled the things out of her bag, and laid them on the table in front of them. She slowly and carefully explained what each of the items were, and how they were used.

"This right here…is a cellular telephone."

"That can't be a phone. It isn't connected to anything." Thomas picked it up, and turned it over in his hand. "It has to be connected to something, or you wouldn't be able to talk to anyone. You'd almost be better off yelling."

It wasn't until the maid came out to inform them that dinner was served, that they shoved everything back into her bag. Odette and Thomas were very intrigued and fascinated by Alison and her bag of futuristic items, but as excited as they were, they kept their promise to not speak a word to anyone about it, or her. Instead, their conversation turned to what Alison was going to do until she was able to find a way home.

"You said that you were unemployed. What happened to your job back home?" Odette inquired, using her napkin to wipe her mouth.

"I worked at a nursing home…a home for the elderly. We cared for those who were unable to care for themselves, when their children weren't equipped, emotionally or financially."

"That is quite scary…to be put in a building all together, like animals, once we come to a certain age." Thomas cringed at the thought.

"Oh, all of the people I worked with were quite happy and comfortable there. It's like a large hotel, and we have all sorts of activities for them to do. Their children and grandchildren would come visit often."

"That doesn't sound so bad. When you say it that way, I wouldn't be opposed to retiring at a place like that. However, visitation day would be lonely for us. We have no children, as you may have guessed." Odette sighed, sadly.

"But your home is so big…I would have thought that you had at least two or three." Alison tried to sound as if she hadn't guessed their situation before they told her.

"We wanted to have children, but the Lord above had different plans for us." Thomas patted his wife's hand, knowing that their inability to have a family weighed hard on her heart.

"I'm so sorry. Have you thought about adoption?" The words slid out of her mouth before she had a chance to consider whether that was even an option back in the thirties.

"We have considered that option, too, but Thomas and I really wanted a child of our own, too. Now, with Thomas being the Mayor, we barely have time to get things done for the town, nonetheless raise a child."

"That's too bad. You have this huge home, and no one to share it with." Alison sighed, and began to nibble on a piece of buttered bread. However, Odette looked to her husband, and with a smile and a glint in her eye, looked to their guest.

"Alison, we would really love for you to stay here with us, you know, so we can learn more about you and the life you had." Odette chirped.

"It would be much more comfortable here than at the inn, and you would get three good, home-cooked meals a day." Thomas added, a glint in his eye.

"I couldn't possibly impose on you. You have been so kind to me already. Besides, I really don't want to impact anything that is supposed to happen by telling you too much about the future. You know what they say… 'If you change the past even in a small, seemingly insignificant way, it could change the future in a big way.' Knowing my luck, just by showing you my things and telling you about the future, I could have caused a catastrophe to happen in my time."

"Well, we just would love to have you here. And we don't have to know anything that you don't want us to know. It would just be nice to have a young person in the house, even if for a short while. The invitation is there if you change your mind." Thomas smiled and finished his meal, placing his napkin on the table next to his plate.

"Actually, I could really use your help with something. I don't know how long I will be here, and I cannot keep asking you for things, nor would I expect you to offer. I need a job."

"Well, I know that you were talking about your previous job, caring for the elderly. You speak of it with such passion and enthusiasm. What exactly did you do there?" Odette inquired, as she rose from the table and got a writing pad and something to write with.

Alison spoke of her duties, both with the able minded, and with the sickly and disabled clients. She went into detail of her day-to-day responsibilities. As she did, Odette wrote them all down. Thomas was confused at first, but then caught on, and just sat and listened.

After dinner was over, they went back to the sitting room and talked more, not about things from the future, but about Alison herself. Thomas was very impressed with how humble she was. She didn't speak of anyone she knew in an ill manner, even if her face may have spoken for her. She was passionate about reading and she stated, without being asked, that she attended church services regularly back home.

The more that the Gentry's got to know her, the more that they both agreed that they knew the perfect job for her.

After dropping her off at the Inn, and paying for a few nights, up front, for her to stay there, they went home and Odette began to compose a letter to a good friend of hers, in need of some assistance, someone who was reserved and subtle.

To my oldest and dearest friend, Lizzie:

I hope that this letter finds you in good health. I know that things have been hard for you the past month, and that coping with your current situation has been nothing short of heartbreaking. How is Arthur holding up?

To see your grandson in such a fragile state, especially after the loss of your son and the rest of his family, this situation must weigh down hard on you both.

I am writing you this letter to let you know that I may have found a solution to your problem, in a discreet and satisfying way.

Woodcrest has recently acquired a new resident by the name of Alison Moreno. She has previous experience in the healthcare occupation, working in a facility that aids in the rehabilitation of very ill and sometimes incapacitated patients.

She is friendly, humble, kind-hearted, and has a passion for helping others. After a long, and very interesting conversation in our home, we feel that she would be exactly what poor Addison needs. As she is not from Woodcrest, her knowledge of your family's history and reputation is only minimal, so her discretion is almost certain.

If you feel that you might be interested, I have enclosed a list of all the duties that she performed at her previous place of employment. You can either reach her here, at our home, or at Millie's Inn. Please give her a chance. I promise that you won't regret it.

Sincerely yours,
Odette Gentry.

She folded the letter and the notes she took, and placed them in an envelope. In the morning, she would call and make certain to let them know that she was putting the letter in the post office box that was secretly assigned to the ad in the paper.

"That is a really nice thing that you are doing, my love. I am sure that Elizabeth and Arthur will appreciate it. Alison seems like the type of pure hearted person that might just do that whole family some good." Thomas kissed his wife on the top of her head, and stroked her cheek with his hand.

"If anyone can turn things around, Alison Moreno can do it...our friend from the future." She smiled, and then took her husband's hand, and they both turned in for the night.

Chapter Seven

Her heart was pounding wildly as she approached the home of Elizabeth Thatcher, the woman she had spoken to on the phone just the day prior. Before she had gathered up the nerve to knock on the door, she took one last look in the reflective glass window, making sure that she looked presentable and professional.

Her dark chocolate hair, which normally was pulled up into a ponytail or messy bun, was now smoothed out and tamed into a beautiful curled up do. Odette had assisted her in choosing the right outfit to impress her oldest friend, as she knew her so well, a peach and blue dress, with a lovely eggshell-colored sash. Her feet, which usually looked awkwardly shoved into anything with a heel, looked rather lovely in the off-white pumps that were on them. If people thought that she looked out of place before, they couldn't say that by looking at her now. She fit in with all the high society ladies, right down to the way she carried herself.

She raised her hand, which was covered by little white gloves, and knocked on the door. After a moment or so went by, a balding man in a suit answered the door, a smile on his face.

"Hello, Miss. May I help you?" Roger asked, quite taken by Alison's sweet smile and beautiful sapphire eyes.

"I am here to see Mrs. Thatcher. I have an appointment." She kept her head held high, not in an indignant way, but the way someone who had self-confidence would.

"Ah, yes! You must be Ms. Moreno. She and Master Thatcher are waiting for you in the study. Please…please, come in. I will let them know that you have arrived." He stepped aside to allow her to enter into the foyer. "I'm Roger." He gave a courteous bow to her. She giggled, and gave him a curtsy.

"A pleasure to meet you, Roger."

"The pleasure is all mine, young lady." And he shuffled off to the office, a little pep in his step, to announce her arrival. His footsteps echoed across the marble floor, and she began to look around her.

The foyer, alone, was impressive, and spoke of the type of people who lived here. She took a few steps further into the grand room, and saw the antique oak railing that ran along the outside of the curved grand staircase on the left. To the right, there were massive French doors, which undoubtedly led to a ballroom of some sort, probably where they hosted parties and get-togethers. And just past the doors was a beautiful fireplace with a large family portrait. She felt compelled to examine the people in it, and walked slowly toward it.

In the painting, there was a very handsome man with a very clean beard and moustache standing next to a beautiful, ginger-haired woman, who was seated. On either side of her, there stood two very lovely young girls, in matching white dresses. And seated on the woman's lap was a very cheeky little boy, a smile that stretched from ear-to-ear, with the longest eyelashes she had ever seen on a boy. It was a beautiful family portrait, and she was so entranced by the happiness that was captured, that she didn't hear the older man approach.

Her first indication that her admiration of the painted family was not going unwitnessed was the smell of pipe tobacco. For some reason she absolutely loved the sweet smell that it emitted, and she inhaled through her nose.

"Lovely family, are they not?"

"They all look so happy. How I wish that my family could have a picture taken like that. It is absolutely beautiful, and I can't seem to take my eyes off the boy. His smile shines all the way into his eyes." She pointed at the child, and smiled.

"He had a very contagious smile and laugh at that age. That is my grandson, Addison. The two young girls were my granddaughters, Cassandra and Alicia. They were the spitting image of their mother, Madeline. And that fine looking man there…that's my son, Landon…God rest his soul. He was a good husband, and a loving father. He is missed terribly." The sorrow in his voice caused Alison to turn her head, and place a hand gently on the older man's arm, which he had crossed over his chest.

"I'm so sorry."

"There is no need to be, my darling girl, but thank you." He patted her gloved hand, softly, and removed the pipe from between his teeth. "I'm Arthur Thatcher. And you must be Ms. Moreno." He took her hand in his, and kissed it. "The mayor and his wife spoke very highly of you."

"They did? They barely know me, really. I just…moved here a few days ago." She tried to be as careful as possible to stick to what she and Odette had discussed about her being in Woodcrest.

"Well, then, you made quite the first impression on them." He let out a hearty laugh, and led her to the study. "Come with me, my dear. My wife is expecting you. We can speak more once you have gotten the job." He seemed almost sure that she was a shoe-in for the position, though she was not a hundred percent sure, herself.

He walked her to the hallway and led her to the door, opening it for her.

The study was lovely, and something that you would find in an old movie. Books were lining the mahogany shelves, and there was a roll-top antique desk positioned against the wall, behind where a lovely silver-haired woman was standing.

"What took the two of you so long?" She spoke, with a smile on her face, her eyes narrowed as if they were being sneaky by not coming immediately.

"She was entranced by the portrait of Landon, Madeline, and the children." He closed the door behind him as he spoke.

"Oh, well, it is a lovely painting, and the children were exceptionally patient, standing there for all that time. It has a very welcoming and inviting quality to it, so I am not surprised that she was drawn to it." Elizabeth motioned for Alison to take a seat on the couch across from her. She, herself, sat down in her desk chair, and Arthur chose to stand behind her, and smoke his pipe.

"Shall we get on with this interview, then?" Elizabeth waited until Alison had seated herself on the plush cushions of the couch, before pulling out a notepad, and a pen, placing them on her lap.

"I am ready to begin, when you are." Alison stated, politely.

"Alright. First thing is first, my name is Elizabeth Thatcher, and if you are hired, you will answer directly to me or my husband, Arthur. Is that understood? If any other person tells you how to do your job, and it is not directly from us, you need to let us know."

"I understand perfectly, Ma'am. You are the bosses...no one else." Her confidence and ability to follow along made the corners of Elizabeth's mouth twitch upward.

"Secondly, I have spoken extensively to Mrs. Gentry upon her recommendation for this position. She has informed me that you are used to working long hours, and dealing with unusual circumstances and conditions. Is she correct in telling me this?"

"Yes, Ma'am." She nodded, a smile on her face.

"She also assures me that you are discreet and will, per our wishes, not discuss anything about your job or your duties here with anyone outside the home's walls. Are we clear?" Though she tried her hardest to be stern with the young woman in front of her, she didn't blink once or waver in her answering respectfully.

"I understand, perfectly. If I were to obtain the position, I will only discuss job-related information with you and Mr. Thatcher, unless otherwise asked to do so by you personally."

"And whom do you believe we would want you to discuss these matters with, other than us, may I ask?"

"Perhaps his doctor, in certain cases, Mrs. Thatcher. There is no one else that I would believe would even need that kind of personal and confidential information. I may be trained but even I don't have all of the answers, and I may need to speak to a medical professional for advice or assistance. However, it would only be with your permission."

"That is quite acceptable and understandable, Ms. Moreno." Elizabeth looked over her shoulder at her husband, a look of surprise and awe. She was thoroughly impressed by Alison's answer.

"Lastly, you will need to be professional and mature in how you handle certain duties. I know you are young, and that you are used to dealing with the elderly. My grandson, Addison, is not what you are used to. He is a very handsome man…virile, and young, and has been known to make girls your age act irrationally, and foolishly…in short, they do tend to lose their inhibitions and act less than tactfully when they are presented with the type of duties that your job would entail."

"If you are referring to bathing him, and grooming him…" She looked directly into Elizabeth's eyes, and said with confidence and absolute surety. "…I am professional in what I do. I may be young, and he may, as you say, be handsome, but my hormones, raging or not, will not interfere with my job. I will not violate his person, or act in an uncouth manner, that would be unbefitting of a lady."

"Well, I think that that last answer just made my decision for me." She turned to the man behind her, a smile on her face, which she hid from Alison. Arthur's eyebrows raised, and he winked at Alison, and then nodded to his wife. Removing the mouthpiece of his pipe, he pointed at the young lady in front of them. "That young lady right there…she is a diamond in the rough. She has an honest, trustworthy, noble air about her, and I have no doubts in my mind that she was sent to us from the great beyond…as the answer to our prayers. That, and she has gumption!"

"I would have to agree with my husband. Alison, if you want the job, it is yours." With a smile, she extended her hand to the young woman.

"I appreciate it, thank you. When would you like me to start?" Alison placed her hand in the hand offered to her, and Elizabeth put her other hand atop of it, giving it a soft squeeze.

"We can have your things brought over from the Inn, immediately if you would like to start now." She rolled her eyes, hearing screaming coming from the floor above them. "I just need to deal with a pest problem first." Alison jumped at the sudden shrill noise, and looked to Arthur, who didn't even bat an eye. Rather than seem nosey, she remained in the study, but listened to the proceedings, as the door was left open for them to hear.

Down the stairs, in an indignant manner, Lena stomped, dripping wet and gagging.

"Oh my, Lena…what on earth happened to you? You look like a drowned rat!" Elizabeth sarcastically asked, though she wanted it to sound sincere.

"Oh, wouldn't you like to know! Let's just say that I have had enough of this, and I refuse to carry on with this charade. I am covered in human urine, and you are standing there, patronizing me!" She had to grasp the railing to keep from slipping on the liquid that was dripping from her, and onto the marble steps. "I have been trying to be the patient, selfless woman that Addison deserves, but enough is enough. This is just too hard, and I am not cut out to do this manual labor." She gagged a few more times, and then stopped dead, at the foot of the steps. Alison could see the blonde girl through the crack in the door, but the door blocked the girl's sight of her and Mr. Thatcher, that was now laughing and choking on his pipe at hearing what had just happened. Lena continued to gag, and then stomped her foot on the floor.

"Lena, I am sure that he didn't do it on purpose. After all, he's in a coma. You are supposed to change the bag, not wear the contents." She tried to keep from laughing, but it was very difficult.

"You win! I quit. He's gorgeous, true…he could have made my life a cake-walk, definitely true…I could have had enough money that I could bath in it like a queen…but he is soooo not worth this. I may be a money hungry wench, as you've undoubtedly called me, but even I have my limits." She pried the ring off her left hand, and threw it to the ground at Mrs. Thatcher's feet. "I am so out of here. I cannot believe that I am covered in human excrement. I smell like a septic tank!" She stomped passed the older woman, and came to the front door, where Roger was holding it open for her, a huge smile on his face. She stuck her nose up at him, and stomped out the front door.

Right after the door slammed, a young, red-headed girl came stumbling down the stairs in a fit of laughter, attempting to clean the trail of liquid that Lena had dripped on her way out the door. By this time, Arthur and Alison had come out to join the others. Arthur removed a handkerchief from his pocket and retrieved the soiled engagement ring. He handed it to Roger.

"Please take this to the jewelers and have them clean it...thoroughly." He asked politely of the other man, who was chuckling as he took the balled up cloth from his boss.

"Rebecca, as elated as I am at the outcome of whatever transpired, please explain to me why Lena was covered in the contents of Addison's..." She couldn't even stand to say what she was thinking.

"Mum, she went to switch out the bag, and I told her to twist the little red thing to seal it, before removing it from the tube. She told me to mind my own business, and she proceeded to yank the bag off of the tubing. Needless to say, mum, that she got a face full of Master Addison's....bodily liquids" Her Irish accent only made the story that much funnier. Even Alison couldn't help but snicker, but she put her hand over her mouth to muffle the sound. Arthur looked at Alison, and smiled, a twinkle in his eye.

"I take it that she was the pest control problem you spoke of." Alison tried to compose herself, but Rebecca's infectious laughter was getting to her.

"Well, yes. She was his fiancé..." Elizabeth cleared her throat.

"...Emphasis on the word *was*." Alison snickered.

"You know what, I like you, Ms. Moreno! You will fit in here very well." Elizabeth began to laugh harder. "Could you please assist Rebecca in cleaning this up before someone slips on it?"

"Of course." She stepped around the puddles, and motioned to the young girl to hand her some towels. "I'm Alison, the new in-home caregiver." She held out her hand to the young woman, and gave her hand a shake.

"I'm Rebecca, but yeh can just call me Becky. Welcome to the Thatcher Estate."

Chapter Eight

After Becky and Alison had finished cleaning up the mess left behind by Lena, they took the soiled cloth out back, and put them in a wash tub to soak. Becky showed Alison around the estate, and then took her upstairs, where she would show her to her new living quarters. As they headed up the stairs, she began to ask her guide some questions, trying to get a feel for what she was in for, and what she had witnessed earlier.

"So, the girl…she was engaged to Addison. How long had they been together? Obviously, it couldn't have been that long." Alison ran her hand along the railing as they ascended, loving the ridging and beautiful details etched into the wood.

"Oh, they have been together for quite a while, miss."

"Did they love one another?"

"He loved her. She loved his social status and his money. But, sadly, she never loved *him*."

"Well, that is obvious." Looking around her, she became confused, as the rooms they passed didn't look like servants' quarters. "Um, Becky, aren't you supposed to be showing me where I will be staying?"

"I am, Miss. And here it is…through this door." She smiled and turned the knob on the large oak door. As it swung open, she felt like she was dreaming.

"This is one of the bedrooms, Becky. I am supposed to be in the Servant's quarters, aren't I?" She went to close the door, but she was stopped by a familiar voice.

"There aren't servant's quarters in this house, Alison. No one is treated like property." Elizabeth came up from behind them. "Arthur and I chose this room for you, so that you could be close to Addison. He's in that room, there. Arthur and I are in that room down there, just in case you need to know, for emergencies."

"No servant's quarters, Ma'am?"

"Please, call me Elizabeth or Liz. Calling me ma'am makes me sound so old." She smiled, and guided Alison forward into her new room. "Something that you will learn about the Thatcher's is that we are not above anyone who is worthy of respect, like Rebecca and her family. They work to make a living, and they do their jobs well."

"Becky's family works here too?"

"You have already met her father, Roger. And her mother, Corrine, works in the kitchen and she also assists with the housekeeping."

"We love it here, Miss. We are treated like family. I've lived here since I was about five or six years old. I used to play with…" Her emerald eyes filled with tears, and she had to turn away for a moment.

"What's wrong?" Alison tried to console the weeping girl.

"She and my granddaughters were quite close, and used to play together when they would come to visit us. Everyone was devastated when we lost them. Thank the Heavens that Addison survived the crash." Elizabeth took Becky into her arms, and embraced her.

"So, that portrait above the fireplace…they all died…his parents and sisters, I mean?"

"I'm afraid so. Addison only survived because he was seated between the girls, and they took the impact when the car rolled. But, enough of the sadness…We have to get you settled, and then I will accompany you to Addison's room myself." She brushed a tear from Becky's cheek, and one from hers as well.

The bed that sat off to the left of the door was beautiful. It had gorgeous wood posts at each corner, and the mattresses were very thick and plush. There was even a little sitting area, and a small table with some books.

Just past the bed was a large, intricate wardrobe, where her things had already been put away. Amazingly, the Thatchers had managed to have her bags brought from the inn in the time between the interview and now.

"The room is absolutely beautiful, Elizabeth, but it really is too much."

"Nonsense, child. You'll be caring for my grandson until he wakes. I only wish that I could make it feel more like home for you. Now, if you will follow me, I will take you to Addison."

Alison followed the woman back out into the hallway and down to the room next to hers.

"You will have full access to this room, day or night. I will show you where we keep all the supplies that you need, and so on, and then leave you to your job. Dinner is served at six o'clock, sharp. After dinner, you will come to my study to discuss pay and so on, and for you to sign some papers."

"Alright." Despite her confidence, the butterflies in her stomach were fluttering like mad. After seeing the portrait of him as a child, and to hear about how handsome he was, she was nervous to actually lay eyes on him.

The room was dark, and dreary. The heavy curtains that hung on the windows were drawn closed. There was a lamp lit on the far side of his bed. It cast an eerie shadow as it revealed his silhouette behind the sheer curtains around Addison's bed, where he was lying, motionless, except for the rise and fall of his chest. They didn't get close enough to the bed for her to get a good look at him, which sent a feeling of disappointment through her. Elizabeth led her to a large cabinet. Behind the mahogany doors, there were shelves stocked with everything that she could possibly need; catheter bags, gauze, bandages, bed pan, wet pads, a blood pressure cuff, and stethoscope.

After she had the walkthrough of where everything she would need could be located, Elizabeth left the room.

Alison slowly walked over to the bed, and stood at the foot of the giant footboard, and looked in on him through the curtains. As if a nervous tick, she started to fidget, and bite her lower lip.

"Um, hello Addison...my name is Alison, and I am here to take care of you now. I am sure that you would rather have your fiancé here to care for you, as she should, but she needed to take some time off. I hope that you don't mind. I promise that I will be gentle and try not to..." She felt silly, talking to him, but it was a proven fact that coma patients could hear everything around them. "Let's see here...I need more light." She walked to the side of the bed closest to the door, and turned on the other lamp. The visibility improved dramatically, but her vision of him was still impaired because of the sheer curtains that went around the bed.

She moved them out of her way, and tied them to the posts, and sat down on the bed at his hip. Anger and disgust welled up inside of her as she got a good look at him. She leaned forward, and got poked with something sharp. Upon investigation, she gently lifted his hand, and found what had jabbed her leg. She felt a slight shudder of his hand.

"It's alright. I am here to help." She said softly.

His nails were longer than hers. They were jagged, and rough, and a couple were cracked and split.

"This is not healthy or sanitary." She carefully slid off the bed, setting his hand back down at his side. She looked in his night stands for a nail grooming kit. She found one, as well as a shaving razor, strap, brush, and lotion bowl. She looked at his face, and pulled them from the drawer, as well as a pair of scissors and a comb.

As she stood back, and surveyed his current appearance, she became even angrier at his condition. Even in a coma, personal hygiene was very important. She was grateful for her years of experience with the elderly men at the home, because she knew how to use all the things that she had found.

"I think that I am going to need some help. I need to bathe you, before I do anything about your beard, nails and hair. I will be back very soon." And suddenly, she felt like she was back at the home again, and began to go to work.

Her first mission was to get into some comfortable clothes that would make it easier to move around, because the dress and little white gloves would not do. She rushed to her room, and rummaged through her things. She found a set of plain scrubs, and put them on. She slipped on her tennis shoes, and took her hair down, and pulled it back into a ponytail. If she was going to do her job right, she needed to be dressed for the job, contrary to what nurses in the current decade wore. If asked, she would come up with something to tell them.

She flew past Becky in the hall, and then came to a halt, turning on her heels.

"Becky, please do me a favor and find your father for me. Also, if you would grab some fresh sheets and meet me in Addison's room. Please and thank you."

"Miss Alison, your clothes…" The girl gaped at her, her mouth wide open."

"They are the new style for nurses now. It makes it easier to work. Dresses are too constrictive." She said quickly, not even thinking of what to say. "The sheets…Roger…please."

"Yes, miss. I'm going." The girl sped down the hall and retrieved sheets and then went to find her father.

After a fast ten minutes passed, Alison had gotten everything that she needed to do what was needed, except for one thing. She walked, calmly to the study door, and knocked.

She heard Elizabeth say to come in, so she slowly opened the door and stuck her head in.

"Elizabeth, I don't mean to bother you, but would you happen to have a recent picture of Addison?"

"It's no bother, my dear. If you don't mind my asking, what do you need a picture of him for, exactly?" She disregarded the apparel that Alison was donning, as unorthodox as it may seem. It covered what needed to be covered, and looked rather comfortable.

"Have you seen your grandson's current appearance? That fiancé of his didn't care for him as she should have, if at all. I need the picture as reference."

"Very well. Right there, on my desk. It was taken last Christmas." She got up, and handed the frame to Alison. "I have to admit, I have seen him, though I have never actually gotten close enough to see the true extent of his appearance. My heart breaks to see him in that bed, knowing there is nothing I can do for him. I talked to Lena about his hair and nails...and she said that she would take care of it, but it is painfully obvious, by the look of disgust on your face, that she didn't do as promised."

"Not to worry, because I will take care of it. That is what you hired me for, right?" she grasped the woman's hand. "You may not be able to bring him out of the coma, Elizabeth, but he needs to know that you are still here, and that you love him. He may not be able to respond to you, but he will hear you if you talk to him. Go in there, and talk to him...hold his hand."

"He can hear me?" Her eyes shot open wide.

"He is not deaf, so he had got to hear what is going on even if he can't respond. Addison is still in there, somewhere." She took a look at the clock on the desk. "I need to go get to work. I have a lot to do before dinnertime." She gave Elizabeth's hand one last squeeze, and then left.

"What did I tell you, Lizzie....Gumption!" Arthur removed the pipe from between his teeth long enough to say his bit, then stuck it back in his mouth, took a couple puffs, and continued to read his paper on the couch, his legs crossed.

With Roger's assistance, Alison was able to thoroughly clean Addison from head to toe, change his clothes, and get the sheets changed. After she cut his hair, she decided to treat the beginnings of bedsores developing, which she caught before any real damage had been done.

She put one last bandage with cream over the sore that was developing on his shoulder. She slipped him into an undershirt. She was going to put on a regular shirt, but decided against it, because of how warm it was in the room. She trimmed Addison's nails, and filed them so they were smooth again.

"In all honesty, Roger, I am surprised that he was not covered with sores. The bandages should help to remove the irritation."

"We did have a few nurses come here from the hospital, to prevent them from developing, but Lena kept chasing them off. The last one stopped coming over a week ago. I would have done it, but I wasn't sure what needed to be done. However, even if I had known, Lena wouldn't have let me do it. I truly believe that she was trying to kill him, which wouldn't have helped her at all, since they hadn't gotten married yet. Good thing, too." He helped to lay Addison back down. "I have to admit, you are exactly what he needed right now. You really know what you are doing."

"If I didn't, I wouldn't be here, Roger." She smiled at him, as she began to mix the shaving lotion.

After brushing the white lather onto his face, she used precision to get as close of a shave as possible. Roger stood and watched her work, and was shocked that she had not nicked him once.

"You're good. I may have to ask for you to do mine, too. I always cut myself."

"Oh, come now, Roger. You are perfect, just as you are. But, if you would like me to, I will do yours too." She felt an overwhelming sense of pride at her handiwork, but the gratification that Roger gave her only made her feel better about it.

After another ten minutes, not only had she given Roger the best shave he had ever gotten, but she trimmed his beard and moustache, and gave him a quick haircut to finish. He looked at himself in the mirror, and smiled.

She took the time to clean up after herself and change back into proper clothing, and walk into the dining room before the clock in the foyer chimed six times.

Everyone was gathered around the table, and the meal was not only delicious, but there was more than enough for everyone to eat as much as they wanted with plenty left over.

After everyone had had their fill, Corrine gathered the leftovers, and took them to the kitchen. Alison, grateful for the good meal, went to help put things away.

"Do you have something for me to put this into?" She asked the Irish woman, who was busy doing something at the counter.

"Bring them here, love. We don't waste food. We are blessed and so we bless others who cannot do for themselves." As Alison came closer, she saw what Corrine was doing. Carefully, she was wrapping the leftover food up and putting it in a basket. "Please get Rebecca and ask her that the basket is ready to go. The Harpers are waiting, and I would hate for the food to get cold before they could eat it."

The fact that the food being wrapped carefully was to feed another family made her heart swell.

"That is absolutely beautiful. No food goes to waste."

"Not in this house it doesn't. Mrs. Thatcher likes to help others out, because that is just who she is. Now, could you get my daughter, please?"

Alison walked out into the dining room, and everyone was smiling at her. Roger was standing amidst the rest of them, and Arthur was examining the closeness of his shave.

"You did this, my dear?" Arthur crooned, the gruffness of his voice sounded like a cat purring.

"Yes, sir, I did." She blushed. Suddenly realizing what she had come back into the dining room for, she looked to Becky. "Becky, your mother asked me to come get you. The food is ready to go to the Harper's."

"Very well." Becky sighed, and went through the open door, as Alison joined the others.

"This is like a work of art in itself, Miss Moreno. Where in the world did you acquire the knowledge to do this?" Arthur put his hand on her shoulder, as if willing her to tell him her secret.

"My father taught me. Would you like me to give you a shave too, sir?"

"You would do that for me?" He was like a child, being offered a big surprise.

"It's the least I can do. Have a seat in the sitting room. I will get the things I need, and be right back." She ran up the stairs, and quietly crept into Addison's room, to retrieve the things she needed. Not even thinking about it, she began to talk to Addison, as if he had just asked her what she was doing. "Obviously, I did such a good job of shaving you, and Roger…now your grandfather is asking that I do his as well. So, I have come up to borrow your straight razor and other things. After I am done, I will return them to you. I hope you don't mind." She looked over at him, and felt like slapping herself in the head. "Of course, you don't mind. You aren't exactly about to say no, now are you?" She giggled to herself.

After collecting the items she needed, she wrapped them in a towel, and held them with one hand, as she swept a strand of hair from his face.

"You just rest. I will be up again soon, to check on you." She smiled at him, and she could have sworn that the corner of his mouth twitched, but figured it was just her imagination.

Chapter Nine

After a week or so of caring for Addison, she had fallen into a routine, and she felt like, unlike at the retirement home, she had a little more freedom and say as to what was done when. She changed his catheter bag twice a day, as she made sure that he was being hydrated the way he was supposed to, and not the way that his ex-fiancé had been doing it, which left him severely dehydrated and gaunt. She was able to remove the bandages from his body, as there was no longer a risk of bed sores. She exercised and massaged his muscles every morning, and every evening before she retired to her room for the night.

Unlike her job at the retirement home, she didn't end the day exhausted, but rather went to bed so that she was sure to get a little time to herself every day. She would bathe, get into comfortable sleeping clothes, read a little, and Becky would bring her a cup of herbal tea. After her tea, she would climb into her plush bed, and sleep soundly, until she had to rise to start the next day over again. She rose with the sun, went to the kitchen and made herself toast, as she was up before everyone else, and then enter Addison's room for her morning conversation with the comatose man.

As his physical health and overall appearance improved in her care, she noticed that there was something rather appealing about his features, and she would often just sit and study his face.

His eyes were no longer sunken in, but rather surrounded by smooth skin, and his long eyelashes were laying softly on the top of his rosy cheeks. He had a very masculine jawline, and a small dimple in his chin. His lips were a healthy pink color, and every now and again, she felt the temptation to touch them. With his hair cut and his face shaved, he now resembled an older version of the young boy in the portrait downstairs.

He had a physique that would make you think that he hadn't stopped working out, as his muscles were still quite toned, despite lack of physical activity. She put the fact that she worked his muscles everyday into account for his maintenance of tone. He had long, strong looking arms, and soft, flawless hands. She noticed that, every once in a while a finger or two would twitch, but that was only natural, especially for coma patients.

Just like that first evening, she found herself talking to him, as if he were just lying there, listening to her every word and taking an interest. Sometimes she would even imagine that he responded to her, though she knew he hadn't. It started out as a game to pass the time, but she found that she was able to speak freely to him about certain things that she couldn't speak to others about, knowing that he would not tell anyone, or freak out and run. And though she knew that he could in fact hear her voice, at least to an extent, she had no worried of being exposed. He was the perfect secret keeper.

His condition hadn't changed, as far as showing signs of waking up, and that concerned Elizabeth and Arthur. The doctors had said that the longer it took him to wake up, the more possibility there was that permanent damage could be done. However, medical science and research was not as advanced as it was in Alison's time, so she was not nearly as worried, as long as he didn't run a fever or show any issues. The trust that the Thatcher's had put in her, when it came to their grandson, was quite overwhelming for her.

One night, after her bath, Becky came to bring her nightly tea, and Alison asked her to stay and talk for a bit. She wanted to know more of the gentleman she was caring for, not only medically but quite recently, emotionally.

"What was he like before his accident, Becky? What kind of person was he?" She took a sip of her tea, and held it in her hands.

"Addison? Do you want to know what he was like before the accident, or before Lena?"

"Was there a difference?" This confused Alison, as being in a relationship very seldom changed a person that drastically, in her experience.

"There is a huge difference, Miss. When he started dating Lena, he became a very unlikable person. He got into a lot of trouble because of her, and the crowd that they associated themselves with." She had a grimace on her freckled face. "He started to treat me, as well as my mum and dad, like his personal slaves…because that is how *she* treated us. He was mean and he barked orders at us, as if he owned us."

"Oh, that is just terrible, considering how his grandparents feel about you. You are like family, not pieces of property."

"Try and convince Lena of that, would ya…cuz no amount of talking to her got anywhere. She had corrupted everything that was good about him and I miss how he used to be."

"He wasn't always like that? Not even a little?"

"Not even slightly…He was my friend. We grew up together. Like Ma'am told you earlier, I used to play with his sisters when they would come here to visit, and the four of us would romp through the halls like mad. When they passed, we comforted each other. He was like me big brother. As we got older, he was very protective of me, and he would help me with the wash, and errands that needed to be ran. He was the model of a good guy here in Woodcrest, and when he came of age, the object of many a girl's affections. Don't get me wrong, he has always been a looker, but it was his personality that everyone loved the most. For a while, even *I* had a crush on him. He was the whole package. But, when he started hanging with the group from the east side of town, things went bad."

"How long had he been this way…you know, behaving badly, before his accident? Is that what caused the coma, something he did, or got involved in?" She asked before taking another sip of tea.

"It was only within the past year that all this started happening, but I don't think that his accident had anything to do with that. The morning of his accident, he and his grands got into it over Lena, and he ran off. The next thing we know, he's in the hospital. Doctors can't explain why he is in the coma. No head trauma or nothin'…other than a minor concussion, but the doctors say that that wouldn't have caused this. Someone just hit his car and then…"

"That is very odd."

"Yeah, I know. Personally, I think it had a lot to do with Lena. Maybe he found out that she never loved him, just his money and connections. Maybe he couldn't cope with the truth."

"I really hate people like that, only out for what they can get from other people. Just between you and me, Becky, I think that this coma may be like a reset button for him. When he wakes up, he may be the same Addison you knew."

"Reset button, miss?" She inquired, confused.

"Oh, sorry. It's a saying where I come from…it means that he will go back to being the Addison that you once knew, before all the bad stuff." Alison needed to remind herself that certain sayings were not understood here, especially ones that referred to technology from her time. "He looks like he is at peace, and I usually have a knack for reading people. He seems like he is the kind of guy that you described…sweet, honorable, and respectful."

"That he was, plus some. I really pray you are right, provided he wakes up." Becky got a sad look on her face, as though she felt like she had lost her favorite toy or security blanket.

"He will wake up, Becky. I promise that I will do everything I can to make that happen."

"Ma'am said that you have a kind, giving heart. You are selfless. You truly want to help him, don't you?"

"Of course I do." She found it odd that Becky would even question her motives, especially after seeing firsthand what she had already done. He no longer looked sickly and frail, like he had under Lena's care. He looked healthy, and aside from being hooked up to feeding tubes and such, he looked as though he was just sleeping. At the mere thought of him, a smile crept across her face. How she longed to see him open his eyes, to see him flash her that brilliant, dimpled smile of his. Becky watched Alison's expression change, and she began to smile as well, as she finally figured out what was making her smile.

"You have taken a liking to him, as well, haven't ya? I can tell it just by lookin' at ya." Her little Irish voice twittered, quietly. "I walk by the room sometimes, and can hear ya talk to him, as if you are carrying on a full conversation."

"You've heard that?!" Alison whispered, startled.

"Well, I mean, it is all garbled and muffled by the doors, but I do hear ya, yeah. How does it feel to talk to yourself? Some might think that you have gone off the tizzy if they heard you going on and on like that, knowing that you are talking to an unconscious person, who won't answer back."

"It sounds crazy, I know, but it is therapeutic for both of us. Just because he doesn't respond as you or I would, doesn't mean that he can't hear. I talk to him, directly, because he can hear me. Eventually, something in his brain will click back on, and he will wake up."

"I love your optimism, Miss." She smiled.

"Becky, why do you call me Miss? I am no different than you."

"It's a sign of respect, Miss."

"I know you respect me, just as I respect you, and your mother and father. Please, do me a favor. Just call me Alison, or Allie, okay?" She put her free hand on Becky's shoulder, and gave it a gentle squeeze. Becky nodded, liking the fact that she could address her by her name. It made her feel as though they were more like friends, and less like acquaintances.

"Ms. Elizabeth was right about one thing. You were sent to us like an angel, to mend our hearts and bring Mr. Addison back to us, fully restored."

"I don't know how soon that will be, but I will do my best to bring him back to us...uh...you...all of you." She stumbled over her words.

"You *HAVE* taken a liking to him. You've got it bad, too. I knew it. I mean, who wouldn't? Ever since you have cared for him, he looks like a whole new man. He is sinfully handsome, and I love that you have left his hair a bit long. It is very becoming of him."

"Oh, Becky, please don't tell anyone. He's a man in a coma, and I am caring for him. It would look unprofessional and very inappropriate." She blushed.

"You needn't worry, Allie. Your secret is safe with me. Well, I need to go to bed. You should do the same. I know that you are an early riser." She rose from her chair, across from Alison, took the empty tea cup from her and left her, quietly closing the door as she left the room.

Thoughts of Addison's face, and fantasies of him awake, smiling and laughing filled her dreams that night.

Alison resigned herself to the fact that she was falling for the man under her care, but was unsure as to what she was going to do about it. She knew that it was inappropriate and unprofessional, especially considering certain things that were included in her duties, such as bathing him and changing his clothing. However, she never did those things alone, and those that helped her never saw her do anything that would jeopardize her morality and professionalism. She had learned to balance her job with her innermost feelings, and compartmentalize things. She had to admit, though, that she had never been in this situation before with any previous clients, as all of them were elderly, and that would have been worse than the situation she was facing, presently.

Aside from her physical attraction to Addison, there was this sinking feeling in her gut that caused her to want to be close to him, like a magnetic pull. She couldn't explain it, but it was getting progressively stronger as the days passed by.

What was it about him that made her want to be so close? She felt like he was a drug to her, unable to resist and so enticing. When she would read to him, she would sit with him, on his bed, or she would sit on a chair next to him, and hold the book in one hand and his hand in the other. When she had to turn the page, she would set the book down on the bed, turn the page with her free hand, and then pick it back up, never letting go of his hand for a second.

She had learned in school, aside from talking to a comatose patient, they benefitted from real physical contact; a hand to hold, massages, a caress of some kind. Alison was more than happy to comply.

Suddenly, after realizing that her feelings were overshadowing her judgement, she felt guilty for taking advantage of the fact that she spent a large majority of her time with him alone. Knowing that she needed to be careful of how wrapped up in him she got, Alison made a point to involve Becky or Roger in a lot of her duties. It allowed her an excuse to distance herself a bit, to restrain herself, for her sake and for Addison's.

Alison was a very emotionally oriented person, and when she fell for someone, she didn't just fall gradually; she fell really hard, and with everything she had. She practically wore her heart on her sleeve. She had learned the hard way; her emotional attachment to people would sometimes get her nothing but heartache in the end. Distancing herself from him was the best way to guard her heart.

One evening, she invited Becky to come into Addison's room with her, while she did his nightly exercising, and she used Becky to distract her from her innermost feelings. And, amazingly, it worked. On this particular night, the subject of how Becky and her family came to work for the Thatcher's was the topic of discussion.

"So, my dad had lost his job, because of budget cutbacks, and limited funds available to the factories. I was pretty small then, and mom wasn't getting business anymore as a seamstress, and housekeeper. Mum and dad would skip meals just to make sure that I was fed. They would save their money on doing wash, by just washing my clothes, and then rinsing their clothes in the lake, and banging them on rocks. It got really bad." She took over the exercises, allowing Alison to rest for a moment. She lifted his left leg, bending it at the knee, and then setting it back down.

"Anyhow, dad was waiting outside the grocer's, offering to carry people's purchases to their cars for them. Mrs. Thatcher came there one day, but the owner of the grocery didn't want my dad to loiter outside his store anymore. He started to holler at dad, and tell him that the people were capable of carrying their own things. Mrs. Thatcher thought that the way my dad was treated was absolutely horrible, so she offered to pay my dad to carry her groceries, right in front of the man. It burned him up something awful." She switched to Addison's other leg. "Dad and Ma'am started talking by her car, and he told her what had happened and that he, mum and I were going to lose our home, and that I was still pretty small. She said she would not have that happen. She offered mum and dad jobs in her home. She said that, as long as they worked for her, they would never have to want for anything. Their son had moved out, gotten married, and had a family of his own, and since they were up there in age, she couldn't maintain the home as she used to. Mum and dad agreed, and we have been here ever since. When I turned five, she paid to have me go to a private school. I got a top notch education, thanks to them; the kind of education my parents would never have been able to afford. And when I got old enough, I took on some responsibilities of my own. The rest is history, I suppose."

"Wow, Becky. That is the best story I have heard in a while. And I don't think that I have ever heard you talk so much at once before." She laughed, admiring how Becky just rambled on and on.

"I'm sorry."

"No need to be, Becky. It's nice to hear another person's voice for a change. I have to admit, I have spent so much time in here, talking to myself, and I was starting to go crazy." She laughed, taking back over with Addison. Becky sat on the edge of the bed.

"You aren't going crazy. He needed to hear your voice. You have a very sweet voice, and you are very comforting. I am sure that he enjoys hearing you talk to him."

"That's nice of you to say, Becky, but what good has it done so far? He hasn't even moved his arm, or fluttered an eyelash to show that it is making a difference. Besides, my voice won't matter in the end."

"Why is that? Your voice matters."

"To you, maybe. To a guy like Addison, unless it has a beautiful woman attached to it, it will make little to no difference whether my voice is sweet or soothing…He will look right through me. Knowing my luck, the first person he calls for when he wakes up will be that Ninny, Lena."

"Ewww…that won't happen. He's heard your voice all this time, not hers. He will know that she hasn't been here for him at all. And even if he doesn't, I will tell him myself." Becky rose to her feet. "You deserve the recognition for all that you have done for him."

"I don't want you to do that. If I had it my way, he would wake up, see me, and know in an instant who I am." She looked over at his face. "He will look at me, smile, and he would just know…That is what I want to happen. Nothing more, and nothing less than that will make this all worth it." She smiled, and then looked at Becky, and they continued to do his exercises in silence.

Chapter Ten

First thing in the morning, she rose and stretched her arms, ready for another day of caring for Addison. She straightened her bed, and then went to the windows and threw the curtains open. It was beautiful and warm, and she closed her eyes, taking in the sunshine and magnificence of a new day. That night, as she dreamt of the man in the room next to hers, she had a revelation.

As he laid in that bed, day after day, relying on her for everything, he was hers. She swore to herself that she would not get caught up in the fantasy, but it was hard not to. He depended on her. He listened to her. He was a constant in her everyday life, and a part of her hoped that he would wake and look at her, and smile that brilliant smile. She longed to hear him speak, telling her that he knew her and that he wanted her.

The feelings in her heart seemed to override the rational thought in her head, and as she stood in the glow of the sunlight, she knew that she couldn't deny that she had feelings for him. However, she knew that the feelings were short lived. Her feelings were for the man that she hoped he'd be, the one that would love her in return, that was kind and gentle. But, no matter how much she looked forward to the day that he'd awaken and pledge his heart to her, realistically, that may never be the case.

Alison was not the typical 1930's image of beauty. She was not tall, and slender. She was rather average in height, and she was not slender at all, but rather round. She had a full figure, like her mother. And though she was told that bigger was beautiful by her parents and the very few friends she had back home, it was not the same here. The only time that bigger was beautiful *here* was when you were with child, which Alison Moreno was not. There was no promise that Addison would look at her and find her the least bit attractive. However, until the day he opened his eyes, he belonged to her, and she to him. She needed him as much as he needed her right now, and she was okay with that.

She crept into his room, and walked to his bedside. As he lay there in the bed, she looked down on his childlike but masculine features, she couldn't help wonder; when he *did* wake, would he see her face, and feel something for her? She reached over and ran her fingers through his soft hair, sweeping some of the deep brown strands from his face.

"Do you have any idea how much you mean to a lot of people, Adam?" She whispered softly, calling him by the nickname that she had given him over the time that she had cared for him. "You are sleeping your life away." She sat at his side, and took his hand in hers. His hand and arm were limp and showed no sign of voluntary movement. "You need to come back to us."

In the midst of her speech to him, she concentrated on his hand, and was oblivious to the smile that tugged at the corners of him mouth and the slight rising of his brows when she took his hand in hers.

"You need to open your amazing brown eyes and see the world fresh." She felt slight trembling, but nothing to cause alarm. As she held his hand softly in hers, she began to sing, starting off with a hum.

The only place she had ever really sung aloud was in the church choir on Sundays, but she was so comfortable there with him, and she thought that anything she could do to get through to him would help.

This became a normal thing for them from that day on. Every morning, she would sit beside him holding his hand, and sing to him.

But, as she sat beside him every morning, her feelings for him deepening, she had to keep in mind that she wasn't from this time, and eventually find a way home. The thought of him sent a warm wave through her body, and it saddened her to think that returning home would mean that she would have to leave him. He was her reason for waking every morning, but she had to be practical about it. She, also, had to be practical in the thought that he may never feel for her as she did for him. She may never feel his arms around her, or have him hold her hand as lovingly as she held his.

It had already been more than five weeks since she had started taking care of him, and there was no sign of him waking. Her heart was aching for his family, as they became more and more discouraged at every day that passed. Alison, however, never gave up hope that he would regain consciousness and open his eyes, so much so, that she started to sleep in his room, either in the big comfy armchair, or laying at the foot of his enormous king sized bed. She did this to ensure that when he *were* to wake, he wouldn't be alone.

There were times when Roger would come in, and find her in the room, a chair pulled up to his bedside, and her holding a book, fast asleep. He would take the book, mark its page, and cover her before being on his way.

It went on like this for another two and a half weeks, until one morning, something woke her from her sleep at dawn.

She had fallen asleep at his side, a book in one hand, and his hand in the other. The sun came shining through a slit between the curtains, and it was shining right into her face. She was roused awake when she felt something shift beneath the covers. There was a thundering ruckus from the floor below, and she was about to get up to go to the door. She closed the book, and was about to slide her hand out from his, which had somehow ended up underneath his. When she went to pull away, his grip suddenly tightened.

Her eyes widened, and shock surged through her, and he was now gripping her hand tightly, as if unwilling to let her leave his side. She leaned forward, and put her face near his, her free hand on his cheek.

"Adam? Adam, can you hear me? Addison, if you can hear me, open your eyes." She whispered, a certain desperation in her voice that resembled both a cry for help, and a cry of hope. The noise from downstairs was getting closer, and she was torn between wanting the first face he saw when he opened his eyes to be hers and wanting to let others know what was happening. Unfortunately, she didn't get to make the choice as the door flew open, and a very loud and annoying screech bellowed through the room.

"Get your greasy, nasty pig hooves off my fiancé, you fat cow!" The blonde with the bird beak had returned with a vengeance. As tightly as Addison had been holding to Alison's hand, it didn't matter anymore because Lena's voice had startled him and he released it. She stumbled back in surprise, and hit the floor with a loud thud. "How dare you! He is not your personal plaything. He is my fiancé, you trollop!

"Lena, how dare you speak to her in that manner?! Get the hell out of my home. You are no longer welcome here. Get out!" Elizabeth ordered, her voice booming louder than Lena's had, yet with a more controlled tone.

"She is just as much allowed to be here, as that tart you call a nurse is! She's his fiancé!" Mr. Thorton voiced his opinion, waddling himself over to the other side of the bed and grabbing Alison by the arm. "I don't know what you think you are up to, but the game is over now. Go back to the brothel you came from."

"You let her go, this instant! How dare you touch her!" Arthur went storming after Lena's father, wielding his walking stick like a sword, ready to defend Alison's honor.

"Stop this! All of you!! Stop this at once...something has happened! Let me through!" Alison, in a fit of panic, got to her feet, and tried to get to Addison's bedside, but Lena and her father blocked her way. "Please! Let me through...It's Addison!!" She tried to break through, but Lena shoved her away, then turned at the sound of Addison's name.

While Alison fought to return to Addison's side, and Arthur and Lena's father were screaming at one another, Elizabeth, and Lena saw something amazing happen.

Raising his hands to his head, and rubbing his eyes, Addison was attempting to sit up.

"Addie...baby? You're awake..." Lena leapt onto the bed, and was now straddling him.

"For goodness sake, Lena, get down from there this instant!" Elizabeth ordered, hardly believing what she was seeing.

"Aspirin...I need aspirin..." Addison whispered, and was surprised that he was unable to speak any louder than that. "What in heaven's name is wrong with my voice?"

"Oh, my love...how I've missed you!" Lena squealed, and began to kiss him. After a few minutes, she pulled away, and he coughed.

"I guess I missed you too. Did I go somewhere?" A small chuckle escaped him, as he tried to clear his throat, and catch his breath.

Alison's heart fell into her stomach, and she swallowed hard, as her throat became restricted. She shut her eyes to keep the group that had barged in from seeing the tears that were welling up in them.

Silently, she crept from the room, and quickly retreated to her room. As her door began to shut behind her, Rebecca saw her friend burst into tears, and throw herself to the floor next to her bed, a look of absolute despair on her sweet face. A fury raged in the petite Irish girl, and she stormed into Addison's room.

"You are Savages…no consideration for anyone else in this house with all the yelling and ruckus…" It was then that she saw Addison's face. Something clicked in her head, and her heart ached for Alison.

"Be gone, you little guttersnipe!" Lena spoke in a very demeaning tone, and Addison immediately reacted.

"Lena! Who on earth do you think you are talking to?! Don't ever let me hear you speak like that to Rebecca again!" He shoved her off of him, and threw back his covers.
"Becky...Sweet, sweet Becky!" As he attempted to get up and walk over to his old friend, his legs suddenly gave out. Becky rushed over him, and caught him, before he hit the floor, and she embraced him tightly, taking on his full weight until he had the strength to stand on his own. Alison was right. Something had happened to him, and he was acting like the old friend she used to know.

"Addison, I cannot even begin to say how glad I am to hear you call me that again."

"Why? Did I stop?"

"Let's just say that you were under the influence..."

"My boy!" Arthur, eyes full of tears, whacked Mr. Thorton over the head with his stick, and rushed to his grandson's side. Elizabeth joined him, and they embraced him.

Becky suddenly remembered a certain teary-eyed girl in the room next door.

"Oh my goodness…Alison!" She removed herself from the group hug, and took off out into the hallway.

Chapter Eleven

With all the excitement of Addison's return to consciousness, the sobbing in the next room was only heard by one person for a while. Becky had slid down onto the floor, and was caressing Alison's hair, while she sobbed. She had no way of consoling her heartbroken friend, though she could understand fully. Endless nights at his side, countless hours of reading, massaging, exercising, cleaning…and her reward at the end was not the one which she sought. Instead, she was brushed aside and made invisible in the eyes of the one she sacrificed so much for. Was it Addison's fault? Of course it wasn't his fault. How could Allie have expected him to see her, when the only thing that he saw when he opened his eyes was a blonde, screeching vulture in his face? The scene had escalated so quickly that even Becky had a lot of trouble registering what was what.

A good half hour of time lapsed by, and finally a couple familiar faces peeked through the opening in the door. When Elizabeth and Arthur saw the state of Alison, they rushed over to her, just as they had done for Addison.

"Dear God! What happened? Alison, darling…are you alright?" Elizabeth whispered softly, laying her hand on her cheek.

"Did Lena or Mr. Thorton do or say something to you? I mean, other than what we had witnessed?" Arthur, still vibrating with fury over the short, filthy, waddling man who had put a crack in his walking stick.

"Did any of you even stop to think that there was one person in the room that Addison should have met…spoken to…or even thanked? Does he even know about Alison?"

"Of course he does. I mean, she was right there when he woke up…wasn't she?" Arthur stated, and then looked like he wasn't quite sure.

"He had to have seen her. She was next to him when he woke up, at his side." Even Elizabeth's words weren't as certain as they should have been.

"I can understand the two of you being caught up in the moment, but how quickly you forget the one who spent countless tiring hours at your grandson's bedside, willing him to awaken." A familiar voice was heard from the doorway behind them. "It sounds as if you are unsure about Addison's knowledge of his caretaker. If I had been there, I would have made her presence obvious."

Roger looked aged, as he had just finally gotten the two unwanted guests out of the house, trying to convince them that though Addison had just awoken from a three and a half month slumber, he still needed his rest.

"Thank you, Roger, but my feelings are inconsequential. All that matters is that he is awake now." Alison sniffled, and wiped her puffy eyes with the back of her hand. "It doesn't matter anymore, anyway. The moment that mattered the most came and went, and I am just happy that he is awake." She sat up, and attempted to salvage what was left of her dignity. "Maybe it's better that he not know about me."

"Of course he needs to know about you, sweetheart. How would we explain who took care of him? None of us have the medical knowledge that you do. And goodness knows, Lena wouldn't be able to find her way out of a cardboard box without directions." Arthur sighed.

"He had doctors and nurses."

"No, Allie! It was you! You brought him back to us, not some doctors or nurses. You performed a miracle, and you should be acknowledged for it." Roger walked over, past the others, and helped her to her feet. Becky got up too, and quickly wiped her eyes with a handkerchief, and straightened her friend's hair.

"I agree, papa. Now that the dust has settled, she needs to meet Addison, and he needs to meet her."

"I can't. I look a wreck. I'm not ready. I don't want to. It will only confuse him. He needs to rest right now. That was too much excitement to deal with right away." She was rambling as she was being dragged out the door, and down the twenty feet to his door.

"What are you so afraid of, my dear? If he can deal with all that right away, he will welcome a quiet, calmer meeting. Your voice, by far, is more pleasing to the ear." Arthur insisted, as he passed them, and headed down the stairs, to commence with is morning routine of reading the paper. "It will do you both some good."

One last shove by Becky, and Alison was now standing by his door, her hand on the handle. She looked back at the three people still watching from a distance. She turned back, and grasped the handle, trying to muster up the courage. She raised her other hand to knock, but it hung in the air inches from the mahogany barrier.

"What's taking you so long? Knock on the door and go in!" Becky whispered loudly. "Go!" She motioned for her to knock, and so Alison did.

She only knocked one time, her hand still on the handle. The door swung open, pulling her into the room, awkwardly, and her face made contact with a chest of warm muscle.

"Ooh...careful, sweetheart!" A husky, partially hoarse voice quickly responded, catching the stumbling girl who had practically kissed his bare skin. But the instant that he grabbed her hand, a shock of electricity jolted though them both. There was something strangely familiar about her touch, a calming sensation coursed through his body, and he looked at her. She looked to her hand, which was in his, and saw the way his fingers curved around her palm, firm but gentle. Slowly, she looked up at his face.

"I...uh...I'm sorry. I didn't mean to...I didn't expect you to..." Unable to get the words out, she seemed to melt beneath the stare of the deep cocoa and caramel colored eyes. She began to shake, her knees about to give out beneath her. Suddenly, she felt the room spin, and her head got heavy. Everything got dark, and she collapsed.

His quick reflexes kicked in and he caught her before she hit the floor. The awkwardness of the situation caused him to blush as he looked around.

"Oh, good gracious! She's passed out!" Roger rushed forward, to assist in helping Addison get her safely to the floor.

"Even after all this time, Roger, I still have the ability to make girls swoon." Addison chuckled, sweeping hair from the face of this strangely familiar girl. There was something about her, something that he couldn't quite put a finger on. It was almost as if he had seen her in a dream he'd had. He looked at Roger, and gave him a shrug.

"Well, that didn't go the way it was supposed to." Becky sighed, disappointed, as she came to her friend's side. "Addison, shouldn't you be in bed, resting?"

"If I had been, she would have hit the floor like a bag of rocks." He snipped back, giving the ginger girl a grin and a wink.

"She wouldn't have passed out, if you had been in bed, and not in her face like a mammoth brick wall!" Becky quipped back. He responded by giving her a raspberry.

"Who is she?" His attention was oddly drawn back to the girl he was cradling in his lap.

"This is Alison Moreno." She smiled at him.

"Do I know her? What is she doing here?" He shifted his position, cradling her head more carefully.

"You should know her. She's the one who has been taking care of you for the past two and a half months." Elizabeth, stepped over, handing her grandson a small vile she had retrieved from her pocket.

"Was she assisting Lena? I mean, obviously, she must have been. Lena couldn't have done everything all alone." He opened the vial, and waved it below the girl's nose. As Alison began to awaken, she looked up, and the first thing she saw was his lips, and brilliantly white teeth.

"Oy, angel eyes…hope I didn't frighten you. I must look a shambles." He smiled at her, and she slowly began to open and close her eyes.

"You're perfect…" She sighed at the sight of his smile and his dimples, then realized what she had just said, and her eyes shot open. "…I meant, perfectly fine. I just didn't expect you to open the door just then. They told me that you were in bed, resting." She noticed his arms, where the I.V.'s were. "My God…did you pull your tubes out yourself?!? You're bleeding!" She jumped up, and attempted to run into the room for bandages, but was still light headed, and so she stumbled and hit the floor.

"Great Scott! I *am* bleeding." He got up, and followed her into the room, helping her to her feet without getting any more blood on her. He helped her to the couch by the fireplace, and Elizabeth handed her a glass of water to drink. Without needing to be asked, Rebecca and Roger retrieved the bandages and soapy water for her.

After she had composed herself enough, she had Addison sit on a chair in front of her. Gently washing the blood from his arms, she bandaged where the I.V. ports had been.

"I should have waited for Lena to return, so she could have taken them out, shouldn't I have?" He rubbed the gauze on his arm. Unintentionally, Alison snickered.

"I'm sorry to say, but no." She said, a smile still on her face, amused at his assumption that his mentally-insufficient ex-fiancé would have known what to do.

"Why not? She must know what to do, right? I mean, she's taken care for me for the last couple months."

"Unfortunately, she wouldn't, unless she was a nurse. That's why I am here."

"Oh…well, then I guess I am glad that I waited to remove the other thing." He pointed down at his groin area.

"OKAY!! I am out of here!" Becky squealed, highly embarrassed at his reference to the catheter tube in his man parts. She grabbed her father's hand, and gestured for Elizabeth to follow. "They are going to need a little privacy for this one. I will lock the door behind me. We don't want a certain someone to burst through the door, you know, in the middle of you doing that little task. You don't need to be startled." She made a gesture that only Alison could see, and it shocked her so much that she burst out laughing at the pure obscenity of it. Addison jerked his head around, to see what had made her laugh, but he just saw the door shut behind them.

"What was so funny?" He smiled, wanting to be in on the joke, which he obviously didn't get.

"Don't trouble yourself. You *really* don't want to know." She was still laughing as she gathered the things that she needed.

"Isn't this going to be a little awkward for you? You know, working down there?" He blushed, looking at her, and then down at his lap.

"No more awkward than it was to bathe you." She was slightly amused at the shocked expression on his face at her admittance that she had already been south of his navel. He crossed his legs, and blushed. "If it makes you feel any better, I used to work with the elderly. You are a vast improvement over that…and much more pleasing to the eyes." She saw him grab a towel from the shelf, and place it over his lap, as she was sure that that had literally perked him up slightly. She shot him a sideways smile, and then returned her attention to the supplies. "Now, go lie down on the bed, and I will be there to remove that, momentarily. Grab the bedpan on your way over. You are going to need it."

"Bedpan?" He stood up, and looked around for what she had asked for.

"It looks like a metal toilet seat. It's up on the top shelf…just there." She pointed up to where it was located in the cupboard, and then continued to look for the things she would need.

As he slid himself onto the bed, and positioned himself, a weird feeling went through him. Why was he so willing to lie there, and allow a stranger, who wasn't his fiancé, to handle his...man parts? Was it that she was a nurse? Or was there something else there, some subconscious familiarity between this russet-haired girl across the room and himself? The strong feeling of trust he had in her was bewildering to him, and yet he was not about to argue with his instincts.

"Just so you know, you are going to have to go to see the doctors at the hospital to remove the feeding tube." She stated, as she walked over to the bed, and set the tray down on the table.

"Okay...if you say so." He laid there, feeling very strange. He looked at Alison, and studied her movements. "So, are you sure that you feel comfortable doing this? I am sure that Lena..." He started, but she interrupted him before he had a chance to finish his statement.

"Alright, stop right there. Your female friend is neither trained, nor mature enough to be able to remove this catheter correctly. So, if you think she is more equipped to do this, without causing damage, by all means. I will step aside, and we will have her do it, but it will cause you a lot of pain, not to mention that, if not done correctly, it could cause serious medical issues. It's your choice." She stepped back, and threw her hands up in the air.

"I just...I mean, have you done this before?" He asked, and to answer his question, she pulled his pants, and undergarments down, placed the bedpan between his legs, snipped, and then he heard liquid draining into the metal pan. He was about to panic, but then he felt a weird sensation, and she was done. He barely felt anything, and she was walking away. He thought he caught a smirk on her face, but she walked away so quickly he couldn't tell.

"I think I liked you better when you were in a coma, Addison. You never questioned my ability to care for you before. It is quite irritating."

"I'm sorry. Am I inconveniencing you? I said that I could have had Lena do it." He sounded a little upset, but she just walked over to him, and crossed her arms over her chest.

"It's not an inconvenience...it's my job. Now, before you start getting indignant with me, I suggest that you *have* some dignity, and pull up your pants. Just be careful. You are going to be a little uncomfortable for a few days." He quickly pulled his pants up, and got off the bed, and felt discomfort, but that didn't stop him from standing up in front of her, and blocking her from walking away.

"I'm sorry." His tone was no longer harsh, but very calm and apologetic. "I really am. I appreciate you being here, now, and the last couple months to help Lena. This couldn't have been that easy on her." He had this look in his eyes, as though he wasn't quite sure that he believed what he was saying.

"Addison...about that...um..." She wanted to set him straight, but then he began talking again.

"I know that it was probably hard on you, as well. Lena is not exactly easy to get along with, but I love her. And, she loves me, too. So, thank you for enduring her constant moodiness, and ill-nature. She didn't exactly grow up with the best role model as far as social etiquette." He went to the window, and looked out. The sun shined in, and revealed hues of lighter browns and crimson in his dark hair. She decided that she needed to be honest with him, even if it meant that he would be mad, and probably call her a liar.

"Addison, the truth is...Lena didn't...Lena wasn't..." She stumbled to get the words out.

"I think I know what you are trying to say, and I am inclined to believe you, just because I know Lena better than anyone else does." He turned his head, and looked at Alison, and there was a clarity in his eyes. "But, for now, can you just let me believe that Lena loved me enough to stick around and take care of me, instead of ditching me and making someone else get their hands dirty?"

The sadness in his voice was almost heart-breaking. She nodded, and began to walk away. Against her better judgment, she turned back to him, and said something that she never thought she would say. After all, it was already clear to him that she had been there, caring for him, and not Lena. He had acknowledged the fact that he knew the truth, but that acknowledgement was hard to deal with, considering that he obviously still loved her, despite the truth.

"If it makes any difference, she *was* here the first month. She *did* make an effort to care for you, herself. But, when you are not mentally or physically equipped to deal with the stresses of what all is required of you, in this situation, there is only so much you can do before it just overwhelms you. I just wanted you to know that."

The gratitude that shined in his eyes was like a reward to her. Though she stretched the truth a bit, and made it seem as though Lena made an ***actual*** effort to care for him, the fact that she even said anything to him about it seemed to make a difference in his eyes. She could have just walked away, and left him feeling disheartened, but she had decided to speak on his fiancé's behalf, and he felt his heart swell with gratitude for her kindness. He shot her a smile, and then looked back to the sunshine. She stood there, admiring the sight of him, basking in the warm sunlight. For a moment, she was jealous of the ray of warmth that glowed on his skin. She sighed, and finished cleaning up, and then excused herself without another word.

Alison had made peace with the fact that she had pretty much tightened the noose around her neck that day. Not only had she lost the opportunity of a lifetime, being the first face that he saw when he woke from his coma, but then she actually made Addison believe that Lena actually cared enough to make an effort to take care of him. When she told Becky what she had told him, she had to sit down.

"Why would you say that to him? You and I both know that what you said about her was a lie. The only things she did when she was here were go through his things, complain, and steal from him. What part of that signified that she cared about him?"

"Becky, you should have seen the look on his face. He looked so defeated and depressed. I had to say something to him."

"All I have to say is that you are a better person than I would have been in your situation. Knowing that he actually knew the truth, I would have just walked my happy arse right outta there, without a word." She tried to see the situation from Alison's point of view, but she just couldn't understand why she would do what she did, especially after what Lena had called her.

Alison regretted lying to Addison, but to give him that hope, despite the fact that it was false hope, it was worth it to her.

"All I have to say is this…it was a stupid move on your part, Allie. You just shot yourself in the foot. But, if I were

Addison, I'd strongly consider his choices before making a decision."

As if Alison didn't already regret not keeping her mouth shut, what happened a few days later was a clincher.

Lena came over to retrieve her engagement ring, and spotted Alison coming out of Addison's room. It made no difference that she just went in to borrow a book, or that he wasn't even in there at the time. Lena felt the need to lay down the law as far as Alison's involvement in Addison's life. She came charging up the stairs, and cornered Allie, and stuck her finger in her face.

"Let's get something straight, right here and right now. Addison is *mine*! That being said, stay away from him! Your job is completed. There is no reason why you should continue to even be here, but since you are, you need to become invisible to him. You don't talk to him, you don't look at him, don't even breathe the same air he does. If he comes into a room, you leave. If he is in a room that you enter, you leave. If you don't stay away from him, I will make your life Hell. Understood?"

"If you say so, Lena. Quite honestly, I don't see why it should matter to you what I do. You are the one he wants. I am just the nurse that took care of him. Nothing more. I mean nothing to him."

"I want your word that you will stay the heck away from him. And if I catch you even pass by his room again…"

"I have to pass his room to get to mine." Alison stated.

"I want you to move into the servants' quarters then…"

"There are no servants, so why would there be servants' quarters? My room is perfectly fine, thank you very much."

"You are next to his room, so you need to move to a different room, effective immediately." She began to sound like she was having a tantrum.

"Listen, Lena. This is the deal. I will stay away from Addison like you want. I won't talk to him or look at him, and if by chance I do need to speak to him about something, I will do so in your presence." She spoke softly, and slowly so she would comprehend.

"Perfect!" Lena looked satisfied that her orders were going to be followed.

"However, I will NOT move to a different room to satisfy your jealous spoiled brat whim. Do not forget that I am the one that was here, taking care of him for two months. I was the one who shaved him, cut his hair, BATHED him, and held his frail hand, while you were off somewhere in a gutter. I have never done anything to you, have never treated you badly, have never spoke badly to your face or otherwise, yet you have a personal vendetta against me, because I did what you couldn't. You don't have to like me, and I most certainly don't have to like you, but I live here. You don't. So, if you have a problem with the bedroom arrangements...take it up with Elizabeth and Arthur!" And she shoved past Lena, and slammed the door in her face.

"You are still a disgusting, fat...if I find so much as one of your little piggy hoof prints on his door handle, I will have you out of this house faster than you can say 'OINK,' do you hear me!?" Lena screeched at the large thick door.

Inside the room, Alison had to bury her face in the pillow to muffle the screams and sobs. She had just exiled herself from the man that she had come to care very deeply for, all for the sake of not having to endure Lena's heartless name calling and harassment. True, she was not the thinnest girl in the world, but why must that twig consistently berate her with the same insults. She had never done anything to her. Had it not been for Alison, Addison would still be laid up in the bed next door.

The next day, when Addison came up to her to ask her how she was liking the book she borrowed, she handed it to him, and walked away without a word. When he would come to the dinner table to eat, she would not talk to him, hurry to finish her meal or not finish at all, but take her dish to the kitchen and then go out the back door and into the garden.

It broke her heart to do this to him, without explanation, but she figured that this was the best way to eliminate herself from his life, and therefore make it easier to go back home when she had figured out how.

As bad as it was that she was avoiding him, the gut wrenching heartbreak was when he stopped trying to talk to her, and he would avoid her as well.

He couldn't understand why she refused to talk to him, or even acknowledge him. He wanted to find out what he had said or done wrong, to cause her to be so cold towards him. He needed to know the truth, no matter how he had to go about getting it.

As he stood at his bedroom window, watching her in the garden, he thought about the first few days after he had awoken from his coma. It was only after his first day out of the house that he noticed a change in Alison's behavior towards him. He remembered her asking him if she could borrow one of his books before he walked out the door. When he came home that evening, she had handed him the book back with not so much as a word. And since then, she had avoided even being in the same room as him.

As he stood at the window contemplating it, Becky entered the room with fresh towels. It wasn't until she was leaving the room that he said something to her.

"Becky…you have become friends with Alison, haven't you? I mean, you guys seem to spend time together, so I assume that the two of you talk to one another. Am I right?" He turned his head slightly.

"We are friends, and we do talk, yes. Why? Is she not allowed to talk to me either?" Rebecca snarled. Her accusatory question caught him off guard, and he turned around to face her.

"What is that supposed to mean? I just asked you a question. Why on earth would I stop the two of you from talking?"

"I don't know…why do you want to know if we talk?" She crossed her arms over her chest, and shifted her weight to one side.

"I was just curious as to whether she has said anything to you as to why she is avoiding me. Did I say or do anything to offend her?" He walked over to her, and looked as though he was really bothered by the situation. Her expression softened as she searched his eyes.

"You really don't know, do you?"

"I haven't the faintest clue what I did wrong? One moment she is talking to me and we are fine, but then the next moment, she has stopped talking to me, and she is avoiding me completely. How can I fix this? I cannot apologize for what I did wrong if I have no clue what I did." The frustration and desperation in his voice pulled at Becky's mind.

"Why do you care so much? I mean, she served her purpose. Her job is complete here, because you are healthy and back to normal. That's all she was to you…your nurse. Why does it bother you so much that she isn't giving you any attention?"

"Why are you attacking me, Becky? What did I do to her that was so bad that you are mad at me, too?" He flung his arms up in the air. "Have I been such a horrible person since I woke up that everyone is angry with me? I don't know what I have done that would have caused everyone to turn on me like this."

"If you want answers, why don't you ask your fiancé?" Becky screeched and then left, slamming the door in his face before he could ask any more questions. She walked down the stairs, thinking about the conversation that they had just had. *Did he really not know that Lena had confronted Alison? Did he really believe that he had done something to cause Alison to stop talking to him?* She really couldn't put blame on him for Lena's actions, as she had a habit of causing disruption wherever she went without Addison's knowledge. As much as Becky would have liked to blame him for Alison's pain and loneliness, it was Lena's demands, not his, which stated she stay away from him.

Addison felt as though Becky was telling him something without actually telling him. She had asked if Alison was not allowed to talk to her *either*, which meant that someone had told her that she wasn't allowed to speak to someone else. The only person that she had not been talking to was him.

"Did someone forbid her from talking to me?" He thought to himself, spotting her walking out of the garden. Without a second thought, he raced out of his room and down the stairs, past Becky, and headed towards the kitchen. He blasted out the back door, and headed in the direction of the stables with a determined pace.

Alison sat on the bench in the garden, staring off at the distant line of trees that surrounded Woodcrest, thinking about how she was going to get home. Despite the fact that she still harbored deep feelings for Addison, she knew that her feelings weren't reciprocated. The man that she had loved and cared for was going to marry another woman; a woman who did not love or deserve him.

Lena had her engagement ring back on her finger, and she flaunted it to everyone, especially to the one person she knew it would hurt the worst...Alison. And so, because of Lena's constant torment, which Alison concluded was completely intentional, she made a point to avoid her as well. When Lena was at the house, Alison would retreat to her room, or to the garden, where she knew Lena would never be for fear of bugs.

As she contemplated her plans to get home, and away from the daily reminders of her broken heart, she rose from the bench and began to walk along the cobblestone path that led to the field of wildflowers. When she was about halfway into the field, she heard faint thudding behind her. The breeze that blew freely in the field, unencumbered by the trees, blew her auburn tresses about, and temporarily blocked her sight. Because of this, she didn't see a large black and white horse and its rider swiftly head in her direction. The thudding became louder and quicker, and she swept her hair from her eyes just a moment before the source of the galloping was right next to her, and an arm had swept down, grasping her around the waist. She was hoisted up onto the massive equine before she had a chance to react.

"What in Heaven's name!?!" She turned her head, and yelped in protest as the horse was urged into a full-out run.

"This is the only thing I could think of to get your attention. It's just you and I now. Talk to me." He commanded, sternly, looking to where the horse was running and not at her.

"I have nothing to say. Now, let me down." She looked at him, a dozen emotions running through her mind.

"Don't lie to me. I hate liars. Now, talk to me. Why have you been avoiding me and giving me the silent treatment? What could I possibly have said or done to you that would make you give me the cold shoulder?"

"What makes you think that you said or did anything? Do you have a guilty conscience?" She refused to look at him, because she knew that her face would give her away.

"That's the thing…I can't think of anything that I did wrong, so I need to know the truth. Why are you treating me like this? Why do you hate me so much?" He brought the horse to a slow saunter. "I need to know. Please, Alison."

"You think I hate you?" She whipped her head around and looked at him, tears in her eyes. "I don't hate you. Why would I hate you?" Her heart ached to hear him ask her such a question, especially considering that hatred was the furthest from the truth.

"Well, then explain it to me, Alison! Because, honestly, I have been racking my brain, trying to figure out what would cause you to…"

"If you must know…if it is that important to know, I will tell you, but you won't like it. Heck, you probably won't even believe me…"

"I need to know. Whatever you have to say has to be better than what I have been going through. It's been agony, not knowing what I could have done to make you mad at me."

"I'm not mad at you either, Addison. You did nothing to cause this…"

"Then, who did? I don't care if it upsets me…I need to know."

In the few moments that lapsed between his pleading and her answering him, so many things ran through her mind. If she told him the truth, that his beloved fiancé had given her the unfair demands, it would truly crush him. However, if she didn't tell him the truth, he would never forgive her for lying to him, because he *would* eventually figure it out. She searched his eyes, and a sadness filled her, and she hung her head under the weight of what she was about to confess.

"Well, Alison…who was it?"

"It was Lena. Lena told me that I was not to speak to you, look at you…she even forbade me from breathing the same air as you, which is kinda impossible but whatever. I didn't want to tell you, because she's your fiancé, but you kind of left me with no choice." She refused to look at his face, because she was sure that his facial expression was one of anger. She saw him tense up, and he let out a rattled huff, and then signaled for the horse to start walking at a quicker pace.

"I was hoping that you wouldn't say her name."

"I'm sorry, Addison. I wouldn't have told you, but that would have meant that I would have had to lie, and I can't lie to you."

"You have no reason to apologize. You were honest with me. And, to tell you the truth, I am not shocked that you said it was her, just disappointed that my assumptions were correct. At least you had the courage to tell me, even though you knew the truth would hurt."

"I never intended to hurt you, Addison. That was why I chose not to say anything to you about it. I did as she said, and stayed away. It wasn't easy, but I figured that it would keep the peace."

"I know. And I understand your reasons for not telling me, but…" His tone was soft, and soothing.

"But what?" She turned her head away, afraid to hear what he was about to say.

"I appreciate that you were trying to spare my feelings, but what you need to understand is that she has no right to demand such things of anyone, especially you. You are not her property."

"I know I'm not her property, but I just figured it would be easier to just do as she asked…or demanded…because…" She paused, trying to figure out how to justify her obedience to such unjustified orders. "…Because you had been through so much already, and I didn't want to do anything to upset things for you. You seemed happy. I didn't want to be the one to ruin that."

Chapter Twelve

They rode on through the fields for a while after the truth had been told. The silence between them was almost deafening. Alison feared that, though she had been honest with him, it would backfire and she caused things to get worse with Lena.

The main thing that was going through Addison's mind, as they headed back to the house, was that he wanted to get his hands on Lena, and let her know what was on his mind. After he had decided to confront Lena about this newest revelation the next time her saw her, he put it to the back of his mind.

Something else was resonating in his mind now, and it was that there was something going on between him and Alison, and he couldn't explain it at all. He barely knew her, and yet he felt like he knew everything about her. The questions that Rebecca asked him earlier really struck a chord. *Why does it bother me so much that Alison had stopped talking to me? Why did I feel as though I had done something wrong to hurt or offend her?* There was a strange feeling of needing to be close to her, as though he only felt safe when he was near her. An odd feeling coursed through him the first time he touched her, and it returned today when he lifted her onto the horse.

A sense of security and confidence filled him completely as they trotted along on the horse together. He felt this odd compulsion to wrap his arms around her, like a child would cling to a security blanket. He shook his head, trying to shake these thoughts from his mind, but they only got stronger.

The large weeping willow came into view as they approached the edge of the property. He brought the horse to a halt, and slid down to the ground. Alison reached for him to help her down from the massive steed, but he signaled for her to stay there, and to stay quiet. He spoke in slow, soothing words to the horse, and they crept to the edge of the trees. Making certain that no one could see them, he quickly mounted the horse again, and raced to the stable, his one arm around Alison's waist to keep her from falling off the horse at the pace they were moving.

When they were safely hidden by the large wooden structure, he dismounted and reached up to help her down. He took the reins in one hand, and gripped her hand in his other, and they entered the stables.

The instant that their hands touched, a strange warm feeling ran up Addison's arm, and his heart began to beat harder and faster. Alison's first reaction was to pull her hand away, but instead, she tightened her grip. It was as if her body was fighting for her heart, and overruling her mind. She let out a staggered breath and followed him to the stall without argument.

"I really should be getting back inside. If Lena catches me here with you…" She went to pull away, thinking that he was distracted by returning his horse to its stall.

"I'll take care of Lena, don't worry. We need to talk." He gripped her hand firmly, and closed the gate until it locked. He led her over to a corner of the stable that was filled with bales of hay, hidden from view of the doors or windows. "Please sit down."

"Seriously, Addison. I wish that you would just let this go." She watched him sit down on the bale of hay that he had just motioned for her to sit on. "You are making a bigger deal over this than you should. First, you abduct me on horseback. Now, you are holding me hostage in a stable. Back home, they would consider this kidnapping." A part of her was amused by his persistence, and had once fantasized of this very situation with a handsome rogue. However, in her fantasy, the scene ended in a passionate confession of undying love and then a kiss. She knew that this was not her fantasy in any shape or form, despite her feelings for the man sitting in front of her.

"Alison, this is not a kidnapping. This is me, trying to talk to you, privately. Please, sit down." He looked at her with such desperation, that she found herself sitting down next to him, despite her mind telling her to run.

"Are you feeling alright? Are you in pain?" Her concern for any aftereffects of the coma were evident.

"I am fine...well, at least, I think I am...as far as I can tell."

"Then, what is this about, Addison? There is really nothing else that we would have to talk about, other than medical issues..."

"It's my head...and my heart..." He didn't look at her, but rather, he stared at his riding boots as he kicked straw around on the wood floorboards, as if he was not sure how to say what he had to say without sounding crazy.

"Headaches? Chest pains? Explain it to me. I can't help if you don't tell me what's going on." There was panic in her voice.

"I'm trying, dammit!!! Just shut up and listen to me!!!" He barked, unintentionally, as he rose from his seat and punched a wooden plank. She jumped, and instantly got up and backed away from him. Realizing that he had just scared her, and she was going to run, he swiftly walked toward her. She turned, a look of fear on her face, and went for the door. He picked up his pace, and caught her before she got the door open to leave. He slammed the door shut, and she stood there, trembling, her forehead leaning against the wood that blocked her escape, her fingertips digging into the old wood, as if trying to claw her way free. Her shoulders were hunched and she appeared to be cowering, like a frightened animal.

"Please, Addison. Just let me go. I don't know what I did to anger you. I was just trying to help. Please…" The sobs came out, though she tried to control them.

"I'm sorry, Alison. I didn't mean to yell. I didn't mean to react like that." He let out a sigh, and leaned his head against hers. "It's just that…I have been trying to talk to you about this for a while, but you have been avoiding me."

"Fine…talk. Tell me what symptoms you are having, and I will see if I can help." She whimpered, her bottom lip trembling.

"It is nothing like that. Please, look at me." He lifted his head, and cocked it to the side, trying to see her face, but she turned away.

"No."

"Please, Alison." He put his hands on her arms, and she flinched. "Please don't be afraid of me. I honestly never meant to scare you. I'm just so frustrated, and I needed to talk to you about it."

"And this is something that you couldn't talk to Lena about? Or your grandparents? Anyone you know and trust?" She tried to shrug his hands off of her, but they didn't budge.

"I definitely couldn't talk to Lena about it. That would be like adding fuel to a fire. And my grandparents wouldn't understand. As far as someone I know and trust…" He gently urged her to turn around, so that he could say what needed to be said without having to talk to the back of her head. She leaned against the door, and he positioned one hand on either side of her, which brought his face just inches from hers. "I trust you, Alison. And though I don't know you that well, strangely, I feel like I know you better than anyone else. I feel like you are the only person that can explain to me what is going on."

"Why do you think that I have all the answers? I can't read your mind." She took a breath, and then looked to him, a vacant expression on her face. "I…am…just…a…nurse. That's all. If it was medical, I could give you some kind of explanation, but, it doesn't sound like it has anything to do with your health. I'm sorry. I can't help. May I please go now?" She reached up and got a grip on his wrists, attempting to free herself. She knew in an instant that that was a mistake. She released his wrists, and tried to push him away, but he grabbed her hands, and pinned them against the door, leaning closer, so she could feel his breath on her cheek.

"You are wrong!" An odd smile crept across his face, as though he knew something she didn't. "You are so much more than just a nurse! You may think that you don't have any answers for what I am going through, but you are the *only one* who can tell me why…"

"Why you have lost your mind and are acting like a complete nut? I haven't the vaguest idea!" She let out a panicked laugh.

"No…I haven't lost my mind. That is just it. I am thinking and seeing clearer than I ever have before." His eyes lit up, like he had had an epiphany.

"You have lost your mind! Why are you looking at me like that? You look like a hungry wolf, ready to feast."

"Maybe I am…who knows? All I know is that you are the only one that can explain to me…why is it that you have managed to invade every cell in my bloodstream? No woman has ever excited me and infuriated me as much as you do." His voice was a low growl in her ear, and it scared and aroused her at the same time. "Ever since I woke up, and saw you at my door…I see your face everywhere. Your voice haunts my dreams. I feel your eyes watching me all the time, yet you are nowhere near."

"This could be a psychotic episode…a side effect of the coma. You need to see a real doctor, Addison!"

"What kind of nurse are you?" His eyes narrowed, as though searching her face for something. "When I was in the coma, what did you do to me?"

"I am a normal, run-of-the-mill nurse. There is nothing special about me. I just did what I was taught at school."

"Well, whatever you did...I feel like I am under some kind of spell. When you are not near me, I feel anxious and restless. I feel like I am lost, and disoriented."

"And, now? Do you feel better, now that you have me pinned to this door...under your control?" At hearing her words and the terror in her voice, a panic rushed over him and he quickly released her and backed away, having seen that he had left deep red marks on her wrists. His reaction caught her off guard. She watched him as he backed away, staring at his hands like they had done something horrible. He stumbled and hit the floor, a look of both horror and disbelief.

"I'm sorry. I...I don't want to control you. I don't know what's wrong with...I didn't mean to hurt you. I just feel like I am on a constant downward spiral, out of control. I can't catch my breath, like I am drowning in my thoughts and these unexplainable feelings." He just sat there, mortified by his behavior, and a look of confusion filled his brown eyes. Any other person would have taken this opportunity to run in the opposite direction, thinking that he was trying to trick them. However, Alison couldn't leave him there. She was a nurse, his nurse, and she cared about him more than she would ever admit. It was in that one moment, watching him gasp for air, that she realized she was never in any danger. He was suffering with something, and she needed to help him. She walked over to him, and fell to the floor at his side.

"I'm right here. You need to take deep breathes, and calm yourself. Listen to me, Addison. If you need to talk to someone, I can go phone someone to help." She took his face in her hands and tried to get him to focus.

When he was not calming down, she decided to get help. She attempted to get up, but he grabbed her arm.

"Please, don't…leave…me!" he gasped.

"I going to get help."

"I don't need help. I need…I need you!"

Against her better judgement, she moved towards him on her knees, and stopped right next to him. He reached out, and took her hand in his. The sensation that he had gotten the last few times that they touched returned, and it calmed his nerves almost immediately.

"Alright. I'm here. If you need to talk about what's going on, you have my undivided attention." She held his hand, and waited for him to start talking.

He swallowed hard, and closed his eyes to try to get his thoughts straight. After a few moments of silence, his eyes opened, and he found himself lost in an ocean of sapphire and steel.

"You have the most beautiful eyes…like a clear pool of water…" Addison whispered softly to her, reaching up to brush a strand of hair from her face. His fingers brushed her cheek, and the feeling of electricity shot through his fingers onto her olive skin. She jerked her head back, and retracted her hand.

"What's all this about, Addison? Why did you bring me here? You were talking nonsense…"

"It's not important." He rubbed his head, and then put his hands over his face, almost like he was embarrassed for his behavior.

"It had to have been important…" She sensed that he was shutting down on her.

"Important enough to kidnap you, right?" He gave a nervous laugh.

"So, you admit it. You kidnapped me and held me captive in a horse stable." She joked, trying to get him to open up. She was now leaning next to him, her hand braced across him. He leaned back on his elbows, and looked at her, a smile tugging at the corners of his mouth. "Seriously, Addison...what is wrong?"

"It's just...I feel like the only time I feel like myself, like I can make sense of anything...is when I am with you."

"That makes no sense. You are engaged to Lena. She is supposed to make you feel like that, not me. I am just the nurse."

"As I said before, Alison...you are more than just a nurse. You are an extraordinarily kind and sweet person. Your smile lights up a room, and your laughter is like music. You are selfless and honest. You are everything that anyone could ever ask for, wrapped up in a cute little package." He reached forward and tweaked her nose.

"Whatever you say. I think that the coma has messed with your eyesight. Cute little package? Seriously?!?" She looked down at the floor, and her wavy russet hair cascaded down like a mudslide to hide her face from view.

He sat up more, and propped himself with one hand. He craned his neck so that he could see her face. He swept the curtain of hair that blocked his view, and tucked it behind her ear. When she tried to look away, he caught her chin with his hand, and turned her so she would look at him.

"You think I'm wrong?" he whispered, then bit his lip.

"Yes...about the cute...and the little part."

"You know what? I am wrong. You are more of a beautifully wrapped package with a heart shaped bow."

"Roger was right...you are a smooth talker." She snickered, blushing. She did her best to resist looking him in the eyes, as they had some kind of effect over her that she was not willing to give him yet.

"Usually, I would have to agree. But with you, it's not sweet talk. That is just how I feel. I don't have to sugarcoat anything with you. You think I am trying to sweet talk you with compliments, but it is just me....being honest with you."

"A beautifully wrapped package? That isn't sweet talk? Seriously, if that isn't sweet talk, you need your eyes checked. There is nothing beautiful about me." She stated, picking straw from his hair.

He couldn't believe what she had just said, and he grabbed her hand.

"Alison Moreno...Look at me." He kept following her with his head until he finally got eye contact. "You couldn't be more wrong." There was a kindness in his voice that seemed to capture her attention. "You have the kind of beauty that's rare. You have a beautiful mind, and heart. Your eyes are incredible, and you have a glow that radiates from every pore. Your smile could stop armies, and the way you carry yourself...You could turn heads. If I had met you a couple years ago...I would have had to stand in line for a chance to even be near you."

"You would have been attracted to a girl like me?"

"I highly doubt that there is anyone like you." His face progressively got closer to hers, and his voice was soft and sweet, and very seductive. "But, yes, I would have been attracted to you back then. Hell, I am attracted to you right now."

"Liar." She could barely get the word out louder than a whisper, as she felt like she was being pulled towards him by some invisible force.

"Call me a liar again, and I'll have no choice but to prove it to you." He took in a staggered breath, and licked his lips, scanning her face with his eyes. "Call me a liar again. Go ahead...I dare you." There was an almost primal growl to his voice, and he had a half smile, his lip curled into a sort of snarl.

"You're a liar, Addison Thatcher." The temptation to see what he would do next was irresistible, and the words slipped out, and her breath mingled with his.

"Don't say that I didn't warn you." He gave her a vicious, blood thirsty look, and moved so quick, she felt her breath catch in her throat.

In one swift movement, he swept her over the top of him, and he rolled with her. The next thing she knew, she found herself pinned to the floor. He held her hands above her head, their fingers intertwined. He was straddling her, and the tip of his nose was teasing hers.

"I would fight my way through a hundred men to get to you, to have you look at me with those amazingly sultry eyes of yours…and I'd fight a hundred more just be the one who gets to taste your lips first." He leaned in closer, and she tried to look away from him, but he had her caught, without escape.

"As much as you want to believe that to be true, I don't think that you would actually do that."

"I would, without a doubt." He leaned forward and spoke in her ear. "You can't look at me in the eye and tell me that you think that I would lie about something like that."

"I don't know what to believe right now, Addison. All I know is that I want what you said to be true. But, more so, I want this to be more than just a ploy to get out of telling me what is really going on…a way to prevent me from leaving, like I'd like to."

"You don't want to leave because you are afraid of me, Alison. I can feel your body tremble beneath me. You can feel the connection between us. You can feel this electricity flowing through us…even now." His words were a little more than a whisper, as his face was so close to hers that his breath was lingering with her own.

"And what about Lena? Do you feel the same connection with her as you do with me? Maybe, what you consider to be a connection is actually just lust or sexual frustration."

"Are you my Therapist, now?"

"No, but you are close to doing something that you may decide later to be…"

"…A Mistake? Alison, I may not be sure about a whole lot right now, but…this…It's not a mistake. I want this, and I know you do, too." His lips were right there. She could sense their presence just hovering above hers, and her eyes closed slowly.

Just as she felt his lips barely brush hers, her heart felt like it was going to explode.

"ADDISON!!! ADDISON SWEETIE!!! WHERE ARE YOU?" A shrill voice screamed less than twenty feet from the stable. "HONEY BEAR? ARE YOU IN THERE?"

The door at the far end of the stable began to rattle, and Addison jumped up to his feet, which were still straddling Alison.

"Dammit!!!" He whispered loudly. He looked down at Alison, who looked flushed and quite shocked. He reached down, and hoisted Alison to her feet. Leading her to the corner, out of sight, he leaned forward and whispered in her ear. "I'll get rid of her. Don't say a word. We aren't done yet." He gave her a smile, and kissed her hand before rushing to the door.

"How do you get this darn door open?" Lena screeched, yanking at the door. "Baby, are you in there? Let me in."

He brushed himself off, and pulled the last few pieces of straw from his hair, before lifting the latch and peeking his head out.

"Lena, there is no reason for you to scream. You're scaring the horses."

"What are you doing out here?"

"Brushing Loki…I haven't been a very good master."

"Is that really what you were doing in there? You look like you've been rolling around in the dirt." She picked a piece of straw from his hair, and brushed the dust from his shirt.

"I did roll in the dirt…well, not roll in it, but I do get dirty when I am cleaning the stalls. It's part of the fun."

"You are a terrible liar, Addison. What were you really doing out here?" Lena furrowed her brows, and put her hands on her hips.

"You know what…you're right. I am a bad liar. I wasn't out here, cleaning stalls or brushing my horse." He confessed, his voice changing to one of stern determination.. Lena looked satisfied with herself for calling him out, but it was short lived. When he lifted his head, his facial expression was one of anger. "I was out here, blowing off some steam. Someone told me something that made me very angry and I needed to vent before facing you about it." He swung the large wood door open and urged her to come in, and he slammed the door behind her.

"Whatever you heard, you need to consider the source before you jump to conclusions. No one in that house likes me, and you know that. They would say anything to break us up." She carefully walked forward, trying not to step on anything that would ruin her new shoes.

"I know that, so I took that into account. However, I have a reliable source, and I know you well enough to know whether the information is a lie or the truth."

"Well, then, what horrible thing did I do this time, and to whom?"

"First off, I am the one who will be asking the questions here. You will answer me…truthfully."

"Fine!" She rolled her eyes at him, and crossed her arms.

"What on earth gives you the right to forbid anyone from talking to me? I talked to Becky earlier and she said…"

"Your reliable source is the maid?! Are you seriously going to tell me that she is your reliable source? That is so funny. You are taking the servant's word about something that she claims I did. She hates me almost as much as your grandparents!"

"Becky didn't say that you did anything specific, but I have known her a lot longer than you, and I know when she is telling me something without telling me anything."

"That makes no sense. So, she told you I did what you are accusing me of by not telling you that I did it?"

"Shut up, Lena. You lied to me…to my face."

"About what?"

"I asked you almost a week ago if you knew why, out of the blue, Alison would stop talking to me and why she was avoiding me. You said, and I quote…" He began to imitate Lena. "How am I supposed to know? I'm not her keeper. Go ask her yourself, but don't be surprised if she doesn't answer you."

"I do not sound like that!" She stomped her foot.

"Who cares what you sounded like!?! The point is, you lied to me. You knew the reason why she wasn't talking to me. You *were* the reason why she stopped talking to me and why she was avoiding me like the black plague. And don't bother denying it, because you really don't want to lie to me again."

"Okay, so I told her to stay away from you, and that she needed to not talk to you. She has been trying to break us up since she came here!"

"She has not! She was hired to care for me when you couldn't do it anymore."

"When I couldn't do it anymore? What?" The look of confusion on her face said it all.

"Yes. Had you been trained to handle the stress and struggles of taking care of a comatose person, you wouldn't have had to step aside and let someone else do what you just couldn't. At first, I thought that you had just refused to take care of me and left the hard work to a stranger, but Alison explained to me that you made an effort the first month, but just couldn't do it anymore. She stood up for you, and defended you. And then you repay her by being heartless and accusing her of trying to break us up!" He paced back and forth, trying to keep his voice down and his temper under control.

"Why would she do that?!" The new revelation totally blew Lena's mind, and she had to do something to justify her actions. She knew that it had to be something good, to trump the goodie-goodie nurse. If she told Addison that Alison had lied to him, then she would be confessing to not taking care of him at all. In a moment of desperation, she put her hands to her face, and began to turn on the crocodile tears. She sobbed and carried on. "She wins! I give up!"

"What are you talking about, Lena?" Now, Addison was confused.

"She took care of you when I couldn't. It was she who brought you back to us, not me. Everyone loves her and she is so beautiful, and sweet. How on earth could I ever compete with that? I only told her to stay away from you because I was afraid that if you knew how wonderful she was, that you would fall in love with her and I would lose you! I didn't want to lose you!!!"

"You did that because you felt that she was a threat to us?!"

"Why else would I do that? I am not as bad of a person as everyone thinks I am. True, I should have come to you and told you how I felt, but I was afraid that you would think that I was being jealous or paranoid. And maybe I was, but I was in a panic. I saw the way she looked at you. She wanted you for herself, and she *was* the one who took care of you." Her sobs became wails and she fell to her knees. Hearing her crying, Addison started to feel badly for how upset he had made her. She was not one to just confess to doing anything contemptable or sneaky. He walked forward and put his hand on her shoulder.

"Come on, Lena. Please calm down. I appreciate you telling me how you felt, but the way you went about things was wrong. You treated Alison like she was trash, and you had no right to make demands like that. Though I appreciate you being open to me, it doesn't change the fact that you lied to me about it."

"I never intended for it to go this far. I'm so sorry, Addie darling. I was just so afraid that I would lose you. Please forgive me." She looked up at him, and gave him the most pitiful look she could muster without looking fake.

In the far corner, Alison was steaming. ***Unbelievable! I cannot believe he is buying this horse crap!***

"Let's go in the house and talk. You are not properly dressed to be out here in this cool barn. You are shivering, Lena."

"Alright." She wiped her eyes and took the hand he was offering to her.

"I am hurt that you would have such little faith in me and in our relationship." He walked her to the door and opened it for her. "Go in the house, and go up to my room. Sit in front of my fireplace and warm up."

"Aren't you coming?" She sniffled.

"I'll be there in a few minutes. I need to clean up the mess I made of things in here. Go on!" he urged her out the door and watched her walk towards the house, before he closed the door and ran to the girl waiting on the hay bales.

"My God…I am sorry that you had to witness that. I was just going to send her back to the house, but then I felt compelled to deal with the situation at hand." He sat on the bale next to Alison, but she got up and moved away. "Come here, please."

"No…not if you honestly believe that load of malarkey that she just fed you." She put her hands behind her back, and looked to the floor.

"Alison, she was afraid of what is between you and I."

"There is nothing between us. You were confused…stressed because you are still recovering from being in a coma for three months. We had a moment of weakness, nothing more."

"How can you say that?" He was hurt that she was trying to give excuses for what had happened between them.

"Because…because it's the truth. You obviously love Lena very much. I am a complication. Maybe she had the right idea, making me keep my distance. As far as I am concerned, all this…the horseback ride and the things that happened afterward…they never happened. I let my emotions get the best of me. I won't make the same mistake twice."

"What are you saying, Alison?"

"I have a confession, and I think that I need to do it now, before I lose my nerve." She straightened up, and cleared her throat. "Addison, I *am* a threat to your relationship because I allowed you to do something that never should have even gone as far as it had. What happened between us today…it was a mistake."

"This is not exactly what I expected it to feel like."

"What exactly were you expecting to feel?"

"I don't know, but this wasn't it. You may think that it was a mistake, but it was more of a revelation." He looked at her with his deep brown eyes, and he seemed to have been sincere, but she was upset, so she couldn't quite tell. "And just for the record, it may have been a moment of weakness for you, but it was a moment of clarity for me. I meant every word I said to you. Were it not for Lena and our engagement…I wouldn't be wasting time alone with you, talking about my feelings. I would be doing an interactive demonstration." He winked at her, and flashed her a smile, his one dimple sinking deeply into his cheek. He got up off the hay bale, and offered her his hand.

"You cannot say those things to me. It isn't fair. You can't flirt with me and offer me your hand like everything is fine. When we leave this stable, I know exactly where you are going and who you are going to be with. I am not some play thing you can toy with a little before you tie yourself to that...that…to HER!" She shook her head, and refused to stoop to name calling.

She walked past him and went to the back entrance. She stopped, her hand on the handle and looked at him.

"You are seriously going to just leave things like this?"

"I have to leave, because if I don't…" she paused, so he took the small window of opportunity to keep her from leaving.

"Are you afraid that I may say something to make you change your mind?"

"To be totally honest, yes. And that is exactly why I have to go. I am walking a very thin line right now, and you could pretty much say anything, and I would stay and listen to it. That is my weakness…YOU are my weakness."

"And you are mine, my dear...But, no matter what I do or say right now, I won't be able to convince you that what we had…what happened between us…despite what you may feel or think, it was real…not just some male indulgence or momentary weakness. You are not just some play thing to me. You are the culmination of the woman I could honestly see myself spending eternity with. However, much to my dismay, you are obviously unattainable." He leaned forward, kissed her head, and then walked towards the other door. She opened her mouth to say something, but he was gone before she could ask him what he meant by "unattainable."

As she stood in the stable, alone, she still shook with the vibrations of what had happened between them. They had come so close.

Maybe this was just Karma kicking her when she was down. She was right there when he began to wake up, but Lena was there to steal the moment from her. Just now, she was literally breathing the same air as he was, and his lips had just slightly brushed hers, and Lena was there.

The last words that he spoke to her were that she was unattainable, and she would have loved to have heard his explanation. As far as attainability, she was more than that for him. She was his puppet, his wooden model…he could make her do just about anything, feel anything and she would have no control over herself.

The moment that he walked away, he had sucked the air from her lungs. She was befuddled, disoriented, and lost in her own little fantasy of what could have possibly happened.

She slid down the surface of the door, onto the straw-covered floor and stared at the other end of the barn.

By the time that she had made her way back into the house, the sun had gone down, and the crickets were chirping. All she wanted was to crawl into her bed, and curl up into a ball.

After she ascended the stairs, she stopped at his door, and was about to knock, but she just put her hand to the wood for a moment. She proceeded to her room, emotionally drained.

Addison had watched Alison leave the barn, moving toward the house as if in a daze. He had just come back to his room from saying goodnight to Lena after an exhausting conversation. A moment later, he heard footsteps, and saw a shadow appear under his door, hold there for a moment, and then move on. He catapulted his bed, and raced to catch Alison before she entered her room.

He whipped his door open, slid on the hardwood floor, and tried to get to her door before it clicked shut, but was just a moment too late. He quietly approached the door and stopped.

"It wasn't a mistake, Alison. It was anything but. I really wish you could understand that." He thought this as braced himself against the door frame. When she didn't make a sound, he returned to his room, and quietly shut the door. Suddenly her door creaked open, and she peered out, because she swore she heard someone approach it. When she saw no one, she shut her door again, and went to bed.

Chapter Thirteen

Alison spent a large amount of her, now abundant, free time walking in the garden. She found herself quite bored at times, and would actually go out of her way to try to help Becky or Corrine with something. However, by direct orders of Elizabeth and Arthur, that Alison not be allowed to do work and take a little vacation, they would always shoo her away. Every book in the house had been read twice, and she didn't have green thumb, so even trying to weed the garden was out of the question.

One evening, she sat out on the tree swing, which she assumed was Addison's when he was a child, and stared at the sky. It was peaceful, and quiet. And she was content in thinking about what her mother and father were doing at that moment, but her thoughts were interrupted.

"Hey you, there! Come here. I need to speak with you." A high-pitched voice called from the back patio area.

"There is nothing that you have to say to me, that I would want to hear, Lena. Shouldn't you be clinging to Addison like the leech that you are, sucking him dry? Maybe you should just start crying again. Perhaps he'll ask me to leave, to make you feel more secure in your farce of an engagement." She muttered to herself, and yet she got up off the swing and reluctantly walked over to the yellow haired prima Donna. "What on earth can I do for you, Lena?"

"Did you talk to Addison about me?"

"No. That would require me actually being permitted to speak with him without you present." She stated, cordially.

"So, you didn't tell him that I had made an effort to take care of him right after his accident, even though everyone knows that I really didn't make any effort...in the least...You didn't tell him that?"

"Even if I did, why does it matter? I am just a greasy, fat pig, and I am to keep my pig hooves off of him. You have made it painfully clear that I am to stay away from him, in every sense of the word, or you will make my life miserable. I have done just that. But, obviously, that isn't enough for you. What I told him just makes you look good, and that should make you happy, yet you are out here, harassing me about it."

"Why would you lie to him? What is in it for you?" Lena crossed her slender, stick-like arms over her chest, and gave her a skeptical look.

"I told him what I thought he wanted to hear. And obviously, there is nothing in it for me to make you look like you actually care for him. Are we done?"

"No, we are not done. I know you are not telling me the whole truth."

"Why should I tell you anything? I shouldn't have to explain my actions and motives to you. I don't answer to you. I answer to the Thatchers, which last time I checked, you are not."

"Not that it is any of your business, but the wedding is in a matter of just a couple weeks, then, I *will* be a Thatcher." She got a slimy grin on her face.

"Well, then, I will be sure to take my leave before that day comes."

"You can't." She tapped her foot, and rolled her eyes.

"Are you kidding me? And who says I can't? You?" Anger rose in Alison, as she stepped towards the stick figure in front of her.

"What I meant to say is that you can't leave, because Addison wants you at our wedding, and the events leading up to it. That was his only request."

Alison's heart both jumped and sank at the same time. Despite the fact that she had avoided him after what happened in the stables, he still wanted to see her, to have her there. As much as his one request made her feel honored, she felt as though it was more of a punishment; it would be torture to take part in festivities that led up to this prissy gold digging witch binding herself to the man that Allie had fallen in love with.

"Fine. I'll stay...for him. But, just because I am staying, that doesn't mean that I will remain here after the farce you call a wedding takes place. Once you say your 'I do's,' I am gone." She turned on her heels, and headed back to the swing.

As she got back to the swing, she got the feeling that she was being watched. After looking around, she looked up and spotted who was making the hair stand on her neck. Addison was standing at his window, and he smiled slightly, and gave her a wave as she sat down on the swing in the moonlight. She blushed, smiled and waved back. He smiled bigger when she actually responded to him, and she could see the dimples in his cheeks deepen.

"Oh, so you can finally look at him now, huh?" A familiar voice rang from behind her. "And here I thought that *any kind* of communication was forbidden."

"What can I say? I am a glutton for punishment, Roger." She smiled, as she felt him pull the rope back and begin to swing her.

"You know, if you really want to tick Lena off, you should start eating with us again, and not rush away, or skip meals just so you abide by her rules. You aren't looking so hot lately. You need to get more sleep and you need to eat."

"I appreciate you trying to help, but I am fine. I could use to lose a few pounds. Maybe, just maybe, Lena will stop with her name calling and just let me be." Alison said, weakly. Roger stopped the swing, and stepped around to kneel in front of her.

"Alison, do you not see how perfect you are? You are beautiful, and funny, and loving. No one has the right to make you feel badly about yourself, not even you. It worries all of us who actually care about you. Even Addison sees what is happening to you, and it worries him."

"Addison doesn't care. He has his skinny doll. I'm more like an old used beach ball." She looked at the ground, because she was afraid to meet Roger's gaze.

"Is that what you think? That Addison doesn't care about you? That, just because he has Lena, someone who would blow away if hit with a strong wind, that he doesn't care what happens to you?"

"Pretty much, yes, I do."

"Well, then, you are fooling yourself, and you're selling him short. Does he even know how you feel about him? Does he know how much you love him?" His questions caught her off-guard, and she looked at him, shocked and embarrassed.

"She promised me she wouldn't tell anyone!" Fury ran her blood cold, as she thought that her one real friend had betrayed her.

"If you are referring to my daughter, get that nasty look off your face. Rebecca hasn't said a word to anyone, as I am sure she promised not to. I can tell, just by the way that you look at him that you are in love with him, and from what I can tell, it started back when he was still in a coma, am I right?" She looked at him, and her anger ebbed away. "There is nothing to be ashamed or embarrassed about, child. You are blessed, because you can feel something that strongly for someone and show restraint as you have at the sight of the one you love with another."

"I hate her. I hate that he loves her."

"He only thinks he still loves her, my sweet. He doesn't look at her the same way that he used to. He doesn't look at her the same way that you look at him. He thinks that he wants to be with her, that he still has that passion for her that he did before his accident. However, it just isn't the case anymore."

"I wouldn't know. I wasn't here then."

"No you weren't, and thank goodness for that. He was a totally different person then. So much has changed in him, but he just doesn't see it yet. He hasn't come to grips with what he went through during his coma, or even before. He hasn't faced any of it, and I think he is using this relationship with Lena as a distraction."

Alison hadn't really thought about what Addison had gone through, nor had she taken the time to talk to him about it. She hadn't given him much of anything the last few weeks, except the cold shoulder, and an impromptu roll in the hay…literally. At that moment, Alison decided that Lena was no longer going to dictate anyone's lives. True, she had threatened to make her miserable if she went against her orders, but it was time to take her life back.

*****

Preparations for the wedding were well underway, and though no one in the house really wanted it to happen, they were all willing to do it for Addison. Against Lena's orders, Alison started to rejoin family meals, and even talked to Addison at the table, though it was just polite conversation. Her smile began to return, and she looked much healthier now that she was eating again, and sleeping well.

A box had arrived for Alison on the morning of the Pre-wedding party, and she and Becky both had to work together to carry it to her room. It was wrapped in a big blue bow, and Alison could hardly stand the anticipation.

"Why would a box come for me? I am not the one getting married."

"According to the tag, it's from Miss Morton's dress shop. Maybe Ms. Elizabeth bought you a dress to wear for tonight. It is a really fancy party, and I am sure that she would want you to look absolutely gorgeous." They both started to laugh as they opened the box to reveal the most beautiful baby blue ball gown.

It was made of Satin, taffeta and silk, and it looked extremely expensive. Becky felt that she had to get her mother to help her figure out how they were going to do Allie's hair. She raced out of the room, almost running Addison over in the effort to get to the stairs. He was going to enter his room, but something caught his ear, and he stopped dead. As if like a siren's song, he was drawn to the beautifully haunting melody. He stopped short of Alison's bedroom, and looked in.

She had the dress up and out of its box, and pressed up against her body. She was twirling around, her eyes closed, and she was singing and humming. Addison's heart began to beat like mad. He immediately ran to his room, as his head began to throb.

Alison heard the rapid footsteps from the hallway, and placed the dress on her bed before going to investigate, but no one was to be seen. She heard the sound of creaking hinges, and then a slam, but couldn't figure out where it was coming from.

Addison stood against the closed door, and slid down to the floor, clutching his head. Sights, sounds, and feelings began to bombard him all at once, and his heart was racing more so than before. He got a strange feeling in his chest, and suddenly everything was so clear. After a few moments, he rose to his feet, and walked to his mirror, staring at his reflection. He saw everything differently now, felt differently, and he knew what need to be done. All the things that were stuck in his subconscious seemed to flash before his eyes. The image of the first time that he has seen her face and moments since were all he could think about now.

Chapter Fourteen

The party was underway when the clock struck seven o'clock, and everyone who was anyone was there, dancing and laughing and celebrating the upcoming nuptials of Addison and Lena. Even her father had cleaned himself up a bit. He shaved, and slicked his hair back with what looked like grease. He was in a black and white suit, and carried a strange cane with a bird at the top. He looked more like a penguin than an actual person, and the way he laughed only fit.

Addison had made his rounds, greeting all of his guests. He was dressed in a very handsome steel grey and white tuxedo. His shoulder length hair was pulled back into a neat pony at the nape of his neck and he looked quite dashing. Every few minutes, he'd look towards the doors to the ballroom, hoping to see Alison enter. After about an hour, he became very discouraged.

Lena was dressed like a big golden goose in a bright golden dress with sequins and feathers everywhere. She looked ridiculous, however, no one seemed to have the heart to tell her. She had taken notice of her husband-to-be's strange behavior, and went to find out what was wrong.

"Why do you keep looking at the doors? Everyone is here already. Your grandparents are talking to the Ballisters and Lancasters, Mayor and Mrs. Gentry are over there, talking to daddy. And we are here, with our friends. Tonight is perfect. The band is playing our song. Let's go dance."

There *was* someone missing, Addison thought, and she was a very important part of the night.

To humor Lena, he led her to the dance floor. He was very uncomfortable, as the feathers from her dress kept hitting him in the face, and the lights bouncing off her dress were practically blinding him. But, as miserable as he was, the only thing that would be worth the torture would be to see those French doors open and the beautiful girl in baby blue enter.

"You aren't having fun, are you, baby?" Lena whined once the dance was over.

"Couldn't you have worn a dress that was less like a peacock? If you were trying to get noticed, you didn't need to dress like this. I think I got a sequin in my eye." Addison blinked hard, trying to get something out of his eye.

"I thought you would like this dress. I brought three others. Would you like me to go change?" She gave him a pouty smile.

"Please…if you wouldn't mind. I would appreciate it. This one is really too much." He watched her as she grabbed a couple of her female friends. "Oh, please…no feathers!" He called after her. She blew him a kiss, and left the ballroom.

He made his way around the room while she was gone, until he came to his grandparents. They were still talking to the Ballisters and Lancasters, whom were laughing and having a good time, despite the reason for the party.

"Oh, look who it is!!" Dorothy Ballister squealed, and slid her arm into the crook of Addison's elbow. "The man of the hour! How are you, my boy? You look quite dashing and handsome. No one would even imagine you were laid up for three months."

"Thank you, I guess. I am good, better than good. I am happy. Nothing could be better." At the sound of that, Arthur rolled his eyes, and took a puff of his pipe to keep from saying anything.

"Grandmother, you wouldn't happen to know where Alison is, would you? She was supposed to be here a while ago." He leaned towards the woman in deep plum colored chiffon.

"Last I heard, she was still getting ready. That dress you chose was very complicated, but I am sure it will be worth it. She is going to look beautiful."

"She's already is, grandmother. She doesn't need a fancy dress to prove that." He smiled, glancing to the door and then smiling at the two couples with his grandmother and grandfather.

"Who, may I ask, is Alison? I thought the bride's name was Lena." Eloise Lannister piped in, holding her glasses up to her eyes so she could see her companions.

"She is the lovely girl who nursed our Addison back to health. She is magnificent, and so sweet. Just wait until you meet her. She is positively enchanting." Elizabeth twittered, excited when talking about Alison.

Addison's heart leapt, as he saw the doors open, but then got a sick feeling in his stomach, as he saw the most revolting sight he had ever thought he'd see tonight.

Accompanied by her two friends, Lena re-entered the ball room wearing a replica of the dress that had been bought for Alison. He thought that he was literally going to throw up. The dress looked horrible on her, as it was made for girls with fuller figures, and breasts bigger than apples. He rushed over to her, and pulled her aside by the arm.

"Where did you get that dress, Lena?" he spoke through his teeth.

"From Miss Morton's dress shop, of course. Why? Do you like it? She said that you ordered one just like it earlier this week. Thankfully, she had the display, because the one you ordered for me never got delivered to my house today. I will take it up with her after the wedding." She shifted the bodice, slightly, because it kept sliding down. "Let's hope she doesn't lose my wedding dress too. That thing cost you nearly four hundred dollars!" At hearing how much she had spent on her wedding gown, which she would only wear once, Addison nearly choked.

"Lena, please go change your dress this instant. Of all the dresses that you could have put on, you chose this one?" He tried to look like he was smiling, as she spoke through his teeth once more. "The dress is like three sizes too big on you."

"Miss Morton said that you said that the girl you were buying the dress for was going to look absolutely ravishing in it. It isn't my fault that mine didn't come. It would probably have fit me better than this one."

"Just go change, please."

"Okay. If you insist…" She signaled to the other girls, and they followed her, once more, to change her clothes.

Twenty more minutes passed, and Lena had put on an emerald green gown. She had sent the other girls ahead, so she could check herself out in the mirror in the foyer, before rejoining her party. That was when she saw something that made her blood boil like lava. Coming out of her room, a huge smile on her face, and looking like an angel in a powder blue dress just like the one that Addison had just ordered her to change out of, was Alison. It took a whole two seconds for the pieces to fit together in her brain. The dress that Miss Morton had shipped out was not for Lena after all. It never got delivered to her house, because it was not bought for her. It was ordered and bought for Alison…his nurse. And she looked like the dress had been designed just for her.

A line of beautiful jewels ran along the top of the bodice, and sparkled in the lights of the chandelier in the foyer. The dress flared out from just below her breasts, with layer after layer of light, fluffy, flowy material. Alison's hair was in a beautiful curly up do, with tendrils of chocolate and auburn hair hanging and bouncing with every movement.

Lena decided that she was going to put an end to this madness before it even started. She ran back into her dressing room, grabbed her dress, and ran up the stairs to cut off Alison before she had a chance to be seen by Addison.

"What are you doing, Lena? I am already very late. Shouldn't you be in the ball room already?" Alison panicked, when Lena grabbed her arm, and turned her back to the bedroom.

"Oh, dear sweet Alison! I cannot believe that he would do this to you, especially after all you've done for him…" She acted all weepy and upset.

"What are you up to, Lena?" Becky grumbled.

"You need to shush. I am saving Alison from a world of embarrassment." She looked back at Allie, and held her dress up for her to see. "Addison gave me this dress, and told me to go put it on, because he said that he bought it for me, especially for tonight. He said that I was going to be the most beautiful woman, and insisted that I put it on immediately."

"That's impossible. That dress looks like it is about five sizes too big for you." The confusion on her face made Lena's insides jump.

"That is what I said to him, but he insisted. Sweetie, everyone saw the dress. He was showing it off to everyone in there. If I had not caught you before you went in there, you would have been laughed at for wearing the dress that he had bought me."

"Well, Allison looks amazing in it, so she should just go down there anyway. It probably isn't even the same exact dress. Come on, Allie." Becky urged Alison to follow her.

"Becky's probably right. Maybe no one will notice. But, then again, Addison said that if it didn't fit, he would just complain, because she shouldn't even have clothes for fat girls in her store in the first place. He says that fat girls nauseate him. That is probably why he said that you were starting to actually look more attractive when you stopped eating, and started to lose all that weight." She looked away. "Maybe that is the real reason he wanted you to come to the dance, so he could match you up with one of our friends, since you were losing the weight, but that you would have to keep going until you were an appropriate size. Then again, what do men know anyhow, right?" She let go of Alison's arm, after giving it a gentle squeeze. "Well, good luck down there. You are gonna need it. Stay away from the pastry table, please, for your own good." She turned around and walked down the stairs, and hid a very devious look and an evil smile from them. As she got to the bottom of the stairs, she looked up, and gave her a pitying look, shook her head. "You know what, I think I would complain to Miss Morton as well, I am not gonna wear this circus tent. I wouldn't wear it if you paid me." She dumped it on the floor, and went into the ballroom.

"Alison, don't you dare listen to her! Just consider who it was coming from…You look amazing, and she is just jealous." Becky pleaded with her friend, who had tears welling in her eyes.

"If she was lying, why was she carrying the same exact dress as I am wearing now? We saw her come from the ballroom with it. Maybe she was actually just trying to save me from being laughed at. Maybe she actually was trying to do me a favor, rather than trying to hurt me." She sniffed, as a tear fell, and then another.

"Alison, you look amazing. Please don't do this." Becky grabbed her by the arm, and pulled her towards the stairs. We are going down there."

"How can I face him, looking like this?"

"You love him! You need to tell him, before it's too late. Papa told you that Addison isn't really in love with her, he's just confused, doing what he thinks he is supposed to do. You need to go in there, and set him straight…give him a better alternative to what he is heading towards. He will live a life of loveless misery if you don't."

"I don't think I can. You heard what she said…"

"Do it now, or spend the rest of your life regretting not taking a chance. Your choice! But you need to decide right now. What's it going to be, Alison?" Becky looked at her, a fiery determination in her eyes.

Lena walked, with a new determination, towards Addison, and flung her arms around him, pretending to sob. Confused by his fiancé's behavior, he pulled her back, and looked at her.

"What in the world is wrong with you?"

"Oh, Addison…my darling, Addison. That girl is wretched and awful. I tried to convince her to stay, but she said the most awful things to me."

"What are you talking about, Lena? What girl are you speaking of?" He searched her face.

"That nurse…Alison. She said that she had been given the same dress as I was wearing, and it made her laugh. She said that you were a sad excuse for a man, and that I was nothing but a gold-digging wench, and that it was sickening that you would think that you meant anything to her, other than a paycheck. All I did was go up to find out why she hadn't joined up at the party. I knew you were expecting her, so I went to see if she needed help getting ready. Instead, the dress was shredded all over the floor, and she was packing her bags."

Lena was speaking so loud, making certain that everyone in the ballroom was now listening to what she had just dealt with. She buried her face in his shoulder and continued to pretend to cry. She felt his chest tighten, and him take in a deep breath.

"The dress was shredded all over the floor?"

"Yes, it was absolutely horrid."

"It looks like it is all in one piece to me." He sighed, and smiled at the sight in the doorway.

"WHAT?!" Lena's head popped up, and she spun around and looked at what everyone had fallen silent for.

She was like a vision, a dream…and she was walking straight for Lena and Addison. Actually, she didn't look like she was walking, but rather floating, and she had locked eyes with Addison's.

The crowd in the room seemed to part between them, and Addison pushed Lena to the side.

"Don't push me!" She squealed. "Addison, what are you doing? Where are you going? Come back here, now." She stomped her foot. Contrary to her squealing, he kept moving, taking slow precise steps toward his goal.

As Alison closed the gap between her and Addison, she had built up enough courage to say what she needed to say, and she didn't want to wait to get him alone. She got about twenty feet from him, and stopped. Everyone was staring at her, in awe, as she began to speak.

"Adam…I need to tell you something, now, before I lose my nerve…about what we talked about in the Stables…" That was all she could get out. A smile crossed Addison's face, and it stretched all the way to his eyes, and it left her breathless and frozen. He started to step slowly towards her. Right before he got to her, he reached out his hands, taking hers in his.

"You look amazing, Alison."

"Thank you. Now, I know this your party, but I really need to speak with you." She whispered.

"Whatever you need to say can wait. I have been waiting for you to get here. Come with me." He took her hand, and led her to the front of the room. He left Alison with his grandparents, and then stepped up on the platform, where the band's microphone was. "Excuse me! Can I have everyone's attention, please?"

Lena's father made his way to his daughter and her friends, and yanked her arm so he could whisper in her ear.

"What is he up to? Shouldn't you be up there with him? And who is that girl?"

"I don't know what is going on, daddy. That tart over there is his nurse. You saw her…the day Addison woke up. He better not be doing anything stupid, or I am going to have to resort to 'Plan B.' She has been a thorn in my side for too long." She crossed her arms over her chest, and glared at the couple up on the platform.

"Ladies and gentlemen…friends and family. Firstly, I would like to thank you for coming to this party." Addison spoke to the hushed crowd. Alison stood near the platform, watching Addison. She was blushing, and covering her face from everyone who was now staring at her.

"Addison, what are you doing? I need to talk to you. Can your speech wait a few minutes?" She whispered to him.

"As you all know, you were invited here this evening to celebrate mine and Lena's wedding tomorrow. Lena, where are you? Could you come up here, please?" He waited until she came up and stood next to him. She attempted to grab his hand, but he pulled it away. "For those of you who haven't met her yet, this is Lena." A few people began to clap, but Addison cut them off. "There is no need to clap. I assure you, she doesn't deserve the attention."

"Addie, honey, what are you up to?" Lena seethed through a wide, toothy smile.

"For quite some time now, I was known in Woodcrest as the 'Bad Seed of the Thatcher Family.' It is not something I am proud of. I did some things that were unbecoming of my social standing. But, in my defense, I was in love. Love makes you do crazy things." He cleared his throat, and then continued, occasionally glancing to Alison. "It is also known that I had an accident earlier this year, spending three long months in a coma." As he proceeded with the next part, he began to pace on the stage. "Was my loving fiancé at my side the whole time, nursing me back to health?" He looked at Lena, and then back to his guests. "I'm afraid not. Instead, she stole things from me, and then, when she had driven off all of the nurses and couldn't handle the pressure of doing simple duties to help me recover, she ran off to God knows where." Hushed disapproving comments were made, and everyone looked at Lena with narrowed eyes. "My grandparents, fortunately, were able to hire a well-trained live-in nurse to care for me instead. Under her care, I came out of my coma. It was this loving, kind, beautiful woman who changed my life forever." He glanced at the girl standing next to his grandparents, and smiled slightly, then turned his attention to the attentive crowd.

"I cannot believe you are doing this, Addison. This is our pre-wedding party." Lena pouted. He ignored her.

"Now, I am sure that you are wondering why, after finding out the truth about Lena, I decided to go through with marrying Lena. The truth is, a part of me still loved her. The funny thing is, it wasn't until I knew what it felt like to feel real love for someone that I realized my feelings for Lena were not of love, but of a sense of..."

"I think he's having a mental breakdown. The coma took its toll on him. Honey, let's go upstairs so you can lie down. You look like hell." Lena laughed nervously as she tried to convince their guests that he was not well. She grabbed his arm, and tried to pull him from the stage. "You really don't want to continue this, Addison. You really don't know who you are messing with." She grumbled through a smile.

"On the contrary, that coma did wonders for me, mentally. I am finally seeing things clearer than ever. And right now, I see right through your act of doting wife-to-be. You claimed that you loved me, but you love my family's money and social standing a lot more. However, I was so sure that you loved me, not my family and legacy that I made a deal with my grandparents…I marry you, and I get nothing. I am out of the house, and out of their wills."

"What?! You can't be serious!!!"

"I am dead serious, sweetheart. So, I want to present a toast to you. Tomorrow, you get me…that's it." He reached down and grabbed a flute of champagne and raised it into the air.

"I don't believe you. You would never give up your life to marry me!"

"Addison, I think that I need to go. This doesn't involve me. I shouldn't be here. This is between the two of you." Alison whispered and decided to leave the party, but Arthur grasped her hand, gently, and shook his head. She turned around, and he put a loving arm around her shoulder.

"Yeah, you better get the hell out of here! Leave! You aren't welcome here, at my party. Everything was fine until you came along! You probably put this idea in his head."

"Actually, Lena…this was discussed the morning I came to your house, to ask you to elope…the day of my accident." Addison glared at his fiancé.

"Fine, so she didn't give you the idea to bankrupt yourself…why is she here, then? This is our party."

"She's here because I asked her to come. I wanted her here because I needed to tell her something important, before I went and married another woman out of obligation."

"Obligation?!" Lena, Elizabeth, and Alison said in unison, though the tones in their voices were completely different.

"Yes, obligation. I asked Lena to marry me because I was a stupid drunk and I went against my morals, and slept with her. That one night of drunken idiocy produced a child." He confessed to his grandparents and Alison, who were staring at him, oblivious to what he meant.

"You are marrying her because you got her pregnant?" Alison was in shock. She looked at Lena, and looked at where her baby bump was, or should've been. Her eyes narrowed, suspiciously.

"Yes. I made a mistake, and now I have to do the right thing by her and my unborn child. I thought I loved her back then, and so it only seemed natural."

The whole room erupted in chatter at the new revelation.

"Please, don't think ill of me, Alison. This was before you came here...before the accident. I made a mistake and I have to make things right." He pleaded with Alison, but she didn't seem phased by his confession except for a sense of relief. Lena stood next to Addison, a devious smirk on her face.

"What is so funny, Lena? Do you really think that trapping a man into marrying you is funny? This doesn't change the fact that you get nothing when you marry our grandson." Elizabeth piped in, stepping closer to the platform.

"You would allow your great-grandchild to grow up in squalor?" Lena appeared appalled and disgusted, putting her hand to her belly.

"If there was a great-grandchild, I am sure that she wouldn't do that." Alison stated loud enough for everyone to hear. She grabbed the skirt of her dress, and took off towards the stage steps.

"There is, so I guess plans are changing..." Lena sighed.

"Plans are changing, but it isn't because of a baby..." Alison smiled and looked at Addison, putting her hand on his arm. "Don't you get it, Addison?"

"I really don't. What are you talking about?"

"When did she tell you that she was pregnant? How long before your accident?"

"About two or three months before, why?"

Alison walked around Addison, and walked up to Lena.

"What are you up to?" She squealed, as Alison placed her hand on Lena's stomach. "Get your hand off of my stomach!"

"Did you go to a doctor, Lena? Did the doctor tell you that you were pregnant?"

"Yes...of course." There was a bit of hesitation.

"A doctor in Woodcrest?"

"No. It was a secret, so I went to a doctor out of town."

"The nearest doctor is almost ten miles away. You don't have a car. How did you get there?"

"None of your business!"

"Alison, what are you getting at?" Addison was both confused and suspicious about Alison's questioning, but he was beginning to understand. When Alison suddenly turned on her heels, and faced him, he looked shocked.

"If she found out a couple months before your accident, she would be about eight months pregnant right now, and you would be able to tell by the bulge around her midsection....is there a bulge?" She pointed to Lena's stomach.

"Women in my family never look pregnant. We are lucky in that way."

"You are so full of it, Lena. You lied to him..." Alison laughed. She turned back around, and a bit of her Italian side came out, as she began to talk with her hands. "I am a nurse! There is no way, with how small you are, that you can go eight months without showing *at all*...that is, unless women in your family carry in their back ends!!" Alison, amused at the fact that she had revealed Lena's little deception, walked to the other side of Addison, so that he could deal with the situation himself.

There was an outcry of different opinions about what Alison was bringing to light.

"Addison, baby...are you really going to listen to her? She said she's a nurse...not a doctor. How the heck would she know if I was pregnant or not? She is trying to turn you against me!" She began to cry her crocodile tears again. "She is trying to break up our family."

"I thought it was odd that you haven't gained any weight…and that you refuse to let me come with you to the doctor appointments…" Addison looked astonished, and he put his hand to his head, as though he was getting a headache from the situation. "Were you ever pregnant, Lena? Tell me the truth."

Lena stood there, frozen, in front of her fiancé, his nurse, his grandparents, and half of Woodcrest's residents. Everyone waited, wanting to hear what she was going to say. Arthur was so angry that he was puffing away at his pipe with vigor, though there was nothing left in it to smoke. Elizabeth was wringing her hands, a look of pure fury burning a hole into Lena's face.

"No. I thought I was…I was almost positive. I was late. There was no other possible reason…I'm never late."

"You just got done telling us that you were, and that it was verified by a doctor from 'out-of-town.' Now, you are telling me that you were never pregnant with my child in the first place."

"You couldn't have gotten me pregnant, anyway. We never slept together. I just told you that because you passed out, and couldn't remember what happened that night. It was a perfect opportunity. I had to do something. You never would have married me otherwise." Lena actually looked ashamed of what she had done. She looked at Addison, and had real tears in her eyes. "I wanted to marry you. You were slipping away. I was desperate. Please forgive me. I only did it because I loved you."

"Could this party get any more interesting? Do you think he'll marry her anyway, Thomas?" Odette whispered in her husband's ear.

"If he does, then he really has suffered damage from the coma." Thomas Gentry replied, then watched the three people up on the stage.

"You told me that I was going to be a father. You knew that I would not let my child be a bastard. You knew I would do the right thing. You lied to me over and over and over." He had to walk away from her for a moment.

He was trying to keep his temper, especially in front of Alison. The last time that he lost his temper, he frightened her so bad, she nearly ran from him. After he had calmed himself slightly, he turned and looked at his fiancé.

"If you had told me the truth when I came out of my coma, I might have been able to forgive you. Instead, I proposed to you again, under the assumption that you were still pregnant with my child." He started to step toward her, but his temper began to build again. He motioned for Alison to go back with his grandparents, and she did, quickly. He glared at Lena, pointing at her, his hand shaking. "You put a wedge between my family and I. You hurt the people I love. You were going to walk down the aisle tomorrow, and force me to marry you under false pretenses."

"I want to marry you, Addison. I want to be the one you love. I don't care about your money. I don't care about the social standing…not anymore. We have been together for too long to just stop now. I will learn to love you like you love me."

"Well, then you don't have to learn anything." He laughed, angrily. "I stopped loving you a while ago. As I said before, the only reason I was still going to marry you was for our child. But, since there isn't a child, there will be no wedding..." He was calm and spoke with a very controlled tone. He felt as if a weight had been lifted from his chest. He took a deep breath and looked down and to the right, where a pair of sweet blue eyes met his gaze.

"Are you alright?" she mouthed to him, and a tear ran down her cheek. He may not have appeared heartbroken to everyone else, but she knew how devastated he was, and she was feeling it for him.

"In light of the party's purpose becoming null and void, I think it only appropriate that we have something else to celebrate." He turned his back to Lena, who was still standing on the stage, but had stepped back to the far end, appearing to be in denial of what had just happened. "I am sure that everyone knows Miss Alison Moreno by now. I don't know of too many people who don't know who she is and why she is here. She was my nurse, and she saved my life…twice now; she cared for me and brought me out of my coma, and now she saved me from marrying a woman I didn't love...a woman who deceived me."

"I just did the job I was hired to do, Addison. And as far as Lena, I just stated the obvious." She said in a hushed voice, embarrassed at the scene he was making. "Now, can we go talk?"

"Give me a few minutes more to say what I need to say in front of our guests, and then I am all yours." He whispered back to her. "I was ready to face the repercussions of my actions, even if it meant a lifetime of misery. I was going to marry a woman who…what I mean to say is…" He directed the next part to the brunette standing by the stage. "Alison, when you took on the job as my nurse, your job was to care for me until I woke from my coma, and you did that. But, when you did, you not only brought me back to my family, but you woke something within me…feelings, thoughts, emotions. It was as if I was not whole until now. I see things so much more clearly than I ever have. Sights are more beautiful, words have new meaning, and a fire has ignited."

"Sounds like he really is suffering a mental breakdown." Harvey Thorton grumbled.

"Sounds like he is coming down with something." Killian Callahan, Becky's date, snickered in her ear.

"No, Killian, what it sounds like…" She sighed.

"It sounds like he is in love." Arthur finished Becky's thought, and relit his pipe. Elizabeth slapped her hands together and put them to her lips to cover the widest of smiles.

"I guess we can call the lawyer and have our wills redone…again."

Addison walked to the steps, and motioned for Alison to join him. With some reluctance, she took his hand and slowly joined him on stage.

"Alison, I have never met anyone like you before. You are kind, and generous, and selfless. You brighten every room that you enter, your smile is like pure joy, and laughter is contagious. You look at a person and see who they really are, not who they are trying to be." He released her hand and brushed a finger along her arm.

"What are you doing? You just broke off your engagement with Lena. This is neither the time nor place to be doing this." Alison giggled quietly, as she began to blush again. In response to her objection of his speech, he put the microphone back on its stand.

"I want you to know the truth. I need you to know…that day in the stable…I remember what we talked about, and I have regretted how things ended ever since. I chose to listen to my head and my sense of duty…and not my heart. I left my heart in that stable that day." He whispered in her ear. What he did next was the last thing that she expected, even though her heart was willing it to happen.

He stepped toward her, until he was just an inch from her, his eyes drawing her in. He slipped one hand around to the base of her back, and slid the other to the nape of her neck. With a tenderness that she never expected, he pulled her to him, pressing her to his body, and he kissed her.

The kiss awakened something in her that she had suppressed for quite a while, and she grasped the front of his waistcoat. She forgot how to breathe, and didn't care, because

~ 143 ~

she was getting everything that she needed from him. Her heart seemed to explode in loud booms and bangs as the fireworks within her were ignited.

He had lived in complete darkness for the first month in his coma, and it was like Hell for him. Then one day, a spark ignited, and it progressively got brighter and brighter. The spark grew, and as it grew, he felt warmth and love and yearning. He was drawn to it, needing it to survive. He had found the one thing that would help him get free, and he clung to it with everything he had. And, as he cared for and nurtured the flame that had been his saving grace, it rewarded him with the most beautiful sound, like a choir of Angels singing to him, all combined into one majestic voice. On the day that he woke up, he felt like the flame was being ripped from his very hand, so he gripped it tight, and it pulled him from the darkness and into the light. However, when he opened his eyes, he was looking through fog, and there was a dark storm cloud over his head, ready to rain down on him with despair and emptiness.

He had been feeling strangely drawn to Alison since the day he saw her at his door, but it wasn't until today, when he heard Alison singing in her room, that he realize why he felt that gravitational pull. *She* was the flame, *she* was the light, and *she* was the choir of angels singing him home.

He held her to him, and kissed her with all the passion that he could possibly convey through a kiss. He wanted to pull that light from her for the whole world to see, to make her glow brighter than any supernova could even be, because compared to her, a supernova was nothing but match light.

Lena stood there, watching the scene, and she began to lose control. She screamed, and lunged forward.

"YOU RUINED EVERYTHING!!!!!"

At the sound of Lena's scream, Alison opened her eyes.

"Adam, look out!!" She pushed Addison out of the way, before being thrown off the platform, and onto the floor. Lena stumbled at the impact, and then went to jump off the stage, on top of her, but Addison grabbed her, and threw her at a group of guys near the steps leading to the stage, before jumping off the stage, himself, and rushing to Alison's side. When she pushed Addison out of the way, she assumed that Lena was charging at him. However, she was the one that Lena was after.

Had someone been standing close enough to catch her when she flew off the stage, she would have been fine. However, no one was there, and it had happened so fast that no one could react in time. As the crowd gasped and screamed, they watched her fly through the air as if in slow motion. She tried to turn, and reach her arms out to brace the impact, but she hit the floor with such force that her arms slid out from under her, and she bashed her head on the floor, knocking her out.

"Lena!! What have you done?!" He tried to wake Alison, but she had hit her head quite hard on the marble floor. Furious beyond any reason, he turned on Lena, and the look on his face was almost murderous. It took seven guys, including the Mayor, Arthur, and Roger to restrain him.

"Someone call for help! She's bleeding!" Elizabeth cried out, kneeling next to Alison, and holding her hand.

"Get her out of here, we can't hold him much longer!" Thomas Gentry screamed, and rounded on Addison. "Addison, listen to me, man. She isn't worth it. We have to get Alison to the hospital. Do you hear me? Alison's hurt bad!" He tried to snap him out of it, but Addison was ready to tear Lena limb-from-limb.

"Oh My God! Addison, please….You have to help her! She's fading. I can't find a pulse!!" Elizabeth cried, holding Alison's wrist between her fingers.

"NO!!!" His head turned at hearing his grandmother cry. "No, Allie…no, no…stay with me, please…Alison, please don't leave me…." He fell to the floor, and picked her up in his arms, holding her and covered in her blood from the large gash across her head. "I need you, please…you can't do this…don't let go, stay with me." He sobbed, kissing her lips, but they didn't kiss him back.

Lena heard everything as her father dragged her from the ballroom, and at hearing how bad it was, she stopped smiling, and her laughter ceased.

"I told you to stay away from him, Alison. He was mine." She murmured as she and her father were thrown out into the rain, which had just began to fall hard from a freak thunderstorm overhead. The sirens could be heard off in the distance.

The crowd stood around and watched Addison rock the woman he had just professed his feelings for, by way of an unbelievably passionate kiss. He spoke softly to her through the sobs.

The ambulance arrived soon after, and Addison was forced to step aside, to allow them to take care of her. When he heard them say that she had stopped breathing, his heart fell. He collapsed to the floor near her, and watched as the medics worked feverishly to revive her. They began to perform CPR on her, and it was more than he could bear. All he could think of was that he was to blame. He should have told her how he felt when it was just the two of them. Instead, he put his feelings and Alison out on display in front of half of Woodcrest, and within striking distance of the woman he had just scorned and called out.

He made a plea to the heavens as he groveled on the marble floor; He asked the powers that be to take him instead, to spare the life of Alison and damn him to hell for putting her in danger.

"We have a pulse, but it's faint!" One of the men cried out. "Let's get her to the hospital ASAP. She's lost a lot of blood, and she may not make it. Clear a path, people!"

Chapter Fifteen

The clock ticked away as the Thatchers took turns pacing the waiting room, waiting to get word on Alison's condition. Becky was sitting in the corner, but she wasn't alone. Though Roger and Corrine had stayed behind to make sure that all the guests had departed, taking their gifts with them, Becky had been brought to the hospital by her date, Killian.

Killian Callahan was a sweet boy, and was related, indirectly, to one of the founding families of Woodcrest. He hadn't know the Thatchers well, but he did know Addison, as he had gone to school with him.

He held Becky's hand, and stood in silence at her side.

"This is driving me crazy. What is taking them so long?" Addison got up, wringing his hands.

"The doctors had to stitch her head, and do an examination to see if more damage had been done. That takes time." Elizabeth sighed, putting her hand on his arm.

"She didn't deserve this. That should have been me, not her. I was the one who kissed *her*."

"It kind of looked like you were kissing each other to me." Killian piped in, trying to lighten the mood slightly.

"That's true, Casey." Becky sighed, calling him by his nickname. "But I don't think that that is helping."

"Sorry, man. I am sure she is going to be alright. If anything had gone wrong, they would have been out here by now." He said, patting Addison on the shoulder.

"If anyone is to blame for this...it's me. I was the one who urged her to come down after Lena had screwed with her head. She wanted to go back to her room, but I told her that she needed to go to the party. I was the one who said that she needed to tell you how she felt, before it was too late. If I had just kept my nose out of it, she would have been safe and sound in her room." Becky began to sob, and Killian hugged her. Addison looked at his friend, and got up. He walked over to her, and pulled her to him, and hugged her, kissing her on the top of her head.

"Becky, this was not your fault. Lena stepped over the line, saying those horrible things to Alison. I am glad you were there with her, or she may have left the estate, and been gone before any of us knew what had happened. Thank you for giving her the courage to do what she needed to do." He pulled her back from him for a moment. "I could say that it was my fault, because I didn't have to put my feelings for Alison on display in front of all of those people, but I did. We could all point fingers at ourselves for something that we could have done to prevent this horrible thing from happening, but instead...let's put the blame where it really belongs." He took her hands in his, and kissed her knuckles. "Lena manipulated all of us, but no one more than me. I am so sorry that I almost brought that into our family. She hurt a lot of people. What she said to Alison was despicable and loathsome, but what she did to her...That cannot be forgiven. She will pay for what she has done. I will make certain of it."

"Are you the family of Alison Moreno?" An aged man in a long white coat approached them.

"Yes...yes! How is she? Please tell me she's alright."

"Calm yourself, son." The doctor could sense the urgency and worry, and tried to have him lower his voice. When Addison had calmed slightly, the doctor continued. "We managed to stop the bleeding, and stitch her head up, but she will have a scar there, about this big." He used his fingers to show a length of about six inches right at her hairline. "Because of the impact, she does have a concussion, and a bit of swelling, but that is perfectly normal for head trauma of this sort. We are going to keep her for at least a week or so, to make sure that the swelling goes down."

"Can I go see her?" Addison urged.

"Yes, but just bear in mind, she is still not awake yet." Fully aware of Addison's case, he added to his statement quickly. "However, that has a lot to do with the sedative that we gave her. She should be awake soon, but she is going to be groggy."

Addison didn't wait to hear the rest of what the doctor had to say, as he raced down the hall to Allie's room. Seeing her lying there, so pale, and a bandage across her head, he felt like crying. He walked over to her, and pulled the chair up next to her bed. He picked up her hand, and leaned over to kiss her softly on the lips, before sitting down next to her, and holding her hand to his cheek, watching her attentively.

"I never meant for this to happen, Alison. I never meant for you to get hurt." He sobbed.

Soon he was joined by the others, but he paid no mind to them entering, because he was not going to leave her side. Arthur came over, and kissed her on the forehead. Elizabeth did the same, and brushed her pink cheek with her hand. Becky came in, and pulled up the other chair, and sat down next to her, and Killian stood directly behind her. Becky took Allie's other hand and held it for a few minutes, then got up for Addison's grandmother to sit down. Addison got up, and offered his chair to his grandfather, and he sat on the bed next to Alison instead. He felt like he needed to be closer to her. She needed to feel him close by.

About an hour passed, and the nurse came in to tell them that visiting hours were ending, and that they had a few minutes, but that they had to leave until the next morning.

"I don't care what your visiting hours are...I'm not leaving her. I will be quiet, and not disturb the other patients, but I am not going anywhere." Addison grumbled.

"Sir, I'm sorry, but you have to go. We can't make exceptions."

"Like hell you can't! Do you have any idea who I am?" He raised his voice slightly.

"I don't care if you are the king of England... you are not staying. Rules are rules. If I bend the rules for you, I will have to do it for everyone else with a sick loved one."

"Grandmother, please do something. I can't leave her...not tonight...not until she wakes up." He pleaded with his grandmother, and then he looked at the nurse. "I don't want her to wake up alone. Can't I, at least, stay until she wake up? Please..." He begged, tears filling his eyes.

"Let me talk to the doctor. If he says it's alright, then I suppose you can stay for a little while longer, but the rest of you will have to leave. I will be right back." The nurse rolled her eyes, and walked out.

"Well, I am sure they will at least let *you* stay for a bit. We will go." Elizabeth whispered. "Give her our love and let her know we are thinking of her, and will see her soon." She kissed her grandson on the top of the head, and took her husband's arm. "I will talk to the doctor, myself."

"We'll go too. I'll take Rebecca home." Killian said, taking Becky's hand.

"Hey, Killian…" Addison looked at his old schoolmate.

"Yeah?"

"You know…Becky is like my sister. Treat her like a lady. I'll be watching." He gave him a look, and smiled at them. "Thank you."

"Give her a hug and kiss from me, please."

"I will." He took Becky's hand, and gave it a squeeze, and then watched her and Killian leave together, hand-in-hand. A few minutes later, the nurse came back to tell them that only one of them could stay, but she saw that the only one that remained was Addison, so she closed the shades, handed him a pillow and blanket and closed the door behind her.

It was the longest couple hours of his life. He thought that being in a coma was the worst he would ever have to endure. Yet, faced with waiting for her to wake up, to see her brilliant cerulean eyes look at him, it was pure torture.

He thought over the past twenty four hours, the past forty-eight, the past couple months…He thought about every look, every sideways glance, every smirk, and every little quirk that had clearly registered in his mind of Alison, yet they seemed trivial at the time. He thought about the day at the stables, and the look in her eyes when he walked out to go be with Lena. He came back from his three months in a coma with a better understanding of what being loved felt like. Even when she was purposely avoiding him, she still managed to give him a look or a secret smile.

That kind of love, adoration, and devotion despite the circumstances of their relationship…it made him think about all the times that Lena had claimed she loved him. With her, he needed to hear her say the words out loud, and even then, that feeling of love wasn't there. But with Alison, she never needed to utter a single word to him…he felt it in abundance every moment of every day, even before he knew who she was.

He sat there, holding and caressing her hand, rubbing his cheek against her soft skin and he smiled when he remembered the moment that he saw here walk through the French doors in that beautiful gown, looking like the angel she was. Suddenly, he felt her fingers twitch, and heard a small giggle.

"Stop doing that. That tickles. I need to teach you how to shave." It came out of her like a whisper, but he jumped as though she had just screamed it. He turned his face and smiled at her, running his lips along her knuckles.

"I am a really bad student…it may take you a long time to teach me." He whispered against her knuckles, kissed them, and then got up to kiss her forehead. She grunted, and sucked in air through her teeth. "Ooh…sorry."

"No, don't be sorry." She looked around her, and after a moment, she realized where she was, and looked at him with panic in her eyes. "What happened? Why am I in the hospital?" She used her free hand to reach up and feel her head. She let out a small cry of pain.

"Ooh, baby, you need to be careful. They just stitched you up." He grabbed her other hand, and held it as well. "What do you remember?"

"I remember…um…coming out of my room in a beautiful blue party dress…and Lena, she said the most horrible things. I wanted to run away. But, Becky told me that Lena was just trying to hurt me. She told me to go to the party, despite Lena, and to…" She tried hard to remember, but everything was hazy and broken up in her mind, like trying to put a puzzle together in a thick fog.

"You are doing well. Keep going, but take your time. Let it come back to you." He encouraged her, but was not trying to rush her. She closed her eyes, and tried to let the fog clear on its own. If she didn't try to force it, her head hurt less.

"Becky said that I needed to tell you how I felt. She said that if I didn't let you know as soon as possible, I would live to regret it, because you had a right to know. I guess that I realized that she was right, because I went to the doors, and opened them, and there you were. Lena was hanging on you, and I wanted to hurt her like she had hurt me…at least I did at first. Then I saw your eyes, and they were filled with this…I don't know…It was like they were calling to me. I decided that I wasn't doing it to hurt her at all…I needed to tell you, before it was too late…before I lost my chance…before you married her." She looked at him, and there were tears glittering in her silvery blue eyes, and there was a hint of clarity in them.

"You needed to tell me something. You said, 'Adam, I need to tell you something very important...' and then what? What happened next, sweetheart? Do you remember?" A glint of excitement was in his eyes, and she smiled.

"I think I stopped, because I realized that you already knew what I was going to say. You started to walk towards me." She readjusted herself, trying to get comfortable. After a few deep breathes, she continued. "You took me up to the stage...made a crazy speech. Lena was up there, too. You said that you no longer loved her, that the marriage was out of obligation."

"And you removed me from that obligation by revealing the truth." He seemed sad, and almost disappointed that the pregnancy had been a lie.

"You started talking about clarity and you whispered in my ear. Then, I saw the look in your eyes, and I felt my whole world just explode." She closed her eyes, and began to raise her fingers to her lips, but he stopped her, pressing his lips tenderly to hers. Her fingers tightened around his, and she moaned softly. A few moments passed by, and suddenly her eyes shot open, and she squeaked. He pulled his lips from hers. She heard Lena's scream echo though her head. As before, she shoved him back, and cried. "She lunged at you...or me...I'm not quite sure anymore, and I pushed you out of the way, I felt like I was falling. Next, I felt a sharp pain on my head, and everything went black!" Her eyes were wide, and she began to shake.

"Shh, it's alright. You are okay, I promise. You are safe and sound." He tried to calm her.

"I don't care about me!?! Are you alright? Did she hurt *you*?" She began to scan his face, feverishly, as if looking to see if he was injured in any way.

"As a matter of fact, she hurt me worse than I even thought was possible, yet she didn't lay a hand on me." He sat down on the bed next to her, and held her hands between his, pressing them to his lips. She felt them tremble, and she saw the look in his eyes.

"What happened? Tell me!" She demanded, sitting up, despite the pressure in her head. "What did she do to you?!"

"She shoved you so hard, that you slammed your head against the marble floor. You lost consciousness immediately, and…You stopped breathing…your heart stopped, Alison." He bent his head down, and pressed her knuckles into his forehead. She saw his shoulders shake, and heard him sniffle. The reality of what had happened, the depth of his words sunk in and she stretched her fingers, and ran them through his hair. She gently curled her fingers around the back of his head, and pulled him closer, and he instantly wound his arms around her. She wound her arms around his neck and the back of his head, and let him release whatever fears he had been feeling. He buried his face in her neck, and gripped her with a fierceness that she had never encountered before in her life. It scared her. She wasn't scared of *him*, but of the absolute terror that had caused him to react in such a manner that had him shaking so violently.

"I'm still here, Adam. I'm right here. I'm not going anywhere, I promise you." She stroked the back of his head, and neck. She had to let him work through it, to let his body release all the anger, and helplessness that he had to have felt when he, undoubtedly, held her lifeless body in his arms. What she wondered now was this: *if he is reacting this way, knowing that I'm alive, what on Earth did he do to Lena, when he thought that she had caused my death?*

When the trembling and sobs subsided, and he had loosened his tight grip on her, and was now, just holding onto her, gently, she could pull her head back enough that she saw the dried blood on his collar, and all over his neck and shoulder. He had held her in his arms, her warm blood flowing over his skin, and though they got her to the hospital, he had yet to wash it off. It had even gotten in his hair, because it was stiff in spots, and stuck together. She hadn't noticed it until just then.

"Addison, I need you to look at me." There was a seriousness in her voice, and he lifted his head, but not before kissing her neck, where her pulse had been beating against his cheek. He laid his forehead against the side of her forehead that wasn't bandaged, and lazily opened his eyes to look into hers. When she was sure that he was listening, she asked him the question that was burning in her mind. "Addison, where's Lena? What did you do to her, after I fell? You need to tell me, please"

"I don't give a damn where she is, Alison. She could be in a gutter somewhere, for all I care." He answered softly.

"What did you do to her?" Her voice was stern, and demanding.

"I didn't touch her…I wanted to kill her, to rip her apart for what she had done, but I never laid a finger on her."

"So, what happened? Did she leave? Did she get taken out…" She swallowed hard.

"Are you asking if she got carried out in a body bag? If so, the answer is still no. She would have been if I had gotten ahold of her, but I was being restrained. She and her sleazy father were thrown out of the house, into the rain. Where they went from there, who knows? I honestly don't care."

"That's the thing, Addison…You should care. You loved her. You were going to marry her." She whispered to him, trying to understand what was going on in his head. He had lost all sense of logic, of right and wrong because of his grief and pain. "As bad as it was that she did what she did…I do not believe that she intentionally was trying to cause the kind of damage that was caused."

"Are you trying to tell me that it wasn't her fault? That, despite the fact that she damn near *killed* you…that I should care about her?" He couldn't believe what he was hearing. He pulled his head back, and focused on her face.

"I'm not saying that what she did was right, or that she didn't deserve to be thrown to the streets. I'm not saying that she shouldn't be punished for what she did, but…" She bit her lip. "Addison, even the most poisonous snake deserves compassion. If you didn't care at all for her, then why were you willing to marry her in the first place? Or were you marrying her simply because she told you she was pregnant?"

"I don't know, anymore." A sense of shame came over him, and he understood what she was trying to say. "I guess, a part of me loved her, and I was trying to be the bigger man, despite all the hurt and pain that she had caused so many people. I mean, she was to be the mother of my child…or she would have been if she had been pregnant. I hate that she chose that to try to trap me. I thought I was going to be a father, and now I hate her for taking that from me, too."

"Be angry…Be furious…but don't let hatred consume you. You can't just stop loving someone, altogether, for making a mistake. What happened at the party was an accident. She was angry. Angry at me, for standing in the way of her getting what she wanted… Angry at you for finally seeing through her deception, and choosing to love someone who would love you back. She was so angry, she lashed out." Her words were soft, and gentle, and there was no evidence of contempt or hatred in her voice, despite all the things that Lena had done to her. It shook him to the core. "Forgive her for what she did. You don't have to forgive the way she went about it, but you need to forgive her. I have."

"But, I almost lost you tonight, Alison. I held you in my arms as you were slipping away. I kissed you, and there was nothing…no breath, no life in you…" His lip began to tremble again, as he touched her lips, which were warm with breath and pulsing with blood beneath the surface. "How can you forgive someone for nearly taking your life? How can you just let that go?" He tried to understand, and she could see that he was struggling with it. She put her hands on the sides of his face, and he laid his on top of hers.

"I'm still here, and I am looking at what I got out of it. You're in front of me, looking at me with those beautiful brown eyes of yours…you are why I can forgive her. She will have to spend the rest of her life, knowing that, despite her best efforts to trap you or thwart me, *I* am the one who wound up getting what both of us ultimately wanted…you! You and I could be dirt poor, living on a desert island, living off of coconuts and rum for the rest of our lives…wearing nothing but palm tree leaves, and I would be the happiest woman in the world, because I would have you." She smiled at him, and the light that had filled her eyes before had finally pushed away the darkness, and he smiled back.

"You are the most beautiful person that I have ever met." He took a deep breath and cleared his throat. "I need to be honest with you about something." He kissed her knuckles again, and the leaned over and whispered in her ear.

"Before you say anything, I have had a question on my mind…"

"What is it?"

"That day, at the stables…before you walked out… you said that I was unattainable. Why? Why did you say that I was unattainable?"

"You pushed me away. You said that what happened between us was a mistake, that it was a moment of weakness for you, nothing more."

"Addison…you have to understand something. I was already in a very emotional state, then you said those things to me, and nearly kissed me. I would have been yours right then and there if you had asked me to. But, Lena came in, gave you that sob story, and the next thing I know, you are telling her that you will meet her in your room, and you acted like it was no big deal."

"I didn't mean to make you feel like you did. I didn't want her to see you, and I couldn't think of any other way to get her away from the stables. When you said that stuff to me…accusing me of considering you like a play thing…that hurt my feelings. I felt something for you, something I couldn't explain, and when you shot me down, I felt as though…"

"You thought that I didn't want you…that, even if you hadn't been with Lena, I would not have wanted you. Is that what you meant by me being 'Unattainable?' That I didn't want you, regardless?"

"Pretty much. When I didn't see you for the rest of the evening, and then I spotted you coming from the stables after dark, looking like you had been waiting for me to return…I knew that I had made a critical mistake."

"I did wait for you to come back. I sat there and waited, and cried, and thought about what had happened, and I wanted you to come back."

Addison thought about what he was going to tell her, when he went to her door that night.

"That night was a turning point for us, and we can linger on it, or be honest with how we really feel here and now. So, getting back to what you were saying…you said that you needed to be honest about something. What was it? What were you going to say?"

"Alison, I…after all the clouds had cleared, I finally realized why I was so messed up that day, so lost in how I felt because I was unsure. Alison, what I'm trying to tell you is…I've fallen in love with you."

The words that he said to her, words that she had only dreamt him saying to her, laid on her heart like a warm blanket, and she kissed him so sweetly, that his breath caught in the lump in his throat. She didn't have to say anything. He could feel how she felt in the way she kissed him and the way she looked at him.

After he got her settled and comfortable, he took the pillow that the nurse had supplied him, and laid it on the edge of the bed, and sat with her, until they both drifted off to sleep.

Chapter Sixteen

What happened between the two of them the night before was not brought up again, as there was nothing left to be said.

Though it was going to take him some time to get past her malicious actions, Addison had made a promise to himself, and Alison, that he would work hard to forgive Lena for what she had done. However, thoughts of her were not going to consume him, as he had more important things and people to think about.

Alison's doctor said that her swelling was improved when he examined her the next morning, but that they were still going to keep her for another few days or so, just to make sure. She didn't like that very much, as she wanted to get past the whole situation and get on with her life. What she didn't want to say was that she was used to doing the nursing, not being the one nursed. When it came to being taken care of, she was very stubborn and pig headed. She had been very self-sufficient from a young age, and to have people falling all over themselves to take care of her drove her crazy.

The nurse had brought her breakfast, and she was about to reach for her orange juice, but Addison felt the need to step in.

"Let me get that for you." He snatched it off the tray, and opened it.

"I can do it myself."

"I'm sure you can, but you don't need to be reaching and stretching like that." He smiled at her, and handed it to her.

"Thank you." She gave him a little smile.

"My pleasure. Is there anything else I can get for you? Do you need me to fluff your pillows? Are you warm enough? Do you need an extra blanket?"

"Adam, stop! Please. I am fine." Her mild annoyance at his incessant helping seemed to come out in her voice.

"I'm sorry." He backed away, momentarily. "I thought that you were a morning person. Roger and Corrine said that you were up every morning before anyone else, every day. You seem kind of cranky in the morning to me. Maybe that is why. You don't deal with people well, first thing in the morning." He sat down, slightly put out.

"I am a morning person, but you really don't have to take care of me. I have a mild concussion, and a bump on the head. I am still capable of doing things for myself."

"Actually, it's not just a mild concussion, and it's far more than just a bump on your head. You need to take it easy, like the doctor said. I understand that you're very capable, but I *want* to take care of you. It is my job to take care of you."

"Who told you it was your job to take care of me?"

"Oh, let's see…I did!" He laughed, and sat on the edge of the bed, taking the bowl of creamy oatmeal off her tray, grabbing the spoon, and began to stir it and cool it, by blowing on it.

"What are you doing with that? Put it down, now." She motioned for him to return the bowl to the tray.

"No. I am gonna feed you. You just sit back and relax."

"I don't wanna sit back and relax. I wanna eat my breakfast."

"And you will eat it…because I am going to feed it to you."

"No, you're not. I can…"

"I know you are capable of feeding yourself, but guess what? I don't care. Now, open up." He spooned some out, and held it above the bowl.

"No!" She pouted, shut her mouth tight, and crossed her arms over her chest.

"Alison, come on. Open up, before it gets cold." She responded, by shaking her head slightly, grunting, and gave him a look of defiance that reminded him of a child. "Real mature, Alison. Now, come on, and open your mouth. Don't make me do the airplane!" He found the way that she was acting to be both infuriating and highly amusing at the same time, and he gave her a stern look, with a smile tugging at the corner of his mouth. She turned her head away, closed her eyes, and clenched her jaw shut. He grunted at her.

"Aw…look, darling. They are having their first fight already. How cute!" Elizabeth smiled from the doorway, and Arthur peeked around his wife, an eyebrow raised.

"Grandmother, I am so glad you are here. Please tell her that she needs to eat to keep her strength up."

"It's true, Alison. You still look pale, and you need to eat."

"I will eat, just as soon as he sets the bowl down, so I can feed myself." She watched him from the corner of her eye, and spoke through her clenched teeth.

"He's just trying to help, honey. Why won't you let him help?" Arthur chimed in.

"She won't let me help because she's acting like a stubborn child!" Addison barked.

"I am NOT…" That was all she got out, and he quickly spooned the oatmeal into her open mouth, before she could prevent it. She turned her head, and gave him a deadly look, her cheeks puffed out like a chipmunk.

"Now, was that so hard?" He snickered, proud of himself, and his grandparents gave him a thumbs up when she wasn't looking. Alison grunted, and kicked him in the side from beneath the covers. "Ow. That was completely unnecessary!"

He reprimanded her, shaking his finger at her, like he was scolding a child.

Knowing that she was now outnumbered, and that she needed to just deal with the torture of being babied, she reluctantly swallowed, and then opened her mouth again, her arms still crossed over her chest.

By midday, everyone she knew in Woodcrest had come to see her, minus the Thortons, but then, she really had no desire to see them at all.

Mayor Gentry and his lovely wife, Odette, brought her beautiful purple orchids. The women talked for a while, making the men leave, so they could have some girl time.

"So…How are things between you and Addison? Last night was…I am still reeling." Odette asked.

"You and me both. To be honest, it all happened so fast…" She took a drink of water. "…as I was saying, it happened so fast, I am still trying to figure it all out. And as far as Addison and I, there is still a lot to be said. He shocked me last night. I was not expecting that kiss, especially considering that he and Lena were to be married today."

"What got into him? Well, I can imagine. He's a man. He saw you, looking like an absolute vision, and I suppose his hormones took over."

"I am not sure it had anything to do with hormones, Odette. I honestly believe that he felt something, deep inside, and he had no control over his actions."

"No self-control…that was obvious. You should have seen him after you got hurt. He wanted to kill Lena, and I am not talking figuratively. It took seven men to hold him back, and even that many were having trouble restraining him."

"I know, and that scares me." Alison looked at Odette, and then looked out into the hall, where Thomas and Addison were standing and talking. "What scares me even more is that, had the situation been reversed, I would not have reacted any differently than he did."

In the hallway, the men were chatting, and Addison could sense that Thomas was refraining from looking him in the eye. This bothered him, as Thomas was focused and he always made eye contact with those he spoke with.

"You have been acting strangely, Mayor. Is there something wrong?"

"No, Addison. Nothing is wrong. I just have been thinking about Ms. Moreno's place here in Woodcrest."

"Her place?"

"Well, yes. I mean, haven't you noticed that she is different than all the other girls here? She dresses different, acts different, talks different...she is very educated and knowledgeable about things that we can't even fathom to understand..."

"What's wrong with that?" Addison got defensive.

"Nothing is wrong with that, Addison. In fact, it's refreshing to have someone here that stirs the pot a bit, as they say. I just want you to be careful...careful as to how you carry on a prospective relationship with her. She did not move to Woodcrest. She was just passing through. I was the first person to speak with her when she arrived."

"So, you think that now that her job here is finished, she is just going to be on her way? She wouldn't do that."

"At least not right away, no...especially since you have feelings for each other. But, you must be prepared for the inevitable, because she *will* choose to leave eventually, and you will be left behind."

"No I won't. If she leaves Woodcrest, I will be at her side."

"No, you can't." The abrupt way that Mayor Gentry answered Addison, made him agitated.

"And who is going to stop me? You? My grandparents?" He folded his arms over his chest. Thomas looked in the room, exchanged looks with his wife, and then looked at Addison, eye-to-eye.

"Alison will. I assure you…she will not take you with her."

"Odette, is there something wrong?" Alison asked, noticing that the woman in front of her was distracted.

"What does Addison know about you? For instance, does he know about where you are from, or should I say, *when*?"

"Not exactly. I mean, He knows that I am not from Woodcrest. And he knows I have family in Philly, but aside from that…he doesn't have a clue about the other details." Allie looked over her shoulder, and then back to Odette. "You guys aren't going to tell him, are you? You both promised me." She grasped her hand, and gave a pleading look.

"We won't say a word to him. We made you a promise, and we keep our promises."

"You are right, though. He needs to know. If I truly care for him, I need to be honest with him, about everything. I may lose him, though. I really doubt that he will be as understanding as you and your husband are."

"He may surprise you. He may even love you more for being brave enough to tell him the truth, despite the chance of losing him. If he truly loves you that much, he will learn to accept it."

"Maybe it would be better if he told me to leave, or thought I was crazy. God only knows how he would react if one day, I went back. I can't stay here forever. I would love to…to stay with him till the bitter end, but I *have* to go back. And as hard as it is to face, he *cannot* come with me." That realization brought tears to her eyes.

Chapter Seventeen

It had been a few days since she was released from the hospital, and yet, the conversation with Odette was lingering in her mind. Addison was also distracted after speaking with Thomas, but it was good to have Alison home. He still insisted on trying to take care of her, despite her resistance. She did, however, insist on changing her own bandages, and he didn't argue, but rather helped her by getting the things from the cupboard for her.

He watched her, contently, as she removed the soiled bandage, and looked at the gash. It was looking better every day, and almost all the swelling was gone. As she applied the cream to it, he watched her face, and decided to talk to her.

"So, Alison…um…being that this relationship started out on a bumpy road, I would love it if you and I could spend as much time together as possible, getting to know one another." She turned her head, and there was a smile on her face, and it calmed his nerves a bit.

"I would love that, Adam. I was hoping that we could spend some time together, just the two of us."

"What do you say that we have a picnic out in the garden tonight? I am sure that Corrine can put together a basket for us. The leaves are changing, and the sunset is beautiful in the evening…then again, you already knew that. I used to watch you out there, sometimes. Lena hated heights, so she never came near the windows to see what I was looking at."

"I know. I saw you standing there." She placed the new bandage over the treated gash, and took the pieces of tape that Addison had ripped off for her.

After she had put the tape on, her and Addison went downstairs, and prepared for their picnic. When Corrine was finished filling the basket with lots of goodies, Addison grabbed a blanket and they went out to the large willow tree.

It was quiet, aside from the breeze blowing through the tree branches, and the other sounds of nature. Corrine had made them turkey and cheese sandwiches and some selected fruits and vegetables to munch on. After they had finished eating, Addison leaned against the trunk of the tree, and Allison leaned against his chest. They sat and enjoyed the quiet alone time, but then Addison started to talk.

"Do you like it in Woodcrest, Allie?"

"I love it here. It is so much less busy than back home, and the people here care a lot for one another."

"So, I take it that you are thinking of staying here, then."

"Not forever, but for a while, I suppose."

"You wouldn't want to live here, with me?"

"There is a whole world out there, Adam. There are still a lot of places that I would love to travel, like Europe, and across the United States. There is so much to see. As much as I love it here, I don't see myself staying here forever." She played with his fingers, which suddenly got stiff and tense.

"If you were to travel, would you want me to come with you?"

"Of course I would. Traveling is more fun when you do it with people to share it with." She looked up at him, and the tension in his face seemed to melt away. "However, there may come a day, when I am going to have to go on my own." The tension returned.

"Why would you go on your own? Why wouldn't you want me to come with you?" There was a strain in his voice. She sat up and turned around, so she could face him, tucking her dress beneath her knees.

"I am sure that there are places that you would want to go on your own, right?"

"I am content staying right here with you. There is no place I would want to be, if you weren't there with me, at my side."

"That couldn't possibly be true. There has to be somewhere..."

"Nope. Which makes me wonder...where on earth you would want to go, that you would insist I not come." He gave her a look.

"If you really must know..." She swallowed hard, and turned back around, leaning against his chest again, because she couldn't bear to see the look on his face. "That would be the day I go home."

"But....I thought this was home."

"It is, at least for now, anyway. Can we talk about this all later? I really would like to just sit here, and enjoy this sunset with you, if that's alright." She tried to avoid talking about the whole subject, but she could feel the tension in his chest.

"Why can't we talk about all this now?" He began to sit up, but she grabbed his hands, and wrapped them around her.

"Because I just don't want to. I don't want to talk about leaving, or why, or when...I want to sit here, in your arms..." The defiant child in her was beginning to throw a temper tantrum, because she didn't want to talk about the inevitable, and he was pushing the issue.

"There is something you aren't telling me, and though you don't want to talk about it right now, we are going to talk about it, anyways. You can't just come into my life, steal my heart, and run. That is not how relationships work."

"I know that, Addison." She turned her upper body to look at him. "Do you honestly think I want to go? That I would leave you for any reason if I had any other choice? I spent way too many nights, holding your hand, praying that you would open your eyes…I wanted to be the first face that you saw when you woke up. I wanted to be the one that brought you from your mental prison…"

"You *were* the one who brought me out of it, Alison. I thought you knew that already. Just because Lena's face was the first one I saw…it doesn't mean that she was the one who brought me out of it." He sat up, and swung himself around, so he was looking at her, without her having to twist so far to look at him.

"You had no idea who I was, when I came to your door. You hadn't the vaguest idea. So, how can you sit there and tell me that I was the one who brought me out of your coma, if you had no idea I even existed until later?" She was both confused, and angry at the thought of being lied to.

"I didn't realize until it was almost too late, but the truth is, I think a part of me knew…when you fell against me, and touched me…it was the same spark that went through me as that first day that you came here, the first time that I felt anything since I was in that dark prison in my head."

"I remember that day. I touched your hand and it shuddered slightly." Her cheeks became slightly pink.

"It wasn't until I heard you sing…the day of the party, that I knew, with absolute certainty, that it *had* been you. Your touch, your voice…it is what pulled me from the never-ending darkness. I have been basking in your light ever since. If you were to leave, I am pretty sure that the light would follow, and only darkness would remain."

Her heart felt like breaking and swelling with overwhelming love at the same time. She searched his eyes, trying to tell if he was being sincere, or if he was just feeding her poetry to make her tell him what she was not quite ready to tell him. Parts of her knew that there was, in fact, a spoiled rich boy in him; a part of him that always seemed to get what he wanted, when he wanted it. Behind the golden caramel flecks in his deep brown eyes, she saw a hint of fear.

"I just don't understand this at all…it is a total mystery to me." She got an almost amused look on her face.

"What don't you understand? Please, enlighten me."

"How can two people, from totally different backgrounds, with barely anything in common…who honestly don't know much about one another…How can we feel for each other as we do? It makes no sense. You barely even knew me, broke off your engagement, and were willing to literally rip your soon-to-be bride apart for me. And I fell in love with you while you were in a coma…Hypothetically speaking, it is absolutely beyond reason that we should even feel even a fraction of what we do for one another."

"Are you doubting how much I care for you?"

"No…no, not at all. I should, but I don't doubt it for a second. Are you? Are you doubting my feelings for you?" She laid her hand on his cheek, realizing how absolutely certain she was in her feelings.

"Well, I am the best looking guy in Woodcrest, and you saw parts of me that would make any woman swoon…" He joked, but the look in her eyes made his expression of amusement die down to seriousness. "…but aside from that, the things that you did for me, the extents that you went to…the amount of emotion that you had invested in making sure that I was safe and cared for…I don't doubt that you have to feel something for me, something stronger than just affection."

"Nurses get emotionally invested in their patients all the time, Addison. That is why we are so distraught when we lose them."

"But, then I look in your eyes…there is something far deeper in there than casual affection, Alison. I see an ocean of emotions, and the depth of those emotions…they would drive any other person insane. You invested your time, your knowledge, your emotion…your heart and your soul…you laid your cards on the table, win or lose. You put all in, and hoped for the best. No one, outside of my family, has ever done that for me before." He swept a stray strand of her hair from her face, and tucked it behind her ear, brushing her cheek with his fingers.

"I know that I owe you the truth…you deserve to know. However, as much as it pains me to keep it from you, I fear that telling you now…I'm just not ready to lose you quite yet."

"What on earth makes you think that telling me the truth about something that affects us in such a drastic way…why would you lose me over something as important as honesty?"

"Because this truth…You may not want to believe." She ran her fingers though his hair, the softness of his locks tickled her fingertips. "You may even call me crazy, out of my mind, delusional…you may want to have me committed to a mental hospital."

"That wouldn't happen, no matter how crazy you may sound…I mean, honestly, it isn't like you are going to tell me you are here from outer space, or you travelled through a wormhole in time or something *that* absolutely insane, right?" He kind of gave a nervous laugh.

"Yeah…right… An alien from outer space is pretty hard to believe…" Her laugh was even more nervous, and she turned away, biting her lip. "I assure you, Adam…I am no Alien."

Chapter Eighteen

They both laughed for a moment, and then Addison caught on to what she said, or rather didn't say, and stopped abruptly.

"Wait...You aren't an alien...but what about the wormhole thing...you didn't say anything about the wormhole thing..."

"You're right. I didn't." She got to her feet and brushed herself off. She could have denied that too, but then that would have meant that she was lying to him, and she refused to lie, especially if she was planning to tell him the truth later on down the line anyway. She really had wanted to wait to talk to him about it, but he pretty much put it out there, so there was no getting around it. She turned and faced him, her arms crossed over her chest, awkwardly.

"You *are* gonna tell me that you traveling through a wormhole is preposterous too, right?" He laughed, looking up at her, hoping that she would laugh again. He was hoping that she was just trying to be funny or play a little joke, but the look in her eyes was the complete opposite. She had a pained look on her face, and her bottom lip began to tremble. She couldn't even make eye contact with him. "Alison, you are joking, right? I mean, it's impossible. There is absolutely no way that that could happen...Alison? Allie...tell me it's impossible." He got to his feet and stood in front of her, trying to get her to look him in the eye and agree with him. When she kept looking away, and then bowed her head focusing on the ground, he began to laugh, almost hysterically. "Unbelievable...Impossible...You are messing with me. You have to be."

"I really wish I was...I wish it was just a little joke, but I am not going to look you in the face and tell you that, cuz I would be lying to you. I knew you would react this way, which is why I wasn't ready to tell you yet. But, since you know the truth now, I will go pack." She turned toward the house, and began to head in, her head still hung low.

"Wait a second! Can't we talk about this for a minute? You drop this huge bombshell on me, and then just walk off?! No way! Explain this to me, please" He stood there, frozen in his spot, unsure what had just happened or what had just been said. She rounded on her spot, looking at him, her head cocked to one side, squinting against the sunset with one eye, the breeze blowing through her hair.

"What is there to explain? I am literally out of time. End of discussion. I knew that all of this perfection and happiness...I knew it would end as soon as you found out the truth. I didn't want to tell you, or even talk about it, because I knew that I would have to go back eventually, and I can't take you with me. I will never get my happily ever after with you. I will never grow old with you, because I don't know how much time I have left here, but I wasn't ready to give you up just yet."

"So what? You were gonna wait until right before you left to tell me? You were gonna spring it on me right before you walked through a giant swirling...thingy..." He made a gesture to illustrate what he was talking about. "...you were gonna look at me, and say 'By the way, Adam...I have to go back home. I'm from the future or something, and guess what, you can't come. It's been fun, but I have to go. Bye.' Were you gonna wait until then to tell me?" He was actually getting angry at her.

"No, I was not going to wait until then. I was going to tell you, but I was just not ready to do it tonight! I wanted to have at least a little time with you before you found out that I was out of my mind crazy...I wanted a little bit of the fairy tale to carry with me, before it was gone forever, you know...Was that too much to ask?" She flailed her arms, a bit of her Italian nature coming out of her, tears in her eyes. "As far as the giant swirly...thingy..." She motioned the same way he did. "...I didn't come through a big swirly thingy...I drove through a bunch of trees and ended up here. I don't know how and I don't know why, and I don't know how long I will be here...but I am. And I have a reason why I should be happy about it...or I *had* a reason to." She turned around and ran to the house before he could stop her.

She rushed up the stairs and went to her room, slamming the door behind her. Immediately, she began to pack her things. She removed all the things that would remind her of her time here, and hung all the garments in the wardrobe. All she wanted was one night, one solitary night of complete and utter happiness, but she shortly came to the realization that she wasn't supposed to.

Maybe the reason she came back in time was to keep Addison from marrying Lena. Maybe, by doing that, she had fulfilled her purpose, stopping something bad that was going to happen. The fact that she fell in love with him was just a side effect, and was not supposed to happen. It was better that it ended this way. Despite that fact, it didn't change the fact that her heart was breaking.

As she sat at the edge of the bed, holding the dress from the dance, which had been cleaned to look like new even though she knew that it had to have been covered in blood, she knew that the truth needed to come out and now a weight was lifted slightly from her shoulders.

The door swung wide, and she jumped. Addison stood in the doorway, a look unfamiliar to her on his face. She tried to figure out what he was thinking, but his expression was so strange, that she couldn't even fathom what was going through his mind.

"Let me just finish packing my things. Don't worry. I will be gone before dark. I apologize for coming into your life, and screwing everything up for you." She turned around, and laid the dress on the bed, and finished gathering her things.

"How did you screw everything up for me? Alison, you are the best thing that has ever happened to me. I am not quite ready to accept the whole time travel stuff, but…regardless of how or why you are here, you are here, and I am not gonna let you run out on me. Not now...not ever. I just wish that you had had a bit more faith in me."

"Whatever, Addison. I saw how you reacted. I had the courage to be honest with you. The least you could do is have the same respect to be honest with me. The idea of falling in love with a psychologically unbalanced girl was not something you were counting on. It is good that we didn't go any further than this. It makes it easier to just go our separate ways, with little to no pain." He was in denial, she thought, unable to mentally register the reality of the situation.

"Alison, stop packing." He stormed over to her, and grabbed her by the arms. "I said, stop packing. You aren't going anywhere. We need to talk about this."

"Just let me go, Addison. Let me go. You will move on once I am gone, and you will live a very long and happy life, and never give me a second thought. And if you think that we will meet again later in life...it is highly doubtful."

"Okay, so let's say I believe that you are from the future or something…exactly how far in the future are you from...like twenty...thirty years?"

"Try seventy-seven. I am from the year..." She whispered the next part. "...I'm from the year two-thousand fifteen." She took her opportunity to pull her arms from his grip, as he froze in shock. "So, unless my calculations are incorrect, when I go back home, you will be..."

"Old enough to be your grandfather...I would be a hundred and five years old in 2015. No wonder you felt so comfortable taking care of me. It would be like caring for one of your little old men at those retirement homes." His hands dropped to his side, and he slumped onto the edge of the bed. "Now, I am severely depressed."

"You know what? I didn't even think about that." She stopped packing, momentarily, and thought about what he had just said. "But, no, that is not why I felt so comfortable taking care of you. I felt comfortable taking care of you because I take great pride in taking care of people, regardless of their age. Not to mention, that I felt connected to you for some reason. That connection turned to fondness, and fondness into more...much more."

"It doesn't matter now. No matter what happens from here on out, I cannot move on with my life. And not a moment goes by that I am not thinking of you. You and I belong together." He looked at her, his hand reaching for hers. "Now please, stop packing and talk to me. If you are hell-bent on leaving me, I don't want it to end like this. I don't want our last moments together to be spent like this."

"I don't *want* to leave. God knows, I would have given anything to avoid this for as long as possible. You insisted on talking about this, about where I must go, about where I am from. I can only blame Thomas and Odette Gentry for this, as they were the only ones that knew. I am planning on having some strong words with them when I see them." She flung her clothes, aggressively, into her bag. "Just ONCE...I would love to be happy without everything going wrong!" Her anger and temper got the best of her, and she flung her bag across the room, and slid onto the floor, and buried her face in her hands.

"Then, let's pretend that we didn't talk about it. Let's go back outside, sit by the tree again, and just enjoy the evening like none of this even came up. We can do that, can't we?'" he knelt in front of her. "I am willing to start the evening over again...clean slate."

"Yeah...like that could happen. You know my big secret, where I am from...when I am from. That is all you are going to be thinking about. We can't go back to how it was." Tears streamed down her face, and she wiped them away.

"Why can't we go back to how it was? I don't feel any differently for you, knowing what I know, than I did before. It doesn't change how I feel or how I look at you. It *does*, however, answer some questions that I have had, but it makes me feel closer to you."

"So, you are telling me that...knowing what you know now, you aren't totally freaking out? I'm freaking out, just talking about it."

"You weren't ready to talk about it yet, so let's not talk about it anymore until you are ready. We will just get up, you will take my hand, and we will go back out and finish our picnic. I am not ready to let you go just yet." He got up, and offered her his hand. She stared at his outstretched hand for a few minutes, before taking it.

They returned to the garden, and he sat back down on the blanket, after straightening it back out. When he was sitting comfortably, he gestured for her to join him on the ground. When she sat down, he wrapped his arms around her, and pulled her closer, and held onto her. He swept her hair to one side, and laid his chin on her shoulder, so they were cheek to cheek. She took a deep breath, and leaned her head back, and began to relax. Not another word was spoken for the rest of the evening, though their thoughts of the new information being out in the open was speaking louder than anything. Every time that she would move, he would tighten his grip on her. Neither of them wanted to let go of what they had, and so they both fought hard not to.

After about three hours of just sitting out in the beautiful and peaceful night air, Alison felt the need to speak.

"As great as this is, and how much I hope to do this more..."

"Don't." He whispered in her ear.

"Don't what?"

"We have plenty of time to talk about stuff. Just enjoy this moment. I made the mistake of trying to push the issue, and you almost left. I am not going to question the how's or why's of this...I am going to treasure it, revel in it. We have time...nothing but time. Are you getting tired? It has to be getting close to midnight."

"I'm a little tired, emotionally tired, mostly. However, you are right. I just want to enjoy this. It's a beautiful night."

"The night pales in comparison to the amazing vision in my arms." He nuzzled her ear with his nose, and she giggled slightly, as his gesture of affection tickled. A slight shiver shook her. In a simple motion, he reached over and grabbed a second blanket, and covered her without letting her go. "How's that?"

"You came prepared. Obviously, you had this evening pretty much planned out."

"Yes, I did. Are you comfortable?" He tucked the blanket around her, and then wrapped his arms over the top of the blanket.

"I think I lost the feeling in my bum a while ago. What about you?" She snickered, and shifted her body slightly.

"I think some bugs have taken up residence in my trousers, and my back itches, but I am good, otherwise." He scratched his back against the tree, which caused her to bounce around slightly. She wanted to take mercy on him and suggest they go inside, but he stopped scratching, and pulled her back towards him. "The sky is so clear tonight...so many stars. Is it like this...you know...back home?"

"Not even close. We have smog, and pollution, and half the time, no one wants to be outside in the heat. They would rather be sitting in front of their televisions, in the central air."

"Are televisions like the moving picture shows?"

"Yes, only more advanced and they are in everyone's homes." She laughed, because she had forgotten how far technology had advanced since the nineteen thirties.

"Ah...well, I am not even going to ask about central air. I don't know what you think of it all, but it sounds like pure Hell to me." He laughed. "This is paradise right here...Heaven on Earth...a starry sky, cool clean air, and an angel in my arms." He sighed, and pressed a kiss to her cheek. "In all honesty, I don't care where you are from, because this is where you belong...right here, right now...with me. God had his hand in this, and I am going to give my thanks to him tenfold for bringing you to Woodcrest, and into my life."

She closed her eyes, and thought about what he had just said, and she smiled, leaning her head back to rest on his shoulder. It was so calm, and quiet, not like the city. The sound of his breathing and the rhythm of his heartbeat against her back seemed to lull her to sleep. The last thoughts that crossed her mind before she drifted off was how absolutely happy she was.

Chapter Nineteen

The last thing that Alison remembered was falling asleep under the stars, with Addison holding her in his arms. As her eyes fluttered opened that morning, she was not greeted by the breeze blowing through the large trees, but a soft morning breeze blowing the curtains in her room. She was warm under the covers and cradled comfortably by her large plush mattress. She rolled towards the windows, and was face to face with a sweet sleeping face. Lying atop the comforter, still fully clothed and sleeping peacefully with his arm beneath his head as a pillow, Addison sighed and twitched his nose slightly. She swept a strand of hair from his face, and propped her head up on her hand. *Did he carry her up himself, instead of waking her?* She thought to herself, as she just laid there and observed him.

"Knock knock" A whisper broke the silence, and Becky came creeping through the door. She must have known that he was in there with her, as she was carrying two plates of breakfast on her tray. Alison gestured for Becky to set the tray down on the table over by the chairs, and she put her finger to her lips, and then pointed to next to her. Becky winked and nodded, and then crept over to the door. Alison carefully slid off the bed, and crept over to the door, and closed it most of the way as they stepped into the hall.

"How was your evening? It must have been very romantic. He carried you up here, well after midnight, and I don't think that he has ever been so quiet and careful. I opened the door, and turned down the covers on your bed for him. Sir and Madam hadn't even realized you were back in the house. They thought you were both in the garden when they rose from bed this morning. Papa got the blankets and picnic basket last night, after Addison brought you in."

"He carried me in, all by himself?" Her eyes became wide. "No wonder he slept in there. He must have been exhausted. I am not exactly feather light."

"Actually, he wasn't even winded. He carried you in with such ease, and went up the stairs, and you barely batted an eye. It was so sweet." She blushed, and got a starry eyed look on her face. "I asked him if he wanted me to turn down his bed for him, and he said yes, but when I went in to give him his breakfast, I noticed that his bed hadn't been touched. It doesn't take a genius to figure out where he was. No worries, though. He is very honorable. He probably just wanted to make sure you were okay, and he just drifted off."

"Well thank you, Becky. I think I better get back in there before he wakes up." She patted her friend on the shoulder and then crept back into the room, closing the door quietly behind her.

She walked over to where the tray had been set, and picked up one of the cups of tea, and made her way over to the bed. Propping one hip on the edge of the mattress, she stood there and sipped out of the porcelain cup, just watching him. She observed how much differently he slept than when he was in his coma, and she smiled. His features were less tense, less troubled now. He seemed at peace, and his breathing was slow and constant.

It was a good ten minutes that passed before he even moved, and it was his hand that slid across the covers, almost on its own, to find her. She couldn't put her cup and saucer down fast enough. By the time that she had turned around from setting them carefully and quietly on the side table, and turn back around, his hand had discovered that she was not there, and it woke him from his sleep with a jolt.

"Alison!" He leapt up, screaming, a terrified look on his face.

"Shh...I'm right here...It's okay." She climbed back upon the bed, and sat down by the pillows. His arms, almost instinctively, went around her waist, and his head laid in her lap, as though he were a child who had just woken from a nightmare and needed reassuring.

"Thank Goodness. I thought that you had crept off while I was sleeping."

"Why would I do that?"

"You almost left last night...until I stopped you. What would keep you from doing it while I was sleeping?" He looked up at her, his big brown eyes looking like a pitiful puppy who thought he'd been abandoned. She ran her fingers though his hair, and caressed his cheek. He had a valid point, and it didn't dawn on her, until that moment, that he had stayed there in her room to make certain she wouldn't sneak away.

"Is that why you slept here last night? Because you were afraid that I would leave you?" The look of guilt in his eyes answered her question. "And here, I thought that you were just being incredibly sweet and dozed off, watching me sleep." She gave him a disappointed look, and pouted her lips. "You were just playing guard dog. You don't trust me."

"I'm sorry, Alison. I don't mean to make it seem as though I don't trust you. I do, inexplicably. I am just afraid that you will try to run...like before. I don't want you to leave. I want you to stay here...with me..."

"I have to go back, eventually, Addison. I have to. You know that as well as I do. If I had nothing and no one to go back to...if I thought that my absence would go unnoticed...not to mention..." She sat and thought of her parents, and what they must be going through with every day that passed. "How will my presence here affect the future? I am not supposed to be here. My parents haven't even been born yet. It is like a paradox that I am even here. I wasn't born until 1987…that means that I will not be born for another almost fifty years from now…Ooooh, I have a headache, now." She put her finger to her temple and began to rub it.

"I *am* old enough to be your grandfather…I will be seventy-seven when you are born. Are you certain that I am *not* your grandfather?" He teased her.

"Oh, I know you aren't my grandfather. This is 1938 so that would mean that, about now, my maternal grandfather works in a restaurant in Italy, with my grandmother. And my paternal grandfather is a luchador fighter in Mexico…El Niño Gazpacho" She spoke with a Mexican accent when pronouncing his wrestling name and her nose crinkled in amusement. "He married my grandmother, who was American. Now, unless you are an Italian or a Mexican….there is no way you could be my Noni or Papi." She smiled.

"Good, cuz that would be *really* awkward." He laughed, propping himself on his elbows. They laughed, but then jumped when the door suddenly flew open, as a red head came toppling to the floor. Alison and Addison exchanged terrified looks and then jumped off the bed.

"Becky! What in God's good graces….were you eavesdropping at the door?!?" Addison barked, helping her to her feet.

"What did you hear?" Alison, pulling Becky into the room, closed the door quickly behind her.

"Quite honestly…I am not quite sure I believe what I thought I heard." Becky yanked her arm from Alison's grip, and gave her a horrified look. "Either you guys knew I was there, and are trying to teach me a lesson, or you are speaking absolute nonsense." She backed herself to the door, and gripped the handle, as if ready to make a quick escape.

"What did you hear, Rebecca?" Addison ordered her to answer, and Alison backed away, her hands over her mouth, looking almost as scared as Becky.

"I just came up to see if I could get you two anything, or take your tray…and I heard something about Alison not being born for another forty-nine years and that you could possibly be her grandfather, then I lost my footing." She looked from one to the other, and then smiled, as if she had just figured out a joke. "You guys knew I was there, didn't you? That whole conversation was just something to teach me a lesson…right? I mean, there is no way that you were serious…" Her smile started to fade, as she saw tears build in Alison's eyes, and the color drain from Addison's face. It took her a moment, and then she nearly crawled up the door. "Holy Moses! Yer as mad as a box a frogs, you two are!! There ain't no way…yeh can't be telling me the truth…Allie?" They noticed that her Irish accent became stronger when she was upset.

"I didn't want you to find out this way, Becky…I swear. I was going to tell you, when the time was right."

"Would you please calm down, Becky...?" Addison grabbed the ginger-haired girl and led her away from the doors, and sat her in one of the chairs. Kneeling down in front of her, he held her hands, and tried to get her to focus. "I know that it is unbelievable, and it seems absolutely impossible. I only just found out last night, myself. Just calm down, and breathe. Alison is the same person that she was before…the same sweet, kind, incredible, beautiful, loving person she has been all along…." He looked at Alison, trying to reassure both of the girls there that nothing had changed.

"Please don't tell anyone what you heard…not even your mom and dad…and definitely not Elizabeth and Arthur. I am asking you…as my friend. I just need more time to figure out what I am going to do." Alison was now kneeling in front of Becky, tears streaming down her cheeks. Becky nodded, and then got up, and ran out the door, before either of them could say another word to her.

No one seemed to be acting any differently toward Alison, so she felt sure that Becky hadn't said anything. After all, it was a lot to process. The idea that someone could just step through time as though they were going from one room to another was absolutely ridiculous. Though that isn't exactly how it had happened, Alison thought to herself, it was basically the same theory. Outside of the woods, she was in 2015, but once she passed through the trees, she was transported to 1938, and never felt a thing, except maybe a head rush. Getting out of a chair too fast has the same effect.

The grandfather clock in the foyer had just rung for the sixth time, as the two of them made their way to the dining room for supper. Everyone was gathered around the table, including Becky, as Addison pulled Alison's chair out for her.

"How was your picnic last night?" Elizabeth began, as her grandson took his seat, and laid his napkin in his lap.

"It was nice to spend some time just the two of us, to be honest, Grandmother. Thank you for asking." He found it strange that his grandmother had started with the conversations before they had even taken the time to say grace. "Who is going to say this meal's blessing tonight?"

"I think that we should let the youngest one of us do it tonight." Elizabeth looked to her husband, and then to each of the others, to which they all agreed. They all joined hands, and bowed their heads. When Becky didn't begin right away, Addison opened his eyes, and cleared his throat.

"Becky...say grace, please."

"I'm not the youngest one here." There was a twinkle in her eye, and a slight smirk that tugged at the corner of her mouth.

Chapter Twenty

"What do you mean, Becky? Of course you are!" Addison gave her a look of disapproval, but then his grandfather piped in, saying something that almost made Alison topple over in her chair.

"We aren't waiting on Rebecca...Alison is the youngest one at the table, if I am not mistaken. She hasn't even been born yet." He smirked, and winked at Becky. No one else at the table even flinched.

"What?!?" Alison looked at Becky, hurt and disbelief in her eyes. She stumbled from the chair, throwing her napkin onto it as she got to her feet. "How could you? I begged you not to say anything!" Red hot tears well in her eyes, as she looked at the redhead. Turning her attention, she looked at each of the other people at the table, as though she were a deer caught in headlights.

"I didn't say anything, I swear." Becky leapt from her chair, the look of amusement gone. Her hands were up in a defensive manner, and she tried to go to Alison, but Adam pushed her back into her chair.

"Then, why would my grandfather make a statement like that, unless you said something?" Addison, in defense of Alison, got up from the table as well, and put his arms around the woman he loved, who was now shaking.

"She didn't need to say a word. Your grandfather and I already knew. We knew before you did, my dear grandson. As for Roger and Corinne...they overheard you talking last night, and came to us about it. As soon as they saw Rebecca running from your room this morning, white as a sheet, they knew that she had just found out, so they pulled her into our office and we all had a family meeting...well, without the two of you." She rose from her chair, and approached Alison.

"You knew?"

"Yes, my dear sweet girl. We knew...we've known for quite some time now. However, it is not our secret to tell. It is not our place to share information like that. But, as I told you before, there are no secrets in this house...in this family."

"I'd have told you, but I can hardly believe it myself and I am in the middle of it all. I was afraid that you would think I was insane and not give me a job. I'm sorry if I kept it from you." She sobbed, shaking uncontrollably in Addison's arms. "I was just so afraid."

"Afraid of what, exactly, my dear? That we would have you committed? That we would think that you were mental?" Arthur asked, lighting his pipe, despite the fact that dinner was still sitting on the table. "If you hadn't already noticed, none of us are exactly perfect. We knew that there was something different about you. We couldn't exactly judge you, before we got to know you. You proved yourself to us by doing exactly what we hired you for...to bring our grandson back to us. What more could we ask of you?"

"I honestly have no words...how did you know, if you don't mind me asking?" She staggered forward and sat back down at the table, along with everyone else.

"Little things, really...like your clothes, your mannerisms, your vocabulary...they were signs that something was a bit off. At first, I was honestly put out that you would dare to lie to my face, after we had given you a job, and a place to call home." Elizabeth admitted, looking rather upset. "However, after much thought, and a conversation with the one who had given me the recommendation to hire you, things were clarified. Unlike me, Arthur wasn't the least bit surprised to learn about your...background, so to speak. He acted as if he had experienced something like this before. It was rather puzzling to me that he acted so nonchalant about it. It was only after he told me that he had spoken to the mayor that I realized that he had known about you and where you were from long before I did."

"I should have known that they wouldn't be able to keep it secret." Alison was both amused and disappointed at the revelation.

"Dearie, you needn't worry about it getting out...ya know, yer secret." Corrine spoke up. "Thomas and Odette were jus' tryin' to help. They figured that questions would rise, and knew that if anyone could reassure you of your safety, it would be the Thatchers. They swore that they wouldn't say another word to another living soul of it...heard it with my own ears, I did."

"In all honesty, this is a relief." Alison took a deep breath, and wiped a tear from her cheek. "I hated not telling you all the truth. I hated lying, but you understand why I did it, don't you?" She squeezed Addison's hand, and let out another sigh.

"Now that we have gotten past this, we can move on to more important issues...like grace. I'm hungry." Arthur stared at the food, and he seemed to be salivating. The people around the table began to laugh.

*****

Since the cat had been let out of the bag, life at Thatcher manor was a lot less tense. Alison opened her "secret" bag, and showed off certain items that she had brought with her from the twenty-first century, and everyone found them intriguing and quite strange. Becky liked the mp3 player, and asked to listen to it while she was cleaning. Alison learned very quickly that it may have been a mistake, as Becky learned the songs rather quickly, and was heard singing along quite loudly at times. It was rather strange to hear music from her time being echoed through the halls of the massive 1930's home. However, no one had ever seen Becky clean more efficiently, and actually enjoy it as much as she did now.

      The leaves on the trees covered the ground like a multicolored carpet and dusted with little white crystals of snow, and there was a chill in the air as autumn was in full swing, and nearly Christmas time. The town was decorated for the festivities, ranging from apple picking to their annual Yuletide Festival. Alison had acclimated herself to the town, and volunteered to help out with Corrine's Pie booth, as well as to be a judge at the Christmas Tree Decorating contest.

      As she walked down the street dodging little children dressed in little coats and hats, mittens on their small hands, she felt as though she belonged there. She greeted everyone she passed, even though she didn't know very many of them. Every once in a while, she would catch Addison watching her, a smile on his face. She delivered the last of the pies to Corrine's booth, and then went to join him in the pavilion.

      "I wonder, Mr. Thatcher…what on earth could possibly cause you to wear such a smile?" She sat on his lap, and brushed a stray hair from his face.

      "I'm smiling cuz I am in love with a beautiful woman, and I am the happiest that I could ever be." He brushed his fingers on her flushed cheek and down her neck. She shivered slightly. "Are you cold? Do want me to give you my jacket?"

      "No, I'm not cold. You just gave me goosebumps."

      "I give you goosebumps?"

"Yes, you give me goosebumps. You do a lot more than that, but I am not going to say what else, cuz people are around." Her nose crinkled, and she kissed him, before getting up, and pulling him to his feet. When he was up off the bench he had been sitting on, she slid her arms under his, and nuzzled into his chest.

"Happy Yule, Addison."

"And to you, Beautiful." He wrapped his arms around her, and kissed the top of her head. He felt her shiver again, and he removed his coat, placing it over her shoulders, atop her winter shawl. "Let's go get some hot chocolate." He reached around and took her by the hand. She pulled the coat around her a bit tighter, and descended the few stairs and accompanied Addison over to Odette's booth.

The happiness and contentment that filled her heart as she walked hand in hand with Addison, passing townsfolk, listening to their whispering.

"Look at them…it's so nice to see that someone could bring out the best in him."

"Now, that is one couple that you can tell are in love."

"It is good to have the old Addison back. That girl is the best thing that could have happened to him."

As they approached Odette's table, happy and content, they were approached by someone that could surely ruin their sense of euphoria.

"Hello Addison." She said, a smug look on her face. At the sound of her voice, he instinctively moved between the source of the voice and Alison.

"Lena? What are you doing here?"

"I came to enjoy the winter festivities, same as everyone else. Just because you and I aren't together, that doesn't mean that I cannot take part in the annual fun in Woodcrest. I live here too." Her sly grin annoyed him.

"I realize that, but I thought I told you to stay away from Alison and I. I am sure that I made myself perfectly clear the last time that I saw you." The anger in his voice was very obvious.

"When was that, exactly? Hmm, let me think. Ah, yes." Her expression went from sickeningly sweet to furious. "You said that to me on the night before our *wedding*, when you dumped me for the fat cow you have hiding behind you!!!"

"You lied to me and told me you were pregnant! I broke it off because you weren't pregnant in the first place…and, you nearly killed Alison!"

"She seems alright to me. Obviously, I didn't do too much damage, or you would be crying at her grave, instead of sipping cider hand-in-hand."

"Just stay away from us, Lena. And, for goodness sake, stop feeling sorry for yourself. You never loved me, so it isn't like I broke your heart. You just wanted to marry me for my family's money and social standing." Addison barked out, for everyone else to hear, and Lena didn't even flinch at being called out again. The murmuring of the townspeople was almost as loud as the throbbing in Alison's ears, as her heart beat harder and harder.

"You think that that your new girlfriend isn't the same way? She saw money signs the moment she walked into your grandparents' house, and you know it. You just don't want to admit that you were *that* gullible for the second time in your life." The words that were coming out of Lena's mouth only angered him more, and he began to shake. Thomas quickly came over and tried to diffuse the situation, before Addison did something that he would regret.

"Lena, if you were smart, you would stop talking and start walking. The things you are saying about Miss Alison are very untrue. I suggest that you leave now, before you say anything else."

"I haven't said anything wrong. I am sure that I am not the first person to feel this way about the whole situation. She just appears in Woodcrest, out of nowhere, and now she is dating a man that she had to steal from another woman…on the eve of their wedding. I find that rather suspicious."

"Come on, Lena." Mayor Gentry grasped the boasting blonde by the arm, and tried to escort her away. In the meantime, Alison had swung around and was now holding Addison's face between her hands.

"Adam, I don't care what she says about me, what names she calls me. It doesn't matter. Keep your temper and just consider the source. She is just trying to get a rise out of you. Don't let her, please. Focus on me, and nothing else. Nothing she says can change what we have. Nothing she says matters. Mayor Gentry will take care of her."

"You just keep telling yourself that, sweetheart. We all know what you are up to. Even if you aren't after his money, he is never going to commit to you like he was going to commit to me. You are like an appetizer…you are the promissory plate that comes before the real meal…the salad before the steak!" The sheer ridiculousness of Lena's words seemed to hit Alison, and she began to laugh. Even Addison's anger seemed to lessen at the how silly she sounded. The laughter only made Lena even more upset, and she turned and confronted Alison. "What's so funny?"

"You know, Lena, for someone who gets a kick out of making fat jokes and commenting on my size…for you to use a food analogy…and compare me with salad, of all things…" Alison had to take a couple deep breaths before continuing. "At one time, I thought that you had to be pretty smart to convince a man like Addison that you loved him, when it was painfully clear to everyone else that you were just playing him. However, after hearing the gibberish that you just spewed out of that big mouth of yours, I realize that smarts had nothing to do with it."

"Are you calling me stupid?" Lena got right in Alison's face, but Alison didn't back away or even flinch.

"I wasn't calling you anything. I was just stating an observation. Unfortunately for you, Lena, I have been called every name imaginable, pertaining to my body size, and have learned to ignore what others think of me. There is no insult that you could throw my way that would even get a rise out of me, so you can just stop trying. Now, if you'll excuse us, we are going to enjoy the Yule Festival. I suggest you stop being petty and do the same." She turned on her heels, purposely whacking Lena in the face with her thick chestnut ponytail. Grasping Addison by the hand, they walked a few paced away, and went to speak with Odette. Lena stood in her spot, shocked that Alison had had the nerve to stand up to her.

They enjoyed the rest of the day with friends and neighbors, without even mentioning Lena or the confrontation. Only when Alison was in her room and her door was securely closed, did the things that Lena said get to her. As hard as she tried to act as if the statements made hadn't bothered her, the more it impacted her, and the harder that Alison cried.

"I am not an appetizer, Lena. I am not just some rebound chick that he has settled on, temporarily. True, he probably deserves better..." She stopped pacing and talking to herself and stared out the window. "Not probably...he *does* deserve better...far better than me, in fact." Alison's eyes widened and she began to think about the statements that Lena had made. *"She wasn't wrong. I came in like a wrecking ball and ruined everything the night before they were supposed to get married."* The truth in Lena's spiteful words seemed to resonate in her mind and she slumped down into one of the chairs. Again, she began to think aloud. "If I had been in her place, and another woman had come in and stolen my fiancé away, I would have acted the same way. I would have been just as angry." She stared blankly at the wall, and put her hand to the scar on her head. "I deserved this. I deserved far worse."

She got out of her chair, and began to pack her bags. There was a strong sense of determination in her actions, yet she felt as if she was watching someone else do it. She had no control over what she was doing, as if her mind was set to autopilot. She felt numb and was oblivious to the fact that there was someone watching from the doorway.

"Going somewhere, Miss?" Roger inquired.

"Yes…no…I'm not sure yet." She sighed, with very little emotion.

"Would this have anything to do with the confrontation in town earlier?" He made his approach slowly, and came to a halt at her side.

"Should it? I mean, she made some valid points, and the more I think about the things she said…"

"That is the problem right there. Why would you listen to that girl? She wanted to get into your head, and you let her."

"Roger, Addison deserves better. Sure, I saved him from marrying her, but now I just…Is he with me because he's grateful? Does he feel obligated, out of gratitude, to play the doting boyfriend until he finds someone…am I a place holder, an appetizer?" She turned to the butler, tears in her eyes and a crumpled shirt in her hands.

"Is it common for girls from your time to be so emotional and paranoid; to compare themselves to food? Are men in your time that horrible and unable to commit that they warrant this mass hysteria? If so, you need to remember where you are and take a minute." He removed the crumpled shirt from her grip and laid it down on the bedspread.

"I am not paranoid, Roger. I am being rational and practical. I am a complete mess, a train wreck. I mean, look at me." She held her arms out to the sides, a distressing look in her eyes.

"You look perfectly fine, Miss Alison…very anti-Train wreck." He took her hands, and held them between his, as he did with Rebecca. "There is absolutely nothing wrong with you. You are beautiful, and if you were my daughter, I would tell anyone that said different that they needed their tongue cut out for speaking such lies."

"I appreciate the kind words, but the reality is that I am not what Addison needs or deserves, and it took the scornful words of Lena to make me realize that. He deserves someone who can complement him, socially, visually, and intellectually."

"What does that mean? Explain it to me."

"Addison is the handsome grandson of the most prominent family in Woodcrest, one of the founding families. When he walks down the street, he needs to be seen with someone that is elegant, graceful, and radiant. She needs to be able to speak to others with some sense of intelligence and wisdom. I have never been good at history, and so knowing the history of Woodcrest, and being able to discuss it with others is beyond me. I am still getting used to the way of life here, as opposed to how things are where I am from. I am not elegant, even in the loosest of terms, and I don't have a graceful bone in my body. I am an embarrassment to him, and I don't think that the townsfolk will take him seriously with someone like me at his side."

"And you think that if he had someone like Lena at his side…that he would be taken seriously?" His eyebrow raised, and he gave her a skeptical look. His arms crossed over his chest, and his demeanor changed.

"In a manner of speaking…yes, I do."

"Do you know the only thing that Lena has that you don't?" In answer to his question, she shook her head. "She has self-confidence! That is the only thing that she has over you. She is a gold-digging, hateful, retched girl with no self-respect, but everything she does…everything she says…she is confident.

She holds her head high, and has a 'devil-may-care' attitude. You outweigh her in every other aspect of what it is to be a decent human being…and, no, I was not referring to your physical difference, so don't even start…"

She opened her mouth to say something, her eyebrows furrowed, but Roger's last words made her snap her mouth shut.

He put his hands on her shoulders. Looking her straight in the eye, he gave her the kick that she needed. "Addison doesn't need a trophy to show off on his arm. He needs someone that can keep him humble and grounded. His social standing has nothing to do with the kind of person that he should be. No one wants a conceited, stuffed shirt, swaggering uppity whatever waltzing around town, acting as if he is better than everyone else, above the law, looking down on the little man. What people saw in town today is what they need to see, what Addison needs to be. He is not any more intelligent than anyone else, any better than any man. You speak of him as though he should be a God to be worshipped and adored. He's not a God…he's…" Roger tried to finish his statement, but someone else finished it for him.

"I'm just a man. I am a man who looks at you and sees the most beautiful woman ever to walk into their life. A man who doesn't want some graceful, elegant swan. He…I like that you are a little on the clumsy side, because that means that I can catch you when you fall. I like each and every one of your flaws and quirks, because if you were perfect, you wouldn't be real. I hate fake people." Addison stepped towards her.

Alison's heart began to race as she studied his face thoroughly, trying to find any wavering in his words or the meaning behind them.

"Roger, could we have a moment, please?" He whispered to the older, balding gentleman. He nodded, kissing Alison's hands, and then he took his leave.

Addison closed the gap between them, and took Alison's hands in his own, holding them tenderly, as he caressed them with his thumbs. A moment passed when he was just looking down at her, concern in his eyes.

"Alison, I wish that there was something that I could say to you, one thing that I could say that would explain to you how I feel for you. It seems like, every time that I think that things are going good, something seems to happen and you are ready to run away."

"I'm not trying to run away, Adam."

"Funny…it looks as if you are." He pointed to the bags and suitcases on her bed, filled with clothes.

"You don't get it, do you? I don't belong here. I can try and fool myself into thinking that I can stay here forever, with you, but I can't. You're meant for something great, and with me here, you will never achieve greatness. I am a distraction, an anomaly."

"Who says that I am meant for something great? My Grandmother? My Grandfather?"

"No one said it…I just know it. I've known it since I got here, the first time I set eyes on you. If I stay, I will just stand in your way, holding you back from being the kind of man you are supposed to be."

"Who's to say what kind of man I am meant to be, Allie? Without you in my life, I will never be anything close to the kind of man that I want to become."

"No matter what happens, Adam, I will always be with you…right here." She reached forward and put her hand on his chest. He quickly grasped her hand and held it there, before she could pull away.

"Allie, you don't understand. I am a better man for having known you." His forehead wrinkled as the tension of thinking about her leaving burrowed deep into his mind. He squeezed her hand. "You have a good life here. You have a family that loves you, friends that love you, a town full of people that adore and respect you, a beautiful home to live in…and a man who loves you…"

"What?" Alison felt her heart leap into her throat.

"I said that you have a good life here..."

"No, after that."

"Family that…" He looked at her, and their eyes connected.

"No…no…the very last thing. Did you just say you loved me?" A smile began to stretch across her face.

"I suppose I did, yes. I've told you that before, haven't I?" He smiled at her.

"Not really. Not in those exact words." She tried to remember him actually telling her that he loved her, but her mind was racing with so much, she couldn't remember. "You love me? Like, you *LOVE* me?"

"Yes."

"Don't say it unless you mean it. My heart can't take it if you are just saying it to get me to stay. You need to mean it." She was excited, and anxious.

"If I didn't mean it, I wouldn't say it to get you to stay. On the other hand, if I didn't honestly love you, I would not be trying to get you to stay, would I?"

"I don't know!"

"Okay, let me try this a different way." He reached into his pocket and was getting set to pull something from it, when there was a banging at the door. "Oh, for Pete's sake!! Come back later!!" His euphoria turned to agitation, and he screamed at the door.

"It's important, Sir." Roger said from the other side of the door.

"This is, too!!!" He began to say a choice of unsavory and very vulgar words under his breath. "Go away, Roger! I am in the middle of something. Whatever it is can wait!"

"Addison, don't talk to Roger like that!" Alison gave a very disapproving look, though she was curious as to where their conversation was going.

"I'm sorry." He apologized to Alison, and then turned his head to the door. "I'm sorry, Roger. It's just that your timing is impeccable and very inopportune." He sighed, removing his hand from his pocket. "Is there any way that your important thing can wait five minutes, until I am done with my important thing…please."

"Whining is unbecoming of you, sir."

"Please…" Addison pleaded, and reached back into your pocket.

"I suppose it can wait a few moments…" Roger stated, breathing a heavy sigh. "…but, timing is of the essence, so make it quick." He grumbled. Just as Addison took a breath and opened his mouth to say something, Roger added something. "Oh, and sir, remember that she is a lady, and you must be gentle. Use protection!" Roger had a hint of humor in his voice.

"ROGER!?!" Addison screamed. "Seriously?!?"

"Sorry, sir." There was slight laughter outside the door.

"Where was I?" he shook his head, and tried to regain his focus and remember what he was about to do before the interruption. "Ah, yes…I need to ask you a question."

"Okay. What is it?" Alison's heart was beating hard.

"If there was anything that I could do or say that would give you reason to stay, would you consider it?"

"There is nothing that you could say or do to change the fact that I have to go home, eventually. Why are we doing this right now? We haven't even figured out how to get me back to my time, so why are we talking about this right this minute?"

"You didn't answer my question."

"Okay. If you could think of something to say or do, would I consider staying?" She stopped and thought about if for a moment. "It would have to be huge. Aside from the portal thingy never appearing again, it would have to be a life altering thing like…" She was staring at the ceiling, thinking, until she saw Addison yank his hand from his pocket, and get down on one knee in front of her. "Um…yeah…that'd be something that might work."

"Alison Moreno, I am in love with you, and I want to spend forever with you, whether it be here and now, or seventy some years into the future. Where you go, I go. I want to be tied to you for the rest of my human existence."

"Addison, I don't know what to say." Her hands were over her mouth, so her words were muffled.

"Just say yes!" Voices from outside of the room squealed.

"What they said…I know you love me too. I can see it and feel it. I am your candle and you are my flame. Please, Ms. Moreno…do me the honor of becoming my wife. I will love you until the end of time." Tears welled in his smiling eyes, and she smiled at him, and opened her mouth to reply. However, a thought creeped its way into her mind, and she suddenly got sad.

"I do love you. I love you with every bit of life within me…but…"

"No 'but's.' Just say yes."

"I want to…I do! However…there is one thing that I would need you to do, before I accepted…and it is important...and impossible."

"Whatever it is, I'll do it. Nothing is impossible when you have love on your side. Tell me, and I'll do it. Whatever it is!"

"You can't." She began to cry, heartbroken.

"I can…I will…just tell me. What do I need you to do?" He rose from his feet, the ring box in his hand. The large diamond set on a beautiful white gold band sparkled in the light.

"I...um...I can't accept your proposal until..." Her sobs became harder and it was difficult to understand her. "It's a family tradition...you need...it's impossible..."

"Anything...Nothing is impossible. Tell me, my love."

"I can't marry you until...you get my parents' blessing." She shook from her cries and collapsed onto the floor. Addison's heart broke. He felt as though someone had ripped the air from his lungs. He slumped down on the floor next to Alison just as the door opened, a look of devastation and sorrow on the five people's faces, as they had heard every word.

He wapped his arms around the woman who had turned his world upside down and made him feel alive again. He held her close, and took her hand in his. Gasping for air as he felt consumed by overwhelming love and respect for her plight, he removed the ring from the box, and slipped it on her right hand ring finger.

"If that is what is required of me, I will find a way. As God is my witness, Allie, I will do what you require." He whispered softly in her ear. "Until then, I want you to hold onto this. This ring stands as my promise...it will be done."

Moments went by, and she looked at him, and she saw a glimmer of hope in his eyes.

"If you say you will...I have faith in you." She gave him a small smile.

"I hate to ruin the moment, but..." Roger whispered.

"Then don't!" Addison barked, shooting Roger a look of anger.

"The mayor is downstairs. He says that Alison may not have much time."

"What?" Alison's head shot up, and she looked at the balding man.

"The mayor says that there is something weird going on...down by where you...well, he says you need to come see."

Chapter Twenty-One

"No! No! Not yet! I'm not ready to go yet!" She gripped Addison's hand and let him help her to her feet, as he leapt up when Roger dropped the bomb on them.

"Is he sure that that is what it is? It could be anything!" A fit of fury and panic sent vibrations through his body.

"Come down and talk to him. He's in the foyer." Arthur said. "He sounded pretty sure."

The group raced down the stairs as quickly as their feet would take them, except for Alison, who froze at the top of the stairs, as she looked down at the Mayor.

"Don't kill the messenger. I just came to let you know what is going on. I felt that you had a right to know, considering your situation." Thomas Gentry pleaded as Addison charged at him, fury in his eyes.

As if it wasn't bad enough that he was faced with a virtually impossible task, now the woman he loved was going to be leaving forever. True, it wasn't the Mayor's fault, but that didn't mean that Addison couldn't be furious for his untimely delivery of such devastating news. So many different emotions were flowing through his head as he grabbed Thomas by his waistcoat and drove him back towards the door.

"Calm yourself, Addison." Arthur rushed forward, grabbing his grandson's arm. "You grandmother and I asked him to let us know if they found anything strange. He is just doing as he was asked. This is not his fault."

"Addison…let Mayor Gentry go." Alison's voice echoed from the top of the staircase.

"We should have more time. This is too soon!" Addison yelped. He released Thomas, and straightened his waistcoat before slamming his fist into the front door.

"It could be nothing, Addison." Thomas reached for his friend's arm, but he yanked it away. "In all honesty, I am not sure what I am supposed to be looking for."

"You aren't supposed to be looking for anything. Just let it go, Thomas. I don't care what my grandparents say…stop looking for whatever it is. Stop searching for a way to take Alison away from me. Just…stop." He threw his arms up into the air, and walked away in a huff.

"Addison Xavier Thatcher! My Office! Now!!" Elizabeth sternly pointed to her office door, and began to walk toward it. Arthur walked over to his grandson.

"Come, boy. We need to talk." He led Addison to the room his grandmother had entered.

Alison, unsure as to what she should do, leaned against the railing, and took a few deep breathes. When she had regained some control over her emotions, she looked to Thomas. There was an apologetic sadness in his eyes.

"Roger…Rebecca…could I have your assistance? I need to pack my things…just in case." She didn't wait for them, but turned around and headed back to her room.

After gathering all of her things, which she had started earlier, she lugged her duffle bags and suitcases to the doorway. Roger and Thomas took turns taking the bags to her car, which had been brought from the Inn's parking lot. She changed her clothes, put her dress on a hanger and put it in the large wardrobe. She pinned a note to Becky on it, and closed the door.

Throwing her purse strap over her shoulder, and grabbing her journal off of her nightstand, she backed out of the room, and closed the door. Becky was waiting at the top landing for her.

"Are you sure you want to be doing this right now? I mean, you can just go check it out and then come back. It might be nothing." Rebecca sighed as they descended the staircase slowly.

"It could be nothing, true. But, Becky, this could be the way home, and none of us know how long it will be there…how long it will stay open or whatnot. If I don't go prepared, and it starts closing…I could lose my chance."

"Being stuck here wouldn't be so bad, would it? I mean, Addison's here…I'm here. Mama and Papa and the Thatchers…the mayor and his wife…"

"But, being stuck here means that I will never see my parents again. As much as I love it here…and love you all…I miss my mom and dad. Could you imagine never seeing your mom and dad again…and they not knowing what happened to you? I cannot imagine what my family is going through. I have been here for almost a year. If the time has passed there like it has passed here…they will never stop looking for me. I have to go home."

"When you put it that way, I can see how you must feel." Becky looked sad at the thought of never seeing her mom and dad ever again.

"It isn't like this is an easy decision. I am losing more than I am gaining by returning home. I may see my parents again…but, I will have to say goodbye to you, your parents, Arthur, Elizabeth…and Addison."

"You know, he would follow you to the ends of the Earth. If you asked him, he would go with you. He would leave everything behind to be with you, no matter what the future may be…literally speaking."

"I wish he could come with me…I wish you all could. But the truth is…I don't even know what the future will be like."

"What do you mean? I thought you said you were from the future."

"There is something called the butterfly effect. How it goes is…you step on a butterfly in the past and it causes a hurricane in the future…or something like that. I don't know how the future has been effected by my being here. Knowing my luck, I will go back and there will be flying cars and hover boards or something like that." Even though she was trying to explain the bad things that might have happened since she came, flying cars and hover boards didn't sound so bad to her.

"And you are sure that going through the wormhole or portal thingamajig will take you back to where you need to be?" Addison said as he stepped out of the office, followed by his grandparents.

"If it brought me here one way, I can only assume that it will take me back there when I go the opposite way."

"But, there is a possibility that it could send you somewhere else entirely, right?" Alison answered Addison's question with a shrug. "So, why take the chance of going alone? Let me come with you."

"No, Addison. You can't. I could never ask you to leave your family and your home behind."

"You did it!"

"Yes, but I didn't *choose* to leave them. I didn't know that by taking that detour…that driving through those trees would lead me here." She reached for his hand, but he pulled away.

"So, had you been given the choice…you never would have left your family? You never would have come here?" He looked hurt, and very emotionally injured by her reply.

"Addison…that is not what I said. I do not regret coming here. I don't regret it for a second. If I hadn't, you and I would not have found one another. I am just saying that I will not take you from your grandparents. I won't take on the burden of knowing that you could have a better life than what you will have in my time."

"Isn't that for me to decide? Don't I have a choice as to whether I want to stay or go with you?"

There were a few moments of silence. Alison knew that he was right, but she thought about what the repercussions would be of him coming with her. She thought about how hard it would be for him to adapt to the way things were in the future, as opposed to the simple quiet life here in Woodcrest.

"You have been fighting for me to stay here ever since you found out about where I am from. You kept saying that my life would be so much better here. Now, you want to trade a simple, quiet, calmer life here for the chaotic, busy, loud, dangerous life where I am from?"

"If it is good enough for you, then I will adapt. If it is so bad where you are from, why are you even going back?!"

"You…of all people…should understand, Adam!"

"How do you figure?" Their tempers were flaring as they stood in the foyer, in front of an audience, and had their very first fight. Alison didn't want things to come to this, to bring up a sensitive subject like his family, but if it was the only way she could make him understand, she had to use it.

"If you had a chance to see your family…your mom and dad again…if the situation were reversed, and it was your family that was on the other side of the void…"

"Don't you dare bring my family into this! There is a big difference between your parents and mine. My parents are dead! Yours are still alive, living their lives! Don't you dare try to use my parents to back up your reasoning for abandoning me and the rest of the people here…" His face became a deep shade of red, his breathing becoming heavy.

"Why are you arguing like this? This is stupid!" Becky decided to get between the two of them. "You love each other. Why are you wasting valuable time together, arguing like you hate one another?!" She screamed, trying to reason with them.

"If you had a chance to see them again, you would take it, without hesitation! Don't stand there and act like a martyr!"

"You're right! I would do everything I can to see them again. But, unlike you, I wouldn't want to leave the one I loved behind. I wouldn't have to choose between you and them! I would throw you over my shoulder and take you with me, kicking and screaming!!!" His arms were flailing, and there were tears in his eyes. Alison opened her mouth to reply but something he said struck a chord. She sucked in air, and the tears in her eyes stung.

"You think that I don't want you to come with me? It isn't about that, Addison. I would take you with me in a heartbeat." She choked back tears and her voice was strained against the lump in her throat.

"Then, why won't you let me come with you?"

"THE BUTTERFLY EFFECT!" Becky, just realizing that what Alison had explained earlier worked backwards as well. "Addison, it's the butterfly effect. That is why she can't take you with her."

"What is the butterfly effect? What kind of nonsense is that?" Addison was caught off guard by Becky's strange interruption.

"Alison has already altered things back home by being here…in the past. If you go with her to the future…everything that you would have done between now and then will be erased. Any children or grandchildren you are supposed to have, any significant events that you are supposed to be involved in…they will be erased, and that will alter the future as well. As well as anything that those said children or grandchildren are to do." Becky looked between Alison and Addison.

"Is that true? The butterfly effect? Is that why you can't take me with you?" He looked to Alison for validation of their friend's statement.

"Yes. I have no idea what I have done to the future by being here…but you would make bigger waves if you come to the future with me. You could alter reality so much that it could end up being a war zone if you come along…or worse. Who knows for sure? Do you really want to take the chance?"

"But…I love you. I don't want to lose you. I can't lose you." He walked toward her, and put his hands on her face. "There would be no risk of children or grandchildren being erased. If I lost you, I wouldn't be able to be with anyone else. My world would fade to black."

After much more discussion about it, everyone decided that it would be best to go look at what the Mayor had found before making any definitive decisions or saying their goodbyes.

Arriving in three different vehicles, they pulled up to the woods where Alison had driven out of and ended up on the cobblestone road by Town Hall. All of Alison's possessions were packed in her car, just in case. As they looked at the patch of woods, they all saw the same thing at the same time; a sheer silver, shimmering, water-like area that seemed to move so little that if you blinked, you'd miss it. It almost looked as if someone had taken a piece of silver silk and hung it in midair. They could see the trees beyond it, but they seemed to dance when viewed through the weird area.

"Well, shall we test it?" Roger picked up a clump of snow, and lobbed it at the area. The snowball was suspended in thin air for a moment, and then it seemed to dissolve until it had disappeared. It appeared as if the area was absorbing it. A chill went up Alison's spine.

"Is that what it did when you came through the first time?" Becky seemed to shiver as she imagined her friend going through the same way that the snow did.

"It has been so long…I honestly don't know. I don't think it did. It just looked like a bunch of trees with a path.

"So…" Addison turned to Alison, despair in his eyes, and pulled her to him. His arms wrapped around her, and he clung to her with a fierceness that reminded her of the night of the party, when he told her that he had almost watched her die in his arms. Still clinging to her journal, she nestled her head into his warm chest, and listened to his heart beat. She found solace and peace in the sound of his heartbeat.

"You know, Alison, you don't have to do this right now." Arthur walked over, and laid his hand on her head.

"He's right, sweetheart. If it came back now, it might stay open until you go back through. No one really knows."

"But, what if it is only open for a certain amount of time? If it closes before she goes through, she'll be stuck here." Thomas brought up what a few of them were thinking.

"Mayor Gentry…you aren't helping. We would love for her to stay forever, but we can't keep her here against her will…" Elizabeth sighed.

"Maybe it is just me, but I get the feeling that our dear friend, the Mayor, is in a hurry to send Alison away." Addison looked at the man he called his friend, and there was a glimmer of something in his eye.

"Why would I want to send her away? I care about her as much as the rest of the town. Just because you refuse to accept the fact that this may be her only chance to get home…"

"SHE IS HOME!! THIS IS HER HOME….I'm her home." The tone in Addison's voice went from anger to anguish. The realization of the situation hit everyone pretty hard, and everyone standing there began to tear up.

"Alison…this is your decision. You need to do what you need to do. I love you more than I could ever love anyone, and I want you to stay with me…but this isn't about me." He lifted her chin so she was looking at him. "I want you to understand…I am not giving you permission to leave me. If I thought that it would change your mind, I would get down on my knees and beg."

"I appreciate the fact that you have accepted this. And, in that acceptance, I know that you love me enough to let me go." She pulled away from him slightly. "I wanted to give this to you. This my journal. I kept it the whole time that I have been here, and a bit before I came. I wrote in it every day, sometimes twice a day. I wanted to share everything that I felt, everything that happened while you were in a coma and after."

"Are you sure? I mean, I am sure there is some personal stuff in there."

"There is nothing in there that I wouldn't share with you anyway. This will be a constant reminder of how much I truly love you." She pressed the thick book to his chest.

"There are no words to express what this means..." He placed his hand over hers.

"You don't need to say anything." She kissed him softly on the lips.

Backing away from him, she went to bid farewell to the others. As she approached Becky, she reached into her pocket and pulled her mp3 player and the ear buds out, and laid them in her friend's hand.

"I want you to keep this to remember me. Just make me a promise that you will not show or tell anyone about it than the people here. Remember...butterfly effect. These songs on here don't come out for quite a few years."

"Thank you, Allie." She took the small object and tucked it into her apron pocket, and flung her arms around Alison's neck. "I am going to miss you so much. You are the best friend I have ever had, and I love you so much." She sobbed.

"I will miss you, too, Becks. I will miss our nighttime talks over tea. I left some dresses for you in my wardrobe. Have Ms. Morton alter them and they are all yours. You can wear them on dates with Killian." She looked around, and then looked at Becky. "Where is he, anyway? I would have liked to have said goodbye to him as well."

"He's coming. He had to grab something. He should be here any minute." Just as she finished her statement, they head rapid footsteps approaching.

"Ms. Alison!! Don't go anywhere just yet!" Killian was carrying a package. When he caught up to them, he was winded, but was still clinging to the package. "This…is…for…you!" He handed the package to her, and leaned over to rest his hands on his knees, trying to catch his breath, which came billowing visibly in the form of whitish puffs of air.

"It's from all of us. Rebecca and Addison picked it out and we all put in money to pay for it." Elizabeth sighed. "We figured that you might want something to remember us by. We weren't sure when this day would come, so Killian had to go pick it up from the shop in quite a rush."

"You guys didn't have to do this!" She went to open it, but Addison stopped her.

"Wait until you are home." Tears welled in his eyes as he said the words, as she knew it must have killed him to say those words with how he felt.

"This is home, too. I want to open it here with all of you." Her words brought a smile to his face, as well as the rest of her second family.

She sat down on the hood of her lime green car, and carefully unwrapped the brown paper. Opening the box, her eyes filled with tears, and they began to fall as she reached into the box and removed the beautiful item within.

In her hands, she held the most ornate and magnificent music box she had ever seen in her life. Made from real mahogany, and trimmed in gold, it was the size of a large shoebox, with a gold wind up key on the back of it. She asked Addison to wind it up, and when he did, it played the most beautiful melody.

"This is unbelievable. I love it!" She smiled as the tears fell from her baby blue eyes. She placed it back into the box, and put the box on her front passenger seat.

She finished saying her goodbyes, except for the Thatchers, which she chose to save for last. She approached Arthur first, and gave him a big hug. She stuck he nose to his coat and took in the scent of it. She wanted to make a memory of him. Now, every time she smelled pipe tobacco and earl grey tea, she would think of him. She looked at him, and smiled.

"I am going to miss you, Arthur. Please remember me."

"I will think of you often, my dear. Safe journey."

She gave him one last squeeze, and he kissed her forehead. After she felt she had said what she needed to, she moved on to Elizabeth, who already had her arms open for the young woman.

"Elizabeth, I wanted to thank you for everything. Thank you for trusting me to care for your grandson, for taking me into your home and into your hearts. I will never forget your kind heart and your sweet face." She wrapped her arms around the woman and whispered in her ear. "Please take care of Addison for me, now. He is going to need you, now more than ever."

She held onto Elizabeth for a moment longer, and then she backed away, and turned.

Rather than walking toward Addison right away, she stood, staring at him for a moment. She took him into her memory, and tried to burn a mental picture of him into her mind. The lump in her throat grew as she saw him fight to keep a smile on his face, though the sadness and helplessness was winning the fight.

They had been through so much together, and they had seen both the best and the worst in one another. She finally felt the love that she had waited her whole life to feel, and she knew that something as beautiful as what they had was only short lived. She took a deep breathe, cocked her head to the side, and tried to give him a smile, but her heart was hurting. Lost in a moment of true heartbreak at the reality that she was about to say goodbye, the emotional dam broke and she put her hands to her face.

Deep down, he knew that this wasn't what she really wanted, to have to say goodbye to him, but that she didn't have a choice. He put his hands to his mouth, and exhaled rather shakily, before he threw her journal down to the ground, rushed to her, and lifted her into his arms.

"This is not goodbye...do you hear me?! I am not going to let you say goodbye!" He held her in his arms, and she hugged him with an almost death grip. She released every tear that she had been holding back, and was shaking from the sobs. "We will see one another again. I made you a promise, remember? Don't lose hope. If you start to, just look at that ring on your finger. I will find a way."

"I want to believe that, Adam!" She wept into his shoulder, her grip around him tightening. "I love you, Addison Xavier Thatcher." It came out as a whisper, as he slowly lowered her to the ground.

"Don't do this, Allie. You are saying goodbye, and I will not let you...not to me...not yet." He held her face between his hands.

"Alright, no goodbyes." She began to compose herself, and managed to give him a sad smile. "No matter where I am in my life, no matter what I am doing, I will never be far from you in my heart. You will always be in my soul, a part of my present, and a dream for my future." She ran her hand down his cheek, and swept a tear away that began to fall from his golden brown eyes. "I want you to know one more thing, before I leave." She swallowed hard, and managed to compose herself long enough to get the words out. "I will always be true to you, and I will always love you. My heart is yours and yours alone…from now until the end of time. No amount of time or distance will ever change that."

She kissed him, and savored the feeling of his lips as they connected to hers, devouring her in the most heartfelt kiss that they had ever had.

She quickly pushed from his arms and got into the car, and turned the key in the ignition. The green machine roared to life, and everyone moved out of the way, as she slowly moved toward the opening in the trees beyond the silvery mist.

Addison picked up the journal, which he had thrown to the ground to go to her. Brushing the snow off of it, he held it tight to him, as he sobbed and waved to her as she pulled away.

Alison now had everyone in her rear view mirror, and at the front of the waving group was Addison, just holding his hand up and stationary.

"Goodbye, love." Those were the last words that came out of her mouth as she entered the weird misty air.

The car began to rattle and shake, and she looked into the mirror, seeing his smile fade. This would be the last time that she saw any of the people she had come to love. She had built a life for herself, and she had chosen to leave them behind.

At once, she began to regret her decision. Before she had a chance to stomp on the break, and throw the car into reverse, it felt like a magnet was pulling her forwards. She tried to stop the car, turn the wheel; she tried anything she could think of to try to get back to them, but it was too late, as her car was now surrounded by the strange mist.

Suddenly, there was a flash of light, and she felt light headed, and very sick to her stomach.

"Something is wrong! None of this stuff happened before. What is happening?!" Panic and fear took over and she gripped the first thing she could get her hands on…the open box containing her beautiful music box. She gripped it against her, and prayed that whatever was happening would be over soon.

The car shuttered even harder, and it felt as she was twisting and flipping. After a few moments, the shaking and weird sensations came to a halt. She breathed a sigh of relief, and went to open her eyes. She knew that she had assumed it was over too soon, as it suddenly felt like she was falling from a cliff. She held the box to herself with one hand and braced herself with the other. The fear and heartache was too much to handle, and she couldn't see anything as the blinding light around her car became even brighter.

Right before everything faded to black, she felt the car thud and come to a halt. The engine cut off. There was silence.

Chapter Twenty-Two

Her eyes fluttered open, momentarily, as she felt herself being carried slowly. Whomever was holding her was incredibly strong and yet they held her in their arms with such care and gentleness. She tried to focus her eyes over their shoulders, but it was hard, as her head was pounding and swirling erratically. She could barely make out the shape and color of her lime green beetle as the distance increased between it and her. *What had happened when she went through those woods? Why was she so woozy, nauseated, and disoriented? It wasn't like that before.*

The person carrying her was unfamiliar. His smell was of the outdoors, like pine, leather, and musk. She felt the feeling of worn suede against her cheek and the gentle brush of his hair as it blew in the gentle breeze. She could just make out the sound of their footsteps against the gravel as he stepped gingerly and carefully along the side of the road. Her heart called out for Addison, though her throat burned and she could not get the words out, before everything fell to black again.

Her eyes opened again, slightly, and the scenery had changed. There was bright white all around her, and she was lying flat, lights passing above her, as if she were being wheeled, swiftly, down a long hallway. There were people on either side of her that were chattering and talking, but their voices were garbled and incoherent. She tried to call out, but her throat still felt like it was aflame. She was too weak to move and her eyelids were like heavy rock. She couldn't keep her eyes open any longer.

Thoughts and frozen visions of the last moments with Addison floated around in her mind, like puzzle pieces that were submerged in water. She tried to swallow, but it hurt terribly. *What was wrong with her? Did something go wrong when she came back?* She could no longer smell anything familiar to her. The clean scent of Adam's cologne was but a memory, momentarily replaced by the stranger's rugged odor, only to be replaced by bleach and disinfectant. Trying to figure out where she was, and how she got there made her head pound. Her heart was beating like mad and her body felt strangely cool against the air around her. Her breathing was labored, and it felt as though there was a large rock on her chest. She heard whispering, and then felt as they transferred her to another bed-like platform. She felt the sharp pinch of needles or daggers in her arms, and then felt the people place a tube in her nose and around her ears. Everything faded again after that.

As she lay in the bed, liquids being given to her intravenously, a gentle hand took hers in his, and he sat there with her, not wanting her to be alone.

"Is she going to be okay?" the stranger asked, looking up at the nurse, as she adjusted the saline drip.

"Thanks to you, yes. She was severely dehydrated and had you not gotten her here when you did, there might have been some serious damage done to her internal organs." She looked at the man. "Is there anything that I can get you? Would you like some food, something to drink? It's the least that we can do, considering that you saved her life. That couldn't have been an easy trek. You must be exhausted."

"I'm fine. Did someone get in touch with her family yet?" He asked, his voice reflecting the apparent weariness he felt.

"Yes, someone got ahold of her parents in Philadelphia. They are on their way. Why don't you rest? I am sure they are going to want to talk to you."

"If you don't mind, I'll just wait here with her until her family comes. Thank you." He spoke softly, but firmly, as if to dismiss the nurse, so he could be alone with the woman he had rescued.

The man didn't leave her side, not once, until he saw two older folks rushing to her room. As they halted in the doorway, only able to see part of his face beneath the brim of his worn leather hat. He looked like he had spent a long time in nature, as his skin was tanned. When the doctors had called, they told them about the stranger. Seeing him in front of her, Alison's mother, Maria, still couldn't believe that he'd saved a girl he had found on the side of the road.

Mr. Moreno went to shake his hand and thank him, but he stepped aside, motioning for them to be with their daughter. Tipping his hat to them, he ducked out of the room, before they could ask who he was. When he went after the man, it was as if he had disappeared.

The doctor came in to explain how she was bought in; the man had carried her for the six miles between where he had found her to the hospital in Lancaster. He had carried her, on foot the whole way.

"That dear man…he saved our little girl, and didn't even stay for us to thank him." Mrs. Moreno sighed, taking her daughter's clammy hand in hers.

"If he walked that whole way, carrying her…Who would do that for a total stranger? Who would carry someone six miles to a hospital? Did he not have a phone? Did he not have a car?" Mr. Moreno stared down the hallways, trying to figure out where the man may have gone.

It took her two days, and lots of liquids pumped into her system, before she was even lucid enough to interact with anyone. When she finally came to, her first thoughts were not of home but of the dark haired handsome man she had left behind. She woke with a start and called out to him.

"Sweetie! It's alright! Mama's here, honey." Maria grasped Alison's hand tightly, and tried to help her.

"Mama?! Mom…" she blinked a few times, trying to get her bearings. "Mama…Where am I?" Alison gasped, gripping to her mother's hand as though she were her lifeline to reality.

"You are in Trinity Medical Hospital, in Lancaster. A stranger found you on the side of the interstate, and brought you here. You were severely dehydrated, and your car was in a ditch."

"How long have I been here?" She prayed not to hear her mother say that she had been there for months.

"You have been missing for about four days, but we got the call that you were found and brought here just day before yesterday. What happened to you, baby girl?"

"I've been missing for only four days? That's impossible!"

"You were supposed to be home on Friday evening, sweetie. Today is Thursday, April sixteenth."

"What year is it?" Her inquiry confused her mother and the doctor and nurse that were standing nearby.

"It is two thousand fifteen, sweetie. Are you alright?" Maria looked at the doctor, as he approached her. "Is she alright?"

"Sometimes, severe dehydration can mess with the memory, neuropathways in the brain. She should be back to normal in just a few more days." He checked her eyes, and made some notes in her chart. "Just make certain that she gets lots of rest for the next few days and that she stays hydrated."

"I will do that, Doctor." Maria held her daughter's hand tightly in hers. They both watched as the doctor left, and then Alison turned to her mother.

"Mom, it can't still be twenty fifteen. I have been gone nearly a year…I took a wrong turn, a detour, and ended up in this quaint little town…" She purposely was going to leave out the difference in years, so as not to look completely insane. "I was there nearly a whole year, mama."

"Now, sweetheart, I know that you have been through a lot, and you are disoriented, but like I told you…you have only been missing for a few days. The dehydration and maybe a slight bump on the head…" She noticed what looked like a scar on her forehead. "…Maybe you just need to get some rest. You have been through so much already."

"Mom…I'm serious. I was there…in Woodcrest…for almost a whole year. Why don't you believe me?"

"Alison, you need to calm down. I believe that *you* believe you were there. That is good enough for me, but I am just telling you that you had only been missing for four days. Had that kind young man not found you and brought you here…"

"What young man? Who was here, mama? Who found me?" She began to look around, feverishly.

"A man in a suede jacket and old hat found you on the side of the road, and brought you here. He stayed with you until we got here." She gave Alison's hand a squeeze. "As I was saying, had he not found you and brought you here, Heaven only knows what would have happened to you."

"Where's my car?"

"Your father has gone with Anthony Marconi to retrieve it from the ditch that you drove into. It's only six or so miles from here. Marconi said that he will take it back to Philly with him, and give it a look over, make sure it can be repaired.

"It's in a ditch? How'd it end up in a ditch?"

"I don't have the vaguest idea. I really don't care about the car. It is you whom I am worried about, sweetheart. Now, lie down and rest. The doctors are going to release you soon, and then you can come home with us and recuperate from this traumatic experience. I will contact Jeanie and let her know that you are alright. She's been worried sick about you as well, the poor dear."

"Call Dad! Tell him to grab the box in my front seat…It is about the size of a large shoe box. Tell him to get it. Please!"

"I'll call and tell him, but you need to calm down and relax!" Maria replied to her daughter's frantic demand.

As Alison laid back on the pillows, she was trying to sort through all the new information that she had been given. She was very confused and distraught. She was sure that she had been in Woodcrest for at least eight months, and yet everyone else was telling her it had only been four days. She was found in a ditch, by a strange man, and brought to the hospital for severe dehydration. It had felt like only that moments ago that she had left Addison standing at the edge of woods. She was wishing, now more than ever, that she had just waited a few more days to come back. Her heart ached to have Addison's arms around her. As comforting as her mother could be, she was not Addison.

Alison let out a sigh and looked at her mom.

"Mama, you do believe me, right? I mean, about me being in Woodcrest…you do believe me?"

"My sweet little girl, if you say that you were in this little town, well, then you were there. Who am I to argue with you? You have always been honest with me. Strange things happen to us when we suffer trauma."

"But, mama….it has nothing to do with trauma. I was there. I don't understand how the length of time is different but I am sure that there is a logical explanation. There has to be."

"We'll talk about it more when you come home. Just rest right now, sweetie."

Chapter Twenty-three

It had been a few long months since Alison had come home to Philadelphia, heartbroken and highly disoriented. Despite the doctors and her family telling her that she had only been missing for a few days, she knew that nearly a year had gone by in Woodcrest.

More so, they insisted that there was no way that she could have been in Woodcrest because it no longer existed, and hadn't for about thirty years, at least not as a thriving town. It had been abandoned and was now in ruins. Alison had to see for herself, and so she made the journey back to the dirt road that took her to the forest, which hid the town she had called home.

The trees were gone, cut down to the ground, exposing the ghost town to all whom drove the interstate. Half the buildings were tattered and worn from the elements. The other half were barely standing. Many of the shops were all boarded up, and there was graffiti everywhere. There was nothing left that even remotely resembled the beautiful place she knew.

Even the Thatcher estate was gone, no doubt torn down, or destroyed by years of neglect and abandonment. All that was left of it was the few steps that led up to the entrance doors. Alison found herself sitting on the front stoop, crying. Her father walked to her from the car and sat next to her.

"You really thought that you had been in this place, don't you?"

"I don't *think*, dad, I know!" She glared at the man standing in front of her, her eyes bloodshot and puffy.

"That is impossible and you know it. Stop trying to convince yourself that the stuff you saw when you were unconscious were real. Your mother may tolerate you delusions, but I will not stand for it any longer." His stern tone, which used to make her cringe, had no effect on her now. She knew the truth, and no one was going to convince her otherwise. *Let them think I am delusional…crazy. I know what I saw, what I experienced, what I felt.* She stood up, and walked past the man without even looking at him, and got into the car. He let out a grunt and followed suit.

The ride back to Philly was very quiet, and no attempt to even break the silence was made. She knew that she would have to convince everyone that she wasn't imagining what happened. She just didn't know how.

When they pulled into their driveway, she didn't even wait until he had turned off the ignition, and she was out of her seatbelt and out of the car. She came in the back door, kissed her mother, who was standing at the stove, and then proceeded up the stairs to her room.

"Why in the world would I choose this over what I had? Why would I choose to come back here? Screw the time space continuum or whatever it's called!! I try to do what's right, and what did it get me?! A broken heart, and a community and family that think I have gone off the deep end." She muttered to herself, as she pulled out her sketch book, and flipped through all the pages of doodles and drawings of her time in the peaceful haven that she missed so. She flipped through countless pages of doodles of Elizabeth, and the Gentry's, Becky, Roger, and the landmarks until she came to the last few pages. She ran her fingers over the smiling face of the man she had come to love deeply, and intimately. His smiling eyes, and his dimples in the sketch of him laughing made her smile, though her eyes filled with tears. "Dear, sweet Adam…I regret every day that I chose to come back. Nothing has changed here, so my staying there

~ 224 ~

indefinitely would not have effected anything at all, and we could have been together. I just pray that your life went on, and you found your happy ending." She set the book down next to the gorgeous mahogany music box that she had placed on her bedside table. She ran her finger over the key.

A light switched on in her head, and leapt from her bed. She grabbed her purse, and her car keys, and she sped through the kitchen.

"Alison, darling…where are you off to in such a hurry? Dinner is almost ready." Mrs. Moreno called to her daughter as she sped out the back door.

"I am going to the library, mama. I will be back in a while. Love you!" That was all she said before the screen door slammed behind her. As her mother heard her car's engine start, her husband came into the kitchen, to see what all the commotion was about.

"It's almost dinner! Where in the world is she off to, now?" He folded his paper and slammed it onto the counter, and leaned his hip against the lower cabinets. "I swear to you, Maria. Ever since her accident, she had been acting like a crazy person. I knew that we should have had that psychological evaluation done on her at the hospital, when they suggested it."

Maria didn't even hesitate a second at hearing her husband's words. She snatched up the biggest knife from the butcher's block and held it up in front of his face, a look of fury in her eyes.

"Do not say that about my daughter! She is not crazy! If she believes, in her heart, that she was in some strange town…then she was there. We were not! Who knows what happened to her in those few days that she was missing. She could have been in excruciating pain, near death…we know nothing! Had that young man not found her, and taken action…" Her voice became strained, and her eyes welled up with tears. "Just because you do not believe in magic…that does not mean that the rest of us can't either. Praise Santa Maria for bringing our baby girl home safely to us. Do not let me hear you speak ill of that poor girl again, or I will use this on you!" She waved the sharp blade in his face again, before returning it to its spot. He held up his hands in surrender, snatched his paper back up, and went back to the living room.

Alison entered the library, and went straight to the librarian, requesting exactly what she was after. The older woman took her to the microfilm room. The librarian told her where all the microfilm was and then left her be. She immediately started to open drawers, and searched through the files until she found what she was after.

After ten minutes, she found an article about Woodcrest, dated just a few days after she had left.

Thatcher Heir Missing
Could Mystery Girl be Involved?

Her heart jumped into her throat, as she read the article. After she had driven into the woods, watching Woodcrest and Addison disappear forever, she never imagined that he would turn up missing. She flipped through more articles, trying to find more information.

The fact that there were actual articles, involving people she had come to care about, made her feel closer to them. She read about Mayor Gentry's re-election, and also the joyous news of an addition to their family, as Odette had finally given birth to a beautiful baby girl, whom they named Alison. However, as warm as that news made her feel, the next article tore her heart right from her chest.

Body found in Lake Woodcrest
M.E. identifies it as Missing Thatcher Heir

After days of endless searching, the body of Addison Thatcher was found Tuesday afternoon, washed up on the south shore of Berber Lake. Due to the condition of the body, which was a direct result of prolonged exposure to the water and other elements, it was very difficult to identify the body. All that the Medical examiner had to go on was dental records, and personal effects. Unfortunately, the dental records were not definitive, but the personal effects, including wallet and identification as well as clothing, led the M.E. to conclude that the remains found were that of Addison Thatcher, Grandson of Arthur and Elizabeth Thatcher of Wellington Circle. When questioned of their thoughts on the Medical examiner's reports, they refused to comment.

No one knows the nature of the death, but many have commented that it had to have something to do with a young lady whom had spent some time in Woodcrest. It was said that she was employed by the family to care for him when he was taken ill, but only one person, Mr. Thatcher's ex-fiancé, Lena Thorton, chose to make a statement:

"The girl had to have had something to do with this. She corrupted him into dumping me on the eve of our wedding, but I think that she thought that he would fall in love with her. What probably happened was that he turned her down, and she took her revenge, thinking that if she couldn't have him, then no one could. My poor Addison…I forgive you, and I will always love you. I hope that they find that wretched girl, and throw her in prison for the rest of her days for what she has done."

The Local authorities have no leads or evidence to coincide with the accusations of Ms. Thorton, and have ruled his death, temporarily, as an accident.

She removed the microfilm and put it back into the file, furiously. Alison couldn't believe what she'd just read. Not only was the love of her life gone, but she was being blamed for his death. Her breathing became labored and she became increasingly light-headed. As quick as she could, she ran to a trash can, and instantly began to retch and choke.

The Librarian came over to see if she was okay, and handed her a few tissues. She also pulled a chair up to Alison, and had her sit down.

"Is there anyone you would like me to call?"

"No. I'll be okay. I just need to get some air. Thank you, though."

One of the gentlemen in the library walked her out to her car, and made sure she was alright before heading back in to help close up for the night.

Alison sat there in her car, and stared at her steering wheel, wishing that she had not gone to the library, had not looked for information on Addison. Her heart ached for him, and she prayed that he had not felt pain. Tears fell like waterfalls from her eyes, and she wept for him.

When she pulled into the driveway, over an hour later, her mother was sitting on the porch swing, waiting for her daughter to return.

"Did you find what you were looking for, my darling?" Maria rose from the seat as her daughter approached, eyes red and bloodshot. "Oh, my sweet...come to mama." She held out her arms, and Alison ran into them as she had always done, for comfort and love. They sat on the front porch and Maria just let her cry. She just caressed her daughter's dark mane, as it hung over her face.

The days that followed were very melancholy and quiet. Alison went through the motions, but didn't speak of what she had discovered at the library. She tried not to let her sadness and loss affect her job performance, as she went from room to room at Bruckner's Rehabilitation Center, treating her patients.

When she arrived home from work on the fifth day, she found a large, fancy envelope on the dining room table, her name was written in beautiful Calligraphy upon the front of the black paper in silver.

"Mama, what is this?" She picked it up and walked into the living room, where her mother was sitting, doing needlepoint.

"It was delivered for you this evening by special courier. It looks very lovely." The shine in her eyes just showed how intrigued she was by the large envelope. Alison came over, and sat on the couch with her mother, her father sitting in his chair, hiding behind his evening paper. He bent down the corner to see what was going on, but did not utter a word.

As Alison's finger slid under the flap, and broke the beautiful wax seal, a sense of wonder and excitement seemed to tug at her. She opened the envelope and slid the thick paper out.

It was a fancy and intricate invitation. It was black cardstock with white in the center, and on top of that, there was thin rice paper over the top. Tying all the layers together was a black satin ribbon. Alison had not seen an invitation like this in her whole life, and handled it with extreme care.

"Well, what on earth is it, girl? For Goodness sake, read it." Her father piped up, when nothing but silence fell after the adoring sighs and "ooh's" and "ah's."

"Alright….It says, 'Callahan Banking and Trust Inc. Cordially invite you to our very exclusive Annual Halloween Gala as we celebrate our 70th Anniversary. All expenses paid, including transportation, attire, and grooming (hair/Make-up)

Please RSVP by October 10th." Her heart was skipping, as she stared at the words, and read them over and over again in silence.

"My goodness, Alison. Why in Heavens would you receive an invitation to that? It is the most exclusive event in Philadelphia. Only the rich and extremely connected hoity-toity folks get an invitation to that party. You have to practically be a celebrity to even be considered for the guest list." Salvador dropped his paper on the floor, and didn't bother to pick it up. "What did you do? Who did you…"

"Daddy!!!!! I didn't do anything! I don't know why I got the invitation, and I didn't con my way onto the invitation list, by ANY means. There has to be a mistake. There is a number here, to RSVP…I'll figure this out right now." She pulled her phone out of her pocket, and dialed the number, putting it on speaker. Her mother took the invitation, gently from her and held it, while she spoke on the phone.

"Callahan Banking and Trust Inc. This is Simone. How can I help you?" The sweet voice on the other spoke.

"I received an invitation to the Gala…"

"Are you calling to RSVP? How many will be in attendance?"

"That's the thing…I think that I received the invitation by mistake."

"May I have your name, please?"

"Alison Moreno."

"There was no mistake, Ms. Moreno. You are at the top of our list of invites."

"I am? I'm at the top?" Alison began to shake.

"Yes, miss. You are a VIP! Were you calling to RSVP?" The girl on the other end was speaking as if Alison were the President of the United States, such reverence and respect in her voice.

"I suppose I am. How many guests am I permitted to bring?"

"You may bring three guests."

"Alright, well, I suppose I am RSVP'ing for four people, myself and three guests."

"Very well, Ms. Moreno. Expect to be picked up by limousine at precisely five o'clock p.m. on the thirtieth of this month. Be certain to show the limo driver your invitation at time of pick-up, and bring it with you. We will see you there. Thank you. Have a good day." Then the girl hung up on her end.

Alison sat, staring at the phone in her hand, as if she could not believe the conversation that she had just had.

"A V.I.P., ay? Wow, baby girl. It was unbelievable that you even got an invitation, but you are a VIP! I don't know how you managed that, but wow. Who are your three guests, if you don't mind me asking?"

"Well, Jeanie is supposed to be coming into town that week to visit, so I suppose she will be one of my guests."

"And the other two?" Her mother breathed, on the edge of her seat, clutching the invitation to her chest.

"The two of you, of course. That is, if you want to go. I mean, it is like a dance. I know that loud music bothers you, dad. And large crowds make you nervous, mama."

"I can deal with large crowds, my darling, especially if there are good looking celebrities among them." Her grin went from ear to ear.

"And if it gets too loud, I'll just turn down my hearing aids." Her father said, in a matter-of-fact tone.

"Alright. I better let Jeanie know. She is going to be so excited." She snatched the invitation out of her mother's hand, and raced up the stairs to her room, to call her friend and old roommate. As she closed the door, and went to sit on her bed, she caught her music box and sketchbook out of the corner of her eye.

For just a few moments, she had put her sadness into the back of her mind and was happy, and it felt good. But, as happy and excited as she wanted to be about this, she couldn't help but become sad at the fact that there was one person she would have wanted to have with her; a specific doe-eyed, handsome faced gentleman that she knew would have enjoyed the chance to sweep her off her feet on the dance floor.

"I wish you were here, Adam. Having you beside me, dancing me across the floor as only you could…that would have made this so much better. I am sorry that I broke your heart and left you behind. Not a day goes by that I don't regret my decision." She closed her eyes, and sighed, thinking of his smiling face. "I know you may not believe this, but I love you still, and I always will. You will be there with me, and in every day that passes. You will always be in my heart. I hope that you are at peace, with your family."

She dialed the phone, and nearly jumped out of her skin with excitement when her friend picked up the other end of the phone.

The Gala was all she could talk about at work, and her coworkers were so excited for her, but none of them were as nearly excited as a certain patient of hers, Mrs. Callahan, who was somehow related to the Gala to which she was going to attend.

"What I don't understand is…why me?" She brushed the woman's hair carefully as she spoke to her.

"Why not you? You are as special as anyone who attends those events. You deserve to have a night of fun, and romance, and wonder."

"Romance? It will be anything but romantic, Mrs. Callahan." There was a sadness in her voice that the woman immediately picked up on it.

"Why not romance? You are a beautiful young lady, and plenty of single men attend the party every year. You may find your prince charming. It's happened more than you think."

"Mrs. Callahan, I gave my love and my heart to someone, and I lost them, tragically. I am afraid that romance is the furthest thing from my mind. I am not looking for love."

"Yes…I remember you told me about your beloved. But, in all honesty, I don't think that he would want you to spend the rest of your days alone. You have so much love to offer. Just because you find someone new, that doesn't mean that you love him any less."

"Yes, but even if I was *looking* for love…The type of men that attend the Gala every year are extremely wealthy, and very handsome, and I cannot compete with the women who attend, even if I wanted to." She recalled a time, back in Woodcrest, when she thought the same thing.

"Love does not seek out wealth or outer beauty, my dear child…Love seeks out the heart that is pure, true and rich with desire to love and be loved by others. Seeking out love with the eyes of conceit and wealth is not love…it is lust and greed. True love transcends that which cannot be seen with our eyes, but with the pull of our innermost spirit." The elderly woman's words seemed to reach Alison on a level that she didn't expect, as it described the love between her and Addison perfectly. She stopped brushing and wrapped her arms, gently, around the woman's shoulders.

"Thank you, Mrs. Callahan. I needed that."

"Please dear…call me Becky." That statement caught Alison's attention, and she smiled, remembering the first time that she had met her petite ginger-headed friend. She had said the same to her that day.

Little things that have been said seemed to remind her of her family that she had left behind, and she was filled with happiness. As long as she was given little reminders here and there, the memory of what had happened would live on.

Alison's bond with Ms. Callahan was one of the most special of all the older folks that she had ever cared for. She missed he old patients back at the home in Pittsburg, but when she spoke to Jeanie, she found out that they were all doing well, and missed her back.

Jeanie also informed her that they had found out what, or who had started the fire. It was the one patient that Alison never had missed, Mrs. Helena Bancroft.

Helena Bancroft was a nasty old woman with a bad attitude and a vendetta against Alison. Whenever she could make her job a bit more frustrating or difficult, she would. She was sweet as pie to every other nurse or orderly that worked there, but never missed her chance to make Alison miserable. If she wasn't dumping her bedpan, or defecating directly on the bed, she would throw things, scream, and accuse Allie of hurting her. She even had the nerve to spit in her face a few times. Alison didn't hate her, but she was actually grateful when she didn't have to take her abuse any longer.

According to Alison's boss and supervisor, Madison, Mrs. Bancroft was very happy to confess to setting the fire.

Something that startled Alison was that she was not the only one that Helena hated and treated like she had been treated. She had been equally cruel and harsh to the newest overnight orderly. But, though she had treated him so horrible, he made certain to pull her from the fire and smoke filled building. She was actually the last one to be rescued before the building became engulfed in flames. The orderly had told Madison that she was hiding in the bathroom, and he had almost missed seeing her. Had she been in the orderly's place, despite how she had been treated, she would have pulled the cruel and hateful woman from the building without question, as well.

As far as the orderly, and who he was, Madison couldn't remember his name except for senile Mrs. Evie Appleton said that the orderly and she needed to get back to their garden and ask God for forgiveness.

Chapter Twenty-four

Just as Simone had stated on the phone weeks before, the limousine arrived in front of their home at promptly five o'clock. A tall, thin man in a suit walked up to the door and rang the doorbell. Alison and Jeanie squealed quietly before Salvador Moreno opened the door.

"I am here to pick up Ms. Alison Moreno, and three guests for the Halloween Gala." The man stated, dryly. Alison stepped forward, and showed him the invitation, to which he nodded and walked down to the limo and opened the door for them to enter. The four of them filed out of the house, and neighbors came out to see what was going on. Mrs. Moreno waved at her friends, as she entered the limo and scooted along the seat to allow the rest to fit in there comfortably.

The limo would have been big enough to fit about ten more people, and it was well stocked with everything that you could imagine. There was an ice bucket, chilling four bottles of very fancy French champagne, and crystal flutes hanging securely from a rack above. Alison and Jeanie sat right by the doors, and just looked at one another, laughing at the sheer excitement of being in an actual limousine. Mr. Moreno was playing with the skylight and the buttons that changed the lighting in the back of the limo. He was like a kid in a toy store, and Maria had to keep him from breaking anything.

The first place that they were taken to was an extravagant salon. The stylists took one look at the invitation, and then to Alison and, wide-eyed, went to work. She got the star treatment, including a facial, manicure and pedicure, and massage. While that was being done, her mother, father, and best friend were getting their hair and makeup done to go perfectly with pre-selected Halloween attire. When they were done, they were sent next door to the place where they were put into their costumes, complete with masks.

They went all out with Alison's hair and make-up, and she felt like absolute royalty. But, though they adorned her with make-up to match with her costume, her true beauty shined through with the color palate that they had chosen. There were a lot of golds and silvers, and shimmery jewels, which were delicately fastened to her face, at the corners of her eyes. There were beautiful jewels in her hair, with ringlets hanging down at her temples and a few beautiful ivory ostrich feathers fasted into her up do.

When she was escorted to be fitted for her costume, she found that she looked like a princess. She watched in the mirror, as they tightened the bodice of the beautifully elegant white gown. It had a long train of light, flowing satin and silk, with the thinnest chiffon sleeves. Before placing her sheer glittery lace mask to her face with little pieces of tacky putty, they attached what looked like angel's wings to the back of her dress.

Her heart thumped in her chest as she looked into the multi-surfaced mirror. She was about to return to the limo, to go to the Gala, when one of the girls came up to her, holding something that sparkled in the lights of the shop.

"I almost forgot this." She fastened a very delicate chain around Alison's neck, and adjusted the charm on it, so it set almost right in her cleavage. "Now, my sweet…you are all set. Have a beautiful time at the party."

"Thank you. Happy All Hallows Eve." She smiled and went out to the limo.

Standing outside the limo, waiting to see her, were her mother, father and friend, and they looked absolutely wonderful.

Her father was dressed as a war hero, with a very accurate looking Army uniform, and a black mask, with gold trim. He looked very handsome and it made Alison smile.

Her mother, a very full figured Italian woman, was actually dressed as a Spanish salsa dancer. She had a red and black frilly dress on that was mid-thigh on one side and down almost to the ground on the other. She had her hair up in curls, with red flowers adorning the one side, and a black and red lacy mask to match.

Jeanie was dressed as the black swan from the ballet, with feathers in her hair, down her sheer sleeves, and attached to the side of her glittery sequined mask, which was held on by a strap around her head, hidden by her dark hair. A lovely, and seemingly authentic black tutu was around her waist as well as satin ballet slippers on her feet, with satin straps going up her legs.

But as delighted as she was at the sight of the three of them, the looks on *their* faces at seeing her were priceless. Wide eyed and mesmerized by how absolutely breathtaking she looked in her costume, they had no words to describe how they were feeling. Maria's hands shot to her smiling lips, and her eyes filled with tears. She had never seen her daughter look so angelic.

They all carefully got into the limousine and were soon on their way to the biggest social event in Philadelphia. They could see the lights as they flashed in the sky from the large machine in front of the grandest hotel in all of Pennsylvania, the Grand Florian Hotel.

There was a red carpet out front and the hotel entrance was decked out for the event, with all the flashiest Halloween décor imaginable.

The limo came to a stop, and a man in a black tuxedo stepped over to open the door for them. The limo driver told the other three to exit first, and stand aside.

There were hundreds of people lined up behind velvet ropes, trying to snap pictures of celebrities as they exited their cars, and though none of the people in this specific limousine were celebrities by any means, it didn't stop the people from snapping pictures and squealing when they saw them. The paparazzi were going crazy, but an awed hush came over the crowd as Alison was assisted out of the limo and stood in front of all of them. The photographers politely walked around and snapped picture after picture of her, as though she was to be adored and treated carefully. They got the shots that they needed and then parted so that she could enter the building.

The music was already playing and there were at least a hundred people in attendance so far. It was like a dream. Alison didn't want to wake anytime soon. Her parents and Jeanie came in first, caught by the spotlight, but unlike other guests, the spotlights didn't follow them down the grand staircase. They stayed on her, and suddenly the orchestra began to play a soft melody, and everyone turned their attention to her, even if they were in the middle of a conversation.

"Is it just me, or is everyone staring at you, Allie?" Jeanie whispered to her friend. "It's like Cinderella's entrance at the prince's ball. And that would make me…the ugly step sister…" She laughed nervously, as she adjusted her mask, and descended the stairs.

"Even as the black swan, Jeanie, you are beautiful as well. I am no Cinderella. I don't get the prince at the end of the night. My prince will never find me…" She lowered her voice, so she couldn't be heard. "…My prince is dead."

After another half hour had passed, the orchestra stopped playing, and the spotlight moved to the stage, where a Princess in blue taffeta and a Beast with a top hat stepped to the microphone, and the crowd came to a hush.

"Welcome honored guests, friends, and family to our 70th Annual Halloween Gala for Callahan Banking and Trust Inc. I am Caitlin and this strapping beast next to me is my brother, Ian. We are acting CEO's and your host and hostess for tonight." The princess spoke with sweet conviction.

"As my adorable sister said, this is the 70th birthday for CBT Inc., and it is very special to have you all here to celebrate it with us. As you all may know, our grandparents, Killian and Rebecca Callahan started this company, with an anonymous investor, shortly after the end of the Great Depression. It was their dream that no one would ever have to fear poverty again. With the assistance of their private investors, they were able to build this company from the ground up, making it possible for, even the most destitute, to rely on the knowledge that they were not alone. Through charities, fundraisers, and Galas such as this, over the past Seventy years, we have managed to raise millions upon millions of dollars to assist those in need." The handsome man spoke, a smile across his face.

"It was our grandmother's hope that we take care of family, as they take care of us. She knew, first hand, the kindness of those who were willing to look past the social and economic standing, and nurture the human spirit." The girl spoke again. Her brother wasn't paying attention, so she gave him a nudge.

"Unfortunately, Grandmother isn't able to be here with us tonight. Her health is not at its best, but she gave us her blessings and hoped that tonight's celebrations and festivities would stand as a reminder that, though we come from different places and live differently, when together we are but the same."

"So, please, enjoy each other's company. Meet someone new. Dance with a stranger. And don't forget…at the stroke of midnight, you must remove your masks, no matter who you are with." Caitlin concluded, and winked.

"Happy Haunting!" They both said in unison, before waving and exiting the stage, after a booming round of applause. The orchestra began to play again, and a woman took the microphone from the stand and began to croon a Halloween tune.

Alison turned to her parents and Jeanie, a sly grin on her face.

"Well, that explains it." She chuckled to herself.

"What? What explains what, Sweetheart?" Maria asked, curious as to why Alison was laughing and smiling.

"Do you remember me telling you about that sweet old Irish lady that I take care of at the center?"

"Yes, the one that is so interested in your little fantasy world that you have created, to explain why you went missing…" Salvador grumbled, until his wife smacked him.

"Well, dad…That lady that is so interested hearing about where I went…she is THE Rebecca Callahan, as in Rebecca Callahan of Callahan Banking and Trust, Inc. I bet that she is the reason that I got the invite to this Gala tonight."

"Wow, so you *are* well connected. I guess it just goes to show…if you schmooze up to the right people, you get rewarded for it." Salvador commented, sarcastically.

"I didn't 'schmooze,' up to anyone, dad. I take care of her, and I guess she just appreciates having someone spend time with her without wanting anything in return. Seriously, dad, I just don't understand how you can be so bitter, and judgmental. Not everyone is out to get stuff from others. I honestly didn't know that she was the same woman that started this company."

"I am not bitter. I am a realist." He grimaced.

"Yeah… a realist." She laughed, and turned to her friend, who was now flirting with a handsome man in a Phantom mask, and cape. A soft melody floated through the air, and the mysterious man whisked her off to the dance floor, without a word to anyone.

"If you will excuse me, I am going to get real as only a realist could, and go dance with your mother. Will you be okay?" He took Maria's hand, and didn't wait for his daughter to respond. He tweaked her nose, and then she was left standing alone against a large pillar.

She stood there for a while, watching her parents dance their way across the floor, and then she would spot her best friend, attempting to stand on the tips of the ballet slippers she was wearing. It amused her, and smiled.

As much as she knew that she was not looking to find someone tonight, she felt as though her costume was going to waste as she remained standing there, alone. Again, her thoughts wandered to Addison, and the dance in the moonlight. A smile tugged at the corner of her mouth, and suddenly her attention was pulled back to the present. All of a sudden, a white rose popped up in front of her face, the stem held by a white glove.

"A beautiful flower for a beautiful Wallflower." A husky, yet oddly familiar voice said.

"No, thank you." She whispered out of the corner her mouth.

"I'm sorry?" He asked, puzzled.

"No offense, but I am not interested. Thank you." She tried to be polite.

"It's just a flower. I wasn't proposing." A hint of amusement came out in his words. "You just looked a little sad, over here alone. I thought I would be nice. Do you not like Random acts of kindness by handsome strangers?"

"A handsome stranger, huh? A little full of yourself, if you think that your good looks are going to get any girl you offer a flower to." She still had not turned her eyes from the dance floor.

"How about two flowers? Will two flowers at least get you to turn around and talk to me?" He held up a second rose.

"Nope. Still not interested. Sorry. Try your suave pick-up lines on another girl." She was a little amused with the man's persistence, as well as slightly flattered.

"Well, I have obviously picked the wrong girl to be a nice guy to. You're just like all the other girls." There was a pang of disappointment and anger in his voice, and he lowered the flowers that he had held out to her. Feeling as though she had actually hurt his feelings, she turned her head, and gently grabbed his wrist.

"I'm sorry if I seem cold and rude. I'm just not very good company right now. Please forgive me if I have offended you. You seem like a very sweet guy."

"I assure you, my intentions were not to 'pick you up.' I just saw you standing here, looking absolutely beautiful, but very sad and alone." His tone softened. She took that moment to turn to him, and gently take the flowers from his hand. She smelled the beautiful roses, and looked up at him.

He wore a large brimmed hat with a few giant feathers sticking out the one side, and had a mask the covered nearly his entire face. She could not make out any of his features, but his eyes seemed soft and warm through the holes. He wore an intricately decorated costume, with a long sweeping Cape, and boots that came up to his knees. On his hands he wore gloves of deep onyx, and he offered her his hand, and motioned to an unoccupied table and chairs a few feet away.

"May I have the pleasure of knowing your name?" He sighed, his husky voice low and gentle.

"I'm...Cinderella." She reluctantly placed her hand in his, and blushed.

"Well, then, Cinderella...I am Prince Charming. Would you care to sit and keep me company?" He kissed her hand, and she felt an electric current run through her at the touch of his lips to her skin. She just nodded, and was led her over to the chairs, where he pulled one out for her.

As they sat, and talked, she couldn't help but notice that he never looked away from her, but seemed to hang on her every word. She also noticed that the lighting was better where they were sitting, and so she could see his eyes and lips more so than before.

His eyes were oddly familiar in color, a deep chocolate brown, with caramel flecks around the edges. They were kind, and clear, and focused on her, despite the fact that women were walking past the table every few moments, some of them obviously trying to sway his attention.

His smile, though partially covered by the bottom of the mask, was sweet, and slightly crooked. He made no indication that he was going to make a move, and Alison thought it strange, as men usually don't respect women's personal space or boundaries. He just sat there, a few feet from her, with one arm leaning on the table and the other laying in his lap.

They sat there talking, for what seemed like hours, and amazingly the rest of the party seemed to dissolve away around them. It is only when she stopped talking, and looked around, that she remembered where she was.

"I don't mean to be rude, but I really must find my family. I cannot see them on the dance floor anymore." She looked over, and none of them were anywhere to be seen.

"Would you like me to help you look for them? What are they dressed as?" His willingness to assist her in looking for them, instead of trying to keep her to himself, caught her off guard.

"Um...well, my father is dressed as a soldier, and he is probably standing or sitting close to a very full figured Salsa dancer in a black and red dress. And my friend is a Black Swan ballet dancer." She said as she attempted to lean further over to look at more of the dance floor. Just then, a gloved hand appeared in front of her. She took it, without hesitation, and stood up. He tucked her arm under his, and put her hand on his wrist, as a gentleman would, and they walked out onto the dance floor to get a better look.

After walking around the whole dance floor, and ascending some stairs to another seating area, he spotted her mother and father, or at least people that fit her description.

"Are those your parents...over there? The ones talking to the Callahan's?" He leaned in so she could hear him over the talking guests around them. She looked and confirmed that it was them, and not too far away was Jeanie, who was sitting on the lap of the man whom had whisked her away to dance. "I suppose then, I should bid you Adieu, since you found those whom you came with." There was sadness in his eyes, as he gave her hand a soft squeeze.

"Actually, they look like they are busy right now. I would hate to disturb them. But, if you have to get back to your date, far be it for me to keep you from her. I have already taken up enough of your time."

"I have no date for tonight."

"Well, then, since neither of us have any other plans..." She looked down at his hand, which still was laying atop hers.

"Would you like to go out and get some air?" He motioned to a set of beautifully intricate French doors, which led to a gorgeous balcony overlooking the Philadelphia Skyline.

"I would love that, thank you." And she allowed him to lead her past all the tables and people until they stepped out into the wide open air.

The moonlight was purely magnificent, and the breeze swept her ringlets gently across her cheeks. She closed her eyes, and took a deep breath, and got lost in the moment, unaware that the man with her was watching her, and smiling. The moonlight made the jewels in her hair, and on her face shimmer and shine, and they reflected in his eyes.

When she finally became aware that he was watching her, she blushed and looked away. Slipping her hand from his grip, she placed her hands on her cheeks, and felt the warmth that had risen to the surface.

"Why are you watching me like that?" She laughed, meekly, and looked at him out of the corner of her eye.

"I was just admiring your beauty, and the fact that the lights inside do not do you justice. You are breathtaking." He gave her a look of absolute amazement, and she couldn't help but believe that he was not lying or trying to con her.

"I don't know what to say...except thank you. I'm sorry if I seem a bit apprehensive. It's just, I am not used to people saying that kind of stuff to me, especially men I have only just met."

"I'm sorry if my blunt honesty makes you uncomfortable. I just couldn't help myself. You really are a vision, especially in the moonlight." He looked away for a moment, and spotted a few stone benches near the railing of the balcony, by a potted Cherry blossom tree, which had beautiful lights strewn through its branches. "Please, come sit with me, and we will talk some more...or not at all, if that is what you prefer." Again, he offered his hand to her. He noticed that she was more willing to take his hand each time that he offered it to her. She walked with him to the benches, and they sat down.

"May I ask you a question?" She looked at him, and smoothed the dress material on her lap.

"By all means, please ask me anything." He responded, almost sounding eager to hear her speak again.

"Well, I know this is going to sound very odd, but I get the funny feeling that I know you. Do you get that feeling too? Like you know me? Like we have met before?" She studied his face for any indication that he felt as she did.

"It doesn't sound odd at all." He paused, and proceeded to remove his gloves, laying them neatly next to him on the bench. Without warning, he slid his hands under hers, and held them, softly. Her first instinct was to pull her hands away, but the warmth of his skin against the cool October air felt very nice. "The truth is, I do get the feeling like I know you, like we have met before. You remind me of someone from a long time ago. That feeling is what drew me to you. The sadness and longing in your eyes, the way that you seemed to be looking for someone in the crowd that you knew wouldn't be there...It was like déjà vu." The strain in his voice made her believe that he had lost someone that he loved as well, though, she was certain that they were different circumstances entirely. "I'm sorry if my approaching you like that was strange and uncomfortable. I guess that I was hoping that maybe we could keep one another company, even for a short while. You are entirely too beautiful to look that sad. I much prefer your smile." He smiled at her, his eyes locking hers.

"And I'm sorry if I seemed rather frigid and bothered by your methods of striking up conversation. I must be honest with you, in that, I am not looking for any sort of...whirlwind romance or torrid affair." She began to blush again, and she went to turn her face away, but his hand caught her chin.

As she looked into his eyes, she saw a flicker of something that she hadn't seen in a long time, and it drew her full attention and focus. Her pulse began to pick up speed, and her fingers began to tighten around his right hand, which still remained in her lap. As though there were magnets pulling them closer together, they both leaned towards one another. Things began to get a little hazy, and she slowly blinked her eyes. He caressed her cheek with his thumb, and then his hand returned to lay on top of hers.

Chapter Twenty-Five

"Dance with me...please. Just once. Just tonight." That was all that came out of his mouth, in a low, raspy growl. When she smiled and nodded in agreement, he got up off the bench, her hands still in his, and helped her up. Tucking her arm back under his, as before, he reached down, put his gloves back on, and led her back inside.

The atmosphere inside the grand ballroom of the hotel had changed from before. And as they made their way slowly to the dance floor, the heads of everyone they passed seemed to turn and watch them. Even Mr. And Mrs. Moreno had taken notice, and were now watching the couple's descent down the grand staircase to the dance floor. Jeanie got to her feet, and rushed to the banister, to watch from above. The spotlight, which had followed Alison's entrance earlier, was now following the two of them down, and across the marble floor.

The handsome stranger led Alison to the center of the floor, and turned her so that she was facing him. She quickly grasped the train of her gown, and held it up, as he placed his hand on her hip. Without breaking eye contact, he took her other hand in his, and they began to move in sync with the music and with one another.

All of the guests watched the two of them, as they danced in the soft glow of the mirror ball and spotlight. Even Ian and Caitlin took notice, and joined the rest of Alison's group at the railing to watch in awe and amazement.

The music seemed to follow their lead as they took to the floor in a slow sweeping motion, like out of an old movie.

Alison felt as though there was magic in the air, and she closed her eyes, and continued to move in unison with this handsome man holding her firmly, yet gently. And though she was aware that it was impossible, she imagined that it was Addison that had his arm around her waist. This was the dance, amidst hundreds of onlookers, that she would have had with Addison the night of the party, had Lena not acted out and brought the night to a screeching halt. She felt like the most beautiful, most cherished, most wanted woman in the room...and yet, the man she was with was not the one she wanted, though he was a very good substitute.

"Oh my, Sal...look at our baby girl down there. She is the belle of the ball, dancing with..." She squinted, and leaned her head closer to see if she recognized the gentleman dancing with her daughter. Looking to Jeanie, she whispered, not taking her eyes off the scene below. "Jeanie, darling...who is that masked man?"

"I don't know, Mrs. Moreno, but right now, every guy in the room wishes he was dancing *with* Allie, and every girl in the room is wishing they *were* Allie."

Soon, other people joined the two of them on the dance floor, and everyone circled the floor, twirling and spinning. It was mystical and magical, and Alison felt like she could have gone on like this forever. As the song being played came to an end, the mystery guy took a step back, giving a low bow, and removing his hat, then replacing it on his head on his way back up to stand in front of her. As he looked at her, and stepped forward, the magnetic pull became stronger. She leaned her head back, and looked at him; her body pressed against his. As she felt his hand slide across the small of her back, she took a deep breath. Her hand slid up his chest, and laid right above his heart.

His body heat radiated off of him, and his breathing deepened as he pulled her closer, leaning his head down. All reasoning and rational thought had left her, and she felt numb. She knew that it was too soon to be in the arms of someone else, but it was if she had no control over her body. Just as their lips were about to make contact with each other, something stopped them.

Alison's mother and friend were watching from above, and both were whispering prayers, though Maria's were in very rapidly spoken Italian, and she was crossing herself over and over again. They were just about to see them kiss, but the large clock struck midnight.

It felt as though the air had been knocked right out of her, and the groan that escaped him was truly a sound of disappointment. As the clock tolled its bells, people began to remove their masks, and look around them. All that Alison could do was to stare into those eyes; the eyes that had yearned to say so much, to speak words that would not escape him. She felt a tremor of anticipation, both in his touch and inside of her.

"I think that I will just leave my mask on. If I take it off, you may be disappointed at who you find underneath." She murmured, sheepishly.

"I don't think that is possible. When I look at you, I see you, not the mask. We all wear masks, my sweet."

She wanted to see the man behind the mask now more than ever. The clock struck the eleventh time, and she bowed her head down to remove her mask, though she was in no rush. He reached up, while she wasn't looking, and removed his mask, looking around until he had made eye contact with Caitlin and Ian. It was also then, when he saw the familiar faces of Alison's Mother and father. In a panic, he turned and ran up the stairs, dropping his mask to the ground at her feet. When she saw his mask hit the floor, she looked up, her lace mask in her hand, but he was gone.

Salvador and Maria got a good look at his face, and then looked at one another, their mouths gaping wide.

"Could it be?" Sal inquired.

"It was...It was him." Maria's heart swelled, as she looked down at her daughter, who was frantically looking around her for the man with the large brimmed, feathered hat.

"Who was he? Do you know him?" Jeanie asked, needing to know who the handsome young man was.

"It was the young man...the one who found our Alison, the one that saved her. He stayed at the hospital long enough for Alison's father and I to arrive from Philly, and then he took off. However, we got a good look at him before he left."

"So that was him? That was her mystery man." She looked down in wonder, and then saw her friend looking up at her, as if to ask if she had saw where he went. Jeanie pointed to the top of the steps, and ran to meet her there. They met at the top of the steps, and Alison had tears in her eyes.

"Jeanie, where did he go? Why did he just leave?" She held his mask in her hand and looked lost, and confused. "Who was he? Do I know him? I don't understand!" She sobbed.

"We'll find him, Allie. I swear we will. He went this way." She grabbed her friend's hand, and they raced up the rest of the stairs to the top, and out the doors. They asked the ushers and waiters, and everyone who may have seen him pass by, describing his costume to them, but no one seemed to have seen him.

Meanwhile, Mr. And Mrs. Moreno took the time to stop and thank the young Callahan's for inviting them, and for the nice little chat earlier, before taking off after their daughter. Ian looked down at his sister, and then pulled his phone from his pocket, hit a button, and then walked towards the balcony for some privacy. Caitlin walked to the edge of the railing and watched the doors, as Salvador and Maria raced through them, and disappeared into the crowd, before joining her brother.

Chapter Twenty-Six

After several hours of searching the streets around the hotel, the black car pulled up to their house. Alison and Jeanie had ridden the majority of the time they searched standing up, their upper halves sticking out the skylight to get a better view. They sunk back down into the car as the car came to a halt in front of the old colonial.

"I am deeply sorry that we couldn't find him, Miss Moreno. We *did* look everywhere we could." The driver said as he opened the door for them.

As a sign of how saddened and defeated she felt, the wings pinned to her back were drooped as she stumbled up the stairs and into the house. Mascara was running down her cheeks as she ascended the stairs up to her room, followed by her friend.

"We tried to find him, Alison. I swear we did, sweetheart." Salvador said to her. She turned to him, and looked at him, the sadness of a child shimmering in the tears that she shed.

"I know you did, daddy. But, he is gone. He's gone, just like the only man that I ever loved. This is my punishment. I am supposed to live the rest of my life, having perfect moments of pure happiness, just so I can be left heartbroken when they disappear."

"Oh, come now, Alison…you will find your happiness one day, and it will be meant to be. You'll see. Just be patient." Maria sighed, grabbing her daughter's hand, tenderly, and giving it a squeeze.

"Mom, I *had* pure happiness. I could've had it forever. He was perfect, and I abandoned him to do what was 'right.' Now, he's dead. Then, I opened my heart tonight, against my better judgement, and *he* ran away from me. I am seeing a pattern here. I am not going to go through this anymore." She yanked her hand away and ran up the stairs, sobbing. Maria grasped Jeanie's hand, and looked at her.

"She has such a loving heart, and she deserves to be happy. Please talk to her. Don't let her give up on love. She has to realize that there is always more out there...always an explanation. Please, Jeanie. Talk to her!" Maria pleaded.

"I will. I'll do the best I can. But you have to see things from her perspective, Mrs. Moreno. She has never felt as though anyone would ever love her, because she is not tall, skinny, and blonde. How could she ever compete with that...the ideal image that men crave? It's the times we live in, you know. Being a plus-sized woman isn't beautiful to men...it never has been, it never will be. She feels like the ugly duckling, but tonight, she felt like the most beautiful girl in the world, and that jerk still ran away from her..." There was fury in her eyes. "He saw how beautiful she was, he spoke to her, he danced with her, and then he crushed her. If I ever find him, I will make him sorry that he ever even came near her. He broke my friend's heart. He *will* pay." She raced up the stairs after Alison.

*****

A knock came at the door, and Mrs. Callahan turned from her writing desk and called that the door was open. Wheeling herself around, she came face-to-face with the person standing in her doorway, and a look of disappointment and displeasure came across her face.

"I thought I would be seeing you sometime soon."

"Hello, Ma'am." The voice said, sadly.

~ 252 ~

"And what do you have to say for yourself?" She asked, a hint of fury in her voice.

"Honestly, I have no excuse for what happened...except that I got scared."

"You have been planning this...*We* have been planning this for months and months. You were right there, Boy! You had her in your arms. All you had to do was to let her see you! Instead, I had to sit here, comforting a devastated young lady who felt as though she had scared you away. She had finally started to heal, and you crushed her."

"I'm sorry. I panicked. She was there, in my arms, and she was happy. Her eyes were all aglow and her smile was...She had let go of the pain of knowing what happened...she was ready to open her heart, to love again."

"All the more reason for you to have stayed! My grandson told me that you just ran...I understand that you were scared, but honestly..."

"I said I was sorry! What more can I say?" He came over and sat on the chair near the old woman, and put his head in his hands. "I made a mistake. I know that, but there is still time. She didn't see me. She didn't see my face." He looked at her, desperation in his eyes.

"She may not have seen your face, but her parents did. They remember you from the hospital. They remember you."

"I really screwed things up, didn't I?" he despaired and stuck his face back in his hands, leaning back in the chair.

The clock chimed six times, and a smile crossed the old woman's lips. She turned her wheelchair in his direction and looked at him, a feeling of compassion in her eyes.

"Hope may not be lost for you, my good sir."

"What hope is there, dear lady Callahan? I have failed miserably. You are right, I had her right there...and I ran off like a child. If her parents saw me, then they had to have told her who I was by now."

"Oh, don't be silly. Even they don't know who you are…not really. They just think that you were the kind stranger who saved her. There could be many reasons why you left her at the ball, many logical reasons. You can explain it to her yourself."

"Do you really think that she would understand? That she would forgive me for abandoning her there, at that moment?"

"This is Alison we are talking about. She would forgive *you* for anything. But before we get to that, maybe it is time that she reunites with an old friend first." She patted him on the leg, and returned to her writing desk. After she had finished the letter that she had been writing, she folded it, placed it in an envelope and handed it to him. "Deliver this to her home, but be sure not to be seen. If all goes well, every piece of this will fall into place, just as it should be.

"Are you mad? How is a letter going to make any difference?" He held the envelope out in front of him, and flipped it over and over in his hands.

"It's all in the power of words, my dear boy. They can move mountains, stop time, heal pain, etcetera."

"Okay. But can you do me a huge favor, Rebecca? Stop calling me 'dear boy,' please? I mean, in all honesty, I am not exactly a boy anymore." He laughed.

"You are to me! Now, take that letter and do as you were told. Come back here tomorrow at a quarter to eleven tomorrow morning, and don't be late."

He stood up, tucked the letter into his pocket, and kissed her forehead before walking out the door.

As he walked out of the facility, he found himself deep in thought. Thoughts of Alison brought a smile to his lips, and then his eyebrows furrowed at the reality of what he had done to her, how he had hurt her by running out on her, especially after the evening that they had had. His heart ached for her, knowing that her insecurities were confirmed when he took off without even a word. He could have been honest with her, but he took the coward's way out and ran.

He walked, aimlessly, for what seemed like forever. He was so distracted by trying to find the right words to say to her when he saw her again, that his feet seemed to run on autopilot and led him to the front steps of her home. When he finally realized where he was standing, his eyes were filled with tears. His heart thumped wildly as he gazed up at the one illuminated window on the second floor.

She was sitting in the window seat, a saddened look on her face. Her pouty lips were evidence that she had been crying, as were her puffy eyes and flushed cheeks. As he stood watching her, he reached for the envelope in his pocket, and placed it in the mailbox. Letting out a sigh, he watched her for a few minutes more, and then began his journey back to his cabin.

The long trek to his cabin in the woods was not that far, as he had a ride waiting for him outside the city. His transportation was in the form of an old friend; a beautiful ebony and white stallion.

As soon as he reached the horse, wandering happily in the woods for his owner's return, he greeted him with a shake of the head and stomp of his hooves, and he backed away, as if upset with him.

"Yes...I screwed up. Rebecca already yelled at me for it. I don't need grief from you too. Can we talk about this on the way home? I'm tired." The horse answered with a snort and another stomp, then approached his rider.

*****

Alison had just exited the shower, and was walking to her room when she walked past her parents' bedroom. They were having a heated conversation. She was about to keep walking to her room, when she heard her father mention her name. Out of curiosity, she stood by the door, out of sight, and listened.

"She keeps talking about this guy that she lost…someone who died…If it is that guy she claims she met in that fantasy town of hers…" Sal whispered loudly.

"First of all, Salvador, it wasn't a fantasy town. It is a real town, or it was at one time. You went there with her!"

"Yes, and it was horrific, but that is beside the point, Maria. She claims that she was there for almost a year, and yet she was only missing for four days. Something happened to her on that road, and she suffered a mental breakdown. I talked to Dr. Greer at Cliffmoore…"

"Cliffmoore?!? The Sanitarium? Salvador, are you saying that you want to have our little girl committed?"

"If need be, yes. She speaks in riddles, talking about these people that she spent time with in that desolate town…and the man she fell in love with and he died. She's speaking about time travel and all that. It's a bunch of crazy talk. She needs professional help, Maria. And you aren't helping her by listening to it."

"The only one in this house that needs professional help is you!"

"Furthermore, I am going to Bruckner's and I am ordering that they remove that crazy old lady from her rounds as well. She is filling Alison's head with nonsense."

"If you go to Alison's work and start talking to them like you are speaking to me, not only will that cause her to lose her job, but it could ruin her career! No nursing home will hire her if they think she is mentally unstable, and the only one that thinks she is would be you!!"

"Say what you want, Maria, but I am the only one of the two of us who is willing to face the fact that she is losing her mind."

Alison could hardly believe what she was hearing. Her parents were fighting with each other over her. All of their fighting was because her father thought she had lost her mind, and her mother believed her. She couldn't stand the fighting. She knew that she needed to do something, so she took a deep breath and walked through their door without warning.

"If you will give me a chance to say goodbye to everyone, I will resign from Bruckner's and voluntarily commit myself to Cliffmoore. If you really feel that strongly about me being mentally unstable, I will commit myself, but on my own terms."

"You were eavesdropping on our conversation?" Her father looked embarrassed and shocked that she had heard what he said. "And what exactly are your terms? What do they entail?"

"If I commit myself, and they release me with a clean bill of health, you will drop the whole thing. Also, when they release me, I am moving out." Alison saw the look on her mother's face, and walked to her. "Mama, I cannot live under the same roof with someone who doesn't trust or believe me. I am not lying about Woodcrest or anything that has happened to me. I have always been brutally honest with you both, so for him to assume the worst of me…I am not going face him looking at me every day, with doubt in his eyes."

Without waiting for a reply from either of them, she walked out of their room, and closed the door behind her.

The sun shone through her window the following morning, as she rose to the sound of her alarm. Today, she was going to say goodbye to her career, to the people she called friends, and to her patients. The one person that she would have the hardest time saying goodbye to was sweet old Mrs. Callahan. She was the one person who honestly believed every word that Alison told her about Woodcrest and the people. Having heard that Killian Callahan was one of the founders of CBT Inc., she needed to ask Mrs. Callahan if he could be the same Killian than she had known. If it was just a common Irish name, then it was a coincidental connection. However, if it was the same Killian, there were a dozen more questions that would follow. She needed answers before she left the dear woman to someone else and locked herself in a padded cell.

Chapter Twenty-Seven

That morning, he came back as she had requested, and they waited together. As the clock rang its eleventh toll, there was a knock at the door, and a familiar smiling face came through the doorway. Unseen by Alison, Becky put her finger to her lips, giving the gentleman in the shadows the signal that he was not to speak until it was time. She had something to prove, not only to Alison, but also to him. He had been warned not to speak a word, no matter if she spoke of him or not. It was imperative to the old woman's plans.

"Mrs. Callahan…I see that you were waiting for me." Alison smiled half-heartedly, stepping in and closing the door behind her. She observed the elderly woman in front of her, and her smile widened. "I must say, you look absolutely beautiful this moning. Have you gotten your hair done?"

"I have, my dear. Do you like it?" She acted quite pleased with herself.

"I love it. It is very nineteen thirties…" Her speech was slowed at the last few words. A saddened look came over her.

"By any chance, did you get the letter that I sent to you?" She took Alison's hand in hers. Alison reached into the pocket of her scrubs, and pulled out the letter. "Good."

"It said on the envelope that I wasn't to open it until I came to see you. May I open it now?" She inquired, ready to break the wax seal. There was an almost child-like excitement in her voice and in the look on her face.

"By all means, my sweet girl. Open it. We have much to talk about after you have read it." Alison sat on the edge of the bed, and unfolded the parchment within the envelope. It was when she came to the very end, and let out a gasp, that the man in the shadows had to cover his mouth to keep from making a sound. Alison's eyes opened wide, filling with tears. The letter fell from her shaking hands. She turned her head to look at the elderly lady next to her, and for a second no one knew how she was going to react to what she had just read. There was deadening silence in the room, as Mrs. Callahan and the silent spectator watched Alison try to connect all the dots in her head.

"No…it couldn't be…after all this time…" She swallowed hard, and moved her hand from her trembling lips, to reveal a smile that extended from ear to ear. "My dearest Becky…it's you...you're here…you've been here, this whole time…right in front of me and you never said anything…" She slid to the floor to kneel at Mrs. Callahan's feet. She took the lady's hands in her own and laid her forehead against the thin soft skin. "I thought I was going mad. I thought that there was no one alive that would believe me, with certainty, that all that had happened was really real. But you did…from the day I started here, from the first day I started caring for you. You believed me, you listened…and now I understand why. " She lifted her head, and looked into the eyes of the wheelchair-bound woman in front of her. "My dear sweet Becky…You knew because you were there! You were my dearest friend, my beloved Becky!"

She wanted to embrace the woman with a wild fierceness, but she knew that she could hurt her, she slipped her arms gently around the woman, and just held her, sobbing into her sweet, soft shoulder. After a few moments, she pulled from her, and looked at her face, looked deeply into her eyes. As soon as she saw her, the young Irish girl from Woodcrest, her heart leapt.

"I wanted to tell you so many times, Alison. I wanted to make you see me, to see your Becky… but it just wasn't the right time. But, I felt that I had waited long enough." She reached into her pocket and pulled out a small white device with ear buds connected to it. "I still have it. It still works, too."

"Oh my goodness, Becky…my old mp3 player. It still works?" She took the object from her friend's hand, and noticed how much her hands had changed since she placed it in her hands, before she left. "Oh, my Dear…you've gotten so old…" She laughed through her tears, and sniffled. "…but I am so grateful to see you, so relieved…so tired of trying to convince myself that it wasn't just…I have tried so hard. I am so tired, Becky, so tired and so sad."

Becky could see what the last couple months had done to Alison. All of a sudden she looked aged, and worn.

"I know that it has been hard on you. I am sure that you have started doubting yourself, your memories, but I assure you…it was all real. You were in Woodcrest…you were. How else would you explain the scar on your forehead…your memories, your heartache…I know that you have been mourning us. You've told me so. You've been mourning *him.*"

"My Adam." Her eyes filled with tears once more. "Becky, I could have stayed with him. Nothing would have changed…not really. Only a few days had passed here…I was with you for nearly a year, but only a few days had passed here. He and I…we could have been together longer. I could have prevented him…"

"Sweetie, you did what you thought was right. He knew that you didn't want to leave him. He knew that. He knew you loved him." She held Alison's face between her hands, and looked at her with such love and tenderness, as only friends could.

"I loved him more than I think anyone could love someone else. He was my world. He saw me, the real me, and he made me feel like the most important and most beautiful woman on the planet. It devastated me to leave him, to watch his face as I went through the trees and away from him forever. I left my heart with him." Tears poured from Alison's eyes at the very thought of him.

"The moment that you disappeared, he knew that there was no way that he could live without you. I was there, remember? He was so scared, Alison. He was terrified of the darkness, and he was sure that it would come again, once you left. The fear of being alone in the darkness again, of not having his 'light' to keep the demons at bay, it paralyzed him."

"A grown man...afraid of the dark. That doesn't sound like Addison. He wasn't afraid of the dark at all. He spent a lot of time in the dark..."

"Of course...But that is not the kind of darkness he was afraid of, Alison."

"We just talked a lot at night, in the dark. It was quiet and...are you certain that Lena had nothing to do with what happened to him? She seemed quite quick in pointing fingers at me."

"Honestly, I know that Lena was a wretched girl with lots of issues, but I don't think that she would ever have done anything to hurt Addison. Deep down, I really think she did have feeling for him, but her greed...the greed of her father... I think greed and conceit overshadowed the person that she could have been. She was as sad as everyone else in Woodcrest, and was genuinely crying at the memorial service we held for him."

The realization that there had been a memorial service, an actual service to commemorate his life and his passing, broke her heart all over again.

"So, please fill me in on what happened in Woodcrest after I left. I went there after I got back....It's all gone now, completely gone. It was thriving, and now it is wreckage." Alison sat on the bed and was content to hear what had happened.

After thinking about it for a few moments, Rebecca began to recount what became of the people of Woodcrest, those same people whom Alison had come to care for very dearly. A lot of what she told Allie, she already knew through looking through the microfilm at the library; about the Gentry's, and their joyous bundle, and Thomas' re-election. However, Becky was able to fill her in on how she became a Callahan, where CBT came to be, and the involvement of the Thatcher family.

Roger and Corrine, Becky's parents, retired after Becky married Killian and they moved to Ireland to spend the rest of their days. Becky made certain that Mr. and Mrs. Thatcher were cared for until the very end, and they were placed in the family mausoleum with the rest of the Thatchers.

"What happened to Thomas and Odette's daughter?"

"Don't you mean their six children? Yes, my dear, they had six all together; four girls, two boys. They grew, got married and live all over the place. I've kept in contact with most of them, but seeing as they never had the pleasure of knowing you personally, when I spoke of you, they just chalked it up to someone that used to live in Woodcrest but moved on. No one ever had a problem leaving Woodcrest after you did. Soon, more people were venturing out of the town, rather than staying safe within its borders. Life and nature took over from there. Soon, there was no one left to maintain it, and it just fell apart."

"That beautiful little town…it had such potential."

"Without the people, it was nothing but a town. Killian, God rest his soul, wanted to rebuild Woodcrest, to make it fresh and new. He had hopes that he would live long enough to see you again too, but he passed on just last year. I swore that I would live long enough to see you again. I knew that you would go back to work, doing what you spoke so fondly of back then. When I got word that you were back in Philadelphia, and that you were looking for work, I pulled some strings. I am a very powerful woman here, apparently." She seemed very proud of herself, and looked at Alison with a youthful smile that she had come to know so well.

Alison was very flattered at the thought that she meant so much to others, and that she had left such a mark on Rebecca and Killian, that they tried to live long enough to see her again.

"So, aside from Odette and Thomas' children, you are all that is left of 'my Woodcrest,' the Woodcrest I knew and loved?" There was a sadness in her voice.

"Not exactly." Rebecca sighed, and turned her chair in the direction of the stranger, hiding in the shadows. "There's one other…"

"You were the youngest person I really knew, Becky. Everyone else is probably dead by now. Who else would be left?" Alison's heart began to beat faster as she got to her feet and looked in the direction that her friend was facing. There, in the shadows, she could barely make out the silhouette of a person, sitting in an armchair, in the darkness. They had been there the whole time, had been a silent spectator to the whole discussion.

"Oy! You!! Who are you? How'd you get in here?" Alison started to come forth, as if to grab them and throw them out of the room. "This is a private room, you know?! How dare you hide there in the shadows and listen to our conversation. That was private!"

"I invited him here, my sweet. I needed him here, to hear what was said."

"Who is he?" She came around the chair, leaned over and looked at her aged friend.

"You and I had a discussion a week or so back, about you going to the Gala. I told you that there was romance to find there, did I not?"

"Yes, and I came and saw you after the Gala and told you what had happened, didn't I? I opened myself up, met someone, despite my heart still hurting over Addison. I met that mysterious stranger, and he ran off before I could see his face. I looked for him for hours...very nearly until the sun came up the next day. He just vanished."

"I remember that. Well, my grandson and granddaughter also called me when they saw what had happened. They told me and I have to admit, I was very disappointed and angered at that young man for abandoning you like that." She shot the stranger a stern look.

"Did you know him, Becky?"

"Sad to say, yes...but then, so do you. He was also there the day you returned back to this timeline."

"Do you mean to tell me... the masked stranger was the same man who saved my life...the one who carried me over six miles to the hospital and sat with me until my parents arrived? He was the same man?" Her eyes widened, and she looked over her shoulder, then back again.

"Yes, they are one in the same."

"If you knew, Becky, why didn't you tell me? He must think me mad...What on earth would make you keep this from me? You sat here...you watched me cry...and you knew the whole time who he was?"

"It wasn't her fault. I asked her not to say anything to you. I knew you'd be mad, and it really wasn't her fault I ran. That was not part of the plan." The person in the corner sighed.

"Plan? What plan? To deceive me? To crush my heart further than it was already crushed?" She stood up, and went to walk out the door.

"My intention was never to hurt you, to crush you? I just saw how happy you were and I knew that if you saw my face, it would all be over...if you were to see my face, you would run and never look back."

"Well, now you will never know, will you?" She turned and walked closer to the darkness.

"May I explain…Please?"

"Why on Earth would I allow that? What makes you think that I even want to hear your excuses?" She stepped even closer, and went to reach for the pull chain for the lamp nearby.

"Sweet Allie, please hear him out. He has been through so much, just as you have. Please, just listen to what he has to say. If you still want to leave afterward, neither of us will try to stop you." She grasped Alison's hand, and pleaded with her.

"Okay, fine. For Becky…I will hear you out. But, why are you sitting in the dark? Why can't I see your face? You owe me that much, after the other night." The tone in her voice made him chuckle. "What are you laughing for?"

"I've missed that…that cynicism in your voice." He continued to chuckle. Something struck a chord, and she slunk down onto the floor. The moment she heard that laugh, her heart seemed to remember and start beating erratically. "I wished that our reunion would have been better. It should have been magical, whimsical…like the fairy tale that you so deserved, but the fear within me clouded my judgement, and I panicked."

He leaned forward, the old hat on his head, hiding his face from the light that crept in from outside. He took her hands in his. As her hands laid in his, she felt his beating heart, and she found reassurance in them.

"I didn't need a fairy tale. I needed to feel as though I mattered to someone…I needed to feel as though someone could love me for me. I had that once, and I lost him. I can never get his love back, can never feel the warmth of his skin, or the beat…" She swallowed hard, and gripped his hands. "…the beat of his kind, loving heart."

"And, I feared that the darkness would chase you away from me again." His fingers intertwined with hers. "The funny thing about that little batch of woods that you went through…Only four days may have passed by from when you came through, but the portal, or whatever it was, was even

~ 266 ~

crueler to me. It took me to six months *prior* to you even arriving in Woodcrest....I sat there and watched you drive into the dilapidated woods and disappear. Then I had to wait four more days to see you again."

"Wait a second...what?! I'm confused." She blinked, and tried to analyze what he had just said to her.

"I stood at the edge of the woods, right by the junction between the dirt road, and the interstate." He reached behind him, and pulled out a mangled notebook. "It was all written right in here...everything about the day you had arrived, the fact that the interstate was closed, that there was a detour sign, a handwritten sign about Woodcrest...but the strange thing was....there really weren't any of those signs on the road that day. So, I made sure there would be." He unfolded the spiral-bound stack of papers, and held them out to her. She didn't see what he was holding, as she hadn't taken her eyes off of his face, or what she could see of it.

"You put up the detour sign? You closed down the interstate? Why?"

"So that you would go to Woodcrest, of course."

"But that is what is strange...Woodcrest hasn't existed for thirty years...those trees I went though had been long since cut down, exposing the town to all who drove down the dirt road...yet they were towering, alive and strong that day. How did that happen? Did you do that? Did you make the time portal?"

"No...Of course I didn't. But, I knew it would be there, because you came through it that day, and I watched."

"You watched what, exactly?" She gasped, holding his hands still. "You watched me turn down that road? You watched me disappear through...what exactly?"

"I watched...as soon as you turned down the dirt road....the trees were back, as tall and as magnificent as ever. It was the most amazing thing I had ever seen. Your car went into the trees, and then they were gone again." There was wonder and amazement in his voice. "I sat by the edge of the woods, waiting to see you come out again. It was a very long four days...longer than the six months that I waited to see your little green car get there, it felt like."

"You just sat there and watched? You waited for me to come back out? What would have happened, had I chosen to stay in Woodcrest with Addison? Would you have continued to wait?" She rose from her seat on the floor and turned her back to him, tears welling in her eyes, as the realization of his true identity finally hit her.

"Honey, if you had chosen to stay in Woodcrest with me, I would not have been waiting in the woods for six months, waiting for *you*." He paused, not knowing if she realized what he was saying. "If I hadn't followed you back here, I would never have had to trade clothes with the man who originally lived in the woods, and he never would have followed your car into Woodcrest."

"So, you're telling me that you are not just some kind stranger, who just happened to be there when I came through the woods?" She felt her head begin to spin, and a knot tightened in her stomach. "You are trying to tell me that you are...You are not Addison! Addison is dead. I read it. They found him, washed up on the beach. The medical examiner even identified him. They buried him. Even Becky said it herself...she was at his memorial service."

"I did. I was at his Memorial Service, true, but, I never said *he* was the man the family buried in the family plot." Rebecca admitted, saddened that she had deceived her friend. "The man they found...the one that was 'identified' as Addison was buried there."

"Why would they make such a mistake?" Allie looked over her shoulder at Becky, skeptical of what she was hearing.

"That is beside the point." He stepped closer to her, and reached out for her, his hand stretching from the darkness. It was suddenly unfamiliar in appearance. Addison's hands were strong and flawless. They were clean and well-manicured. However, the hand that reached for her was weathered, calloused, and looked older and unkempt. Not willing to accept that it was the same hand that she had held countless times, she pulled away, and stepped further away.

"So, if you are implying what I think you are…an innocent man died in your place? I'm sorry, but I don't believe it…I can't. The Addison that I loved, that I still love, would never have let that happen." Her heart hurt, thinking that he had something to do with the man's unfortunate demise.

"Grandmother and Grandfather just reported me missing. I had nothing to do with what happened to him after he went through, and none of them did either. It just happened. It is unfortunate that that happened, but I had no knowledge of it until I found Becky and she told me." He stepped forward again, still lingering mostly in the shadows.

"Why should I believe you…either of you?" She rounded on her heels, and looked at the woman in the wheelchair. "You sat here, listened to me cry, and didn't give me any indication that my heart was breaking for no reason." Just as quickly, she looked up and pointed her finger at the man in the shadows. "You were right in front of me…you could have said something at the Gala, but you ran away instead of telling me the truth. Even now, you want me to believe that the one man I truly loved…the only man who ever truly loved me…" She had to choke back the tears. "You want me to believe that *you* are my Addison."

"I told you that she wouldn't believe me…" He said to the old woman in the wheelchair. "This is hopeless. I lost her the moment I let her leave Woodcrest." He retracted his hand, and began to fidget.

"My Adam was afraid of returning to the darkness, yet, you have not come out from the shadows. My Adam said that I was…" She whimpered, wrapping her arms around herself, as if to keep from falling apart.

"I said that you were the light that brought me from the darkness, out of the shadows. You are…you always will be. But, I fear that my time here has changed me, and that you will not be happy with the man you see in front of you. I had to rough the winter here, had to hunt for food, and Mother Nature has been cruel."

"Do you really think that I care about what you look like? Do you believe that I am so shallow, that I would shun you for being weathered or disheveled? If you do, then you are definitely *not* Addison Thatcher. Looks have never mattered to me." Red hot tears flowed down her cheeks like molten lava, and she glared into the darkness. She tried to make out the features of the face in the shadow, and had to step towards him a few steps. "I have spent my life, afraid of never being loved because I was not what men wanted, physically. Do you really think that I would be picky? I want to be loved for who I am, inside. Why would I look for love any differently?" Her tone softened. "I didn't fall in love with the face or physical appeal of Addison Thatcher. I fell in love with the person within. I fell in love with his heart and mind."

"I know…I read everything. I know everything from start to finish."

"How do you know so much?"

"You told me…in this!" He stretched his hand out, and handed her the journal she had given to him the day she left.

"I tried to tell him, my darling friend, but he wouldn't listen to an old woman. I am old, yes, but my mind hasn't forgotten those days. But, once he read what you wrote, there was no reason to deny how you felt. He read the words that you wrote with your own hand." The aged hand of the elderly woman reached into the dark, and took him by the hand, and then she reached for Alison's. She put Alison's hand in his. She rolled back, to leave room for them. Alison reached forward, and took some of his hair in her fingers, and it felt like straw between her fingers. "Stop fighting it. Stop trying to make sense of the unimaginable. You are with one another again."

"It was a rather harsh winter, so where did you stay to keep warm?" She turned his hand over and looked at it.

"There was a cabin, but it was not well insulated so the wind blew through. I boarded up the windows, and had to cut down some trees to make firewood, as there was none. But, then I acquired an old truck, and made my way to Pittsburg in March. Got myself a nice little orderly job at this retirement home." There was a glimmer in his eye. "They put me up at a small hotel nearby. But, I lost my job there when the place burned down."

"Wait…what?!? You were the orderly…the new orderly? The one that I had yet to meet? You saved all those people? That was you?"

"Yes. I have a little story to tell you about that, too, but it can wait. Needless to say, after the fire, I knew that your arrival to Woodcrest was coming up quick, so I went back to my cabin to prepare."

"Your facial hair has grown quite a bit. They didn't do a very good job of shaving you for the Gala." She reached up and touched his cheek, feeling a beard grown there in such a short time. She also felt his skin get warmer at her touch, and he leaned his cheek into her palm.

"Your touch…I never thought I would feel that again." His voice was rough, and gruff. "I wore that full mask at the Gala to hide the cuts from my attempts to shave myself. It was bad. I tore my face up something awful."

"Please…come into the light."

"I…I can't…"

"What are you so afraid of?" She squinted, and ducked her head down to try to see under the brim of the hat he was wearing. "You want me to believe that you are my Addison. He trusted me. He knew that I loved him with my whole heart. If you went through all this to be with me, then you can't let your fear keep you from fulfilling what you came to do." She tried to meet his eyes, but he gave a shiver and began to pull away.

"I don't want to scare you."

"I promise you...I am not afraid. Take a leap of faith. I am the same Alison. My heart has not changed." She ran her hand down his chest, and laid it over his heart. Feeling his heart pick up speed beneath her hand, she reached up with her other hand and removed the hat on his head, and dropped it. A bit of dust and dirt puffed up as it hit the floor. Still unable to see his face, she reached over and pulled the chain on the lamp. In reaction to the sudden light, he turned his face away, and shielded his face from the bright glow. His long brown and slightly dirty hair blocked his face as it fell like a curtain over his cheek.

Out of the corner of his eye, he could see that there were tears welling in her beautiful brown eyes. Her light olive skin looked like porcelain in the lamplight, and her cheeks were flushed. She pulled his hand away from his face slowly, and then she began to move his hair from his face. His eyes slowly adjusted to the light, and he turned his face a little towards her, not to reveal his appearance but so he could look at her better. His eyes squinted against the harsh light, but she used her hand to shield them until they were adjusted more.

"Let me see..." She leaned over, but when she still couldn't see his face properly, she stepped around to get a closer look. "...You weren't kidding. What did you use to shave with, a dull blade...tree bark?" She gave him a crooked smile, and he couldn't help but smile back. "It's bad, but I can try to fix that." She laid her hand on his cheek, and he flinched at first, but then put his hand over hers, holding it to his cheek. He squeezed his eyes closed, and one single solitary tear escaped from beneath his eye, and trailed down his dirt covered cheek.

"I am a mess, I know. I don't exactly have a tub to bathe in. The creek is really cold." His voice came out very deep and it sent a shiver down her spine. She moved his hair from his face, and examined every inch of it. There were still hints of him under the dirt, scruff, and chapped skin. Her heart began to grow warm, and her hands began to shake, as she looked at him. She had to grip him, and touch him in some way, or she felt like he was going to fade away. When she looked into his eyes, and saw those same youthful golden brown eyes looking back at her that she had stared into countless times, it felt like something exploded in her. She gripped his hair at the nape of his neck, and pulled him closer to her.

"You're alive, you are here, and you...are...perfect!" She pulled him even closer, and kissed him, which caught him off guard.

It took him less than a second to remember what it felt like to have her this close to him. He flung his arms around her, and held her closely to him, deepening the kiss with a blind, furious wanting that had laid dormant for a while. He felt this sensation wash over him, and he wanted to remove layers of his clothes to feel the warmth of her soft, warm, smooth skin against his, but a few factors prevented him from acting on his impulses. First of all, they weren't alone. There was a giggling old lady less than fifteen feet from them, enjoying the show. Secondly, they were in a retirement home, not in the privacy of a bedroom. And lastly, he respected Alison too much to act so barbaric, though his life in the twenty-first century and living off the land had brought out the animal in him. The reckless abandon that he was feeling would have to wait.

Alison pulled away from him, but didn't let go of him. There was something flashing in her eyes, and he alone could understand its meaning, as it was also present in his eyes as well. Both of them, out of breath, but clinging to one another, they just looked at one another. She began to bite her lower lip, as she always did, and then tugged at his hair rather aggressively.

"Ouch! That hurt! What was that for?" He cried out, a pained look on his face.

"That was for letting me think you were dead!" She yanked again. "That was for running out on me at the Gala!" And one last tug, she growled through her teeth. "And that, Mr. Thatcher, was for...that was for everything else!" She pushed away from him, and she swept off her clothes. "Now, I have to go finish my shift. You will stay right here, and wait for me. No running off on me again. Sit!" She pointed at the chair, and he sat down, or rather fell into the chair, rubbing the back of his head. She backed away from him, and then turned to Mrs. Callahan. "If he tries to leave, run him over. I will be back." She backed up to the door, and opened it. "And don't think you are off the hook, Ms. Becky! You are still in some hot water with me, missy!" With a harsh huff of breath, she exited the room.

"I think that I just fell in love with her all over again!" He laid his head back on the back of the chair and tried to catch his breath, and collect his thoughts. All that Rebecca could do was burst out laughing, and shake her head.

Chapter Twenty-Eight

It was another three hours before Alison returned to the room, and there a rushed anticipation as she clocked out and walked briskly to the room to retrieve the man she had fought through hell to be with. She didn't even knock, but came bursting through the door. His head popped up, his hat slid off his head and into his lap, as he had been dozing in the chair she told him to stay in. Mrs. Callahan was sitting in her bed, reading a book, her bifocals slid to the end of her nose.

"Okay, then. My last shift has ended."

"Last shift?" Becky turned her head, and gave her an inquisitive look.

"Yes. I am no longer your caretaker. Gloria will be taking over for me from now on."

"You are that mad at me, Alison?"

"No…I had no choice. I will call you later and tell you about it, I promise." She looked at the elderly woman, then she signaled to Addison. "*You* are coming with me. Come on!" He jumped up, ran over to Becky, kissed her cheek, and then went over to the brunette in the doorway. She took him by the hand, looked around, and then walked hurriedly to the exit doors, avoiding the other workers, who gave both disgusted and intrigued looks as she passed them, dragging a ruggedly handsome man behind her. He tipped his hat to a few of the women simply out of courtesy.

She got him to her car, buckled him in, and slammed his door. She kept an eye on him as she rounded the front of the car and got in, buckled herself, and put the key in the ignition. The metal monster roared to life, and Addison grabbed the door handle. Since he came here, he had not been in a vehicle much, aside from the old truck he had inherited along with the cabin. The cars back home never sounded like this. He actually looked terrified, which made Alison laugh, but she tried to reassure him.

"No reason to be afraid. I am a good driver. You are safe. Just breathe. We are going to my house. I'm going to get you cleaned up, and then we can talk...or whatever." Her mind was more on the "whatever" than the talking, but she wasn't going to say it out loud.

"We're going to your house…as in, where you live…with your mother and father?" The terror in his eyes intensified.

"That was the plan. My dad is still at work right now."

"But, that still leaves your mother. You looked at me, right? I look more like a homeless man than someone ready to be presented to your parents. I would at least like to make a semi-good impression on them." His voice was shaky and gruff, and she glanced at him from out of the corner of her eye. Maybe he had a valid point.

She pulled to the side of the road, and reached for her purse. She had minimal cash on her, presently, and she knew that he probably didn't have anything on him.

"I would take you to a hotel, but there are two problems with that."

"Two problems…what are they?"

"Well, I have like fifteen dollars cash on me, which wouldn't even pay for an hour. However, I have my credit card…"

"Credit Card? What's that?" He looked at her as if she had just spoken a foreign language.

"Yeah…that's right. You wouldn't know what they are." She went into her wallet and showed him her debit card. "It is a plastic card that you can get, and you can use it in the place of cash, to pay for things. The problem is, it would look suspicious that I have a hotel charge on it."

"Charge? Credit? I'm disliking this time more and more every minute." He smirked. He searched though his pockets, and pulled a card out, handing it to her. "Let's just go talk to Ian." She looked at the business card that he handed her, and there was a number written on the back of it, that resembled an account number.

"You have an account at Callahan Banking and Trust?"

"I don't know. He handed that to me the night of the Gala and said for me to hold onto it. Why don't we just go talk to him? Maybe he can help. Becky said that if I needed anything, that I should either call, or go see him."

"Alright. I mean, it couldn't hurt." She pulled away from the curb, and headed back into the city.

When they pulled into the parking garage, she found a close spot to the entrance, and the two of them went in and immediately felt as though they were severely underdressed.

"Maybe I should have waited in the car." Addison whispered in Alison's ear as they approached the teller window.

Looking around them, it seemed apparent that they did look a bit out of place. There was not a man there that was wasn't in a high-priced designer suit. The women were in dresses and skirts, and they all looked very well-off and professional, and the two of them had drawn quite a bit of attention to themselves. However, Alison was used to being stared at, so she grabbed Addison's arm and stepped up to the counter, ignoring the glares and whispers. The girl at the window gave the two of them a disdainful look, and cleared her throat.

"Welcome to Callahan Banking and Trust. I'm Janette. How can I help you?" She said this with a scowl on her face.

"Hi Janette. I…We would like to speak with Mr. Ian Callahan, please." She tried to be as polite as possible.

"Mr. Callahan is one of our CEO's, and he is a very busy man. Are you sure you wouldn't like to speak with one of our banking managers instead?"

"I'm sure. Could you please tell me where we can find him? Just point us in the right direction, and we won't bother you any longer."

"As I said, he is a…" She said again, but Addison was losing his patience.

"We heard what you said, but the thing is, Janette…I am sure he would take time out of his busy schedule to speak with us. Could you please call him, or whatever you need to do? It is very important."

"I highly doubt that he would take time away from whatever he is doing to speak to…you. If there is nothing else, I have important clients with actual accounts here that need to be taken care of."

"Really?! Do you have any idea who you are speaking to?" Addison was very offended by the teller's attitude, but Alison took over.

"Listen, we were told to come to here, and that we could speak with Mr. Callahan personally. It is a sensitive matter. Can we speak with one of your managers, please?" Her soft tone seemed to have a positive effect on the rude teller, and she signaled a manager to come over.

"Is there a problem here?' the white haired gentleman asked, as he stepped up to them.

"Hi, um…we were told that we could come and speak to Mr. Ian Callahan about this account number. All we want is to speak with him."

"Well, he *is* one of the CEO's, so he is usually very busy. Let's see if I can help you out, and if I can't, then I will give him a call, and see if he can shed light on this situation." He motioned for them to follow him to his desk, and he sat down and punched in the numbers into his computer.

His reaction was not something that they would have expected. Whatever came up on his screen caused all the color to drain from his face, his eyes to widen to an almost cartoonish size, and his jaw to drop. He looked at the two of them, and then immediately straightened his suit.

"May I ask both your names, for security purposes, of course?"

"Addison Thatcher and Alison Moreno." Addison said, calmly.

"I see, okay…Well, I offer my sincerest apologies to you for how you were treated today, Mr. Thatcher…Ms. Moreno. I will let Mr. Callahan know that you are on your way up to his office, and then I will escort you there, personally." He acted all flustered as he picked up his phone, pressed a few buttons, and then mumbled into the receiver. For a moment, he flinched, as though he were being reprimanded. He hung up the phone, and got to his feet. "Follow me, please."

He led them to a hallway, then to an elevator. He reached into his pocket, pulled out a keycard, swiped it in the slot next to the doors, and they immediately opened. He allowed Alison and Addison to enter the elevator, before following them in, and swiped the card again. He pressed a large silver button, and the light around it illuminated a bright blue color. The large box began to move, and Addison's face got white. He gripped Allie's hand tightly. He had never been in an elevator before, and he became slightly claustrophobic in the metal box that was vibrating as it made its ascent.

When the doors opened, there were large windows right across from them, which gave them a beautifully breathtaking view of the Philadelphia skyline. They followed the man out and down the hall to one of two different doors. One had Ian's name on it, and the other had his sister, Caitlin's.

As they entered the large office suite, Ian was on the phone.

"Alright, I will speak with you about this later. Very important clients just arrived, so I need to let you go. Bye." And he slammed the phone down, before rising from his desk, coming around to greet them, a smile on his face.

"Ephraim, I would have expected better of you and the staff. These two people here are very important, and should be treated as such."

"In his defense, we don't exactly look like we belong in an establishment like this." Alison laughed. She was still in her scrubs, and her hair was disheveled. Adam looked as though she had just pulled him from a fight with a bear or wild animal, as he was covered in dust and dirt, and smelled of nature.

"Well, I have to admit…Addison, you have looked better, but that is beside the point. You, Ms. Moreno, are an absolute vision. You are everything that grandmother said and more. Please, have a seat. We have much to talk about." He waved at the older man, excusing him, so that they could get down to business.

After they had sat down, Ian began to type in his computer, and pulling out papers from his desk and filing cabinet.

"Now, I am unsure as to how familiar you are with all of this, Addison. Grandmother was very vague with me about how she knew you, or how you were related to Arthur and Elizabeth Thatcher exactly…"

"It is a long story." Addison gave Alison a sideways glance.

"Well, this account is probably one of the oldest accounts that CBT has on file, aside from Grandmother and Grandfather's account, of course. In fact, it is so old, it pre-dates our computer systems. We actually had to put it in the computer system, manually, from the original paperwork in the basement.

It was started by Mr. and Mrs. Thatcher themselves, in memory of their grandson, whom coincidentally shares your name. I am not going to ask questions about that, because, frankly, it is probably very confusing and so on…" He typed some more and then set some papers in front of Addison. "I just need you to sign these papers right here, stating that you are in fact the rightful owner of the account and all of its contents." He marked where he needed to sign, and handed him a pen. Addison picked up the pen and began to sign.

The anticipation was tugging at Addison's mind, as he signed paper after paper.

"Now that that little detail is taken care of, I need your written permission to allow me to discuss your account and any information about its contents and such in the presence of, as well as, *with* Ms. Moreno, in your absence." Without hesitation, he signed that paperwork. In his mind, the money was just as much hers as it was his.

"Alright. Now, as I was saying, this account is probably our oldest account, meaning that it has been here as long as CBT Inc. has existed. Now, being that it is a high interest-yielding account, what started out as just under $750,000, after compounded interest of over seventy years, we are looking at a monetary value of close to…" He turned his computer monitor, to show them the amount that sat in the account, and Alison nearly hit the floor. "Nice, little chunk of change, huh?"

"Is that good nest egg, Alison?" Addison choked on his amusement, but couldn't figure out why Alison suddenly got pale, and began to sway in her chair. "Allie, are you alright?"

"May I have a glass of water, please?" She gasped, fanning herself. She glanced over at Addison, and could see the sheer confusion on his face. "Do you not understand what that number on the screen means, Adam?" she glanced at him, her eyes as wide as the manager's had been. A young lady came in the office with a pitcher of ice water and a glass, already poured.

She took the glass and drank it, without looking away from his face.

"I see a lot of zeros, yes…but, I am more concerned about you right now."

"I am fine….just a bit in shock…" An anxious laugh escaped her.

"Now, on top of that, there is the matter of land and property ownership." Ian, slightly amused at the difference in their reactions, didn't want to wait to spring more news on them.

"Wait a second….there's more?" Alison struggled to swallow, as her throat went dry, despite just downing a glass of ice water. "I would think that that number on your screen was more than sufficient…but there is more. Oh, Heaven help us."

"Yeah, well, that is nothing compared to what you are about to hear."

"Seriously?!? Can I have a paper bag, too, please? I think that I may hyperventilate if I hear much more." She tried to straighten up in her seat, but her legs were like rubber and her hands were shaking. Ian reached into his desk drawer and handed her a small paper bag.

"Aside from the monetary account, you are also the co-owner of the town, formerly known as Woodcrest, Pennsylvania, as well as five classic town cars, which have been well-maintained and stored for you. There is also a climate-controlled storage warehouse with about thirty crates of classic art work, family heirlooms, etc."

"Adam…Woodcrest!!!" Alison squealed. Then her eyes rolled back and she passed out from utter shock. Addison jumped out of his chair, and ran to her side.

When she came to, she was slumped down on her chair, and Addison was leaning over the top of her, fanning her with his hat.

"Alison, honey…talk to me…You just passed out on me. Say something, sweetheart." He whispered, a look of deep concern on his face.

"I just had the weirdest dream." She sighed. She reached up, and he gripped her hand to help her sit up.

"A weird dream?"

"Yes, I just dreamt that Ian Callahan told you that you were a co-owner of Woodcrest…and that you were a…multi-Billionaire" She let out a half laugh, half squeal. "Isn't that absolutely ridiculous?"

"I hate to break this to you, Ms. Moreno, but that was not a dream. That is exactly what I just told Mr. Thatcher. I know that it is a lot to take in, but I assure you that it is all true." Ian knelt next to Alison's chair, and offered her another glass of water. "Drink this." He waited until she had drank the whole glass and swallowed before he continued. "I know that it is a lot to take in, but I have checked with all of our records, multiple times to make sure that I was giving you accurate information. Even I was in shock when I saw the information."

"Un-freaking-believable…"

"I know. I can only imagine what is going through your mind right now." He laughed, and got to his feet, returning to his seat behind his desk.

Alison sat and tried to absorb all the information that she had just been given, and the first emotion that surfaced was rage.

"So, let me see if I got this straight. He has had this money…sitting in this account for quite some time…just sitting here." Ian answered with a nod. "And yet, he has been living in the woods, off the land, in a crappy little shack for the last eight to nine months. How long ago did you give him this card, with your information the account number on it?"

"I gave him the card at the Gala, but I told him to come and see me when I first met him, about seven months ago. I was wondering when he would come in and finalize the paperwork, to be honest with you."

"Why didn't you take care of this seven months ago?!? You just hand him a card...don't explain anything to him...and expect him to understand how much it could change his life?"

"He didn't look like an ignorant man to me. I didn't think that I needed to explain anything to him." Ian was starting to get defensive at Alison's accusations.

"He isn't ignorant....not in the least, but some things go without saying...." She gripped Addison's hand and squeezed it. She knew that Addison was highly intelligent, but he was going from the early part of the twentieth century into the early part of the twenty-first century, and things were far different in how things worked now.

"I apologize if there was a misunderstanding or miscommunication."

"The money and all that....it is available to him now, right?"

"Of Course! I have his paperwork, the keys to the warehouse, the passcodes to the security systems, his debit cards, all which are right here in this envelope."

"Addison, let's go...before I have a stroke from my blood boiling." She began to mumble what sounded like extremely vulgar Italian swear words under her breath. He just nodded, shook Ian's hand, and took the envelope.

The fury in her subsided as they rode the elevator back to the lobby. Before they exited the elevator, she stashed the envelope in her purse, and held it close to her body as she and Addison made their way toward the doors to the parking garage.

As they were getting into the car, he was watching her.

"What just happened back there?"

"I'm sorry for that. I just find it very unfair that you have had the means to live a better life here, but were forced to live like an animal. We are going to go get you taken care of, right now."

"I know that you are upset, and I don't blame you. But, Alison…the last few months have been life changing for me, eye-opening. I have learned so much about what I am capable of…what I can do to survive on my own. I grew up in a house where others took care of all my needs; someone to cook for me, clean up after me, wash my clothes, dress me. This has been good for me." He looked at his hands, and how much they reminded him of his grandfather's…hard working hands. "Yes, having this money would have made things so much easier for me…but then, I never would have learned how to stand on my own two feet, without money as a cushion."

Alison could see the pride in his eyes at what he had managed to do on his own, even though it changed him vastly. She felt like a complete heel now, and probably made it sound like money was everything to her, when it really wasn't that important in the grand scheme of things.

"You're right. I'm sorry. It is just…You shouldn't have had to live like that. You still could have fended for yourself, and learned those things about yourself, but been able to be warm, and clean, and safe. You went from one extent to the other; from living like royalty to living like a peasant." She pulled out of the parking spot, and headed to a moderately priced hotel. After checking him in, they went to the room in silence.

She barely spoke two words, other than to show him how to use the shower. While he was washing up, she went to a local retail store, and walked out with a couple bags of clothes for him. She had spent so much time with him, dressing him that she knew what size clothes he needed without having to ask.

Her next stop was to a local pharmacy to get him essential things, such as deodorant, toothpaste, and so on.

She returned to the hotel, as he came out of the bathroom, wrapped in a towel. Her cheeks flushed at the sight of him. His physique had changed drastically since she had seen him last. All that manual labor to survive on his own caused his muscles to build quite noticeably. She had to control herself, so she began to remove all the toiletries from the shopping bag. She took the shave cream, razor, and some first aid items she had bought, and set them on the sink area. She set out some clothes for him, and then got a chair for him to sit.

"Come here a minute, please." He sighed, catching her arm as she walked by him. He held her in front of him, the towel still the only thing covering him. When he finally had her attention, he leaned his head down and gave her a feather-sift kiss on the lips. "Thank you for doing all this…buying all this for me. It means a lot, you trying to take care of me…even after all this time."

"Don't mention it. Now, please sit so I get you shaved, and get those cuts and scratches taken care of." Her tone was rather cold, as she pulled away from him. The hurt in his eyes was very clear, but he sat down, and let her get to work.

When she was done, she gave him a kiss on the forehead, and apologized to him once more, before handing him the key to his room, and turning to the door.

"Where are you going? I thought that we were going to talk." He grasped her hand.

"What is the point of talking? You saw how I reacted. You deserve someone who doesn't care about money…and obviously, I care more about it than I thought I did. Maybe Lena was right about me after all. Just like her, I look at you and see money signs. I am just like her."

"Alison…don't be like that, please. You were just worried about my well-being. It has nothing to do with money. You aren't like that, and I know that, whole-heartedly. You and Lena are nothing alike." He pulled her closer, and sat on the edge of the bed. She sat down as well, with her back to him. She felt like a stranger, even to herself.

"You saw how I reacted back there. I was ridiculous. I acted as though that was *my* money, and it isn't." She took the envelope out of her purse. She also handed him the change from the money she withdrew from the bank for his clothes and toiletries, and gave him the receipts. "The receipts for the money I spent are right there. All the money is accounted for. I am going to leave you to do…whatever you need to do."

"Alison, stop this! What has gotten into you?!"

"I just came to the realization that you can now live a full and happy life, and you don't need me. You could own all of Philadelphia if you wanted. You could be with anyone, anyone at all at your side. You don't need frumpy, old me. You said it yourself. You learned to take care of yourself, without having to depend on anyone else. You don't need me to take care of you anymore."

"What has gotten into you, Alison? You are not frumpy. You are beautiful….and I *do* need you. I need you here…with me! Please. Talk to me! If this is about the money, I will donate it all to the bank….I will give it all up. If the money is what has made you feel overwhelmed, it can all go! I don't need it!!! I need you!!" He wrapped his arms around her from behind, and held her close to him. "Don't you understand that you are worth more than any amount of money in the world to me? You are worth more to me than the air I breathe." He whispered in her ear. To hold her so close to him, the scent of her hair lingering in his nostrils, it was like heaven. With his face clean shaven, he could feel the heat from her skin against his.

Her hands, instinctively, went to his and she wove her fingers into his. Her heart hurt, and yet it didn't ache as it had at the thought of never seeing him again. It hurt at the thought that he was back in her life, and she had even less to offer him than before. Both of them had changed since they had parted ways, and she feared that the changes were so drastic that nothing would ever be the same between them.

"Haven't you noticed that both of us have changed since we were together in Woodcrest? How can you say that you still love me the same as before? Were it not for me, you would still be there, happy and with your family."

"No I wouldn't. I would be laying in my bedroom, in a coma, trapped in my own personal hell. You brought me out of it...YOU! You were the tether, the life preserver that saved me from drowning in the darkness. Were it not for you, I would be lost." He held her closely, and continued to whisper in her ear. "True, we have changed...but that doesn't mean that my feelings have changed for you. I went through all this because of you, because I couldn't live my life without you. I changed for you. I wanted to prove to you, and to myself, that I was worthy of all the love and faith you had given me. I didn't want to be the spoiled rich boy. I am more than that, and I needed to prove that."

"I never saw you like that."

"I know, but that is why I had to go through all this; to be the man you saw when you looked at me. Now, I can truly be the man you need, the man that you truly deserve. I can now take care of you, as you took care of me." He set his chin on her shoulder, and held her as she sobbed. "Don't you even think for a second that I don't need you, because that is the farthest from the truth. You say that I could have anyone, but I don't want just anyone...I want you, and only you."

"You only say that because that is what you think I want to hear.

"I am saying it because that is how I feel. You and I are connected." He grabbed her right hand, and held it in front of her face. "Do you see that ring? That was a promise I made to you. And now, the impossible has become possible. All the things that you were worried would happen...altering events and such...did you notice anything different from how things were before?" It took her a few minutes to think. Something struck her odd, so she turned to look at him.

"You said that you were the one who closed off the interstate, that you put the detour sign up, and the city sign…they weren't there until *you* put them there?"

"I swear on my grandparents' graves…I did that. I did it because that is what you wrote in your journal. Same as with the retirement home. It was because of the fire, the loss of your job…that made you have to make the journey to Philadelphia."

"Did you set that fire?! Please tell me you weren't the one who burned down Holly Oaks Retirement Home!"

"You think I did that?!" He rolled his eyes. "Tell me, love, do you believe that I would risk the lives of sixty-some sweet old people just to have you in my life? I love you more than anything, and though I would kill for you, I would not do something like that. They were sweet old people! That would be like killing my grandparents!" He leapt up from the bed, looking appalled. "I was the one who pulled a large majority of them from the building that night. I, however, know who set the fire…and so do you."

"Yes, I do. It was Mrs. Bancroft, that old bat!! She probably tried to frame me and get me fired." Thinking of the old lady made her mad.

"Think about it…can you think of one person, who would be older than dirt by now, who would do everything in their power to ruin your life and make you miserable…and me as well?" He gave her a look, as he leaned over her, a look of blind fury in his eyes.

"Madison told me that Mrs. Bancroft hated the new orderly as much as she hated me…Holy Mary!!!!" her eyes shot wide open, and she could hardly believe that it had never occurred to her before. "Helena Bancroft….That was Lena!?"

"Yes ma'am!"

"Madison also told me that you pulled her from the building just seconds before it went up in flames."

"I know what you are thinking, and sadly, it was one of my weaker moments. I was so tempted to leave her there and let her burn. I found her stuck in her room. She had fallen from her chair, and couldn't get out of her room. I saw her laying there. At first, I didn't know it was her. Then she said that she hoped I burned in Hell for what you and I did to her back in nineteen thirty eight…and that she blamed her horrible life on both of us. Apparently, she was not aware that you had the day off that day."

"Wait a second…she set the fire to punish both of us?"

"Yes."

"But you and I were never there at the same time…if we had been, I would have seen you." Alison gulped.

"Sometimes we were. I would stay hidden and catch glimpses of you coming in for your shift right before I would clock out…or I would come early and watch you leave for the night."

"You sneaky codger!" She laughed as she punched him lightly in the shoulder.

"Anyway, getting back to it, she thought you were on duty and just avoiding her room that day. She was pretty sneaky, because she knew our routines. She had timed it perfectly to coincide with both of us being there at the same time. She also knew that neither of us would run for safety without making sure everyone else was safe."

"If she knew you were there, and she remembered me, why didn't she ever say anything? I just thought she was just a nasty old woman."

"I think that was part of her plan. Neither of us knew what she would look like as an old woman, so she could keep her identity secret."

"So, indirectly, she was part of the reason I came to Woodcrest. She set the fire that made me lose my job…and since I had no job, I couldn't afford my half of the rent. Since I couldn't afford the rent, I had to move back home with my parents, which took me down that interstate…and I had to detour through Woodcrest. Because I came to Woodcrest, I prevented the two of you from getting married, which made her hate us, which led her to harboring a seventy-some year grudge towards us, which led to her setting that fire…" She put her hand to her head. "Oh my. My head hurts now."

"Mine too. However that isn't the end of the craziness."

"I think I have an idea. There was no paradox, no risk of a butterfly effect because it had already happened?"

"Pretty much. You saved the timeline by taking my detour. Had you taken the other road…"

"What other road?! There was no other road. There was only the interstate and the detour." Alison was even more confused.

"There was another road…you turned right to go to Woodcrest. If you had turned left at the junction, it would have taken you about five miles out of the way, but it would have led you back to the interstate. By me putting the Woodcrest sign up, and then the detour sign pointing for you to go right, you never noticed the gravel road to your left. It's called 'Power of Suggestion.' If you had turned left off of the junction, everything would be different, and the timeline would have to adjust accordingly."

"But, if I had turned left, I never would have come to Woodcrest…never would have caused Lena to hate me enough to set that fire."

"Not necessarily. I did some reading in the six months I was here before you. Apparently, by just a change of direction, you would not have stopped the fire, just the circumstances. If you had turned left, you never would have come to Woodcrest, which meant that Lena never would have known you, and just been a normal elderly patient. I also would not have come, which meant that I would not have been there to pull all those people from the fire, and there would have been lives lost that night. And if I never came here after you, then the interstate would have been closed for another reason, and you would have seen Woodcrest as it is now, deserted. You wouldn't have known Becky, and therefore wouldn't have gone to the Gala either."

"Please stop. I have a migraine now."

"But don't you understand, sweetheart. This was all supposed to happen. This was the way it was always supposed to be."

"But, what about your grandparents? Think of the time that you lost with them by coming here."

"That day, when they called me into the office…that is what we were discussing. My grandparents wanted me to be happy, and be with someone who truly loved me. They knew that I wouldn't be able to get on with my life. They knew that I would never be able to find the kind of love with anyone else like I had with you. They gave me their blessing."

"So, they knew that you were going to come after me…Even when I was saying goodbye to them, they knew that you would follow me through."

"Yes. Now, mind you, none of us knew what was going to happen if I followed you. But, I learned from a beautiful person that I needed to take a leap of faith." He tweaked her nose, lovingly. "So, I took a little time to gather a few things, and then, with your journal in my hand, I went through the silver mist. I ended up on the side of the road right outside Woodcrest as she is now."

"You have blown my mind, Addison Xavier Thatcher."

"And you have made me the happiest man on Earth. We are together again." He took her hand and kissed her palm. "Do you forgive me for making you wait so long? For making you cry?"

"You were forgiven as soon as I saw your face." She ran her hand through his wet, tousled hair. "And to be honest, if I was going to fall for your looks, this would be the time. You are seriously…Mmmhmm…you look good enough to eat. You look more like the cover of a smutty romance novel, and less like a preppy, yuppie, rich boy with your hoity-toity waistcoats and pleated slacks…" She ran her hand down the copper skin on his muscular chest.

"Is that so?" There was an animalistic growl in his voice, and he leaned closer to her, grabbing her wrist.

"Oh yes, most definitely. What are you gonna do about it?" The teasing tone in her voice set him off. He pounced at her, and pinned her to the bed, her hands above her head. Alison felt like she had been taken back to the afternoon in the stables, only it was cleaner here, and it smelled significantly better. He straddled her, and leaned in toward her, a low growl in the back of his throat.

"I'll show you what I'm gonna do about it." He whispered, his breath mingling with hers. He closed the gap, and kissed her as he would have in the straw that day, with a wolf-like hunger. It was the most erotic, primal kiss, the kind that you would only read in books or see in the movies.

Her heart, shattered to bits by the pain and heartache, was now whole again and swelling in her chest. Cinderella had found her prince; no glass slipper required.

When they both had satisfied their need of finishing what they had started, they laid on the bed, and just listened to one another breathe. Though they had been tempted to do more than smother each other in kisses, they kept from going farther. Their respect for saving the other things for their wedding night kept them from stripping one another down, and soiling the sheets.

Addison rolled over, and laid on his stomach, propping himself up in his elbows. Looking at the woman he loved, laying on the bed next to him, he had found a kind of contentment that he had been missing for a while. So many times, he was tempted to just show up at her door, and reveal himself to her, just so he could feel the touch of her soft skin, the warmth of her arms around him, and the overwhelming glow that consumed his heart when she smiled at him.

"I want to meet your parents." He bluntly stated.

"Why? When?" She turned her head, and reached up to sweep his hair from his face.

"Because…I have a promise to keep, and I will leave the when up to you. However, I don't want to wait too long."

"Alright. How about next Friday? That will give my mom enough time to plan and prepare food. Come hungry…she's Italian!"

"What about your father?"

"Let me deal with him." She was both excited and nervous. Addison had kept his promise. He was going to be able to ask for her parents' blessing. Knowing her mother, that will be a piece of cake. She was more concerned about her father. He would be the one to convince, and it would take a lot of willpower, and bravery to face him. Her father was a military man, and he was going to be faced with giving his blessing to marry his only daughter to a complete stranger. Alison's stomach began to do somersaults.

Chapter Twenty-Nine

After finding out that the love of her life was alive, the idea of voluntarily admitting herself into Cliffmoore was out of the question. She wasn't crazy, and she had Addison to prove it. Though, telling everyone that he was her boyfriend and he was technically over a hundred years old seemed kind of far-fetched and the men in the Looney Wagon would surely come for her in record time. It was best to keep his origin and year of birth between them.

As far as the discussion had ended, Alison headed home. It was dark outside, and she knew her mom was in a panic, as she had received notifications of five missed calls to her cell phone.

Slowly opening the screen door, she tried to prevent it from creaking, but to no avail. As soon as she swung the door about six inches, the door creaked so loud that you would think that it had never been greased…ever.

"Alison Moreno! Where have you been? You should have been home hours ago. I called at least a dozen times, and you didn't answer. I was afraid that something had happened to you again. Your father, thinking that you had completely gone off your rocker, decided to drive to that town and look for you there."

"First of all, Hi mom. My day was fine, thanks for asking. I quit my job at Bruckner's; a job that I absolutely loved, by the way. Secondly, you only called five times, not a dozen. And lastly, I think that dad is the one that should check into Cliffmoore if he drove all the way out to Woodcrest, thinking I was going to go hide out there. Has he come home yet?" She kissed her mom on the head and then poured herself a glass of wine before sitting at the kitchen table.

"No, he called about twenty minutes ago and said that you weren't at the town, and that he was going to stop at Bruckner's on his way home."

"Good. That gives me about a half an hour to talk to my level-headed parent." She sighed and set her glass down. "Mom, do you remember the guy…from the Gala? The one who swept me off my feet and then ran?"

"Yes…yes, I know who he is. He was the same young man who found you on the side of the road and carried you six miles to the hospital in Lancaster."

"Well, I have good news and bad news…which do you want first?" She got an awkward smirk on her face.

"The good news, I suppose." Maria snatched Alison's wine glass and took a drink.

"Well, I found him…or rather he found me." The look on her face made Maria jump with excitement. "It turns out that his family, and Mrs. Callahan are rather close and he was there, visiting when I went to see her and say goodbye."

"You don't say?! What a small world!" Her over-exuberance at her daughter's news was quite humorous to watch. "So, did he explain to you why he ran off…twice?"

"Twice?"

"Yes, he ran off on you at the party, but he also ran off at the hospital before you father and I had a chance to thank him."

"Well, he probably ran off at the hospital because he was dodging the police…" Alison kept a straight face, and took a sip of her merlot.

"The police?!" Her mother's face got pale and her smile turned to a frown.

"I'm kidding, mama." She laughed, and placed her hand on her mother's. "Actually, he knew that you and dad were grateful, so there was no need to say it. He didn't want to monopolize your time with the niceties when I was laying in the bed. He also said that he was sweaty and dirty. He didn't want to impose." Obviously, that was a legitimate reason for him to leave the hospital, because Maria smiled, and nodded as if she completely understood.

"And what about the Gala?"

"Well, he ate the clams." Alison rubbed her stomach and gave a sour look. After a moment, her mother picked up on the visual hints, and mimicked the face she made. "He had to go…bad. He said that by the time he got back, we were already gone."

"Oh!" She was going to say more, but she watched as a smile grew on Alison's face. "Wait a minute…are you serious? Is that really what happened, or are you just playing with me again?" She pointed her finger at her daughter and gave a suspicious smile.

"I'm joking. No, he got a bad case of nerves. He realized who I was, saw you and dad on the balcony, and panicked."

"Poor dear."

"Yes, but he did apologize to me, sincerely, and asked me out. I couldn't refuse. There was definite chemistry between us…" Alison was trying her best to be as truthful as possible, without giving away too much. "That is where I have been all evening…with him."

"And you enjoyed yourself, yes?" Maria was overjoyed at hearing that her daughter had been on a date with an attractive man…an attractive man who was romantic and had already saved her life. Alison smiled, shyly, and nodded. "So, that was the good news. What is the bad news? He's not married, is he?"

"No, mama, he's not married."

"Is he…" she leaned forward, and whispered the rest of her question. "…gay?" Her volume went back to normal. "I mean, there is absolutely nothing wrong it. They are sweet as pie and they have the best taste in clothes, food, décor…they are wonderful people."

"No, mama. He isn't gay."

"Well, what is the bad news, then?" she took another swig of wine from her daughter's glass.

"He would like to meet you and dad…formally. And he's like to do it next Friday."

"That isn't bad news! That is fabulous news! What kind of food does he like? I can make bruschetta, fried calamari…should we have lasagna or Ragù alla bolognese? Dessert could be homemade gelato or cannoli…Oh, I must make a list." She jumped up from the table and began to buzz around the kitchen, looking at what she had and what she needed.

Alison knew her mother would be excited, not only because she would get to meet a boy interested in her little Alison, but because she loved to cook. She didn't just love to cook, she lived to cook, and when there were guests, and she was in total "Italian mama" mode. Alison hoped that Addison liked Italian food, because there was going to be a lot of it.

After a short while, she heard her father's car pull in the driveway. She settled herself in for a long lecture from her father. Sitting comfortably on the couch, she braced herself. What came from her father was totally unexpected. She watched as he calmly walked through the front door, hung his keys on the hook, remove his coat and hat and hang them on the rack, and then proceed into the kitchen. After hearing her mother scream at him in Italian, he walked swiftly out of the kitchen, and park himself in his chair.

"What has gotten into her?! She's in full-blown 'Italian' mode! Who's coming over for dinner?"

"Hi dad. Nice to see you, too." Alison spoke, sarcastically.

"Hello. Now, answer my question. Why did your mother nearly chop my hand off with the cleaver when I looked into the fridge? Who's coming over to have dinner with us? She's got a shopping list as long as my arm."

"Well, if you must know, I am seeing someone…and he wants to meet my parents. He's coming to dinner next Friday evening." She acted very nonchalant.

"Is it the man that you were seen leaving work with today?" He asked as he picked up his newspaper, and flipped through it to the section he wanted.

"You went to my work…or rather, the place I used to work until I quit so I could admit myself into a psychiatric hospital?" The sarcasm was back.

"Admitting yourself into Cliffmoore will put a damper on your boyfriend coming for dinner, will it not?" He raised the paper so it covered his face.

"Yes, dad. I am pretty sure it will. Can I admit myself after dessert? I would hate to miss out on mama's cannoli." She crossed her arms, upset that her father was acting as if nothing was wrong.

Of all the things to inherit from her parents, she inherited her mother's foul Italian temper and flare for filthy language, but she inherited her father's Mexican sarcasm, stubbornness, and the inability to control herself when she her temper *did* flare up. It was a deadly combination, especially because she used both of them, in quick succession, on her father most of the time.

"Sure, sweetheart. You wouldn't want to miss those cannoli. They are the best in Philly." He replied, dryly.

"Um, dad…aren't you curious as to where I was all afternoon? And why I was leaving work with a strange man?"

"As long as I don't have to hear about your year in that derelict town, I honestly could care less where you have been and whom you have been with. What time will he be here on Friday? I want to clean and polish my shotgun."

"Dad!! For the love of Saint Peter…stop acting like this!" She became rigid and sat at the edge of the couch.

"What would you have me say, Alison? I honestly have nothing to say. You are a grown woman. I hope you have plans as to what you are going to do now that you are unemployed. They told me that you quit, and finished your shift. When I asked what reason you gave them for leaving, you told them that your father was having you committed. They scolded me, and said that I should be ashamed of myself for thinking that you have gone crazy."

"It's the truth. You talked to the doctor there…you were going to have me committed. I heard you talking to mom, remember?"

"That Italian temper is going to get you in trouble one day. If you…and your mother…had let me finish what I was saying, you would have heard me say that I talked to him about your delusions, and he said that it was your mind's way of coping with a traumatic situation, like PTSD. He said to give you time, and to not be so hard on you, because it only makes the situation worse." Throughout the conversation, he never looked out from behind the paper.

"So, you aren't going to have me committed, and I don't have to admit myself? I quit my job for nothing?!" She rose from the couch, and snatched the paper out of her father's hands.

"You still have a job there. They said that they refused to lose one of their best nurses, nor would they accept your resignation. They said they will see you for your shift on Monday. Now, may I have my paper back, please?"

"Sometimes, I wish I had mom's knack of wielding a cleaver. I'd cut that smug look right off your stupid old face, daddy!" She smirked, and put the paper in her father's lap, before kissing his head and heading up to her room.

"You know that you enjoy our talks as much as I do, pumpkin."

Maria had been buzzing around the house, nonstop, for a week. She had cleaned things that didn't need cleaning, just because she saw a speck of dust near it. She wanted everything to be perfect. And as far as preparing a meal for their guest, he was in for a surprise. Alison had to clean off the side table in the dining room to make room for all the food that wouldn't fit on the table.

Her heart was thudding as she looked in the mirror. Tonight was a big night. Tonight, both of her worlds would come together. Her nerves were getting the best of her as she made her way down the stairs. Salvador was in the living room, reading his paper as usual, and Maria was busy in the kitchen, making certain that everything was going to be ready in time.

Alison snuck out the front door, and waited on the front porch for Addison to arrive. She had convinced him to buy a car, as showing up to her parents' house in the beat up truck or on horseback would not make a good impression. He had chosen a modest looking sedan, but insisted that it be fully loaded. She spent the rest of the week helping not to look like a student driver. The cars here were far different from the cars back in his day, and they took some getting used to..

She saw his silver car pull into the driveway, and she rushed to the driver's door just as he cut the engine.

"Any problems?" She whispered to him, hoping that her parents hadn't heard the ca pull in the driveway.

"I drove the way you taught me, with caution. I was aware of my surroundings and I didn't run a stop sign or a red light one time." He seemed so proud of himself, but agitated that Alison was talking to him like a child. "Are you ready for this? It's a big night." The smile on his face was endearing, and she knew what he was referring to.

"Listen…about that…You can't talk to them about that tonight. As far as they know, we have only been seeing each other for a week. This is the first time they are meeting you."

"But, we have been together for longer than a week, Alison."

"You and I know that…but they don't. I have already explained it to you. Be yourself, enjoy tonight, and don't lie when they ask you questions, but don't tell them the whole truth either." She kissed him. "By the way, you look very nice. Where did you get the suit?"

"The lady at Martindale's helped me. She was very courteous." He put his hands in his jacket pockets, and struck a pose. "I almost forgot!" He opened his back door, and pulled two bouquets out. "This is for you…purple orchids are your favorite if I remember correctly." He handed the flowers to her, and kissed her on the cheek.

"They are my favorite, and they are beautiful. Thank you." She cradled the bouquet of flowers on one arm, and took his hand. "I assume those are for my mom."

"No, I got them for your father…figured they would soften him up." He began laughing when she gave him a look of confusion. "Of course they are for your mother. Don't give me that look."

They climbed the stairs and he opened the door for her.

"Mom! Dad! He's here!" It didn't take them long to respond. They both came rather quickly, as though they were waiting anxiously.

"How delightful! Please…come in!" Maria bubbled, and came forward. "Benvenuto!"

"This is my mother, Maria." She leaned closer and began to whisper in his ear. "She said 'Welcome.' If you need me to…" Alison was about to tell Addison that she would translate for him whenever her mother spoke Italian, but he cut her off.

"Molte grazie! è un piacere conoscerla." He leaned forward and kissed Maria sweetly on the cheek and handed her a bouquet of beautiful white lilies.

"Grazie! Parla italiano?" Maria was doe eyes and entranced by Addison.

"Solo un po'." He smiled, and Maria giggled. "Uh…Hai degli occhi bellissimi." At his last words, Maria blushed and began to giggle even more.

"Lei è molto gentile." Maria looked like she was in love.

"Now, hold on…what is going on?" Thoroughly confused, Salvador was getting agitated as he didn't speak Italian and his wife was acting like a teenage girl with a crush. "Alison, what are they saying?" He whispered in his daughter's ear.

"Mama said welcome, then Addison said 'Thank you so much. It's nice to meet you.' Then Addison handed her the flowers and she thanked him. She asked if he spoke Italian and he told he just speaks a little." She smiled and cleared her throat.

"What did he say to her after that? She's mooning over him."

"He told her that she had beautiful eyes. And she said he was very kind." She snickered at the way her parents were acting. Her father seemed jealous, and her mother was about to swoon. "Addison, this is my father, Salvador." She grabbed his arm and turned his attention to the older gentleman, who was currently shooting him dirty looks.

"Ah! Hola, Señor Moreno. Encantado de conocerle." Addison, once again, surprised everyone when he started speaking in Spanish. "Usted tiene una hermosa hija." He gave Salvador a big smile and he couldn't help but to smile back.

"Okay…can we speak English now?" Alison laughed, as she blushed because of what he had just said to her father.

"Sorry. I couldn't help myself." Addison smiled. "He does have a beautiful daughter."

"Alright, Mom...dad... this is Addison Thatcher. You can just call him Adam."

"Well, are you going to stand in the foyer all night, or are you going to come in?" Sal seemed a lot more welcoming now. Alison was both impressed and touched that Adam had learned a bit of both of her parents' languages. The four of them went into the living room, and sat down.

"You have a very lovely home. Thank you so much for inviting me."

"If I'm not mistaken, you planned this little meeting yourself." Salvador said, still smiling.

"Daddy!"

"No, Alison...he's right." He turned his attention back to the other man. "You are not mistaken. I made the statement to Alison that I wanted to meet you, and she suggested us doing it tonight. I was under the assumption that she had asked the both of you if you were alright with that. If this is a bad time, I am sure that we could plan it for a different time."

"No, my dear boy." Maria shot her husband a look and he cleared his throat. "Alison told us you wanted to meet us last week. If there had been a conflict, we would have let you know before now."

"Yes, my wife is right. You are quite welcome. We would actually like to extend our gratitude to you. We know you are the one that got Alison to the hospital in Lancaster a few months back. Since you left before we had a chance to thank you then, we would like to extend our thanks to you now. You saved our little girl's life that day." He held out his hand to Addison, and Addison shook it.

"Sir, I assure you that I only did what any other person would have done, had they been faced with the same situation."

"No, you didn't. You did what you thought was right. I don't know of too many people who would find a stranger and make the decision to help them, let alone, carry that stranger six miles…on foot, to a hospital. Did you not have a vehicle?"

"I had a truck, sir, but it was filthy and rusted. I figured that it would just be easier to carry her. I know it sound strange, but that is just what happened."

"You carried her because you didn't want to get her dirty?!"

"If that is how you want to put it, yes. I didn't want to get her dirty."

"That is the strangest thing that I have ever heard." Perplexed, he looked at Addison and tilted his head as though trying to see his reasoning.

"It doesn't matter how he got her there, Salvador. The point is that he did a good deed and didn't ask for anything in return." Maria chimed in.

"I appreciate the gratitude, but it really isn't necessary. You don't need to thank me, really. I am just glad that she is okay."

"That's all well and good, but could you please explain to me why you ran off on her at the gala? We know it was you. We saw your face. We remembered you from the hospital."

"I already told you why he left, dad."

"I want to hear it from him, sweetheart. I want him to give me a reason for why he abandoned you, and we spent the whole night looking for him. You cried for two days."

"He feels bad enough, daddy. He apologized to me several times for that. Can't you just let it go?" she pleaded with her father.

"No, I can't let it go. I had to watch your face go from happiness to total sadness and desperation. I had to sit here and listen to you cry over it."

"It wasn't all about him…it was about…"

"If I have to hear about this fantasy boyfriend from that town again, I am calling the doctor." His words rang in

Addison's ears, because he knew exactly what he was referring to.

"Sir, in all honesty, I do not have a legitimate excuse for what I did to her that night. Saying that I ran scared, that I chickened out...they aren't good enough reasons for leaving without explanation. It was wrong, and I can never apologize enough for the pain I caused. I am just glad that she was willing to give me another chance. I am grateful that she has such a big heart, that she was willing to put the past aside and start fresh."

"Where's my apology? Maria's? We were out there all night, scouring the streets for you as well."

"Stop this!" Alison had had enough of her father's behavior. "I will not sit here, and listen to you speak to him as if he were a criminal. He is a human being. He made a mistake. Are you so perfect...so without flaws or mistakes...that you can sit there and judge him?" She was so furious. "I think that, if anyone has made a mistake worth apologizing to you for, it's me!"

"What do you have to apologize for?"

"I need to apologize because I thought that, for one night, you could stop being you and just be my father. I thought that you could put aside your feelings and think of mine. I like Addison...a lot. He is the first guy I have ever brought home to meet you and mama...and you are ruining it!" Tears welled in her eyes. "As far as him making me cry, daddy...I cried over what he did for two days. I have cried for a lot longer over the things you've done. If anyone should have to explain himself...it should be you." As soon as the words came out, she walked out of the room, and went to the kitchen.

"You just couldn't resist, could you, Sal? You couldn't just have a nice evening, and keep your opinions and judgements to yourself to make her happy." Maria rose from her chair and walked over to Addison. "Adam, you are a very sweet young man, and you make my daughter smile. That is all that matters to me. I am glad that she found you. Destino!" she bent over and kissed him on one cheek and then the other. She rounded on her heels and looked straight at her husband. "You…go…fix! NOW!" She pointed at him, then the kitchen, and made her orders firm with a stomp of her foot. She looked back at Addison. "We'll be right back. You just make yourself comfortable. Would you like something to drink?"

"No thank you, ma'am." There was a knot in his stomach as he watched Allie's parents follow her into the kitchen. Leaning forward, he put his face in his hands. A part of him was telling him that this was necessary if he ever wanted to get their blessings for him to marry their daughter. However, a part of him was saying that he didn't deserve to be treated with such disrespect. He wanted to go and grab Alison by the hand and leave. Instead of doing what he wanted to do, he was doing what he thought was right for her sake, so he just sat and waited.

By the time that Maria and Salvador had entered the kitchen, Alison was working on her second glass of wine.

"Your father has something that he needs to say to you. Sal?" Maria walked over and put her arm around her daughter.

"You are right, pumpkin. I let my opinions and judgements take over, and I wasn't thinking of what this night meant to you. I am so sorry that I hurt you."

"As bad as it may sound, I don't believe you. I know that mama made you come in here and apologize. But, I am not the one you owe the apology to. I knew how you were, but I thought that you loved me enough that you would…" she stopped, and sniffled. "It doesn't matter. Let's just eat dinner."

"It does matter. I just needed to hear him say that he was sorry for the hurt he caused you."

"Why does he have to apologize to you for hurting me? He apologized to me. I have forgiven him. What happened was in the past. This is the present. He cares about me. He sees me…really sees me. And I am happy. Isn't that enough?" She grabbed the wine bottle off the counter, and was about to refill her glass, but Maria stopped her.

"Yes. It's enough. I'm sorry, Alison." This time, Sal's apology was more sincere.

Alison set her glass down, grabbed the bottle instead, and walked past her father. She was so hurt and extremely upset with the way things had spun out of control. As she made her way through the dining room, she spotted Addison sitting alone in the living room. She just wanted to grab him and run away.

She took a swig from the bottle, set it on the table, and walked over, and stopped in the doorway of the living room.

"Is everything okay?" He asked her, noting that along with her red puffy eyes, she was flushed and her eyes seemed slightly glazed over. He got up and walked to her.

"No. Nothing is okay. This whole night is a disaster. My dad is so hell bent on making me miserable…He doesn't understand how important you are to me."

"It wasn't as bad as you are making it out to be. His questioning bothered you more than it did me. He is your father, Allie. He is just trying to look out for you and protect you. That is what dad's do. He wants what is best for you, sweetheart."

"But, you have already paid your penance for what happened. Why is he pushing so hard?"

"…Because of what I did to you. If tonight had gone perfectly, and he hadn't come down hard on me the way he did, then there would have been something wrong." He made her sit down on the couch because she began to sway. He knelt on the floor in front of her, and held her hands.

"So, you aren't going to run for the hills?"

"No…running away seems to be your forte, if I am not mistaken." He laughed, teasing her about all the times that she had attempted to run when things got dicey. "I am more of the 'dig my heels in and do the impossible, no matter what it takes' kinda guy. We found each other again, didn't we?"

"Why are you so perfect?" She smiled, weakly, as the effects of the wine took effect. She closed her eyes, and opened them slowly, and then hiccupped.

"I'm not perfect."

"No...you are. You are took good to me. You are so understanding, and sweet, and kind, and you speak multiple languages...perfectly, might I add."

"Stay here. You are a bit tipsy. I am gonna help you clear your head, and then we are going to continue the night as planned." He moved a pillow and urged her to lie down until he came back. He got up, and turned to go to the kitchen. That was when he saw her parents standing in the kitchen doorway. He realized at that moment that they had heard the conversation and interaction between their daughter and her new beau.

"She had had a bit too much wine to drink." He grabbed the wine bottle off of the dining room table and walked towards the spectators. "May I have a glass of water, preferably room temperature or cool. Cold water will just upset her stomach." He handed the partially drank bottle to Maria, and leaned against the doorframe, just a few feet from Salvador.

"Did you mean all that stuff you said to Alison? I mean, about you understanding why I was pressing you so hard?"

"Honestly, I think that you had good intentions, but your delivery was a little rusty." He sighed and stared at the floor. Lifting his head, he looked at Sal, and said what was on his mind. "You obviously love Allie very much, and you only want the best for her, sir. But, she was right on one thing. I am only human. I made some mistakes in my life that I am most certainly ashamed of, but none that compare to the night of the gala. I hurt her bad. I made her cry. I made her doubt herself. I will have to live with that. I will have to face that reality every time I look into her eyes." He turned and leaned back against the doorframe, and crossed his arms over his chest.

"She is my little girl…my only little girl. I have to be the father that she deserves, not the one she wants. If that means, at the end of the day, that she hates me…so be it. She hasn't had the easiest life. I wasn't always there for her when she needed me. She had to fend for herself a lot, with her mother and I having to work to make ends meet."

"You were trying to provide for her. There is nothing wrong with that."

"There is when you miss out on watching your only child grow up and you aren't part of it. She has always been heavier than other girls her age, and has had to face rejection more than most. Kids can be cruel, you know?"

"So, you need to be sure that, were a guy to show interest, that their intentions were pure..." He nodded in understanding. "She's had some bad experiences, I take it. Guys out to hurt her for sport?"

"Unfortunately, yes. Even one is too many, and she has had more bad experiences than good ones."

"I know that you have probably been told this before, but I am not out to hurt your little girl. I'm really not." He cleared his throat and looked at Sal again. "I love her."

Just then, Maria walked over with the glass of water, and a cool cloth. He took them from her, and smiled his crooked smile. Without another word, he walked back to the living room, and knelt on the floor. They watched as he helped her to drink the water, and wiped her face with the cloth. They observed how gentle and kind he was, how he looked at her, and then they looked at one another.

"Did I hear him say what I think I did? Did he just tell you he loved her?" Maria asked, watching the heartwarming way that he took care of their child.

"I believe he did, my sweet. And I am inclined to believe him."

After she had drank a few glasses of water, and gotten her bearings, they all sat down at the table for dinner.

Addison had switched out her glass of wine for a cup of tea. Pulling her chair out for her, he allowed the ladies to sit before he took his seat.

"Mrs. Moreno, all this food looks absolutely wonderful. You really didn't have to make so much." He smiled, as he got a sampling of a little of everything.

"Obviously, you have never been to an authentic Italian restaurant, or to the house of an Italian woman. This is a normal Sunday dinner for us." Sal commented, passing the dishes along.

"One thing is for sure, I am planning on spending my Sundays here…This food is delicious. You are a wonderful cook, Ma'am." He lifted a fork full of spaghetti to his mouth, and his eyes rolled back into his head, as he savored the taste of authentic homemade food. He hadn't had it in so long, and he couldn't get enough.

"Eat as much as you like, Addison. There is plenty here. Just make sure that you save room for my Cannoli." Maria laughed.

"That's a typical Italian woman for you…always trying to fatten you up." Alison giggled, feeling much better.

"Let's hope that you got your mother's cooking genes. I could get used to this. I am going to have to buy bigger pants if I am fed like this." Addison smiled as he gave her a sideways glance.

The atmosphere had changed dramatically, and there was no tension in the air. She was oblivious to the conversation that went on between her father and Addison, and they had no intention of mentioning it.

After dinner, the women cleared the table, with a bit of Addison's help, and then he joined Alison's father back in the living room, while the women did the dishes.

"So, Addison...since we got off to a rocky start, I would like to start over fresh. Is that alright with you?" Sal unfastened his belt, and let out a grunt and then a sigh of relief.

"I would like that very much."

"Good." He patted his legs in agreement, and then folded his arms over his chest. "So, Addison, if you don't mind me asking...what do you do for a living?"

"I am a skilled tradesman, self-taught."

"Self-taught, ay? And what exactly do skilled tradesmen do?" He seemed genuinely interested in the answer.

"Well, I do everything really...carpentry, masonry, landscaping...you name it, and I can do it. And if I don't know how to do it, I learn."

"That is wonderful. You are always striving to better yourself...determined and motivated. I like that!" Sal clapped his hands, and looked delighted. "Is the pay pretty good?"

"Generally, it is a moderate wage. However, I don't do it for the money." Addison was being honest, but Sal didn't seem to catch on to what he was saying.

"I see. You don't do it for the money, but because you enjoy your job. It is good to enjoy your work. So, if I recommended you to someone, how much would I be telling them you charge?"

"Nothing."

"Nothing? Do you not take referrals?"

"Oh, no, I take referrals! You asked what I would charge...and I told you. I don't charge. Well, I mean, I charge some folks, but most of the time, I do it free-of-charge."

Sal was both upset and confused by Addison's answer.

"Well, then how do you make a living?"

"In all honesty, sir, I don't really need to work. I have money, enough to last me a lifetime, but I do it to help people."

"If you don't do it for the money, why do you charge some people and do it for free for others?" He was quite put out at what he was hearing.

"I think you are getting the wrong idea."

"What criteria do prospective customers have to meet to get work done for free, exactly?" he began to clench his jaw.

"There is no criteria. Those that pay me for the work, pay in lieu of a donations to homeless shelters, disaster relief, and so on. I never receive any money from my clients, personally." Addison answered his questions without batting an eye. Sal was caught off guard by what he said, as he was under the impression that Addison was out to cheat people of their hard-earned money. His furrowed brows relaxed, and his tone evened out.

"Oh, now I understand. So, you do charity work? If they pay for the work, it goes to charity… I'm impressed."

"I figure that if the Callahans can help people, so can I. They are like family to me. I do my part to lend a helping hand to those who can't afford to pay contractors or do it themselves."

"So, you are on Callahan Banking and Trust's payroll?"

On one hand, he could be honest about where his money came from, but that would just raise more questions. On the other hand, in a way, he was on CBT's payroll, as all of his money came from there.

"Yes…yes, I am. I offered my services to them, and they send me out to help others…"

"And they foot the bill for the work, rather than charging the people that you do the work for. That is both very kind and very smart and selfless. I am thoroughly impressed."

"Thank you, sir."

"Please, call me Sal."

The rest of the evening went very well. There was a lot of small chat here and there. Addison heard about how Maria and Salvador met, where he proposed, and they told him embarrassing stories about Alison, despite her pleas and whining.

When it came to the end of the night, He kissed Maria on the cheek, and shook Sal's hand. Alison walked Addison out to his car after he had exchanged pleasantries with her parents.

"I am so full, I may not eat for a week." Addison laughed.

"Well, maybe you shouldn't have had that third helping of lasagna."

"I couldn't help it. It was so good. And those cannoli...goodness gracious."

"I told you that they were delicious. My mom has gotten so many offers to buy her recipe." She put her hands up, and he did the same. They interlocked their fingers and stood there, talking for another fifteen minutes. It fell silent for a moment and then Addison changed the subject.

"Listen, um...Do you think that when you come over tomorrow, you could bring that thing...the rectangular thing...the one you brought to help me look for cars..."

"My laptop?" She smirked. "I can bring it. Why?"

"I want you to help me look for a place to live."

"Are you getting tired of the hotel?"

"You could say that. It isn't that I am lonely. I mean, I am, but I am used to it...living in that cabin for all that time. It's just...my neighbors are getting to me."

"Did you complain to the hotel manager?" Her look turned from amusement to concern.

"No, it isn't like that. I just...there is a girl across the hall from me. She is very friendly. Maybe too friendly, if you ask me. She reminds me of someone, but I can't seem to put my finger on who, though." He closed his eyes, and cleared his throat. "Anyway, I will see you tomorrow, and we can talk more." He kissed her, and then released her hands, reaching into his pocket for his keys.

Addison arrived at the hotel, and as he got off of the elevator and headed to his room, his neighbor from across the hall peeked her head out of her room.

"How did it go? Do her parents approve?" She inquired, stepping out into the hallway, dressed in a leopard printed negligée. Seeing her so scantily clothed made Addison very uncomfortable.

"It went as well as I could have hoped. Her father is a tough nut to crack, but I am pretty sure I won him over." He didn't look at her when he replied, but faced his door, and messed with the key card. After several attempts to open the door, he began to get frustrated. "What the heck?! Why can't they just use regular keys? I swear that technology hates me."

"Here…let me help." She sighed.

"No thanks, Barb. I will get it eventually. Besides, it is cold out here in the hallway, and you will catch a draft with as little as you are dressed."

"Oh, you don't like my outfit?" She smirked, slyly as she slid the card from Addison's hand and slid it into the slot. The little light turned green, and she pushed the lever, and pushed the door open for him.

"Thanks, Barbara. Good night." He sighed, taking his keycard back, and slipping past her to get into his room. Before he closed the door, he looked the lovely woman in the face and smiled.

The two of them had met a few days before, in the lobby, when he was returning from a day out with Alison. She was trying to carry bags to the elevator, and they all fell off the trolley. He, like the gentleman he was, came to her assistance. They began to talk and he found out that she was in the room directly across the hall from his. He found her to be quite easy on the eyes. However, he was not attracted to her, not like he was attracted to Alison. She wore clothes that left nothing to the imagination, and the way she looked at him made him feel like she was devouring him with her hazel eyes. She was obviously attracted to him, but he was sure to remind her that he was taken. Though she knew that very important fact, it didn't stop her from making advances at him every chance she could.

Her smile was slightly crooked, and her long, waist-length blonde hair looked like a mane. She looked like a model, and was curvy in all the right places. In any other case, he would have steered clear of her. But she had a really nice personality and he enjoyed talking to her, so they had talked occasionally since that day.

Immediately after he closed the door, he dead bolted it, and went directly to the shower. Unable to keep his eyes from wandering, he felt extremely dirty and ashamed for looking at his neighbor in the way that he had. After a long, cool shower, he began to feel his stomach grumble.

"You just ate enough food to feed an army...why would you be hungry again?" He mumbled at his reflection as he pulled his sleep pants on. He walked over to the bed and sat down on the edge. Taking the phone receiver in his hand, he looked at the numbers listed on the phone directory, and dialed.

Ten minutes passed, and there was a knock at his door. As he made his way to the door, dressed in nothing but his sleep pants, he unlocked the dead bolt and opened the door. Just as he looked into the hallway, he heard the click of a door shutting very nearby. His room service cart was just sitting in front of his door, but there was no one around. He grabbed the cart and wheeled it into his room.

As he sat down on the bed to eat his beef stew and bread, he anticipated seeing Alison the next morning. He had a method to his madness, when he asked her to help him look for a house.

He wanted her to like whatever house he chose, because it would be her house too once he asked her to move in with him.

Taking a spoonful of the stew, he put it in his mouth, and smiled. Then he grimaced, as it tasted slightly bitter. He added a few shakes of salt and pepper to it, and that seemed to improve it considerably, as he finished the whole bowl and the bread in record time.

He wheeled the cart with the dirty dishes back into the hallway, and as he turned to go back into his room, Barb's door opened, and her eyes met his. She leaned against the door frame, and smiled. He was going to smile back, and then retrieve to his room, but he suddenly felt funny.

"Is there something wrong, Addison?" Barb asked, with a look of concern on her face.

"I don't know. I feel kind of funny. I had so much food to eat at Alison's parents' house. But, I got hungry again, so I ordered some stew. Maybe the combination of the two isn't sitting with me."

"Well, you know that gluttony is a sin, Addison. You keep eating like that, it is bound to make you sick to the stomach."

"It isn't my stomach that is bothering me."

"Maybe, you should go lie down…let the food digest a little bit." Barb seemed to be genuinely concerned. She stepped out of her room, now covered in a long silken robe, slippers on her feet.

"Maybe, I should. It has been a long and very emotional day. I might just be really tired. I am going to go get some rest. Allie is coming by in the morning to help me look for a house. I am going to ask her to move in with me…so, shh!" He put his finger to his lips, and smiled.

"You really love her, don't you?"

"I don't think I could love anyone more. She is my world, and I want to spend the rest of my life with her." He leaned against the doorframe, as he was beginning to get the sensation as though he was beginning to fall over. "Good night, again, Barbara."

"Night, Addison." She smiled, and watched him.

The hallway and everything else began to tilt and start dancing. He put his hand to his head, and began to back into his room, closing the door behind him. The room was going funky, and he was having a lot of trouble staying upright. He stumbled forward, and the last thing he remembered was thinking that he was obviously very tired as he landed face down on his bed.

Chapter Thirty

Alison pressed the button for Addison's floor, and the doors closed in front of her. With her laptop nestled safely at her side, she rode upward, watching the numbers ascend on the screen above the doors.

Her heart pounded like a hammer as she approached the desired floor, as she thought of who was waiting for her. Last night has been a success, despite her father's militant questioning and her zealous drinking episode.

The bell dinged and the doors slid open, and she didn't wait for them to open completely before darting out and down the hall at a determined pace. As she approached his door, she noticed that it was not closed completely and there was a "Do Not Disturb" sign hanging from the handle. Curious as to why he hadn't closed the door, and why the sign was there, her heart began to bang against her ribcage, and she began to push the door open.

"Adam? Adam, are you alright? Your door was open" She called as she slowing pushed the door open wide. At the sight before her, she felt her heart drop into her stomach, and her bag slid from her shoulder and hit the floor with a thud.

Addison was still in bed, but he wasn't alone. Laying on the bed next to him was a woman with long, mangled, blonde hair. The covers were hanging off the bed, so there was no hiding that they were as bare as the day they had been born, and Addison's arm was draped over the woman in bed with him.

"Addison!!! Why?? How could you…" Alison began to shake as she stood in the doorway of the hotel room, her whole world spinning completely out of control.

At the sound of her cries, Addison jolted upright, and so did the woman next to him. Looking at her, he couldn't believe what he was seeing himself.

"Barb?!?" He gave her a look of disgust, and then looked at Alison. "Allie…sweetie….This isn't what you think…I swear." He searched the floor for his pants, and quickly grabbed them and pulled them on, before lunging at Alison.

"What I think it is…is that you obviously couldn't resist finding yourself in bed with the first skinny blonde that you could get your hands on! What I think is that you needed to please yourself, but couldn't envision yourself with me in that way." She backed away from his outstretched arms and gave him a look of total detestation and loathing. Meanwhile, Barb was snatching up her clothes and things off the floor and trying to slither past the quarreling couple, unnoticed.

"No! I mean, you're wrong! I don't know what happened here, but it wasn't like that! Baby, listen to me. Barbara means nothing to me…absolutely nothing."

"That makes this even worse! Who is she, Addison? And why did I find the two of you in bed together, naked?! If it isn't what it appears to be, what is this?"

"I'm his neighbor, Barb, from across the hall. You must be Alison." Barb approached Alison, still bare, clutching her clothing in her arms against her chest. She had a sheepish grin on her face as she tried to creep by. Addison grabbed her arm, and it startled her, and her clothes hit the floor in a pile.

"Barb, what happened here last night? Why are you in my room? Why were we in bed together…unclothed?!? Explain!!"

"You don't remember? That is kind of hurtful, more hurtful than saying that I mean nothing to you. We made passionate love last night. You said it was the best night of your life and that you felt like you were in ecstasy." She yanked her arm free from him, and picked up her clothes. Turning to Alison, she gave her a sympathetic smile. "I'm so sorry that you had to find out like this, sweetheart. But, if it makes you feel better, he called out your name when he was climaxing…multiple times."

Alison's pain and heartache turned to anger and fury. She had been hurt before, cheated on before, but none of those other times combined compared to this. He had sworn his love and commitment to her, inexplicably, and yet he felt the need to bed a woman that he barely knew just for the sake of satisfying his sexual needs, rather than to come to her for that satisfaction.

"That never happened, Alison. I swear to you, nothing happened…the last thing I remember is ordering room service, eating, and then going to bed. The next thing I knew, you were standing in my doorway, screaming and crying." He reached for Alison, but she backed away.

"Don't…touch…me! Don't come near me, you…you…You stood in front of my parents just last night and told them you *loved* me, and that you would never hurt me again…and then you come back here and do this. You asked me to come and help you look for a house, because of your neighbors…Now I get it! You wanted out of here because you weren't sure that you could control yourself around *her*. Well, obvious you lost your fight with that battle, because I found you both together, in your bed, naked and your arm wrapped around her. I hope that it was worth it!!"

"Alison…I would never cheat on you! I *do* love you. I love you more than I could ever love anyone else. I don't know what happened, but I didn't do what she said! We didn't make love….we didn't! I want to be with you…I asked you to marry me. Doesn't that mean anything to you?" He was both hurt and angry, as he was positive that nothing happened between him and Barbara. He couldn't give an explanation for them being in the bed, stark-naked, but he would have known if they had done anything together. At the mention of his proposal, she slipped the ring off of her finger, and put it on the desk.

"It meant everything to me, but obviously, it meant nothing to you. You would rather…you know…than to touch me in that way. Does the idea of being intimate with me disgust you so much that you have to screw your slutty neighbor instead?"

"I am not a slut!" Barb retorted, standing in the doorway.

"Says the nude woman, standing in the hallway, showing off her goodies to everyone passing by! Leave!" Alison shoved Barb out into the hall and slammed the door in her face. She didn't release the door handle, but rather reached down and grabbed her computer case off the floor, and slid the strap onto her shoulder. "I don't want to hear any of your excuses or explanations, Addison. I thought that you were different. I should have known that your fidelity wouldn't last long here, as opposed to Woodcrest." She paused, and swallowed hard. "The sad thing was that, I never felt that I was good enough for you. I almost expected you to find someone who suited you better than I do, but I never imagined that you would do something like this to me. Though you deserved better than me, I knew that you wouldn't hurt me by lying to my face about your feelings. Once again…I was wrong."

"I have never thought of myself as being too good for you, Alison. And you shouldn't either. Please, believe me. I love you and I would never cheat on you…especially with Barbara." He gripped her and held her to the door, so that she had no choice but to listen to him.

"You're right. You aren't too good for me. I am too good for you!!" She shoved him away, and he hit the floor with a thud. Taking her chance, she raced out of the room, and got to the elevator. As the doors closed in front of her, she saw him race out his room and towards her. She slid down the wall of the elevator, and sobbed.

Chapter Thirty-One

After several attempts to contact her, Addison decided to leave messages at her work and at her house. Sal and Maria were confused, infuriated, and at a loss for words for what they had heard had happened.

Alison threw away the messages that the receptionist had taken for her from him, and only found a release for her broken heart when she was in the privacy of her own bedroom or in the company of her dear friend, Becky.

Since that morning in the hotel, Addison had avoided Becky completely, as he knew that Alison would have told her everything from her point of view, and he couldn't face the look of disappointment on Rebecca's face.

It had been two very long weeks of misery for Alison, and she had gone over that morning again and again, trying to hash out what she had seen and heard as if to try to find Addison's innocence in the whole thing. All that she felt was anger and pain.

"I don't understand why he would go through all that he went through to be with you, just to sleep with some random woman." Rebecca sighed, stroking Alison's hair.

"Whether he did anything or not, he should have been honest."

"Maybe he was being honest with you. Maybe, just maybe, he had no idea how or why that dreadful girl was in his room."

"She said that they had made love, Becky. She looked as if it had been a wild night. The bed was in shambles, there were clothes and such all over the floor and they were both bare naked in bed together. The only way that he could have not known what happened was if he had been in a coma again…and we know he wasn't."

"I have no words, my dear. I really wish that I could think of an explanation to fix all of this, but the only way that it can be fixed is for you and Addison to sit down and talk it out. You love him, and he loves you…I know he does."

"You don't sleep with strangers when you love someone, Becky. If he loved me, he would stop hiding behind his story of not remembering the events of that night and just tell me the truth."

Sitting alone in her room, Barbara thought about all that had happened. She had just hung up the phone, and was now staring out the window. Her heart hurt as she thought about what she had done. She had never seen two people more in love than Addison and Alison, and in one night, she had destroyed that. She yearned to have the love that she saw between the two of them, and at one time, she had that.

He had been the love of her life, but he was tragically taken from her at the hands of a drunk driver. In one fowl swoop, she lost her husband, her child lost their father, and they lost means to survive on their own, as he was the only income that they had. She had to turn to her grandmother for help. The woman was the kind of person that would not do something for nothing, and set terms for her assistance, which included sole custody of her great-granddaughter.

Barbara's grandmother kept her daughter and set her out into the world to find a way to provide for them. She found small jobs here and there, but her desperation and desire to make ends meet and be reunited with the one person she loved more than life itself had led her to do the most despicable and underhanded thing possible.

As much as she loved knowing that she would soon see her little girl again, she knew that she would have to relive that shame every time she looked into her eyes. She would have to carry the guilt with her every day, knowing that she had destroyed Addison and Alison's happiness just so she could have her own. Her little girl deserved a mother who cared for the happiness of the others. Her little girl deserved a mother who would do anything for her, but wouldn't sacrifice other people to do so.

With a deep breath, she finished the glass of whiskey she was drinking with a large gulp, and went to make things right.

After knocking on his door for a good five minutes, she heard the deadbolt unlock and the door opened slightly.

"What do you want?"

"I know that I am the last person that you want to see, but I need to talk to you."

"You *are* the last person I want to see, and I have no desire to hear what you have to say. Whatever happened that night…you know that we did nothing…I did nothing wrong. And yet, you felt the need to lie to her, and now she will not speak to me. You are pure evil. You put a rift between Alison and I that can't be fixed. I cannot even assure her that nothing happened, because it is all a blank to me. *You* alone know the truth, and you could have told her, but you used that forked tongue of yours to spew lies. GO AWAY!!!" He was about to close the door, but she put her hand in the way.

"I need to tell you what really happened. I need to fix what I did. I cannot go another day with these lies. Please…I will fix this. It will cost me everything, but I cannot look my little girl in the face, knowing that I did something so horrible. Please."

The door didn't move for a few moments, and there was silence, then it swung open, allowing her in.

Addison hadn't shaved for the last two weeks, and he looked and smelled as if he hadn't showered either. It was rather saddening to see him looking this way, but it gave her even more motivation to come clean.

After an hour and a half, a lot of screaming and pacing, Addison came to a halt at the window. There was a moment of clarity. He turned on his heels and looked at the girl in the chair five feet away from him.

"And you are willing to confess everything to Alison as well?"

"Of course. If that is what I need to do to fix this mess, I will get down on my hands and knees and beg her to forgive you."

"What on Earth would I need to be forgiven for, Barbara? I did nothing. I was unconscious…you did this whole thing on your own. If anyone needs forgiveness, it's you. I just want Alison to know the truth." He grabbed clean towels, and headed towards the bathroom. "You are not to leave until this has been taken care of. I am going to clean myself up. We are taking a trip to her house to talk to her face-to-face. Don't move." He went into the bathroom and slammed the door. She heard him lock the door.

Alison turned the corner on to her street, on her way home from another long and exhausting day at the rehab center. All she wanted to do was to eat dinner, take a shower and go to bed. As she approached her home, there was a familiar sedan sitting by the curb in front. Fury began to build inside of her as she turned off the ignition, and grabbed her purse. She slammed the car door of the lime green beetle and dashed up the porch steps. She slammed the front door behind her, and stomped into the living room, throwing her purse on the coffee table.

"What on earth are you doing in my house?! Get out…both of you!" Alison was upset that Addison had come here, but was enraged that he had brought his new girlfriend with him. Her mother walked over and put her hands on Alison's shoulders.

"Addison came here to see you, and he brought her with him because she has to talk to you. I think you should hear them out."

"Mama…She's the woman I found him in bed with! She's the one…how could you even let them in this house after what they have done?" She shook off her mother's hands.

"She didn't let them in. I did." Salvador came out of the kitchen, holding two bottles of beer and a bottled water. He handed the water to Barbara, and the beer to Addison, and then sat down. "Alison, you need to hear them out."

"Daddy! I cannot believe you! It was not even a month ago, you were drilling Addison, and laying on a guilt trip about him abandoning me at the Gala. Now, after knowing what they have done, you allow them into our home and serve them drinks like we are all one big happy family."

"I have my reasons, pumpkin. They have been here for some time, and I think you are going to want to hear what they have to say. Now sit down, and listen to them." He pointed at her mother's chair, and Alison obeyed.

"I am going to go make dinner. Do you want anything, Alison?"

"If I am forced to have to sit here and listen to them…bring me a glass of wine…and the bottle, as well." She sat back in the chair and glared at Barb. She wouldn't even look at Addison. A few minutes later, Maria returned with a full glass of wine, and the bottle. She quietly urged Sal to follow her back to the kitchen to give them some privacy. He followed her, without argument.

"I know you are hurting, and that you feel betrayed. What you saw…had to have been devastating." Barb started, her eyes lowered to the ground.

"Do you, now? You know how it feels to have your heart ripped out and stomped on a million times? How tragic for you." Allie snapped back.

"Be angry at me. I deserve it. But I am not here to beg for your forgiveness. I am here for Addison. I am here on his behalf."

"How incredibly sweet of you!"

"Alison…stop interrupting and let her talk!" Addison bellowed, and Alison immediately snapped her mouth shut.

"What you saw…The two of us…Addison was innocent. He did nothing wrong."

"He didn't look innocent. It was his room, his bed…he had his arm wrapped around you."

"He didn't invite me in. Up until you walked in and he woke up, he had no knowledge of me even being there." Barb bit her lip.

"I am supposed to believe that you broke into his room, and crawled into bed with him…and he had no idea. I know what kind of sleeper Addison is…and he wouldn't have slept through all that."

"He didn't wake up because he was…I kind of slipped him a mickey. He was passed out cold before I even came in the room."

"You drugged him?! And how did you do that without him knowing unless you had access to what he was drinking?"

"I put it in his room service. They approached his door, but I caught them before they knocked. I tipped the waiter and then slipped it in his stew. When I saw that it had dissolved, I knocked on his door, and then ran to my room. It took him about a half hour, then I heard him fall onto the bed."

"I can't believe what I am hearing right now."

"Alison, I told you that I didn't remember anything between eating dinner and waking up to you crying and screaming. She told me what she did, and I don't know what a 'mickey' is, but it explains why I couldn't remember anything."

"Isn't that convenient?" She sneered at him, but didn't look at him. "And so, what you are trying to tell me is that she raped you, is that right?"

"That's the thing, Alison. We didn't do anything. I didn't do anything. I just undressed and got into bed with him, and pulled his arm over me to make it look like we were sleeping together."

"Then, if that is the case, he must have been eating his stew in the nude." She finally looked at Addison. "You must think I am a complete idiot."

"I don't!" Addison's eyes shot to hers.

"I undressed him, and threw his clothes around the floor to look like we had…in a fit of passion…" Barb's cheeks were flushed, and she was afraid to look at Alison.

"Okay, so you drugged him…how did you get into his room? He must have left it unlocked, by mistake, right?"

"No. I know the one guy at the front desk. He gave me a spare keycard."

"How long did the two of you sit and work out this story? It is very well constructed."

"It's the truth, Alison. I swear." Barbara pleaded.

"You knew that he and I were together. You knew that what you were up to would hurt us both. What was your motive?"

"I didn't have a choice, Alison. I knew you were together, and that you were happy but if I hadn't done what I was told, I would have been cut off. I have bills, and tuition, and a little girl to take care of."

"What?!" Addison and Alison looked at Barbara.

"Someone told you to break us up? Who on earth would want to break us up? You didn't tell me this part…" Addison jumped up, and looked at her. "I thought you did what you did because…"

"Because I wanted you for myself? That I wanted to be the one you were with?" Barb laughed. "Addison, if I had wanted you, I wouldn't have gone about it like that. Hurting you…breaking the two of you up like that would have just caused you to hate me, not want me."

"Well, if you were forced to do it, who forced you to?" Addison growled. "We have a right to know."

"It was an act of revenge. My grandmother wanted you to pay for what your grandfather did to her. She said that you needed to feel the pain of humiliation, just as she felt, the night before her wedding. She was dumped because he had cheated on her with his nurse."

"My grandfather was a good man! He would never have hurt a woman, let alone humiliate her." Addison barked, coming to his dearly departed grandfather's defense.

"Addison…" Alison processed the information that was just given, and realized what was happening before he had caught on. "Stop yelling." She looked at Barb, and asked her about her grandmother. "By any chance, is your grandmother's name Helena Bancroft?" After asking the question, Addison's breath caught in his chest.

"Yes…yes, it is. How did you know that? Do you know her?" Barb's face turned white as a sheet.

"Yes…unfortunately, I do. I know her more than I care to." Alison's expression went from anger to sadness. "I worked in the nursing home that she lived in back in Pittsburg…the one that burned down. She was a hateful old woman who lived to make me miserable…so did Addison." She looked up at Addison, and suddenly, everything made perfect sense. Her heart sank to her stomach, and her eyes welled up with tears. She reached up and grasped Addison's wrist.

"My *grandfather* hurt and humiliated her…so, she enlisted you to carry out her revenge for her?" He pulled his arm from Alison's grip, walked back over to Barbara, sunk down onto the plastic covered couch, and stared at Alison.

"Yes. I know all about Pittsburg…I mean, I knew that Addison worked there, but she never mentioned you." She looked from Allie to Addison. "She had me follow you from there, and find my way into your path somehow. I lost you for a while and so I got a room at the hotel and waited to get instructions. As luck would have it, you ended up at the same hotel, in the room right across from mine."

"So, you got all friendly and then called your grandmother to tell her…"

"Yes, and the rest is history. The only thing is…I felt horrible about it, so I had to come clean." Barbara began to cry. "I am so sorry. I hope that, by telling you the truth, the two of you can fix what I broke."

"I have no words, Barbara." Alison took a shaky breath and looked at Addison. "Adam, can I talk to you for a minute in private, please?" She looked at him. He thought about it for a moment, and then got up off the couch again, the plastic beneath him making a strange squeaky creaking noise.

"No…not right now. I think that whatever was needed to be said is said. There is nothing left to discuss, private or otherwise. Barb and I are done here. The truth is out, and now I am going to take her home." He reached and grabbed Barb by the arm, and pulled her from the couch.

"Please, Addison…" Alison got up and blocked the doorway.

"Alison, please move out of our way. I have heard enough from you already. I'm not sure that I can be with someone who can't trust me."

"But, Addison… Please…" Alison's tears fell like rain as she stepped out of their way. "I saw the two of you…together. I didn't know that it was all staged…I thought you had…" She sobbed.

"Enough, Alison. If you had trusted me…truly believed that I loved you, we wouldn't be doing this right now. However, you called me a liar and cheater, hit me, and insulted my integrity and fidelity. I need to think about things. I will let you know." She watched him walk out, shutting the door behind him and Barbara.

*****

Before walking into Rebecca's room, she made one last effort to get ahold of Addison. The phone just kept ringing and ringing. She closed her cellphone, and knocked on the door.

"Come in." Becky called from the other side of the door.

"Hello, Becky. It's just me." She sighed, wiping a solitary tear from her cheek.

"Still no luck at getting ahold of him?" Becky rose from her bed and slowly walked towards her friend, meeting her halfway.

"I'm pretty sure that it is over now. It's been at least two weeks." She hugged her old friend, and assisted her in getting over to where the comfortable chairs were. "Has he come to see you yet?"

"No, he hasn't. I suppose that he wants to avoid running into you here."

"He should've at least called you. Why should you be punished because of my mistake?" She got Becky settled and then sat on the chair opposite her.

"Because he knows that he is acting foolishly, and that he has to answer to me for his disregard for your feelings."

"That's the thing, Becky. He shouldn't have to answer to you for it. It is between him and I." She looked at her friend. "As much as I love you, and as much as I appreciate that you understand my point of view…he's right. I should have trusted him, unconditionally."

"But, Alison…you walked into his hotel room and found him in a very compromising position. Any woman in your place would have reacted just the same. After all, this isn't the first time that you found someone you were dating in the midst of the same indiscretion."

"True. I have been cheated on more than I care to admit, but that still doesn't excuse the fact that this time is different. This is Adam that we are talking about here. He dove through a time window to be with me, not knowing what he would find on the other side." She swept another tear from her cheek. As her bottom lip began to tremble, she remembered how he had pleaded with her to believe him. "He loved me…truly loved me, and I repaid that love by accusing him of cheating on me. If only I could go back to that night and redo it."

"We aren't talking about messing with that stuff again, are we? I mean, you were very lucky that nothing monumental changed by you being in Woodcrest in the first place. Imagine what would happen if you found a way to go back in time, voluntarily." Rebecca's face got pale.

"It isn't like I could do it, even if I wanted to. I am just saying that I wish I could, because I ripped the heart out of the only man that ever truly loved me."

"You know, you act like he is the only injured party. Do you not remember how much pain you were in when you thought that he had cheated on you? Before that wretched girl came forward and told the truth, you were the injured and heartbroken one, and he was to blame for your pain." Becky reached for Allie's hands, and took them in hers; a calming, soothing feeling flowed though Alison as she realized that Rebecca's words held truth.

"Just promise me that you will let him and I figure things out on our own. You can speak your opinion all you like, but I want him to make the decision on his own, otherwise I will always wonder if..." Alison swallowed hard. "If we are able to fix what is broken, I want it to be because he wants to, and not because of guilt trips or outside influences."

"I understand, sweetie. I will not intervene...at least I will try not to." She smiled. They sat in silence for a while, and then suddenly, Alison's eyes shot wide open.

"I almost forgot! Dr. Largo said that he will be signing your discharge papers today! He said that your hip has healed enough to let you go home. The only thing is that you need to continue physical therapy, and you can't overdo it."

"I finally get to go home? Oh, thank heavens." The young Becky seemed to shine in the old woman's eyes as she realized that she would be free again. After months of being held in captivity, poked and prodded, stretched and bent, she could finally return to the home that she missed.

"I will go see if he has signed them, and then we can pack you up, and I will take you home, myself."

Getting Rebecca packed and set to make her return to her home consumed the rest of the evening. She got hugs and kisses from the staff, and some tears were shed.

Within a half hour, they were pulling up to the gates of Rebecca's grand home. Taking a deep breath as the gates opened before them, they drove up the long drive toward a crowd of people waiting to welcome home their matron. Rebecca smiled, a tear running down her softly wrinkled cheek. She was home.

Chapter Thirty-Two

As she placed the last suitcase in her car, she had to stop and take a breath. Her heart was pounding harder than it ever had before, and her hands were shaking. She turned and sat on the back of her car, and had one last cry before traveling back to Pittsburgh. She needed to get it all out before she got behind the wheel.

After nearly a month of attempting to contact Addison, to reach out and try to fix things, she came to the conclusion that it was over. She didn't want to believe it, but when she went to the hotel, to talk to him face-to-face, she found that he had checked out of the hotel, as did as his blonde neighbor. The concierge couldn't confirm whether they had left together or not, but he did confirm that they checked out on the same day.

This led Alison to realize that it was time to move on. She contacted Jeanie, who invited her to come back and live with her for a while. Without a second thought, she agreed and quit her job at Bruckner's Rehabilitation Center. With Becky back home, she had nothing to tie her to that place anymore. After talking to her parents, and explaining that she needed to get away, and try to rebuild her life again, they assisted her in packing her things. Alison found it quite odd that they were so willing to help her, considering that she had just come home, and they always said that they loved having her there.

She only had one stop left before she hit the interstate to make the trek to Pittsburgh. As she approached the gates, she pressed the button on the intercom, saw the security camera move, and a strange voice speak through the speaker.

"Welcome back, Miss Moreno. Mrs. Callahan has been anxiously awaiting your arrival." The masculine voice said, sweetly, and then the gates opened in front of her. She put the car in gear, and proceeded forward.

The sight of the estate shocked her just as much now as it had the day she had brought Rebecca home. Her heart beat hard as she took in the mere size of it. It was bigger than any house she had seen in a long time. The only house, in her mind, that could compete was that of the Thatchers.

The large stone columns that stood on either side of the front doors were made of marble, and they stretched from the ground to the roof of the two story colonial mansion. The windows were adorned with black shutters and it had a balcony that ran the width of the house. There were large, well-sculpted spiral bushes spaced across the front of the house, and a large fountain stood in the center of the circular driveway.

Alison parked the car, and went to the front door, ringing the bell. This would be the last time that she would see Rebecca, she thought. She had discussed her plans to return to Pittsburgh with her friend before she even mentioned it to her parents or her boss. Rebecca was saddened that Alison had made the decision to go, but understood and respected the decision. Alison needed to start over, start fresh, and she needed to get out of Philadelphia.

As the door opened, it was not Frederick, the Butler, who was standing there. Ian, Becky's grandson, was there to welcome her with a sad smile and outstretched arms.

"Beautiful Alison..." He walked forward, enveloping her in his arms and giving her a light hug.

"Hello Ian. I assume that your grandmother has told you of my plans."

"Indeed, she has, and I am saddened. Please come in. She is waiting for you in the sitting room." He allowed her to enter, before shutting the door behind them. Together, they walked down the hall to the grand sitting room that seemed to take up half of the first floor.

"What made you decide to go back to Pittsburgh? Please tell me that it has nothing to do with Addison and that whole debacle…" Ian sighed, guiding her forward into the room.

"I'm afraid it does, Ian. He has refused to speak to me, or see me since the truth came out."

"He's a fool, in my opinion. If my wife had found me in the same situation, I would not blame her for assuming the worst. Right now, he is just acting like a pride-filled dope. He'll come around, once he realizes how stupid he is acting." He and Alison approached Rebecca. "Am I right, Grandmother?"

"Of course you are, Ian darling." Rebecca chuckled, only hearing the very end of the conversation.

"See, Alison. Just have patience, and he'll come around. Now, I will leave you ladies to visit. If you need anything, Grandmother, Fredrick is around here somewhere. As am I, and Caitlin." He turned back to Alison. "Caitlin is in the study, on the phone, but I'll let her know that you are here. She would like to see you before you leave as well." And with that said, he turned on his heels and walked briskly out of the room.

What started out as a short visit to say her goodbyes to her dear friend turned into an afternoon filled with laughter and tears. They spoke with each other about the days in Woodcrest, things that had happened in Becky's life leading up to their reunion, and many other things. The clock in the sitting room had chimed, and Alison could not believe that she had been there for about four hours. Fredrick came in to ask if Alison was staying for dinner, but she declined, insisting that she needed to get on the road so she would arrive in Pittsburgh before dark.

"You can't go yet, Allie!!" Caitlin came running into the room, slightly out of breath.

"Have you been on the phone all this time, Caitlin?" Rebecca looked rather upset at her granddaughter's absence.

"Off and on, yes. I do apologize. There has been a lot of business to deal with and I had to get everything straightened out. I'm so very sorry." Caitlin looked flushed and exhausted, but her smile was as bright as always.

"You have everything worked out though?" Rebecca rose from her seat.

"Everything is straight and all plans are confirmed, yes."

"What plans?" Alison was very confused.

"You'll see. Come with me." She grasped Alison's hand, and dragged her out the front door to the town car that was waiting for them outside.

"Where are we going? I have to leave for my long trip to Pittsburgh."

"That is out of the question, missy. You are coming with us. I guarantee that you won't want to miss this." She urged Alison into the car, and then climbed in after her. A few moments later, Rebecca joined them.

"Where are we going? What are you up to?" Alison gave them both suspicious glares, and then jumped when a knock came to the window next to her. She rolled down the tinted window to reveal Ian.

"May I have your car keys, please?" He smiled a very bright and conniving smile. Obviously he was in on whatever they had planned. Reluctantly, she pulled the keys from her purse and put them in his palm. Immediately, he ran to her car, got in and started the engine.

With a jerk, the town car was in motion, and Ian followed them closely.

"What exactly is going on? Where are you taking me, and why is Ian following in my car? Jeanie is expecting me tonight." Alison sat perfectly still, but looked between the young ginger and the elderly one.

"You're right, grandmother…she really doesn't like surprises, does she?" Caitlin giggled.

"Some things don't change." Becky laughed back.

"Can you give me a clue, at least?" Alison had a bit of panic in her voice, completely bewildered by her kidnappers' intentions.

"All I can tell you is that I received a call right before you left." Caitlin smirked.

"And? What does that have to do with me?"

"We are taking you home."

"You're taking me home?! Is everything alright? Is it my mom? My Dad?"

"No, Alison…we're taking you *HOME*!" Caitlin emphasized on the last word, and looked her straight in the eye, a sweet smile crossing her lips.

"But, if you are taking me home, we are going the wrong way." She spotted a sign on the side of the road, and looked around. "Home is the other way."

"Alison…" Rebecca took Alison's hand in hers and there were tears welling in her eyes. It took her a moment and then her eyes widened, her bottom jaw dropping.

"But why are we going there? It's been abandoned for thirty years. It is a mess. Are you sure you want to see it like that?"

"I want to return there…one last time…with my old friend…"

"But Rebecca…That was your home…not mine. It has been abandoned since before I was even born…remember?" Alison looked to Caitlin, then to Becky. To her grandchildren, Alison was just the nurse who took care of their grandmother, or so she thought.

"It's your home, too, Alison. You know that. It's where we met, where we spent many nights talking over tea." Rebecca chuckled, knowing that talking of this in front of her granddaughter was making Alison extremely nervous and paranoid.

"No…we met at the rehabilitation center…" Her eyes jetted to Caitlin. Caitlin just sat there, watching Alison squirm in her seat. There was an amused look in her eyes, and a she was biting her lip to keep from laughing at the awkward scene in front of her.

This went on for another few minutes and then Caitlin decided to take mercy on Allie, as she was on the verge of tears.

"Alison…Ian and I know. Grandmother and grandfather told us all about it a long time ago…when we were children, as they did with our mother, and uncles. We know about you and about Woodcrest." She scooted closer and took Alison's other hand. "It's alright. You don't have to continue with the cover story. To most people, it would seem impossible, but how else could we explain grandmother knowing things that she knows, had it not been for your strange magical trip back in time? She knew songs, word for word, when they played for the first time on the radio. She knew things that no one else would know, long before they occurred."

"You told them…everything?" There was a tightness in Alison's throat as she looked to her friend. A part of her felt relieved, as she had begun to make it sound as if Rebecca was becoming senile or delusional. Then she got a little mad, as that information would have been nice to know a while ago. She sat and thought for a moment. "So, the night of the Gala…you knew?"

"Yes, we did."

"You were in on the whole thing? The Gala? The Bank with Ian…He knew everything?"

"Yes. We knew all about you and Addison. Grandmother told us about the two of you when we were small, sort of like a fairy tale, but as we got older, she felt compelled to explain to us that they weren't just stories, and that soon we would finally be able to meet you in person. And I have to say, her stories didn't do you justice." Caitlin's words managed to make her blush.

"That still doesn't explain why we are going back to Woodcrest. I have been there since I got back…it's nothing like it was before. Houses and buildings are barely standing…there's vandalism and it hurts my heart to just think about the state of it."

"You might be surprised what a little paint and some elbow grease can do." Caitlin sat back in her seat once more.

"It would take a lot more than a little paint and elbow grease to fix Woodcrest." Alison's eyes filled with sorrowful tears.

"Caitlin left out one very important ingredient…Love!" Rebecca closed her eyes and tried to envision the Woodcrest she once knew, and what it might look like now. Alison tried to get more details, but neither of them spoke another word the rest of the trip.

It wasn't until they passed a road sign saying, "Woodcrest: Next left," that Alison's heart began to thump hard against her ribcage.

The car made the turn, and Alison nearly leapt from her seat at what she saw out of the car window. There was no longer a dirt road, but a newly paved one, lined by beautiful Apple and Cherry Blossom Trees and tall, old-fashioned street lamps. The huge Pine trees that had been cut down, revealing the derelict town, were replaced with new trees and a tall line of rod-iron fencing. They approached the gate, and the chauffer punched in some numbers on the keypad outside the huge gate. Above the entrance to the town was a beautiful sign made of iron,

"Welcome to Woodcrest." They drove a few minutes more down a straight lane, lined with trees, until the trees angled out to reveal a sight that made Alison dizzy.

There were flutters in Alison's stomach as she felt as though she had just experienced déjà vu. They drove forward through the gates and found themselves on a cobblestone street. Ahead of them, in the square, a beautiful gazebo stood, surrounded by flowers. There were different roads that they could have taken, but they continued around the gazebo, and drove deeper into the heart of the town. Streets were lined with shops. As they drove, they came upon the large park. And standing as tall, and proud as ever was a refinished statue of the four founders.

Alison could barely breathe. It was just as she remembered it, with the exception of the people. There were no people on the streets. No children were playing in the park. There were no cars at the houses that were built along the shady lanes.

"How…when…How can this be? Who did this?" She unbuckled her seatbelt and rolled down her window. Far in the distance, she could see men in bright, reflective vests placing sod and trees into the ground. There were large machines too, but she couldn't hear them running as they were quite a ways from them.

"I cannot believe he pulled it off. Grandmother? Is it as you remember?" Caitlin smiled, looking to her grandmother. Rebecca had her hands to her trembling lips, and her cheeks were wet with the tears that had fallen from her eyes. "Alison…"

"How is this possible?" Alison brought her head back in the car, and had a look on her face that no words could describe.

Ian pulled the green car up next to the town car, and Caitlin rolled the other window down.

"According to this map, we are on West Lampas Blvd. What street are we looking for again?" Ian flashed the map at his sister, and pointed where they were. She looked for a moment, and then put her finger on a spot not far from where Ian was pointing.

"That's it, right there. You lead the way." She closed the window, and sat on the seat between the two speechless, teary-eyed women.

"Where are we going now?" Alison whimpered. She had a feeling that she knew the answer to that question, but her heart couldn't take any more. She reached out and grasped both of Rebecca's hands, and they exchanged looks of longing.

The car took two more turns and they pulled down a road that brought back so many memories that she got pale and had to stick her hands to her eyes to hide the pure emotion.

"Alison…open your eyes, honey…you are not going to believe this." Rebecca grabbed and squeezed her hands again, and Alison could feel Rebecca tremble.

When Alison removed her hands from her eyes, she had to blink at least a half a dozen times before she could believe what she was seeing. Ian had parked about ten feet ahead, and had gotten out to open the town car door for the ladies. It took her a moment to get her bearings before she took Ian's hand. It was beyond comprehension how the sight before her could be anything but an illusion.

The large brown brick structure towered before her, intimidating her just as it did the first day that she approached it. Her heart beat just as hard now as it did the day her whole life changed for the better; that was the day that she was hired as Addison's nurse by Arthur and Elizabeth Thatcher. She remembered the nicked bricks, the weathered look to the railing, and the sleek shine of the large mahogany front doors.

Every detail of the brick and mortar building in front of her was exact and Alison found herself being reaching out to feel it, if only to prove to herself that it was really there, and not a hallucination.

Her hand made contact with the brick, and she nearly jumped out of her skin. She withdrew her hand and took a few steps back, nearly stumbling down the porch steps that she had unconsciously climbed.

"Careful there, Alison." Ian chuckled as he grabbed her before she fell to the ground.

"It's real...it's here. Unbelievable." She turned on her heels and looked at Rebecca. "Please tell me that I am not crazy. You see it too, don't you? It's the house! It's Thatcher Manor....just as I remember it...just as it was when I was here...every last detail...Please tell me you see it too, Becky?" She pleaded, desperate to prove that she had not lost her mind.

"Down to the very last detail...Impossible." Becky stepped forward, putting her hand on the rod iron railing. "You told me it was completely gone. You said that the only thing left undamaged were the steps...that it had looked like it had been burned to the ground. How can it be standing here...the same as it once was?"

"You didn't know about this?" The shock in Alison's voice conveyed that she was under the impression that Becky had known what she was going to see when they got here.

"Honestly...I had no idea. He told me that Woodcrest was being brought back to life, but I had no idea to what extent. He never told me about this, about any of it...not in any detail, anyway."

"He? He Who, Becky? Who did this? Who rebuilt Woodcrest? Who did this?" Alison's desperation to know who had gone to all the trouble to revamp a desolate and abandoned town made her voice waver and break. When she couldn't get an answer out of Becky, she turned to Caitlin. "Caitlin, tell me...who did this? There is no way that anyone would be able to replicate every single detail of Woodcrest."

"There are pictures of Woodcrest on the internet. I am sure that the person...the man behind this had to have just gotten the details from the pictures, or as close to it as possible." The smirk on Caitlin's face revealed that she was hiding something.

"It's possible, yes, but every single detail cannot be matched from a photograph. This house…every detail is perfect, precise, spot on. Who did this? I need to know." Alison grasped Caitlin's shoulders, and looked as though she was about to come apart as the seams if she didn't find out the truth. Caitlin looked at Alison, her smile extending to her emerald eyes. "Please, Caitlin…Who made Woodcrest whole again?"

For a few short moments, the silence was deafening. Alison tried to search the young woman's eyes for a hint of an answer. What she got instead was a widening grin, and a glint of hope from an emerald green ocean.

"If you must know how every detail was matched, why not just ask the only person who could honestly answer you?" Caitlin slid Alison's hands from her shoulders and held them. Her smile widened. She used her eyes to signal for Alison to look behind her.

Slowly, she turned her head. She heard the faint clickity-clack of horseshoes on the cement road become louder as its source got closer. Closing her eyes, she turned the rest of the way around and patiently waited until the sound stopped. However, as soon as she turned in that direction, the sound ceased. Her eyes shot open at the silence, and she felt her heart try to break free from her chest.

Sitting atop a large black and white horse, the man who had turned her world upside down again and again was a vision off the cover of a romance novel. His hair was not tied back, but blowing freely in the gentle breeze that blew. His head was held high, his bronze chest barely covered by a dirty white V-neck t-shirt that clung to him as if it were a second skin. His skin glistened in the sunlight, as he was sweaty and covered in dirt and muck.

He slid from the horse, and locked eyes with her, and she almost felt her heart breaking into a million pieces, as he had no emotion on his face. They stood where they were, staring at one another for what seemed like an eternity. You could have cut the tension and silence with a knife, as their spectators watched them from the walkway in front of the house. The lump in her throat in her throat seemed to grow the longer that he appeared to glare at her.

She could see the muscles in his cheeks and neck seem to twitch and move, even from the distance that they stood from each other. She interpreted this as his reaction to seeing her after their painful last encounter. He obviously was not expecting to see her there, as his facial expression was hard and cold. She was about to realize how badly she read people's faces.

He swallowed hard, put his hands to his face, took a deep breath and then let out huff of air. His expression softened, his eyes seemed to glisten with tears as his lips parted into a wide grin.

Before she had time to react to the sudden change, he was heading straight at her, first at a slow pace, then a brisk walk, then a jog, and then a full out run.

It felt as though time had slowed to a crawl. She wasn't sure what to do, and her feet seemed to be stuck to the ground. Panic and confusion filled her as she watched him come at her at what seemed to be a very determined speed. He had been farther away than he seemed to have been because an eternity passed until he almost ran her down. At the last moment, he skidded to a halt about an arm's length from her.

"I know I am probably the last person that you want to see. I wouldn't have come, but Caitlin, Ian, and Rebecca kind of kidnapped me." She began to babble in a fit of fear. Her emotions were going haywire, being so close to him.

"What are you talking about?" He swept hair from his sweaty brow and looked at her.

"I was at Becky's, saying goodbye. I am leaving Philly, and moving back to Pittsburgh to live with Jeanie. I was just about to go, and they brought me here."

"I'm confused…" Addison looked at the rest of the people standing around, watching the encounter.

"Before I go, I just want to apologize to you for what happened. You never gave me the chance after the truth was told, and I just wanted to let you know that you were right…I should have trusted you…had more faith in you. I messed up, and ruined everything. I'm sorry." She began to back away, and turned toward Ian, her hand out, waiting for him to return her car keys to her, so she could make her quick escape.

"Go? Where are you going?" Addison stepped forward, and reached for her. At his touch, she jumped and seemed to wince.

"I told you…Pittsburgh." She began to shake.

"But, why? Why are you leaving?" He grasped her forearm gently.

"I am leaving because I am miserable. I need a fresh start, without the daily reminder of all the ways I ruined things between us. I can't stand the looks of pity from my parents…I can't go anywhere without seeing your face." The tears welled up in her eyes, and the tightness in her chest was making it hard for her to breath.

"You just got here. Do you not like it?"

"It is just as I remember it. I love it. But, I don't belong here…not anymore." She sobbed.

"But, Allie…I did this for you. All of this…I did it for you." There was something in his voice that made her cease from trying to pull away. His voice was strained and soft, and it seemed to waver slightly.

"You did this? You brought Woodcrest back to life? For me? Why?" She searched his eyes for deception, something which she had neglected to do the morning she found him in bed with Lena's granddaughter. She may not be good at reading faces, but there is no way to hide the truth with your eyes. A person's eyes were like windows, making it possible to see the person within and all their secrets.

Addison cleared his throat, and grasped her hand. He looked to the others, and then back to Alison.

"Please…come with me. We need to talk, and I have to put the horse back in the stable before it gets too dark out."

"We're going to the stables to talk?" She choked back a laugh, remembering the first time that they had been in there together. "Very well. But I really need to go soon, before Jeanie begins to worry about me."

"I am sure that your friend will understand. This is important." He looked up the road, and put his fingers to his lips. With a brief whistle, the horse came running to them. He hoisted Alison onto the horse, and then climbed up behind her. With a clicking noise, they were galloping around the massive manor to the back, where a large wood and steel structure stood.

The stable that was on the grounds before was purely wood, most likely hand built by Arthur himself. This new stable was more structurally sound and sturdy. As they rode the horse in, she found that it was also climate controlled and a lot nicer than the old one.

Addison slid off the horse, reached up to help her down, and then smacked the horse on the backend. It must have known what he wanted, and it proceeded to its stall.

Instead of staying in the stable to talk, he led her out, and towards the house. Even from the back of the house, it was like taking a walk through one of her memories. Everything was the same, down to the old tree, where a swing gently moved in the breeze.

"You said that we needed to talk…so talk." Alison said, with a little more sassiness than she intended.

"Why are you in such a rush to leave?"

"Because I don't belong here anymore. Why did you say that you brought Woodcrest back for me? Why didn't you do it for Barb?" There was a bit of pain in her voice when she said the girl's name.

"Why on earth would I do all this for her? She has never even been here? She would never appreciate it as we did."

"The guy at the front desk told me that you both checked out of the hotel together. I went there to try to talk to you."

"We didn't check out, together. Well, I mean, we checked out together, but we weren't leaving *together*. She went to reclaim her life, and her daughter. I moved into Becky's place, temporarily."

"What? You were at the Callahan's, and she didn't tell me?"

"I asked her not to. I came to her about a week after you and I parted ways, so to speak, and we talked. I told her what happened, and how I felt about the whole situation. I needed her to keep everything secret. It was important."

"What is it with the two of you?" She yanked her hand free and stopped dead in her tracks. "The two of you have been conspiring against me, off and on, since I got back. I have been falling apart since you walked out on me that day. She knew that. Did she tell you? Did she tell you that I have been trying to reach out to you, to apologize, to let you know that you were right about me not trusting you? I have cried every day since you left…" Her eyes were filled with tears, and her face was twisted by the anguish and pain that she has been feeling over losing him.

"We weren't conspiring. This was all my doing. By the time that Rebecca came home from the center, I was already out of the house, and here, working day and night to finish what I had started. I did this for you…only you. I wanted to do something that would make you understand how sorry I am for being so bull-headed and prideful. I couldn't see past my own hurt at your lack of trust that I forgot what you had gone through, thinking that I had betrayed you for some skinny blonde stranger. It took everything I had to keep me from running back to you, and groveling at your feet." She grasped her arms, and looked at her. "We were our happiest here...in Woodcrest...before all the drama and outside noise. This is our home, Allie. This is where we met, where you brought me back to life. No, you gave me a better life than I had before."

"So, to say you are sorry, you ransack a desolated and forgotten town and turned it into what? A hideaway? A private town for the two of us? There is no one here except for you and I, and those three out front...unless you count the landscapers that I saw in the distance."

"There will be people. Good, moral, wonderful people will populate Woodcrest, as it once was. The benefit of doing all the charity work that I had done is that I met people. The people that are coming to inhabit this wonderful town are people that deserve to be here, people that will bring back the magic of what the town stood for back when we met. They will work here, and live here. Their family businesses will be filling those shops in the center of town. No corporations, no franchises, no money hungry mongrels to steal from the mouths of their children. We will be a community, away from the greed and hatred and racism and judgement."

As Alison listened to the man in front of her, talking with such passion and conviction, her heart swelled. To live in a community like the one he spoke of, to be a part of it would be a blessing unto itself. The only thing that would make it better was if she were a part of it with him. Her heart sunk as she thought of the fact that they were no longer together.

"That's all well and good, Addison. You built this town for them...not me. I commend you on the fact that you are going to give good people a chance at a better life, but how does your plan include me, exactly? Am I to run a nursing home, a rehabilitation center?"

"Did I turn you into the cynical person you have become? Did I kill the kind loving Alison that once looked at me with those beautiful blue eyes?" He released her arms and took a step back.

"No." She looked down at the ground, realizing that the hurt that she felt was coming out as something entirely different. "I am not cynical. And the Alison that used to look at you through these eyes is hiding away in a corner, afraid to come out, because she is emotionally destroyed and full of hopelessness."

"I understand that I hurt you. I speak of protecting you from pain and hurt, and yet I continue to plague you with it. Maybe, it was better if I had just let you believe in my accused indiscretion, because then you would have moved on with your life. Instead, I find a way to reveal the truth, and then I leave you to suffer with the words of a wounded pride."

"You honestly think that I wanted to believe that you had slept with her? You think that it would have made the pain of losing you easier to bear?"

"Maybe…I don't know. But, because of all that I have done, you fear me instead of hating me. Don't think for a moment that I didn't see the fear in your eyes when I ran to you, or the fact that you flinched at my touch. I have never physically harmed you, ever. Why are you afraid of me?" Addison walked a bit further from her.

"Your touch frightens me."

"Why, Alison? Why is my touch so terrifying to you? Why are you pulling away from me, when I am trying to pull you close…to fix what I have broken?" He reached for her, but quickly retracted his hands, sticking them into his pants pockets.

At the risk of bearing her soul, every feeling that she had experienced in the time since they saw one another last, she refused to let him know how deep that her hurt went. If he truly knew how much mental, physical and emotional agony she had been in, it would tear him apart. But, as much as she wanted to hate him for leaving her hanging, all she felt was the need to feel him close to her. That fact alone scared her more than anything.

Minutes seemed to drag on, as he awaited the answer to his questions. He paced and watched her, knowing that she was suffering with the internal fight of head versus heart. When he could endure the silence no more, he felt that only one thing would ease his racing mind and his aching heart.

"I'm sorry. I cannot wait for you to explain it to me. I cannot wait any longer to do what I have wanted to do since I saw you in front of the home I rebuilt for us…I cannot go another minute. Hate me for it…that's fine, but it has been far too long, and I must." He charged forward, grasping her face between his hands. "I love you with everything I am, and I cannot go on in my life without you in it. You are the voice that I hear in the dark of the night, calling to me, begging me to come back. You are the light that has sent the shadows away in my darkest moments. I cannot survive without you at my side, Alison Moreno."

He lowered his lips to hers, and slowly began to devour her. He savored the taste of her, as it was a craving that he had been fighting for weeks. She grasped his wrists, as though trying to pull away. The fear that she had of his touch was not that of physical harm, but of the connection that could reignite the flame that had since become the smallest of embers, just clinging to life. She had almost forgotten what his kiss could do to her. With a tenderness beyond measure, he reminded her of what they once had. She gripped his wrists tighter, but it was no longer to pull away, but to stabilize herself as she felt the earth begin to fall away from beneath her feet.

The Sun began to dip lower and lower behind the enormous trees in the horizon, but neither of them paid any mind to the actions of the sun, or the brilliant colors that accompanied it. They were deep in the warm oceans that surrounded them as they stood just a stone's throw from the back door of the house that they had first laid eyes on one another.

When he pulled his lips from hers, they stood together, grasping one another, gasping for air. It took a few moments for reality to come back into focus.

"I cannot promise that I can keep you from pain, but what I can promise is that if I can, I will protect you from being alone in your pain. I cannot get back the time that we have lost, but what I can do is give you every day from here on out…if you still will have me." He pulled away from her and got down on one knee. "I regretted walking away from you the moment that I closed the door behind me. I have hated myself for not answering your calls or texts…for not coming to you sooner. I wanted to, but I needed to make sure that what I could give you was worth it. This is all I have. This is the life that you will have if you decide to find it in your heart to forgive me once more. I have literally invested everything I have into the dream that we can live as we should have. Together." He pulled his mother's ring from his pocket, and held it out to her. "Please forgive me. Please find it in your heart to love and trust me once again. Please say that you will finally marry me?"

Alison looked at the ring in Addison's hand and remembered the first time he had asked her to marry him. She was so overjoyed, but one thing stood in their way then, as she believed it did now.

"Adam, I cannot marry you. You made a promise to me that you would get my…" She knelt down in front of him, and looked him in the eye, but the voice of her father echoed from the direction of the house, and prevented her from finishing her sentence.

Unbeknownst to her, a crowd had gathered at the back of the house. It was not a small crowd like the one that they had left out front, but a bit larger group. Standing with Rebecca, Ian, and

Caitlin were five others; Sal and Maria had gotten the call shortly after Alison had arrived at the Callahan Mansion, as did Jeanie, who drove from Pittsburgh just to witness her friend's heart be healed. And a few feet away, a young slender blonde woman stood holding the hand of a beautiful little girl.

"You have our blessing, Pumpkin. Be happy." Sal said, clinging to his wife's hand.

"He's a good man. He gave you a whole town. If you won't marry him, I will!" Maria concluded.

"You heard them…they gave us their blessing. Now, what were you saying, Allie?" Addison had a glimmer of amusement in his eye as he smiled at the woman he loved.

"Yes."

"I'm sorry…Yes? Was that a yes?"

"Shut up…you are such a child!" She laughed and shoved him to the ground. "I said yes. The answer is yes, okay." She pinned his hands to the ground and kissed him.

Barbara immediately covered her daughter's eyes with her free hand.

"Mommy…what's happening?" the girl whined.

"You'll find out when you're older."

Chapter Thirty-three

The weeks passed as preparations for two huge events approached; The "Woodcrest Reborn" celebration and the wedding of Addison Thatcher and Alison Moreno. Finishing touches were being taken care of by the new inhabitants of the sleepy little town. A freelance Photographer offered her services to the couple for their wedding photos, a baker made the most beautiful cake for the wedding, and had a large order of her best pies, cakes, and pastries for the celebration. And the family owned restaurant offered to cater and host the reception, as well as to supply the celebration with the best food they could offer.

Mostly everyone who were invited to come live in Woodcrest had already moved in and settled with their families. There was a welcoming ceremony, in which Addison announced the appointment of Woodcrest's new Mayor, Stephen Gentry, who happened to be the youngest grandson of Thomas and Odette. Stephen was proud to take his place and stand for something that his grandparents felt so strongly about. His heart swelled with pride as he stood in front of the community that had put their faith in him. He smiled at Addison, and then at Alison. Finally, he squeezed the hand and kissed the cheek of his wife, Sonya, who was six months pregnant and glowing with pride.

Ian and his wife had chosen to move into Woodcrest as well, and open up a small branch of Callahan Banking and Trust for the people there.

Everyone who came to Woodcrest were invited and inducted by making a vow that they would uphold the values, morals and standards that the town and its founders held dear.

As the preparations were well underway, a few of the new residents felt compelled to come up and introduce themselves to the ones who were working so hard to build a community so out of its time that it was practically history-making. And because the community was so small, everyone felt that getting to know their fellow "Woodcrest-ers" would only plant the seeds of true community.

"Are you Alison Moreno?" A young man approached her as she was assisting a new dress shop owner with hanging her sign outside.

"Yes, as a matter of fact, I am. And what can I do for you?" She smiled and held out her hand to shake his.

"My name is Matthew and I am new to Woodcrest, as is my family."

"Well, let me be the first to personally welcome you to Woodcrest, Matthew." She reached out and offered him a hug, which he accepted, with a bit of surprise.

"Thank you, Ma'am. The thing is…my brother, David and I…well, we heard rumor that a long time ago…someone traveled back in time like seventy some years and landed smack dab in the middle of this town…"

"Oh, is that so? And I bet you want to know if it is really true…am I right?" she winked at him, and looked behind him at his lanky brother. "You must be David. Do you believe that someone could travel in time?" She smiled at the two young men, her arms crossed over her chest.

"Personally, miss…it's a tad bit strange if you ask me…a bit wobblety-cobblety. There is no such thing as time travel…except for in the comics or on television."

"You know what, David…I like you! You have a good head on your shoulders. What do you want to be when you grow up?"

"I want to be a Doctor!" He laughed, and they both ran off, still arguing about whether or not time travel and the rumors about the events in the town were true. Alison, on the other hand, knew the truth, and it made the whole thing so much funnier.

As they all prepared to celebrate the rebirth of the town, the townspeople found solace in knowing that they were led by some great people. There was a city council appointed, as well as a small police station. Alison and Addison argued over having a sheriff, as they were trying to establish a community where everyone held each other accountable for their actions.

"Even a small town like this needs some kind of law enforcement, Addison. Though these people were hand-picked by you, you don't know them well enough to say that laws will not be broken." She sighed, rinsing off a soapy dish and then handing it to him to dry and put away.

"I know that, but if we appoint a sheriff, the people will think that we don't trust them to follow the rules. Once you betray trust, everything goes awry. You and I both know that." He placed the dry dish in the cupboard, and put the dish towel on the counter.

"It's not about trust or the lack of it, Adam. Having a sheriff will also show the people that we care about their safety and security. Knowing that laws will be enforced will allow people to breathe easier at night. Do you want people to worry about whether or not the laws set forth in Woodcrest will be unbiased and fair?" She turned off the faucet, handed him the last wet plate, and looked at him. "I am not saying that we need to have to have a full police squad. We still put our faith and trust in the people, but by having a Sheriff, we also prove to them that breaking the law will have consequences. Unless, of course, you would like to resort to the barbaric way of lynching the offender in the town square by a group of their peers…"

She gave him a smirk, then proceeded to wipe her wet hands on the shirt he was wearing. She knew that doing that would just get him worked up, as the towel was closer to her than his shirt was. She quickly walked out of the kitchen, leaving him standing there, shocked that she would use him to dry her dripping wet hands.

"Come on, Alison! The towel was right there!!" He chased after her, waving the damp dish towel at her, dramatically. "Was that completely necessary?!"

"Yes! It was. Why not just take the matter to city council? You feel that between them and the Mayor, they can resolve any issues that may arise in Woodcrest..." She started up the stairs.

"I don't think that your inability to tell the difference between a towel and a shirt are a matter for the council and Mayor Gentry." He followed her, using the towel to pat his shirt dry as best as he could.

"I was talking about the matter of appointing a sheriff, not your wet clothes." She gaped at him, one eyebrow raised. "Seriously, Addison. It's just a shirt. I do the laundry anyway. Sometimes, I think you love your clothes more than me. My hands were wet, you were there. You are such a prissy." She laughed, and picked up her pace slightly.

"I'm a prissy?! Okay, that's it!" He threw the towel to the floor and chased Alison up the stairs. "You're gonna need that Sheriff after I get done with you. Come back here!" He laughed, taking two steps at a time and chasing after her. She let out a squeal and ran the rest of the way up the stairs and down the hall to her room. Slamming the door and locking it, she laughed and gasped for air as she leaned against the door.

"That's not fair. How can I catch you when you lock me out?" He jiggled the door handle. "You know I love you more than my clothes. Come on and unlock the door, sweetie."

"Not until you promise that you aren't gonna retaliate." She giggled as she tried to catch her breath.

"I'm not going to retaliate..."

"Promise me!"

"Okay, I promise." He laughed as he leaned against the door, gripping the handle.

"Okay…I'm going to unlock the door, then."

She flipped the lock on the door, and he immediately burst through the door, and tackled her. He pinned her to the floor and straddled her, holding her hands above her head. He leaned down, so his face was just inches from hers.

"You broke your promise, Adam." She pouted, yet she was still giggling.

"This is not retaliation. This is something else entirely."

"Seems like retaliation to me. You have me pinned to the hardwood floor. I am defenseless."

"Just the way I like it. I cannot wait until we share a bedroom. Why are you staying in here anyway?" He looked around the room. It was almost exactly like her room when she was taking care of him, except that it was filled with more modern items like a flat screen television and a stereo. Most of the furniture was the original furniture from before, which had been in storage for countless years.

"You know why. We aren't married yet. We are already 'living in sin' by living in the same house prior to our wedding." She looked at him, and answered him with an innocent looking expression.

"Well, since you put it that way. Okay. But, in three weeks, you're mine!" He growled, nipped at the tip of her nose with his teeth.

"Can you get off of me now?" She laughed, struggling to free her hands.

"Are you going to apologize for using me as a hand towel?"

"No." She giggled.

"No?"

"Nope. I am not going to apologize for that."

"And, why not?"

"Because…I didn't use you as a hand towel…I used your shirt."

"But, I was wearing the shirt in question at the time of the offense."

"It doesn't matter. I dried my hands on your shirt, not you. So, I am sorry for using your shirt as a hand towel."

"But, since I was wearing the said shirt when you moistened it with your dish-water soaked hands, it dampened my skin…and so therefore you used me as a hand towel as well."

"You are really going to milk this, aren't you? You just don't want to get up."

"Actually, you're right…I don't." He looked at her. "Please…I know we aren't married yet, but…Let me touch something…please." He began to give her puppy dog eyes and outed his lips out.

"How old are you? Five?" She laughed.

"Well, if we go by the year I was born…I am one hundred and five."

"Um…no." she had a disgusted look on her face. "Now, get off me, you dirty old man." The smile that made its way across her face just made him smile back.

"I am not a dirty old man. I am a dirty young man. Now, let me *tooouccch somethhhing.*" He pleaded and begged her. Finally, she pointed at her upper thigh. He smiled as though he were a child getting his way. He put one hand on her thigh and acted as if he were doing something naughty. When he began to slide his hand up further, she grabbed it.

"No, Addison. Anything above that is prohibited until I have a wedding band on my finger."

He didn't care. He got to put his hand on her upper thigh so he was happy in the moment.

Chapter Thirty-Four

The sun was shining through the window, casting beautiful rainbows on the walls as its rays cascaded through a beautiful prism wind chime in the window. Alison was holding the torso of her dress tightly to her abdomen as Barbara and Jeanie buttoned the numerous buttons that ran up the dress. Maria stood off to the side, holding the jeweled toule veil out of the way, so the girls could finish up.

"Alright, last button. And…Done!" Jeanie sighed, relieved as she sucked on the tips of her fingers, which had become sore from having to push small buttons through tight loops. Maria and Barb straightened the veil so it didn't hang funny or catch on her dress. Her mother stepped back from her, and put her hands to her lips.

"Sei troppo Bella!" Maria sighed, taking in the full view of her daughter in her gown.

"Thank you, mama. I feel beautiful…like a princess. Please be sure to thank Carlo Santiago for me when you see him. It is a perfect fit." Alison smiled, looking at herself in the full length mirror.

"Who's Carlo Santiago?" Barbara inquired, fluffing out the layers of crinoline of the skirt.

"Carlo is an old friend of our family's in Sicily. I've known him for years. He designed and made Alison's dress himself and shipped it here."

"How could someone in Italy make a dress for her and it be the right size and fit, without her there to try it on or anything?"

"He has been making dressed like this since before you were a thought in your parents' minds. He has a knack for it. I just sent him her measurements, and he went to work. He had designed and made thousands of wedding dresses for women all over the world." Maria laughed, and smoothed out the dress's silky material.

"Are you talking about…*the* Carlo Santiago? Like the same Carlo Santiago that made that absolutely gorgeous wedding gown for…oh nuts…what is her name…the one that married the guy in the royal family…What's his name?" Barbara began to fiddle and was having trouble remembering their names.

"Yes, the very same one." Alison took pity on Barbara. "Where's Emma? I want to see my flower girl."

"She's with Caitlin and Mrs. Callahan. I'll go get her." Barbara headed for the door, and jumped when she opened it and Alison's dad was on the other side, about to knock. "Hi! I assume you came to see your daughter. Don't worry. She's decent." She stepped aside so he could come in the room, before rushing off to get her daughter.

"Ay Dios Mio!" Salvatore gasped as he set his eyes upon his daughter in her wedding gown, looking as though she had stepped right out of a storybook. "Se mira impresionante!" There were tears in his eyes as he gazed at her.

Alison blushed, and maneuvered herself so that she could hug her father.

"Gracias, papa." She wrapped her arms around her father's neck, and embraced him.

"And for the only English speaking person in the room, may I have a translation…please." Jeanie blushed, embarrassed that she had to ask, as Alison usually translated things said by her parents automatically.

"Sal said, 'Oh my Goodness…you look stunning." Maria spoke up, walking over to the young woman. "I would think that, with all the time that you have spent with Alison, you would have learned Italian and Spanish by now." She laughed.

"I'm not the one you have to worry about. Poor Addison had no idea what he is in for. When she gets mad, she could say things to him that could make his toes curl, and he won't have a clue." Jeanie retorted.

Moments later, the bedroom door opened again, and a small girl walked in, dressed in a white dress very much like Alison's.

"You look absolutely adorable, Emma!" Alison bent down to look at the girl. "Look at how grown up and pretty you look." She turned her head and pointed at the mirror, where the reflection of the two of them was.

"You look very pretty, too, Miss Alison." Emma spoke so quietly, that only Allie could hear her. Smiling, Alison rose back up, and looked at the women who followed Emma in. Both of them were white as a sheet and looked as if they had seen a ghost.

"What is it? What's wrong?" Alison's smile faded away quickly.

"Barb and I need to talk to you." Caitlin tried to be discreet.

"We will leave you to it." Jeanie got the point, and looked to the other three people in the room. "Come on, Emma. Let's go downstairs and wait for the rest of the guests to arrive." She put her hand on the girl's shoulder. "Mr. and Mrs. Moreno, let's let them talk in private."

After the four of them left, Caitlin shut the door and the two women approached Alison, who was beginning to panic.

"Please tell me that Addison is down there, greeting our guests." She grasped the hands of both woman, fearing that they were going to tell her that her groom had not arrived yet.

"He's down there, sweetie. No worries! He looks gorgeous. But, when he sees you...Ooooh honey." Caitlin tried to reassure her friend by giving her a exaggerated smile.

"Okay, Thank Heavens. I was going to have a heart attack." She let out a sigh of relief. "Is the pastor here yet?"

"Yes. Pastor Manning just arrived right before we came up. This is about one of the guests."

"What's wrong? Who didn't show up?" Alison tried to slow her pulse by taking long breathes.

"It isn't about who *didn't* show up...it's about who **did**."

"Who?" Alison looked to both of the women, searching their faces.

"It's my fault. Emma was so excited about being your flower girl. She had to tell anyone and everyone she could tell." Barbara mumbled. "I should have told her to keep it a secret from her, but I couldn't catch her in time."

It took Alison a moment to catch on, but when she did, the color drained from her face.

"Oh dear God, no...no no no no!" She swallowed hard. "Please tell me that she isn't here, Barbara. She could ruin everything."

"I tried to stop Emma from telling her, but she was so excited, and it just kind of flew out of her mouth before I could stop her. I am so sorry, sweetie."

"Does Addison know?" Alison was about to rush to the door.

"Yes, he knows, and everyone else is on red alert. It'll be okay. I am pretty sure that she is not going to make a spectacle of herself. She is, after all, in her late nineties and in a wheelchair." Caitlin tried to diffuse the anxiety in Alison's face. "Ian said that Addison is not worried, but that he didn't want you to know. However, Grandmother said that you needed to be told, so you would be prepared in case you saw her."

"Thank you, Caitlin…Barbara, this isn't your fault. We will just have to prepare ourselves in case she is up to something. I am *not* going to let her ruin my wedding day. We have come too far, and been through far too much to let someone like Helena Bancroft take this away from us. How in the world did she even get here? There are people at the gates, checking invitations for people from outside of Woodcrest."

"I think that she came with your old boss from the nursing home in Pittsburgh. She may have been her plus one or something."

"Okay." Alison took a deep breath, closed her eyes, and focused for a moment. "I am not going to let her get to me. She is an old lady…a mean, conniving, manipulative old lady, true, but an old lady nonetheless. She doesn't scare me." The panic came back to her face. "Oh, who am I kidding? She terrifies me! She's going to ruin everything."

"No! I will not let her. Just because she has a personal vendetta against Addison's grandfather, that doesn't give her the right to take it out on you and Addison. I have had enough. I owe Addison, cuz, he was the one who made it possible for me to get my baby girl back. I was her pawn, and allowed her to manipulate me and it almost destroyed your lives. It will NOT let it happen again…not if I have anything to do about it." Barbara gave a stern look and charged out the door, with a determined pace and a loud slam of the door.

"What in the world!?!" Caitlin laughed, nervously. "Addison's grandfather? Really? That's the story that Lena went with?"

"If Lena had said that it had been Addison, himself, who had broken things off with her the night before their wedding, Barbara would have thought that she was losing her mind." Alison responded, sitting down on the platform that she had been standing on previously. "Why would she come here? How did she convince Madison to bring her as her plus one?"

"No worries, sweetie. Let's just get you ready to go down. You are getting married." She blotted Alison's watery eyes with her handkerchief and helped her up. She straightened her friend's dress and veil and then went to see if everyone had gone outside to the garden by looking out the window. When she saw Addison standing at the altar with the pastor, she knew the coast was clear, and led Alison out of the room and helped her down the large staircase and to the back door. As they passed the large painting of Addison's family, Alison paused and looked at them.

"I love your son, and I promise that I will take very good care of him. I just wish you were here to see how happy he is." She blew a kiss to her soon-to-be mother- and father-in-law and followed Caitlin to the sliding door, where her father, Barbara and Jeanie were waiting with Emma and Nate, Caitlin's son, who was their ring bearer. Alison smiled at how cute the two children looked together.

She took her father's arm, and Jeanie handed her the bridal bouquet. Taking a deep breath, she tried to steady her nerves.

"Are you alright, pumpkin? You look like you are ready to jump out of your skin." Sal said, quietly.

"Everything will be fine, once I am married to the man I love. I'm so ready for this."

The doors in front of them opened, and one by one, the girls walked out and down the silky runner that ran all the way to the altar. Emma went next, sprinkling flower petals on the runner. Then, Nate started out, closing the door behind him just enough to hide the bride. Alison could see Addison perfectly now, through the crack in the door, and Caitlin wasn't joking when she said he looked gorgeous.

Addison had an Ash grey tuxedo on, with a charcoal tie and black vest. His hair was slicked back and tied with a ribbon to match his tuxedo. He looked as nervous as she did, and she smiled.

Off to the one side of the crowd that had gathered to witness their nuptials was a very old woman in a wheelchair. She was just as Alison had remembered her from the home, and seated next to her was her old boss, Maddie, as well as a man appearing to be Madison's husband.

Swallowing hard, knowing that she would be passing next to the woman, she closed her eyes and tried to focus on getting through the next few minutes as she joined the man that she loved at the altar. She refused to let the woman's ominous presence bring a dark cloud to ruin her day. This was a matter of fight-or-flight for her, and she wasn't going down without a fight, even though history has shown that she was more of the flight part.

The music that was playing came to an end, and a sweet, lulling tune began to play from the violinist, signaling that it was time. She exchanged looks with her father, and then waited for the ushers to open the doors in front of them, and the guests to stand.

In the instant that the doors opened, everything changed. There was no one else there. Just him and her. And with instant tears and a smile that weakened her knees, he spoke volumes of what was going through his mind as he set his eyes on her from where he stood. Nothing else mattered. No one else existed in the world.

Addison's bottom lip trembled, and he wiped away the tears in his chestnut eyes that were obscuring his view of the vision coming down the aisle. The tightening in his throat and chest made it difficult to breathe, but he didn't need to do something as trivial as breathing. His heart swelled at the thought that, in a matter of minutes, he would be hers, and she would be his.

Alison clung to her father's arm as she focused on getting to the man waiting for her. Nothing else mattered to her. Everything that they had been through, good and bad, led up to this moment, and all she could think about was making sure that she could stay on her feet long enough to get to him. And as her feet carried her down the stairs that led out to the garden, and down the silken pathway before her, she kept her eyes locked on his. She didn't hear the people around her, whispering to one another, nor did she acknowledge the look on the dreaded uninvited guest's face that she passed.

The sun maneuvered its way through the tree branches to shine on the whole scene, and a gentle breeze carried a familiar scent through the air. As though they both knew what the other was thinking, they looked up at the puffy clouds passing overhead, and blew kisses to the two people that had come to witness the blessed event in spirit. The sunlight kissed Alison's cheek, and she could smell the sweet perfume of Elizabeth mingled with pipe tobacco. In her mind, she thanked them both for coming to share their day.

Sal and Alison reached the altar, after what felt like an eternity, and he lifted her veil, kissed his daughter on the cheek, and then took her hand, and placed it in Addison's.

"Take care of my baby girl, Addison." Sal whispered, placing his hands around theirs. Addison nodded and put his other hand over the man's, giving it a squeeze.

The assembled guests took their seats again, and the pastor began to speak.

"As we gather today, to celebrate the joining of Addison Xavier Thatcher and Alison Selene Consuela Moreno, let us take a moment to reflect on the path that has brought them here today. Let us remember those who, by the mercy of our Heavenly Father and the grace of our Blessed Mother, are here in spirit to bear witness to their Holy union."

Everyone fell silent, and took a moment to honor those who had passed on, and who were watching over them. When the moment of silence passed, everyone turned their attention back to the bride and groom, and the officiant.

Alison was raised in the Catholic Church, and Addison in the Lutheran church. However, despite the differences in their religious backgrounds, they chose to do a less-religiously strict ceremony.

"The union of husband and wife is intended by God for their mutual joy; for the help and comfort given each other in prosperity and adversity; and, when it is God's will, for the procreation of children and their nurture in the knowledge and love of the Lord. Therefore, marriage is not to be entered into unadvisedly or lightly, but reverently, deliberately, and in accordance with the purposes for which it was instituted by God."

The look in Addison's eyes as he looked at the woman he loved was tender and filled Alison's heart with a warm feeling.

But as happy as the two of them were in that moment, the dread that had been in the backs of their minds came forward with the pastor's next statement.

"Into this union Alison and Addison now come to be joined. If any of you can show just cause why they may not be lawfully wed, speak now, or else forever hold your peace."

Alison's heart seemed to stop beating for the short moment that passed, as she waited to hear the dreaded voice from the back of the crowd. Addison sensed her anguish and gripped her hand more firmly, trying to convey in his touch that he was not going to let anything come between them.

Moments ticked by, and when the only sounds heard were the birds in the trees and the wind rustling the leaves overhead, the Pastor continued. Alison let out a slow breath and opened her eyes again. Her heart began to beat again. Addison's shoulders, which were tensed up, began to relax.

"Alison, please present your vows to Addison." The greying man stated, looking to her. As part of the ceremony, they had to memorize their vows and say them to one another. Originally, they had intended on writing their own, but nothing could be said today, that hadn't already been said and expressed already between them.

"I, Alison, take you Addison, for my wedded husband from this day forward, to have and to hold as equal partner in my life, to whom I give my deepest love and devotion. I humbly open my heart to you as a sanctuary of warmth and peace, where you may come and find a refuge of love and strength. I will love you enough to risk being hurt, trust you when I don't understand, weep with you in heartache, and celebrate life with you in joy. I will receive you as my equal throughout all of our days."

"And now you, Addison."

"I, Addison, take you Alison, for my wedded wife from this day forward, to have and to hold as equal partner in my life, to whom I give my deepest love and devotion. I humbly open my heart to you as a sanctuary of warmth and peace, where you may come and find a refuge of love and strength. I will love you enough to risk being hurt, trust you when I don't understand, weep with you in heartache, and celebrate life with you in joy. I will receive you as my equal throughout all of our days."

Pastor Manning held out his bible to Ian, and he placed the wedding band on its pages. Then, the pastor turned to Jeanie, who did the same.

"Bless, O Lord, these rings as a symbol of the vows by which this man and this woman have bound themselves to each other; through Jesus Christ our Lord." He held the bible up in front of him. After a brief prayer, he presented the rings to Addison. He picked up the smaller of the two rings, and took her hand in his.

"As a sign of my love for you, of choosing to share my whole life's journey with you, and of my knowing that in marrying you I shall become much more than I am, I give you this ring, with the pledge that with you, I shall become my highest expression of God, sharing the gifts that I have and I am with you and the world." He gazed into her sapphire eyes. "May this ring always represent my everlasting love and devotion to what we have." He slid the ring onto her finger, and then kissed her hand.

Alison had to fight back tears of happiness as she gripped his ring, and began to slide it over his fingertip. It was then that she noticed how much his hand was trembling.

"As a sign of my love for you, of choosing to share my whole life's journey with you, and of my knowing that in marrying you I shall become much more than I am, I give you this ring, with the pledge that with you, I shall become my highest expression of God, sharing the gifts that I have and I am with you and the world." She slid his ring the rest of the way on, and lifted his hand to her cheek. At the touch of her skin on his palm, the tremors diminished. With his thumb, he swiped away a tear that fell from her eye.

Pastor Manning closed his book, and asked that Alison and Addison place their hands on it.

"Alison and Addison, you have each chosen to be joined in marriage today. The bible states that 'two are better than one; they receive a good reward for their toil, because, if one fails, the other can help the companion up again.' In my presence and in the presence of your family and friends, you have exchanged vows and made promises. You have opened your hearts to one another, declared your love and friendship, and have united yourself with the exchanging of rings. Therefore, with the blessings of God, it is my pleasure to now pronounce you husband and wife." He smiled at the two of them, then looked to Addison. "You may now kiss the bride!"

With a deep breath, they looked to one another, and took in what had just transpired. Addison slid his hands to the base of her spine, and pulled her to him. He teased her by rubbing the tip of her nose with his own. Pressing her body to his, he tightened his grip on her. Unable to resist looking down, he snuck a peek of the bosoms that were practically elusive throughout their entire relationship. They were on display because of the cut of the bodice on the dress and seeing them automatically brought out the animal in Addison. His eyes widened and he seemed to salivate like a wolf spotting a couple of plump juicy bunnies just feet from him.

"Addison!" Alison whispered, giggling as she knew what he was looking at.

"What?!" his eyes snapped back to her face.

"You're drooling! Would you please kiss me already?" She giggled, glancing out of the corner of her eye at the people waiting to see them seal the wedding with a kiss.

"Oh! Sorry. I couldn't help it. I've never met them before and they caught my attention." he wiped his mouth, and refocused his attention on her face. "We did it, Mrs. Thatcher."

"Yes, we did, Mr. Thatcher."

He lowered his lips to hers, and the kiss was by far the most heartfelt and meaningful of all the kisses that they had shared up to that point. The electricity that ran through her just moments ago had made a full circuit, flowing through her and back into him, and she felt like a rocket ship, ready for blast off. He slid his one hand up to the middle of her back to support her, as he leaned into the kiss. She leaned in more too, causing her to go up onto the toes of her high heel shoes. Because her shoes had thicker soles to give a bit of height, she lost her balance. Instinctively, her arms wrapped around his neck, in an effort to catch her balance before she knocked him backwards.

To everyone viewing this, it looked as though they were getting a bit too into the kiss and were going to consummate the marriage right then and there.

"Hey now! We still have a reception to attend. Save that for later on tonight!" Ian jibed, giving Addison's shoulder a shove. Everyone else laughed and began to applaud wildly and cheer loudly.

After they had finished with the receiving line, the marriage licenses had been signed, and pictures were taken, everyone made their way to The Vineyard, a restaurant and banquet hall own by one of the Italian Woodcrest families. It was Addison's insistence that the food at the reception be Italian as he had fallen in love with the taste and aesthetics of Italian food, thanks to Maria's cooking.

Everyone took their seats at the tables and the staff served the food. However, because Alison had not planned on sitting down in her dress, she felt as though she was being shoved through a tight tube. She barely ate anything other than the antipasto salad, and was back onto her feet soon afterward. To save her feet from aching, she had chosen to change her shoes, and found relief in the comfort of her brand new white tennis shoes. Because her dress was long, it dragged the floor slightly without her heels on.

After everyone had digested their food, Addison took Alison by the hand and led her to the dance floor, where they shared their first dance as man and wife. He slid one hand to the small of her back, and took the other hand in his. The lights in the small trees around the dancefloor twinkled as they began to spin and sway.

"I just have to say this, because I haven't gotten the chance to until now." He glanced down, and gazed into her unbelievably beautiful eyes. "When I saw you in the doorway, before you began to walk down the aisle…You are the most beautiful woman I have ever seen and I was tempted to just take you and run. I didn't want to share you with anyone else. I seriously fell in love with you all over again when I saw you there." The dimples in his cheeks deepened, as his smile widened. He couldn't help but smile when he looked at her, especially after seeing her reaction to what he had just said. Her cheeks flushed, and her eyes began to fill with the glitter of tears.

"Addison, please don't make me cry right now. My mascara will run all over the place. I would look awful with runny black streaks on my face."

"You could be covered in mud from head to toe, with leaves and twigs stuck in your hair and I would still think that you are absolute perfection." His words brought more tears to her eyes, and she slid her hand up and put it at the nape of his neck, pulling him closer so she could kiss him.

Laying a feather soft kiss on his lips, she put her forehead to his.

"I love you, Adam...I have loved you from the moment I set eyes on you. I know that it sounds strange, and in light of the circumstances, kind of creepy...but it's the truth."

"I don't think it's creepy. I have loved you since the first time that I heard your voice. I fell in love with you long before I even saw your face." He took his handkerchief from his pocket and blotted her eyes, preventing the mascara from even touching her soft olive toned cheek.

Soon enough, their first dance ended as their song faded and blended into the beginning of another song, and others joined them on the dance floor.

With the wedding ceremony and the festivities that followed, Alison had almost forgotten about Lena's presence until she got a strange feeling at the back of her neck. Turning to see what was behind her, she spotted the aged woman sitting near the edge of the floor, watching them.

"I expected Lena to speak up during the wedding, when Pastor Manning asked if anyone objected. When she didn't, I got even more panicked. How about you? You didn't seem half as afraid as I was." She looked to her new husband and stared into his calm, smiling face. "You still don't seemed bothered by her presence. Why?" Suspicion crept over her.

"Let's just say…the war of wills and revenge has ended." He stopped dancing and took her by the hand. He led her, reluctantly, over to the woman and got behind the chair. "Let's go somewhere a bit more private, and have a little chat…shall we, ladies?" Without waiting for an answer, he proceeded to push Lena out of the room and into the main part of the restaurant, which was empty and secluded, with his new wife trailing closely behind.

Rebecca and her grandchildren sat at their table, watching as the bride and groom walked out of the banquet room, Lena in tow.

"I wonder what that retched woman is doing here. When we told Alison she was here, she darned near had an anxiety attack. Now, she's leaving her own wedding reception with her." Caitlin spoke through her teeth.

"I am sure that they are probably escorting her out, without trying to start anything." Ian scratched his eyebrow, unsure he even believed what he was saying.

"Well, honestly, children…I don't care what that woman has to say, or why she is here. All that matters is that she didn't start anything yet, and she didn't put a stop to the wedding when she had a chance."

"That is rather strange. When the pastor asked if anyone objected, I watched her. She barely even batted an eye. As a matter of fact, she looked down at her watch and then looked as if the service needed to continue quicker." Caitlin sighed.

"Do you mean to tell me…that she appeared to want the wedding to continue quicker?" Becky looked at her granddaughter, a look of disbelief in her eyes. "Are we sure that this Mrs. Bancroft is the same Lena from Woodcrest?"

"I checked into it, Grandmother. I even talked to Barbara. She is the same woman."

"Maybe she didn't hear the pastor ask for any objections until it was already too late to say anything. She's old and old people are deaf."

"Ian Gunther!" Rebecca was appalled at his stereotypical statement.

"Sorry, Grandmother. Not all old people are deaf, but she might be. Maybe what looked like she was getting impatient was he hoping that he come to that part sooner, even though he has already said it."

"Oh, pish posh. Who really cares, anyway? They are married now, so to hell with the old crone! Ian, ask your grandmother to dance before I take you over my knee for forgetting your manners. I want to dance!" Becky ordered, jokingly, wanting to not dwell on Lena any longer than needed.

Chapter Thirty-Five

When they found a good table to sit down and talk, Addison wheeled Lena's chair under the table, locked the wheels, and then pulled out a chair for Alison. She hesitated and then sat down, tucking her layers of dress beneath her. He sat down in the chair between the two of them, and looked at his bride, a smile still lingering on his lips.

"I know that you are quite suspicious of Lena's presence here today. And I have a confession to make. She was, in fact, invited here." He looked at Alison, sheepishly, like a child guilty of directly breaking a rule. "I know what you are thinking, and I know that I should have told you about it before Barbara came and told you that she was here. I know that her being here put more stress on you than you needed, especially today, but I wanted to marry you before I admitted my treacherous plans."

Alison gave Addison a glare that could have melted titanium. She could not understand, after everything that they had gone through, that he would invite the person responsible for almost all of their pain. However, a part of her understood why he waited until after the wedding to drop the bombshell.

"Addison, I am trying to wrap my head around you inviting her to our wedding…I'm trying to find logical reasoning for this, and I can't." There was a pang of both anger and pain in her voice.

"I went to Pittsburgh, while we were apart, and I confronted Lena myself. Everything started with the two of us, and so I felt that it had to end with the two of us. I went with Barb, to help her get her daughter back…and Lena and I talked."

"Is that what you call it…*talking*…It was more like an ambush." Lena spoke up for the first time since she had been there. "He comes charging into my room at the home, and starts to threaten me, telling me that I am nothing more than a spoiled rotten brat who feels that if I don't get my way, I sabotage and take revenge on people's lives." She grumbled.

"But you do, Lena. You lash out…you get downright hateful and dish out revenge like it is sewn into your DNA. You pushed me from the stage the night of the party…"

"My Rehearsal Party for my wedding, which was the next day…"

"…A wedding that was happening because you lied to Addison about being pregnant. You were marrying him under false pretenses, so don't act like he broke your heart." Alison felt her blood pressure rising.

"My heart was broken. Contrary to what everyone thought of me, I did love Addison…very much. Why do you think I made up the pregnancy in the first place? I didn't want to lose him." Lena's tone was cool and calm, and for the first time, Alison caught a hint of raw emotion.

"You mean, you didn't want to lose his money and social standing…You say that you loved him, and yet you felt the need to deceive him…"

"Oh, and you didn't, little miss Time Jumper?! How long was it before you told him where you were really from? You are little miss pure and innocent, judging me for lying to him about a pregnancy…you lied to him about where and *when* you were from. You were a paradox, and anomaly…you weren't even supposed to exist, and yet, there you were." Lena didn't raise her voice, but the look in her eyes spoke for her.

"Addison thought he was going to be a father…you ripped that from him. He was willing to give up everything for you and that baby, even if it meant alienating himself from his own family." Alison crossed her arms over her chest. "I would never have expected him to do that."

"No, instead, you lured him away and his family thought that he was dead! I was there, at his funeral. I saw how devastated they were. At least, with me, he could have reconciled with them after time had passed. You never gave him that chance."

"Alright, ladies…enough. Not one of us stands completely innocent in things that happened." He laid his hands on the table and looked from one of them to the other. "Everyone has blood on their hands for something. Yes, Lena, Alison could have told me the truth about where she really came from in the beginning, but it wouldn't have changed how I felt about her." He turned his head to his wife. "Lena lashed out at you at the party because…well, we know why, but she lied because she was afraid of losing me, and I would have found out her lie eventually…we would have crossed that bridge when we came to it. You busted the bridge down before we even got that far."

"I cannot believe that you just said that to me!" Alison was appalled at what Addison has just said, and got up. "We have been married an hour, and you are talking about, had I not revealed the deception, you would have married her!"

"Sweetheart, if you let me finish…"

"What more is there to say, Addison?"

"A lot, actually. Please…sit back down." He knew that the words had come out wrong as soon as he had said them, and was not the least bit surprised at Alison's reaction. "The point that I was trying to get to is that all of us have blame for what happened back then, on that night. But, after the dust had settled, that should have been the end of it. Instead, Lena felt the need to take it further…seventy-some years further…and throw a wrench into the mix."

"Yes. Despite the fact that it was over and done with, I felt the need to seek my revenge still. I set the fire at the nursing home."

"I know. Your act of revenge could have killed many innocent people, Lena. Do what you must to Adam and I, but those people didn't deserve to almost lose their lives in the process."

"I liked those people. Some of them were my friends. The whole thing got out of hand, and when I tried to put out the fire, I fell from my wheelchair and hit the trash can, and only worsened the situation. It looked as though I was going to be a victim of my own vengeance, and I was ready to face the consequences of my actions. I almost was, but then Addison saved me."

"And to repay him for his mercy, you decided to scheme even further and hurt him by making him out to be a cheater and a liar. And you involved your granddaughter and great granddaughter."

"I wanted to die, to be free of the pain that I felt. When Addison saved me, something clicked in my head. It wasn't about revenge anymore." Lena's eyes filled with tears. "I had not married for love. My husband, George…may he burn in Hell for all eternity…was a heartless, cruel man with no love in his heart. He married me because he needed a pretty trophy wife on his arm, and I just wanted to have…I wanted what the two of you obviously had. In all the time that Addison and I were together, he never kissed me the way he kissed you. He never looked at me the way that he looked at you. I wanted that so badly that I thought that I could get George to love me like that."

Alison slunk down into her chair, and watched as a woman that she despised proceeded to bear her soul.

"George could barely look at me except in public, when he acted as the doting husband. He had lovers on the side, who tended to his manly needs. When I told him that I wanted to be the one to satisfy him, he became enraged and gave me what I wanted. He was so amused that I would have the nerve to speak up to him that he slammed me onto the floor and…it was painful, and he was excessively rough. I ended up with bruises, a broken wrist, and two cracked ribs…and pregnant. He never touched me again after that night. I had Donovan, Barbara's father, nine months later. Donovan was my saving grace. He was the one who loved me, who covered me in kisses every day, and who kept my mind off of being in a loveless marriage."

"Oh my goodness, Lena. That's horrible. Why didn't you leave him? Why didn't you take your son and get out?" Alison was mortified at what she was hearing.

"He wouldn't have let us leave. He was a powerful businessman, and if his wife left him, he would lose credibility in his job. Besides, I am sure that I was not the only woman who was being beaten and tormented by their husband. There was no such thing as divorces when it came to a man beating his wife. And if I tried to get out because of the infidelity, I would be called a liar and laughed at, then punished once I was behind closed doors."

"How on earth did you deal?"

"In all honesty, I wanted out, but my father…you remember that miserable old codger? He told me that I married a man with money, and I had an obligation to stay with him, so that I could provide for him. All those years, I thought that my father wanted what was best for me…but, he only wanted me to marry a wealthy man so that I would take care of him."

"Well, what happened to your husband? Your father?"

"My father died of tuberculosis somewhere around Donovan's freshman year in high school. George…well, let's just say that his excessive drinking became his downfall, literally. He came at me with his shotgun one night, because I added too much pepper to the stew. Donovan came in and saw his father, and shoved him away from me, and George tripped and fell down the basement stairs. The gun went off in his hand on the way down the stairs. He shot himself three times as he fell, so…needless to say, he never felt his neck break. My son saved my life that night. He told the police everything when they showed up."

"Please tell me that everything worked out for him. He was just protecting you. They didn't arrest him, did they?"

"Thank heavens, no. One of my neighbors heard George screaming at me, and there were marks on my face from the muzzle of the gun."

"I am so sorry that you had to live like that, Lena."

"If Addison had married me, I would have at least had a chance at a happy life. It may not have been perfect, but at least I knew that he was a gentleman, and he would never hurt me. But, as luck would have it, you came into his life, and he found his once-in-a-lifetime love. I think that is part of why I was so horrible to you…you had Addison's heart and I didn't."

"I never intended to take him from you, Lena. I fell in love with him, yes, but he had you, he loved you. I was ready to leave as I thought that I would never have his heart."

"No, that is where you are wrong. He didn't love me…"

"That's what I tried to tell you, though, Lena. I did love you. As Alison said before…I was willing to give up everything for you. I wanted to elope, to run away with you. I wanted you, but you made it clear that you wanted my family's money more than you wanted me. I loved you." He looked at Lena, and she could see it in his eyes that he wasn't lying. She smiled, and laid a frail hand on his.

"But not like you loved her…even at our happiest, you never looked at me the way that you looked at her when you thought I wasn't paying attention. And, when I refused to run away with you, it was because I was so afraid what my father would do to me, or to you…I knew that, by refusing you, I would hurt you. But, I knew how my father was. I would much rather you hated me than for him to lay a hand on you."

"I would have protected you, and I would have taken a couple hits from the man if it meant that we could prove everyone wrong." Admitting his feeling for Lena in front of his new bride was awkward, but he refused to lie to save Alison from a little bit of hurt feelings. She knew that he would die for her, that he loved her more than anyone else, and so admitting to a little old lady that he once loved her enough to save her from her life didn't seem so bad. Lena was right, though. Even though he loved her a lot, he was never in love with her as he was and still is with Alison.

"So, that still doesn't explain why you lit that fire…why you sent your granddaughter to break us up." Alison piped in, trying to find out the truth.

"The fire…well, that was a bit of the hurt and pain left from days gone by. I couldn't bear to see the two of you. It took me some time to work out why you were both the same as you were back then. If I had asked questions, I would have been put in the nuthouse. So, I kept my suspicions to myself, and kept my identity a secret. Neither of you recognized me, so I wanted to keep it that way. But, no matter how hard I tried to make your job miserable and make you hate me, you always treated me with kindness. It was then, that I decided that you were everything that Addison had deserved all along. Out of self-pity, I didn't want you to have your 'happily ever after,' because I never got mine. So I lit a fire in my trash bin. The rest of that part is history." She looked at Addison. "As I told you before, Addison, you should have just let me die in that fire. I still don't understand why you chose to save me, especially after you found out who I was and what I had done."

"You may have set the fire, and put people in danger, but you didn't deserve to die such a painful death. No one deserves that." Addison placed his hand on hers.

"As far as Barbara, I wanted to test your relationship...push it past its breaking point and see if the two of you could bounce back. I wanted to prove that true love was not as infallible as you two made it out to be. If I could do that, maybe I could prove that there was no such thing as 'True Love.' I know that what I did was wrong, and I am proud of my granddaughter for doing the right thing in the end. If she hadn't come forward, I fear that she would be doomed to suffer in love as I had."

"But, Addison and Barbara never did anything. She just made it look that way."

"If she had done something with Addison, she would have had to answer to me for it. I just wanted her to put a wedge between the two of you, to put doubt in your mind. She did as she was asked." Lena looked at Addison again. "And that is why I had the papers ready for her when she came to retrieve Emma. At first, I was satisfied with what my little social experiment had proven, but when I saw the look on your face, I knew that I had hurt you more than you ever hurt me. You had love, real love, and I had taken that from you. My heart hurt for you, Addison." She looked back to Alison, and she smiled. "So, I had Donovan gather every picture I owned from my time in Woodcrest, and I mailed them to Addison for him to use for the rebuilding. I knew that that was part of his plan to get you back, and I wanted to make amends. He invited me to come here to be a part of your big day, and I was not going to say no."

"I thought, for sure, you were here to put a stop to our wedding, seeing as I was the reason that you never married Addison."

"I figured that you would, and I had to clamp my mouth shut to keep from laughing at how serious the two of you became up there, waiting for me to jump up and say something." She giggled slightly. "However, I saw the look on your faces, and no matter what I felt, I couldn't take this away from you. So, I would like to call a truce…a cease fire. I am old. I am nearing the end of my time here, and I would like to not leave any enemies." The sincerity in her eyes and in the tone of her voice sent a wave of warmth through Alison. She got up out of her chair and walked over to kneel next to the old lady in the wheelchair. Taking her small, frail hand in her own, she smiled.

"I am so sorry for taking your happy ending from you, and for all that you had to endure since then. You deserved happiness, Lena…just like everyone else. Consider this a new beginning for us. Let's go back in before people start to wonder where we have disappeared to."

As they headed back into the room full of new friends, old friends, and family, something crossed her mind. Had Lena never set that fire, and she not lost her job, she would never have come to Woodcrest in the first place, and Lena and Addison would have gotten married. And then, Lena never would have set the fire in the first place, because she wouldn't have been so miserable. So, by setting the fire at the home, Lena had set in motion a series of events that led to this day. Lena was the reason that Addison and Alison found one another. At the expense of her happiness, she had brought happiness to others.

Alison had a new found respect for her old nemesis. In a moment of deep felt emotion, she brought them to a halt and leaned over, and hugged the woman in the metal chair. At first, Lena found this to be strange and quite uncomfortable, but the longer that Alison hugged her, the more she knew what it felt like to be given a hug that had real meaning behind it. She gripped Alison's hands and gave them a squeeze.

The rest of the evening was filled with memories and laughter. Lena and Rebecca even sat and talked for a bit. They reminisced about the old days, and all the things that had happened since they had seen one another. Tears were shed, and old bridges that seemed to have never been built seemed to spring up out of nowhere. Watching the two old women laughing and talking with one another as though they had been friends their whole lives made Alison snicker to herself. There she sat, the diva who felt that she was above everyone was now sparking up a friendship with the little red headed girl who she treated like a peasant. Alison leaned her head on Addison's shoulder as they swayed to the music being played.

"Penny for your thoughts, My Love?" Addison whispered in her ear, wrapping his arms around her waist.

"I was just thinking…I honestly don't see how this day could have been any more perfect."

"Do you see that man over there?"

"Yes…wasn't he the one who came with Madison and Lena? I believe that he is Madison's husband. I can't remember what his name is. Why?"

"He's Woodcrest's new sheriff. He, his wife, and mother are the newest residents of Woodcrest." He kissed his wife on the cheek, and before spinning her around to face him, he added one last thing. "And, just so you know, his name is Donovan." When Alison caught on and turned her head, he burst out laughing.

"How did I know that you were going to tell me that?" She glared at him through narrowed eyes.

"Because I am very predictable?" He looked down at her, his dimples deeply indented in his cheeks.

"No, you are just you." She kissed him, and then leaned back against his chest. "Thank you…you know, for deciding to talk to the council about a sheriff for Woodcrest. It really is for the best." She looked around at the people around them, and then she began to smile. "I have an idea as to how I can thank you properly!" Her eyes were wide, and she pulled him closer, and whispered in his ear. He got rigid, and cleared his throat, gave a mischievous laugh, and grasped her hand.

"Well, everyone…it's been a great day! Thank you all for coming and sharing this celebration with us. Now, if you'll excuse us…We…um…have things to discuss. Don't forget to lock up after you're done!" He leaned over, and threw his new bride over his shoulder and hauled her out of the building. When they were outside, he set her back down, and kissed her in the moonlight. He put his fingers to his lips and whistled. After a moment, a black and white horse came racing out of the shadowed lane.

"What is he doing here?" Alison put her hands on her hips.

"I wanna get home…like now! I want my thank you's…" He mounted the horse, and reached down. "Come along, Mrs. Thatcher." She took his hand, and he pulled her up onto the horse.

Together they rode off down the cobblestone street toward the place that they called home. The pins that held Alison's veil to her hair came loose, and the sheer toule flew from her head, and blew in the breeze. It finally came to rest at the foot of a statue that stood in the park of four very proud and happy men.

www.ingramcontent.com/pod-product-compliance
Lightning Source LLC
Chambersburg PA
CBHW060148260626
47160CB00001B/178